CW00471124

To David,

M from

Cathy x.

x

Horsing Around

Catherine Rix

Copyright

Dedication

Dedicated to my husband, Peter, who, from the

day we met, has always loved, supported and

encouraged me.

And to my amazing daughter Jessica.

I love you both.

Acknowledgements

I have had the outline plot for this book rattling around in my head for a long time, and finally, here it is!

I have received help and support from many people as I carried out research and worked to add the details to the bones of my original idea. The list of individuals who have helped me would almost be as long as the story, but I must mention the following:

Stephen Hardy and Craig Anderson have been amazing! They provided unlimited access to Burgham International Horse Trials, Alnwick Ford Horse Trials and a wide range of affiliated and unaffiliated competitions at Alnwick Ford Equestrian Centre. Stephen has constantly been at the end of the phone to answer technical questions and explain complicated rules.

All of the staff at Alnwick Ford Equestrian have welcomed me and patiently answered my stream of questions. Stephen and Craig provided me with opportunities to gain first -hand experience as a collecting ring steward, dressage writer and fence judge... In return, I am sure some of my more bizarre questions and observations, along with my attempts to pick up showjumping poles has provided them with some savage amusement.

I have had the privilege of writing for many dressage judges, but I must mention Les Kidd, Les Smith and Sharon Spencer-Mullens, all of whom happily explained the rationale behind their comments to me and answered a multitude of questions.

Special thanks to Debbie Cave and Jill Blackshaw for making me laugh (often inappropriately) and confirming that I am indeed allergic to calculators. One of Jill's horses features in this and the following book, so thank you again! Thanks to Kerry Browning for help regarding the rules of showjumping and proving the walkie-talkie radio works so much better when you know how to turn it on!

A special thank-you to Jess Aitken for her help with the bodies and for her continued agreement that most problems are better tackled with a large slice of cake and a glass of wine, (or bottle of gin.)

Hopefully my enduring love of horses comes through in the narrative so I must acknowledge the part played in shaping the story by every horse or pony I have had the privilege to ride and love.

Thank you also to all of the event riders, owners, grooms and volunteers who were my inspiration and finally, a massive thank you to the staff and horses at Murton Equestrian Centre and Claire Nixon at Swinhoe Farm Riding Centre for helping me to regain my own mojo!

Although every effort has been made to ensure the narrative is as realistic as possible, several technical points / procedures have been adapted to fit the plot and should in no way reflect the expertise of those people who have been kind enough to help; for the same reason, no-one should refer to this work as an accurate guide to the rules of British Eventing, British Dressage, British Showjumping, Breeding or Police procedure etc.

This is a fictitious story, not a how to guide.

Chapter 1

"Yep, she's dead!" Phoebe stepped back from the body which was slumped across the kitchen table and wiped her hands on a tea towel. "What did you do to her?"

I stared at the dead woman. "Nothing. I didn't do anything to her!"

Phoebe dropped the tea towel onto the draining board next to the sink. "And who is she again?"

"I don't know!" I wailed wringing my hands.

"Mm." My friend pulled out a chair next to the body at the table. "So, you have the dead body of an unknown female in your kitchen." She stretched across the table and helped herself to a slice of cake. She paused for a moment and looked from the dead woman to the cake then asked, "Did she...?"

"What? Oh, no. She didn't eat any."

Smiling at the reassurance that my cake had not in fact poisoned the woman slumped next to her and thus been the cause of her untimely demise, Phoebe calmly continued to eat whilst appraising the body. My friend was remarkably calm. In fact, I did find her nonchalant attitude to the situation ever so slightly disturbing.

"What should we do with it... her?" I picked up the tea towel. "Should we wipe the place, you know, remove fingerprints?"

1

"You need to watch fewer crime dramas on the telly for one thing, and unless you did actually murder…" Phoebe waved her hand in the vague direction of the corpse, sprinkling the dead woman with a liberal covering of crumbs, "Does your dead friend have a name?"

I twisted the tea towel in my hands, "I've already told you, she's not my friend. I've never met her before, and I have no idea what her name is. Was."

"Okay, well we'll call her Susan. She looks like a Susan." Phoebe decided, "so anyway, unless you did actually murder Susan, we call the police. But for the record if you do need an alibi, I'm happy to say you were with me. This is very good cake by the way."

"And you have no idea who she is," repeated the Policeman.

"Was," interjected Phoebe.

"No, I'd never met her before."

"But we think she looks like a Susan," added Phoebe. The Policeman raised an eyebrow and politely refused a slice of cake. "It's alright. That's not what killed her," Phoebe reassured him through a mouthful.

"Although," I glared at my friend, "your forensic team might find some evidence of crumbs, especially to the back of her head, but I can confirm they were added to the scene post-mortem."

The Policeman followed the trail of crumbs scattered across the table and Susan's shoulders. "I do hope we haven't contaminated the crime scene!" I added.

The Policeman sighed and sat down opposite Phoebe and Susan.

"Let's start again, shall we?" He flicked through the pages of notes he had scribbled in his little book, perhaps hoping they would make more sense now that he was sitting down.

"So, as I understand it, this woman is a complete stranger."

"That is correct," I confirmed.

"And, she is in fact not called Susan."

2

Again, I nodded my head as I confirmed, "that is correct Sir."

He scratched out something he had earlier written and amended his notes.

"Although, "interrupted Phoebe, "she might be."

The Policeman paused and looked at Phoebe.

"Might be…?"

"She might be called Susan. Well, don't you think she looks like a Susan?" Phoebe waved her slice of cake in the general direction of 'Susan', casting another layer of crumbs over the dead woman. "You know, the hair. It looks very Susanny to me."

The Policeman looked at the wild bird's nest of grey wiry hair. He sighed again before adding to his notes, "might be called Susan, on account of having hair!"

We watched in respectful silence as Susan was covered by a sheet and carried out of my kitchen. "There's nothing in her pockets we can use to identify her, Sir." the Policeman's blue-gloved colleague informed him apologetically.

"Did she have a handbag?" he asked me.

I shook my head, "No Sir."

Again, the Policeman sighed, "Okay. Let's try again. Why don't you tell me exactly, how this dead woman arrived in your kitchen?"

"Well to begin with she wasn't dead when she arrived," I explained.

If this was a film, this is the point where everything would turn hazy and the image would wobble from side to side until returning with vivid clarity to a moment at some point in the past; in this case three hours earlier.

Three hours earlier…

I had just set a large golden Madeira cake to cool on a wire rack when there was a loud thumping on the front door. I looked out of the window and saw a strange car parked in the yard opposite the stables.

I opened the door to be greeted by a thin, confused looking lady. She had a mass of wild grey hair which stood out from her head rather like a halo or the fluff on a dandelion clock. I wondered if it would fly off her head in tufts if a strong wind blew up, thus rendering her bald but with an approximate interpretation of the time. She was wearing a pair of jodhpurs which had probably started off life as being cream or pale beige; now they were a strange washed out biscuit colour with persistent and unremovable stains. They clung to her skinny legs which disappeared into a pair of wellingtons. I couldn't decide whether her boots were overly wide or her pipe-cleaner legs impossibly thin, but it seemed a marvel that the sticks poking out from under her jacket possessed the strength to lift the boots and allow her to walk. The top part of her body at first appeared to be ridiculously inflated in comparison to her flimsy lower portion, however, closer inspection revealed that rather than being a result of her body mass, the disproportionate size of her torso was a result of many, many layers of clothes, held in place by a giant sized Puffa jacket which she was wearing in defence against the biting cold of the January afternoon.

"Hello, I'm looking for the livery stables, I didn't want to go poking around and I did shout but there was no answer and then I thought I'd try the house, but I wasn't sure which door was the right door, are you the owner? I much prefer a yard where the owner lives on site."

She didn't pause for breath.

Before an opening became available in the 'conversation' for me to answer any questions, or even introduce myself, we (or rather she) were interrupted by the sound of the telephone ringing.

I half turned and glanced over my shoulder.

"Go on, you'd best answer that, it might be important," she instructed.

"I'll just be a second."

Turning, I hurried back into the body of the house and into the room I rather grandly referred to as my office. It was actually a dining room, but its proximity to the back door, (the one utilised by most visitors) and the view across the fields in one direction and over to the stables from the other window, made it a perfect room to complete paperwork and deal with any issues relating to the livery stables.

The call was in fact, not important, simply a cold caller offering cheaper gas. I hung up and headed back to the dandelion lady at the door.

But she wasn't there.

The door was closed.

Had she left?

I turned back to the kitchen, intending to look out of the window to see if her car was still there. There was no need. My visitor was sitting at my kitchen table. I didn't know whether to be furious that she had brought herself uninvited into my home or relieved that she wasn't wandering around pilfering. I decided to reserve judgement but wasn't impressed that she was still wearing her enormous boots which were leaving small piles of dried mud, I hoped it was mud, whenever she moved.

"All sorted?" she asked.

"Yes, it wasn't important," I found myself answering.

"Lovely kitchen." She twisted her fluffy head on a scrawny neck, taking in the displays of rosettes and photographs of horses competing in a range of disciplines. "Gosh, I'm tired. Takes it out of you having horses doesn't it?" she yawned.

"Yes, they can be hard work," I agreed.

There was a silence as my visitor folded her arms on my table and laid her head on them. I wasn't sure what to do. It looked for all the world as if she intended to have a nap. "Would you like a coffee?" I asked uncomfortably.

"Mm. Milk no sugar," the woman informed me as she closed her eyes. By the time I had filled the kettle she was snoring gently.

5

"Well, this is awkward," I said to myself. I wasn't sure what the protocol was for dealing with sleeping strangers in one's kitchen, so I decided to continue making the coffee in the hope that she would wake up and we could both pretend the nap incident hadn't taken place. She didn't wake up but continued to sleep while I was banging around making the noisiest pot of coffee ever.

"There you are!" I announced placing a mug in front of her. There was no response.

I decided to drink my coffee while the mug I had placed in front of her slowly cooled.

She was no longer snoring. "Oh hell," I thought to myself, "I hope she isn't drooling onto the table!"

I stood up and coughed.

Nothing.

I coughed again, louder.

Nothing.

I looked at the clock. She had been here for just over an hour. I decided to give her a prod. Just a gentle poke in the arm. However, a gentle poke proved insufficient to penetrate the vast layers of clothing, so I opted for a gentle shake instead.

Nothing.

"Erm, wake up, your coffee's cold." I called as I shook her.

This, I decided was ridiculous; so, I shook harder.

"Wake up!"

As I released her from my shaking grasp, her right arm dropped off the table and dangled by the chair leg and her head, no longer supported by her right arm, slid onto the table with a 'thud'.

I jumped back with a gasp.

"Oh, my god! Are you…? Wake up, please. Oh shit!" I shook her again but there was still no response.

Gingerly I took hold of her wrist. Given the amount of clothes she was wearing, she was surprisingly chilly. I couldn't find a pulse. Grimacing, I tried to find a pulse in her neck, which was slightly clammy.

I stepped back and washed my hands. I needed help. The logical course of action would have been to dial the emergency services, so I phoned my friend; Phoebe.

"Phoebes? Where are you?"

"Just about to drive into your place. Is everything okay?"

"Can you come straight over to the house?" As I spoke, I could see out of the window. Phoebe's car was turning through the gates. I hurried to meet her at the door.

"Are you alright?"

"Phoebe, a woman turned up here just over an hour ago," I glanced at my watch, "actually it might be closer to two hours, but ANYWAY," I paused and took a deep breath, "she followed me into the kitchen, and I think she might be dead!"

Phoebe continued to pull off her boots. "Oh." Phoebe said casually, "what did you do to her?"

"Nothing! I haven't fucking murdered her! She just died!"

Phoebe straightened up and leaving her boots by the door headed to the kitchen." So, she is definitely dead?"

"I don't know," I wailed, "but I think so."

I followed Phoebe into the kitchen. She walked around the table inspecting the woman who was lying exactly as I had left her; slumped on the table with one arm hanging by her side and her head resting on the table with her eyes closed as if she was still deep in slumber. "Is this her?"

"Well can you see any other potentially dead strangers in here?"

"Hey there, strange lady, wake up!" Phoebe shouted.

Unsurprisingly there was no response. She reached out, and taking the dangling arm, searched for a pulse. Having no more luck than I had, Phoebe unceremoniously dropped the woman's arm and reached across her fuzzy head to peel open a lifeless eyelid.

"Yep, she's dead!"

Chapter 2

The Policeman closed his notebook with a snap. "Well, I don't think there is anything else you can tell us at this stage." He stood up to go. "We'll be in touch."

"Thanks. I'll see you out." I began to follow him to the door, "Oh, what about her dog?"

He stopped rather abruptly, and I bumped into him. "Her dog?"

"Yes, her dog. I mean I'm happy to look after it for a bit, but-,"

"What dog?" He interrupted looking around the kitchen, "I didn't see any dog."

I laughed, "Oh it's not in here. It's out there in her car."

"Her car?"

"Yes," I said slowly, "her car."

Honestly, I wondered how any crimes were ever solved if all policemen were as stupid as this one. He seemed intent on repeating everything I said. Perhaps he had a hearing problem.

"You didn't mention a car," he said wearily.

"Well, you didn't ask," I said defensively, "anyway, how do you think she got here? It's pretty much the middle of nowhere."

"Of course," he sighed, "how foolish of me. Which is her car?"

"The small green one," I pointed out of the window.

"The one with the dog," Phoebe added helpfully.

It was quite dark now and the lights in the kitchen made it difficult to see outside. The Policeman squinted into the darkness.

"But the team didn't mention any keys, a phone…" He sighed again, "never mind. I'll go and have a look."

Phoebe and I followed him.

The small green car was unlocked, and the keys were still in the ignition. As soon as the door was opened a brown and white ball of barking fur leapt out, licked everyone, then squatted to do an enormous wee.

Phoebe dropped to her knees. "Oh, you poor little thing, were you desperate for a wee?" The dog wagged its stump of a tail furiously and climbed over Phoebe, licking her at every available opportunity.

"Alright, that's enough now. Get down!" She fended off the dog and stood up to watch with me as the Policeman searched the car for any clue which would help to identify Susan.

It didn't take him long to find a purse in the glovebox. Pulling out his radio, he had a brief, crackly conversation before informing me that someone would be along with a recovery vehicle at some point to collect the car unless a next of kin could be tracked down, in which case someone would bring them to take the car away. The dog was another problem. The Policeman seemed quite relieved when we offered to look after her, at least in the short term.

The little dog was wearing a collar and a tag which informed us that she was called Tilly. "What type of dog do you think she is?" I asked Phoebe as the little dog trotted obediently between us as we headed from the house across the yard to the stables.

"Maybe a Jack Russell," she considered the dog for a moment, "crossed with a sausage dog or something." She picked the dog up and rubbed her behind the ears, "But whatever you are, you're darned cute that's for sure." In

9

reply Tilly licked her nose. "But you can cut that out. I don't lick you, so don't you lick me. Got it." She sighed as the dog licked her cheek.

The stables were old stone buildings which I had worked hard to restore since buying the former racing yard almost a year ago after my rather acrimonious divorce. Twelve years of being told, by my then husband, that I couldn't do something, had easily formed the foundation for a challenge. The desire to put as much distance as possible, both geographical and emotional, between myself and my now ex-husband, as well as my ex-best friend, who, it transpired had been sleeping with my former spouse for ten of our twelve years of marriage, had led me to leave my job and buy a small cottage and the remains of a stable yard in a rural corner of Northumberland, in order to realise a long-time dream of running my own livery stables.

The cottage had originally been built as a tiny bungalow but over the years various owners had extended rooms by knocking down walls, and even moving the bedrooms into the roof space along with a small bathroom. A tumbledown stone wall separated what had once been a neat front garden from the quiet road which ran down the hill and past the cottage towards the village of Stonecross in one direction or continued up the hill towards the moors. A gateway at either end of the wall led into the property. One gate opened onto a short driveway which in turn joined a narrow path. This had been largely reclaimed by an impressive array of weeds; it led around the cottage from the rarely used front door to the back which faced the stable yard.

The second, wider gateway led directly into an open space of gravelly hard standing which separated a small garden at the back of the cottage from the stables which formed three sides of a quadrangle with a low wall and a wooden gate forming the fourth side. To the left of the stables a timber framed barn housed hay and bedding, while the centre of the quadrangle had once been a neat lawn with an apple tree.

10

The tree was still there but the lawn needed some attention to restore it to any semblance of its former glory. The drainage and foundations for an outdoor ménage lay behind the stables, eagerly anticipating the arrival of sand and rubber mixture riding surface. Fields and farmland surrounded the property and stretched as far as the eye could see, eventually blending with the moorland which disappeared over the horizon. Several acres belonged to the cottage, the remainder were the property of the neighbouring farm, whose roof top could be seen in the distance.

My dream of running my own yard had not included having potential customers die in my kitchen.

*****

Susan, it turned out, was in fact called Patricia. Her funeral was not particularly eventful and was held at the crematorium in the nearest town after a brief and somewhat predictable church service. A photograph of the dandelion lady when she was several years younger, standing next to a horse, looked out at the collection of people who had gathered to say goodbye. The same photograph was printed on the front of the order of service.

"I'm going to have a glass coffin." Phoebe whispered, as the small congregation stood up to watch Patricia's coffin glide through the curtains.

"What! Why?" I hissed back.

"So that I can watch. And, I want the mortician to paint open eyes on my eyelids." Phoebe turned to me and closed her eyes so that I could imagine the effect she was describing. I began to giggle until a loud tutting and a furious glare from a lady across the aisle reminded us that this was in fact a solemn, though (based on the number of hip flasks I had observed in operation while waiting for the hearse) a not necessarily sober, occasion.

We lined up with the handful of mourners to shake hands with Patricia's son and daughter, who had travelled up to Northumberland from Yorkshire to arrange her funeral.

"Thank you for coming. Yes, she will be a great miss."

We stepped forward as the lady with the powerful tut dabbed at her eyes and shuffled past the family.

"Thank you for coming." Patricia's son shook my hand. He paused for a moment, still holding my hand; this was not an unpleasant position to be in as Patricia's son was the complete physical antithesis of his mother. Tall, sophisticated appearance; very well dressed in an expensive looking suit and dark, heavy overcoat; he was gorgeous. He had the physique of a professional rugby player and his glossy dark hair was thick and not at all dandelion like.

"I don't think we've met," he smiled, still holding my hand.

I blushed, "I'm Abigail."

"How did you know my mother, Abigail?"

Before I could answer, Phoebe gave me a shove and took the handsome man's hand from mine. "She died in Abi's kitchen," she explained bluntly.

"Oh, we wondered if you would come." I found myself face to face with a small, slight framed woman who, judging by the skinny legs and dandelion hair must, I reasoned, be Patricia's daughter. She held out her hand, "Thank you so much for looking after Tilly."

"You're welcome. It was the least we could do. Did your mother have horses?" I asked her daughter, "I think that's why she came to see me, to ask about livery."

"Yes, she has, sorry had one," she corrected herself. "He's ancient. That's him in the photograph. Fortunately, the man who owns the stables where mother used to keep him has agreed to find a home for him; as a companion. It's nice to have Tilly as a memory of mum, but I've no idea what I would have done with a horse!" she sniffed and wiped away a tear.

I patted her arm.

Patricia's daughter smiled, "It must have been such a shock for you."

"Did they find out what killed her?" interrupted Phoebe, still holding onto the handsome brother.

"Yes, a cerebral aneurysm," Patricia's son explained.

"Well that's good news," said Phoebe.

Patricia's son let go of her hand and turned his attention to the people standing behind us.

"I mean it officially lets you and your cake off the hook," she added quickly, looking at me. "I'm Phoebe." She held out her hand to Patricia's daughter who extended her own hand cautiously.

"Thank you for coming. I'm Susan."

Phoebe's mouth dropped open and her eyes widened. "No bloody way-,"

"We are very sorry for your loss." I hastily cut off Phoebe before she could say any more and dragged her away.

"What is the matter with you? I said she looked Susanny. Are we going to the party?"

"It's called a wake. And I don't think it would be a good idea."

Chapter 3

My daily routine always began with the horses. They were fed while the kettle boiled, then after a coffee it was back over to the stables to change rugs and turn the horses out into one of the fields, before mucking out and preparing haynets or setting beds for later.

Two of the horses were my own; a partially retired chestnut mare called Flame who, at the height of her competition career, had been a successful eventer. She was now enjoying a stress- free life as a 'happy hacker' and I was considering breeding a foal from her. My competitive aspirations had been transferred to Skye, another mare but she was only four. I had owned her since she was a weanling and had spent the years since breaking her in and schooling her.

The third occupant of my new stables belonged to Phoebe. She and I had been friends since I had moved into the cottage and started the renovations a year ago.

A year ago, ...

I burst into the estate agent's office in the small market town of Alnwick. Apart from a woman checking out the details for some rental properties I was the only customer. "I've come to collect the keys for my new house!" I announced to everyone in general and no-one in particular.

The lady working at the rental desk looked up for a moment and smiled. "Hi, which house have you bought?"

"Fellbeck Cottage," I grinned proudly.

"Oh, is that the place near Stonecross?"

Her colleague came out from behind another desk holding an envelope. "That's right," she confirmed, "on the moor road about a mile from the actual village; its where the racehorses used to be, years ago. The keys are in here," she added handing me the envelope.

"Thanks!" I was still grinning. I stuffed the envelope deep into my bag and handed a box of chocolates over in exchange," Drop in for a coffee if you're passing."

"Good luck, and thanks for the chocolates!" both estate agents called as I left. "Congratulations!" said the woman checking the rental properties.

I hurried across the road to where my car was parked and headed off towards my new home. Driving through the town the car behind caught my eye as it jumped through a red light. "Idiot!" I shouted in my mirror. I had been watching the car for a couple of miles and had concluded that the driver was a lunatic. As the road straightened out, and I left the town, exchanging busy streets and houses for countryside and farmland, I slowed down, giving the driver behind the opportunity to pass; however, the car I was trying to lose, slowed down too. I slowed down even more, so did the car behind. I decided to speed up and create a gap between us; the car behind also sped up.

I checked my mirror and slowed down as I pulled out to turn at a roundabout. The car behind followed, planning to take the same exit towards Stonecross. Seeing an opportunity to get away from this fool, I drove all around the roundabout; the car behind continued to follow. I stayed on the roundabout and drove around it again. So, did the car behind. Now I was feeling uncomfortable.

After four complete revolutions of the roundabout I decided that I was definitely being followed.

I took the next exit without signalling and accelerated along the new road. The car was still behind me. Again, without indicating, I left the road and drove into a hotel carpark; checking the mirror, it was no surprise to see the other car follow me. I slammed on the brakes and my car screeched to a halt.

The car behind swerved to avoid crashing into the back of me, and also, screeched to a halt.

Grabbing the only thing I could see, a newspaper from the passenger seat, I got out of my car ready to tackle the other driver.

"Are you following me?" I rolled up the newspaper and pointed it at the woman climbing out of the other car.

"Yes." She answered calmly, "and if you don't mind me saying so, you drive like a crazy person."

"Why? What do you want?" I brandished my rolled -up paper.

"I saw you in the estate agents, picking up the keys for Fellbeck Cottage."

"So? What are you? Some kind of insane stalker?"

She laughed, "I'm not stalking you. I'm looking for somewhere to hide my horse."

"Sorry, for a moment I thought you said hide."

"That's right. Are you going to take liveries?"

"Can we rewind for a moment? Hide? Is your horse stolen?"

"No nothing like that. So, are you?"

"Are I what?"

"Liveries. In the stables up at Fellbeck. Are you taking liveries?"

"Yes. "

"Great!"

"But not yet. There's a ton of work to do before I can take in customers." Her face dropped.

"Look, I'm desperate. Maybe I could help you." She came around from the driver's side of her car towards me. I rolled my paper into a tighter roll. She looked at my weapon and held her hands up in surrender.

"Why do you need to hide you horse?" I asked.

"Because my parents are coming to visit." She said as if this was the most rational explanation I was ever likely to need.

"What are you talking about? Look I'm sorry for … well whatever. But I can't help. I have to go, there's a removal van waiting for me." I got back into my car and left the crazy stalker standing in the carpark.

The following morning, I stood in my new kitchen, looking at the stack of unpacked boxes and wondering where the kettle was when I heard a vehicle slow down on the road outside. A friend was driving my horses to my new home today, but it was too early to be them. A wave of annoyance swept over me as I recognised the car. I gave up looking for the kettle and marched outside to deal with this woman who, despite her protests, was beginning to look more and more like a stalker!

Before I could speak, the stalker had hurried from her car; she met me at the gate leading from the cottage garden. "Hi, I'm Phoebe," she introduced herself, "you might remember me from yesterday."

"Oh, I certainly do!"

"Oh good, you seemed a bit distracted so I wondered if you would remember me."

"I wasn't distracted!"

"Crikey! Do you mean you always drive like that?"

I didn't know how to respond for a moment and gaped at her in disbelief, so she continued. "We were discussing livery…" her voice trailed off hopefully.

"No. As I recall, you were chasing me and driving like a loon before announcing that you needed to hide a horse for some weird reason."

"I'll ignore the driving comment because I was just trying to keep up with you, and it's not a weird reason, I told you, my parents are visiting"

I still didn't understand. "And ...?"

"And if they find out about my horse, I'm in deep trouble. Oo look, a horsebox. I thought you weren't ready for customers," she ended accusingly.

"These are my horses. My friend offered to drive them up from South Tyneside because I haven't sorted myself any transport yet. Now, if you don't mind, I need to help unload." I tried to be assertive. I wanted her to leave because clearly, she was mad as a box of frogs, but I didn't want to be rude because of aforesaid madness.

"Oh absolutely. You crack on." She stepped back as the horsebox negotiated the gateway but didn't leave.

"Yoo- hoo, Abi!" Sue Mason waved out of the cab window.

The large red horsebox shuddered to a standstill in front of the stables.

"Hi!"

"Are you ok?"

"I'm fine Sue, thanks for this."

"Christ Abigail, what kind of god forsaken place is this?" John Mason, Sue's husband jumped down from the driver's side of the wagon scowling. "Well let's get on with it then, come on Sue, get your arse over here and give us a hand."

A small tabby cat which I had noticed hanging around the stables yesterday seemed to have taken up residence in the barn and she ran for cover now as the heavy ramp at the back of the horse box was lowered. The two horses stamped impatiently as one by one they were untied and led down the ramp into the yard.

The first horse to be unloaded was Flame; she stood calmly in the yard while I quickly removed her protective travelling boots. I had cleaned and prepared two stables, the ones with the least number of holes in the roof, and Flame calmly followed as I led her into one of them. A series of stamps and bangs accompanied by shrill screams and calls reminded everyone that Skye was still on board and not at all happy to be kept waiting especially now that she had lost sight of her companion.

She snatched and pulled as John struggled to untie her then leapt down the ramp dragging him with her. "You need to teach this bugger some manners," he grumbled jerking on the headcollar as Sue helped me to remove the mare's travelling things. Her dark bay coat was glistening and flecked with white spots of sweat from the journey. I guessed that John Mason had driven with considerably less care than I would have liked.

Having watched Skye settle into her new home we turned towards the house.

"Would you like a coffee?" I asked.

"Love one," replied John leading the way to the cottage.

In the kitchen, I retrieved two more mugs from the packing cases and, as I still hadn't found the kettle or the spoons, I tipped what I guessed to be a spoonful of coffee into each mug before topping them up with water from the tap. As I put the three mugs into the microwave, I realised that Phoebe, my stalker, had joined us.

"Sue, John, this is Phoebe. Sorry, I'm not sure where the kettle is," I explained handing a mug to John. He simply shrugged and lit a cigarette as he accepted the drink.

"Pleased to meet you, Phoebe. Do you have a horse?" John asked her as he tried to persuade the coffee granules to dissolve with the aid of a biro.

Sue looked suspiciously into her mug, "Milk?"

"I'm afraid I forgot to bring any and I haven't had a chance to go shopping yet," I apologised.

"Yeah I have a horse." Phoebe explained, "A bay gelding, Treasure. We were just discussing me keeping him here when you arrived."

Glad of a distraction from the floating coffee granules which, even with the help of her husband's biro, were refusing to dissolve, Sue began to quiz Phoebe and we all learned that she had recently completed a second master's degree in the history of fine art, at Newcastle University. She worked part time at the 'Dirty Dog', a pub on the other side of Stonecross village; she had only managed to afford to pursue her studies because of the financial support of her parents. However, in return for funding their daughter's continued academic pursuits, Phoebe had reluctantly agreed to sell her horse. Now her parents were planning a long weekend from their home in Surrey to visit, and as the horse in question was currently grazing in a small paddock behind the house where she lived, Phoebe was desperate to find somewhere else to keep him. Somewhere that her parents wouldn't see him.

"To be fair I do need to find somewhere more suitable regardless of the old folks visiting. The paddock is tiny and the kids down the road keep climbing in and feeding him cake and chocolate bars. Plus, the landlord who owns my flat is selling the building, so I need to find somewhere else for me …"

"Why not just sell the horse?" asked John.

"I just couldn't. I mean I, I just couldn't." Her voice cracked and her eyes began to fill with tears.

"Oh, you poor thing!" cried Sue, glaring at her husband. "But don't get upset, you've sorted at least half your problem, haven't you?" She glanced between me and Phoebe.

I shrugged. "It looks like it. But I've warned you, there's a stack of work to get any more stables ready. Even the stables my two are using have holes in the roof."

"Oh, thank you. That's fabulous. I'll call back this afternoon to sort out the details." She kissed everyone on the cheek and bounced out of the kitchen.

In the months that followed Phoebe helped me to turn a semi-derelict racing yard into a smart, professional looking livery stables. Together we sorted through piles of rubble; we made repairs to the roofs of the stables along with painting walls and woodwork. We filled countless skips with miscellaneous piles of rubbish. A local builder, Tom, and his son 'Little Tom' along with an electrician called Paul (Big Tom's brother) came to complete the skilled aspects of the revival, but we did as much as possible to both speed up the process and keep the cost down. As well as repairing the stables, we, with the help of Paul and the two Toms, were able to turn an old stone workshop into a tack room. The Toms lined the walls with some reclaimed wood and fitted a heavy door with a code operated lock; they even managed to turn an adjoining storeroom into a space for the liveries to sit and have a coffee, wait for trainers or just sit and chat.

Treasure had been successfully hidden and in return for paying slightly less livery, Phoebe worked for me on a part time basis when she wasn't working at the Dirty Dog.

After Phoebe, one of my first customers was Felicity; a very quiet, almost timid individual; to be honest I think she was a little bit afraid of Phoebe. In fact, a lot of people were a little bit afraid of Phoebe. Felicity was the sort of woman it was difficult to attach an age to; she could be anywhere between thirty and sixty. She was unmarried, and to the best of my knowledge never had been; although, despite her apparently shy and retiring persona, she often arrived at the stables with a companion.

Always male.

Always gorgeous.

Rarely with any equine knowledge.

Her 'friend' would potter around uncomfortably, usually wearing expensive, fashionable and totally unsuitable clothing. He would fetch and carry various items as directed by Felicity or sit and watch her adoringly from the warmth and safety of the car. After a couple of weeks, he would be replaced. Her horses were her life and she spent hours sifting through their wood shaving beds wearing a pair of pink rubber gloves to remove every last speck of dirt. Their beds were laid with precision; deep, even and so straight that I was convinced she must use a spirit level. Each of her two horses was groomed for hours each day and encased in a variety of expensive rugs. The two recipients of this devotion were an ancient, shaggy, black and white cob sent, I am sure, by the Devil himself to act as a warning to anyone considering becoming involved with horses, and a little black thoroughbred. Both horses were geldings.

The cob, by my estimation was at least thirty and was a testament to the power of modern medicine. His temper and obvious disdain for the human race seemed to be what kept him going. He hadn't been ridden for over ten years and his sole purpose in life appeared to be to kick, bite or barge into anyone foolish enough to come within striking distance. Considering none of his joints seemed to actually bend (I have no idea how he lay down or got up again), he was surprisingly strong and would drag anyone, attempting to lead him, with unstoppable speed and wilful determination. Thankfully, Felicity looked after her horses herself and my only contact with the inappropriately named Romeo, was to give him a feed and turn him out each morning.

Felicity's second horse, Jasper, was a nervous little creature who was terrified of his own shadow. He had originally been bred as a racehorse but his lack of ability and race day nerves, had led to a different life for him as a show jumper. How and why Felicity came to own him was anybody's guess; they were as nervous as each other and neither did anything to instil calmness or confidence. Any unexpected noise sent him into a trembling frenzy and leading him to the field was almost as dangerous as dealing with Romeo. Unlike the cob who stormed from his own predetermined point A to B like a hairy tank, Jasper needed to place his own hooves on the exact spot the human leading him had used for their feet. This delicate tip toeing ballet dance to and from the field was not always executed without said human experiencing some painful toe crushing as Jasper did not always follow in one's footsteps, rather he thought it safer to share the boot sized section of ground with his handler.

The stable next to Romeo was home to a massive bay dressage horse who looked like he was carved from polished mahogany. He was called Eric and was owned by Izzy, a professional divorcee. Along with Eric our final two customers were show ponies; Solo and Symphony. The ponies were never actually ridden, as far as I could tell. They were too small to be ridden by their owners but were very successfully shown 'in-hand'. They were owned by Marc and Henry, who lavished both time and money on their equine prima donnas.

Chapter 4

The day after the funeral was cold and windy. It did nothing to make the task of turning out the horses any easier.

"I can't help thinking Jasper would be less neurotic if Felicity actually did something other than brush and feed him!" grumbled Phoebe as she hobbled through the gateway from the field. "He's just a fizzing bag of nervous energy."

I had to agree with her as we set about mucking out.

"Have you ever seen her ride?" Phoebe continued.

Before I could answer a car drove into the yard. It was a very fancy looking four- wheel drive and judging by the loud gear crunching and long pauses between the various manoeuvres involved in parking, it didn't appear that the driver had owned it for very long. We stopped even pretending to muck out and leaned on our pitch forks to watch. Eventually the driver, a short man, climbed out. He smoothed down his very new looking waxed jacket and reached back into the car for an equally new looking checked cap, which he carefully arranged on his head before walking around the car to open the passenger door and assist out a rather large lady who was swamped in a heavy fur coat with matching fur hat and hand muff.

Phoebe began to snort. "Holy fuck, what the-?"

"Go!" I hissed, "if they are potential customers, I need their money. After the cost of the renovations and the new arena I'm what is technically called 'broke'!"

"Oh, please let me stay. I promise to be good," she giggled.

"Disappear. Now!"

"Spoilsport!" she muttered, balancing her pitchfork on top of her wheelbarrow as she headed, still giggling, towards the muck heap.

The couple from the car picked their way across the car parking area towards the stables. I met them at the gate. "Can I help you?"

"Good morning." The man held out a leather gloved hand, "I'm Jim Thomson-,"

"James!" the woman in fur corrected him.

He coughed, "Erm. Sorry. Yes. I'm James Thompson and this is my wife, Margaret." His wife inclined her head slightly and gave what was either a smile, or a moment of wind as she nodded in acknowledgement. "I've just bought my daughter a horse and we need somewhere to keep it."

"We saw your advertisement online and in Horse and Hound." Margaret emphasised the name of the magazine to ensure I knew they read such equine literature.

"Well, we do have a vacancy for livery. Let me show you around and I'll explain the various packages we offer."

By the time I had shown the couple around and answered their many, many questions, I knew that they had recently celebrated their twenty fifth wedding anniversary with a luxury cruise paid for as a result of matching several numbers in the Lottery. This lucky win had also bought the new car and the horse which their only daughter, Chantelle, had desperately wanted for as long as they could remember.

Chantelle, I discovered, knew everything there was to know about horses and was an absolute natural in the saddle. After having a staggering ten -week package of lessons at the prestigious Riding Academy in Stonecross, the family decided that Chantelle's passion for horses and her natural talent clearly demanded that she have a horse of her own. I was familiar with the Riding Academy. It was a large, well run riding school which catered for an enthusiastic clientele comprised mainly of children under the age of twelve, but with some adult riders. I had met the owner, Camilla and her husband, Steve when I had first moved to the area at a fundraiser for Equine Grass - sickness hosted at the local veterinary centre.

"Did Camilla find the horse for your daughter?" I asked.

"Oh no." Margaret pursed her lips in disapproval, "she's a nice enough woman, but our Chantelle needed something better than those 'ploddy' Bob the Cob types her usual customers shuffle around on."

"Yes, Margaret's right," James smiled in agreement. "Our Chantelle is going to the top and she needs a horse to take her there."

They had then bought a magnificent beast from a girl whose granny went to the bingo with Margaret.

I could see Phoebe out of the corner of my eye. She had moved from mucking out and was pretending to fill haynets. It was clear from the shaking shoulders and lack of hay actually making its way into any nets that she was none too subtly eavesdropping.

After satisfying themselves that this was indeed the perfect place for Chantelle and her new horse, I invited the couple over to the cottage, where we completed some paperwork and finalised arrangements.

"And what type of horse have they bought?" Phoebe asked when I finally waved goodbye to the Thompsons.

"A thoroughbred event prospect apparently."

"Well this should be fun then!" She laughed returning to her still empty haynets. "Are you collecting them?"

"No, they're bringing him themselves, tomorrow after lunch."

"Let me guess, they have a new horsebox."

"Close, a new trailer, hence the fancy four by four."

The following day I sat in the kitchen with Phoebe waiting for the Thompsons to arrive.

"What time did they say they would be here?"

I glanced at the clock, "They didn't give a specific time, just after lunch."

It was almost three o clock, given that it was the middle of January, the light would begin to fail soon.

"Maybe Champion the Wonder Horse doesn't want to move to a new house and is being difficult to load," Phoebe yawned.

"I hope everything's okay; I don't think they have a huge amount of experience."

Phoebe raised an eyebrow in response, "No, really?" Her sarcasm was palpable.

Our musing was interrupted by the arrival of a car. A combination of the failing light and several layers of dried mud made it difficult to be sure of the colour and model, but it certainly wasn't the Thompson family.

"Who's that?" asked Phoebe standing up and peering out of the kitchen window.

"I don't know, but I'm gonna find out."

By the time I had pulled on my boots the driver had left his car and disappeared into the stables. I caught up with him as he was coming out of one of the empty looseboxes. He was a tall man who I guessed to be in his late thirties or early forties and his strong, determined jaw was covered with a sprinkling of dark stubble. His weather -beaten complexion suggested he spent a lot of time out of doors. He was wearing a dark coloured windproof jacket, in a style favoured by horse riders, over a black turtleneck jumper and a pair of blue denim jeans. A dark blue baseball cap, emblazoned with the name of a feed company, was pulled low over his eyes, which I was close enough to see, were a deep sapphire blue; a colour I would have expected with a fair haired person, but if the man's stubble was an indication, he was very dark haired.

"Can I help you?"

He spun around as I spoke.

"Nice place you have here. You've done a lot of work." He continued to look around the yard as he spoke.

"Thanks. Are you looking for livery?"

27

"Mm. Maybe." He walked towards the ménage which was under construction. "Putting in an arena, eh? What surface are you going to put down?" he asked, opening the gate and striding across the layer of rock and drainage material. Before I could answer he spotted the abandoned framework of an old mechanical horse walker, a reminder of the yard's previous racing history; he left the ménage and set off to inspect the machinery. "I can get rid of that, take it off your hands if you want."

I was beginning to feel agitated. This man was striding around what was effectively my home, like he owned the place. "I don't mean to sound rude, but-,"

He turned and looked at me with a grin, "-but?" He tilted his head to one side and waited for a reply.

"But," I took a deep breath and forced myself to smile, "I'm expecting a new client any time now. If you are interested in one of our livery packages why don't you come back tomorrow, then I can show you around properly."

"Is this who you're waiting for?" I turned to see the Thompson's car crawling cautiously through the gateway. "I'll leave you to get on." He walked back to his own car, lifted a hand in greeting to Phoebe who was hurrying across the yard and nodded towards Mr Thompson who by now had stopped his car and trailer combination and was helping the still fur clad Mrs Thompson out of the vehicle. "Bye, I'll see you later Abi!" The stranger called to me, as he got into his own car and drove away.

"Who was that?" asked Phoebe as the illusive visitor drove away.

"I have no idea, but I don't think we've seen the last of him." I watched as the car disappeared into the distance. I didn't like the way he had referred to me as 'Abi', as if we were friends. He had probably been told my name innocently enough by someone in the village, but I still found it un-nerving, especially as I realised, he hadn't told me his name.

Phoebe didn't seem to notice my unease and had gone over to introduce herself to James and Margaret. As I joined them a teenage girl, whom I presumed was their daughter, Chantelle, got out of the rear passenger seat. She yawned then smiled as her father proudly introduced her, before turning her attention back to her phone which she was tapping rapidly with long painted fingernails. She appeared to be snapping a succession of photographs and adding brief comments or animated details before posting them onto social media to alert the world to her present whereabouts. Chantelle was short, like her father and when the two of them stood next to Margaret neither father nor daughter came past her shoulder.

Chantelle had a long blonde ponytail, at least this week she was blonde; her root growth suggested this was not always the case. Enormous gold hooped earrings dangled from her ears. She was wearing a pair of long leather boots and cream jodhpurs with a pale blue padded bomber jacket.

The trailer which was attached to the family's car, began to rock slightly and bounce. The movement was accompanied by a concerning stamping and banging from inside punctuated by loud, shrill whinnies. The Thompson family took a collective step backwards.

Phoebe looked across them towards me. "Sounds like… what's his name?"

"Zeus, "James told her, looking anxiously at the trailer which was becoming more animated and vocal by the minute.

"Yeah. Anyway, sounds like Zeus is becoming a tad impatient. Shall we get him out?"

"Yes, yes. Come on then Chantelle." James smiled nervously and rubbed his hands together but no -one moved.

"Would you like a hand to unload him?" I asked.

Mr Thompson smiled in relief.

"Come on Chantelle, show them how to do it!" Mrs Thompson ordered her daughter. Chantelle reluctantly slid her phone into a back pocket and began to fiddle ineffectually with the catch on the ramp at the back of the trailer.

The protestations from within became louder. "It might be easier to bring him out of this front ramp," Phoebe suggested.

"Oh, that's a good idea. We'll drop the ramp while you hop in through the groom's door, then you can lead him out." James hurried to undo the catch.

"Hang on, I want a photograph of our boy arriving at his new home." His wife produced a small camera from within the folds of the fur muff.

As the front was lowered, I noticed that the plastic covering hadn't been removed from the brand-new ramp. However, Chantelle had already unhooked the breast bar from the inside. The moment the ramp hit the ground and he was able to see the outside world, the mighty Zeus took matters into his own hands, or hooves, and quite literally flew out of the trailer. I needn't have worried about the plastic covered ramp because he barely touched it as he leapt snorting from the trailer into the middle of the yard. Chantelle came with him, travelling in an airborne fashion herself, clinging onto the end of the lead rope. I swear the horse didn't even realise she was there.

Margaret aimed her camera as Phoebe, and I leapt out of the flight path and James was sent spinning into the side of the trailer.

"There's a good boy. Chantelle make him put his ears up."

Zeus paused for a moment and lifted his dark bay head. His nostrils were bright red, and the whites of his eyes showed; lifting his head still higher he trumpeted a loud screaming whinny which was answered by various horses from within the stables.

Margaret clicked her camera in admiration, "Oo, that's lovely. Chantelle smile. And put your shoulders back don't slouch."

"We have a stable ready for him if you'd like to bring him this way."

Chantelle did her best to follow me but every few steps Zeus spun around in circles before launching himself into the shadows dragging Chantelle who was still clinging desperately, though unnoticed by the horse, to his lead rope, with him. Eventually he was safely enclosed in a large loose box and after several attempts and a small nosebleed, (human not equine), Chantelle and her father managed to remove the horse's head collar. Zeus continued to scream to the other horses as he plunged around the stable, tearing nervous mouthfuls of hay from the net.

"Isn't he fabulous?" Margaret crooned offering a mint to Zeus who took absolutely no notice of her. "If it wasn't for the white fur round his front ankle he'd look just like Black Beauty."

I smiled. There was no point explaining that horses have hair not fur and fetlocks not ankles.

"Should we tell her the horse is brown not black?" Phoebe whispered.

I shook my head.

"He needs a bucket of water." Observed James.

"It's okay." I pointed out, "All of the stables have automatic water drinkers." I pointed to the corner of the stable. "It means they have a constant supply of fresh water."

"How will he learn how to use it?" asked Margaret.

"There is always a small amount of water, so when they put their nose in to drink the pressure releases a valve and freshwater flows in."

The Thompson's looked unconvinced. "It looks small."

"Honestly it's great. Easy for us to keep clean and the horses can't kick the bucket over." I reassured him.

Chapter 5

I had almost forgotten about the man who had been snooping around the day that the Thompson family had arrived, when, almost a week later, a shabby maroon coloured car rumbled into the car park, belching black smoke ominously from the exhaust pipe.

I watched from within Eric's stable as the wiry man parked and made his way towards the stables. He stopped on the way to have a look at Marc and Henry's horsebox which was parked next to Phoebe's car. He tried the doors and finding them all locked he moved on and did the same to Izzy's slightly larger horsebox. Finally, he moved to the barn. He disappeared inside. When he hadn't emerged after several minutes, I followed him. I watched for a few seconds as he peered into boxes and baskets stacked in corners and piled next to bales of hay and shavings. As he lifted the lid of a feed bin I spoke; "Can I help?"

He spun around, "Hi. I was looking for you."

"Well you won't find me hiding in a feed bin!"

He laughed, "I don't think we've been properly introduced." He held out his hand, "I'm Dominic. Most people call me Dom."

I took his hand, "I'm- "

"Abigail. I know," he interrupted.

"How? How do you know?"

In reply he simply smiled and led the way out of the barn. "Who's the girl you have working for you? The blonde?"

"Oh, so you don't know everything about me then?"

Again, he laughed. I wanted to say, 'it's none of your business' but instead found myself answering simply, "Phoebe."

"Yeah?" She came around the corner leading Treasure.

"Nice horse." Dom stepped back and ran a professional eye over the horse.

"Thanks," she grinned.

"Phoebes this is Dom."

"Hi. Nice to meet you. Did you need me?" she added looking at me, "I'm just off for a quick ride."

Dom flicked his eyes over her in the same way he had appraised the horse. "Do you want a leg up?"

It was an innocent comment but coupled with the way he had looked at her made me uncomfortable.

"No. I'm fine," Phoebe answered. There was an edge to her voice, "Do you want me to wait for you Abi?"

I assured her that I was fine and watched as she rode out of the yard.

"So, how has your new livery settled in?" smirked Dom. He spoke as if we were the best of friends and had known each other for years.

"Fine thanks. Was there something in particular that you wanted?"

"Maybe. It's a nice yard this. Private. Good grazing," he nodded towards the fields, "decent facilities and no one overlooking you. Mm very nice." He turned slowly, drinking in the entire property and was it my imagination, or had he just run his eye over me?

"Are you looking for livery?" I persisted, determined to retain control over what was beginning to become an uncomfortable situation.

"Perhaps, how many stables do you have?" he looked directly at me and smiled. Rather than settling my feeling of unease, something in his expression made me even more uncomfortable.

"Altogether or empty?" I asked cautiously.

"Both."

33

"We have twelve boxes at the moment and three are empty. Although, I have someone coming to look around later." I added.

"I'll take the empty ones and any extra that become available," he announced, "and I want them together; those ones on the end."

The man's arrogance set my teeth on edge, "I'm sorry but that's not possible."

He looked surprised, "Why?"

He was very direct and the twinkle in his eye which had softened his features vanished.

"For one thing, those stables are already occupied and I'm not moving horses around."

"Oh. What's the other thing?"

"Eh?"

"You said for one thing. Suggests there's another reason." The twinkle was back.

"I do have someone coming later."

"But I'm here now," he smiled.

"I don't want them to come and find there are no stables after all."

"Let me take you for lunch. Perhaps I can persuade you to change your mind…"

"I don't think so."

"Come on, you'll like me when you get to know me. We could be good for each other."

I took a small step back. "What do you mean?"

"I'll take all of your empty boxes, the ones you have and any that become available. I'm a nice guy. Handy to have around"

He raised his eyebrows suggestively and a grin tickled the corner of his narrow lips, "You must get lonely, a recently divorced woman…"

Suddenly I wished I had asked Phoebe to stay. This man seemed to know an awful lot about me.

I took a deep breath, "I'm sorry I don't think I can help you at the moment."

The grin widened, "Are we still talking about the stables?"

I bristled but before I could respond he started to laugh at my obvious discomfort. "I'm sorry, just my sense of humour. Are you certain I can't have those stables?"

I relaxed, slightly. "I'm sure. I don't want to mess these people about."

"Fair enough." His sudden acceptance caught me off guard." How about I leave you my number and if things change, you can give me a ring."

By the time Phoebe returned, my visitor was long gone.

"Urgh!" Phoebe shivered. "I'm glad you said no. I mean he's not bad looking but something about him gives me the creeps. I wonder how he knew you were divorced?"

"I suppose its common knowledge. Most people in the village know."

"True. Anyway, forget about him, who are the new people? When are they coming to look around?"

"There are no new people," I confessed, "it seemed an easy way to get rid of him!"

"Good move! I wonder why he was so particular about the stables he wanted," Phoebe mused.

Any concerns about Dominic were brushed aside with the arrival of Marc and Henry. They parked their car and waved. Marc immediately set off to the field, but Henry headed over towards the house.

"Knock, knock!" he called through the back door.

"Come in!" I called back, "do you want a coffee?"

"No thanks, I've just had one. Have you been to the new coffee shop in the village? OMG! The cakes! I swear I put on a stone just looking at them!" He patted his perfectly flat midriff. "Anyway," he gushed, "I picked this up, thought you might be interested." He handed me a small booklet. "It's the schedule for Stonecross One Day Event. It's unaffiliated, but they run it as close to rules as possible and go all out with all the trimmings. It really is a lovely day, I thought it would be a nice outing for Skye before her affiliated pony parties! Here, let me show you."

He took the booklet back from me and flicked the pages until, satisfied he had found what he was looking for, he handed it back, "Here, the dressage test is quite straightforward, no lateral work in your class."

Phoebe took the booklet from me. "Looks like a laugh. You take Skye and I'll bring Treasure."

"And it's not too far. We're going to watch, it's always a great day. Oh, it will be such fun! We can go in convoy and park next to each other!"

He blew air kisses and disappeared back outside.

Phoebe grinned at me. "I get out of breath just watching him! I wonder if he was on Ritalin as a kid?"

Chapter 6

Flame snorted and tiptoed around a drain in the road. I didn't mind. It was nice to be out alone on my old mare for a change. The last few times I had managed to squeeze enough time into my day for a hack, I had found myself babysitting Chantelle and Zeus. She was a liability, completely unaware of her surroundings. Her parents paid for regular lessons with a never ending, constantly changing, stream of expensive professional trainers, so her basic skills were improving. A more consistent approach would have helped but as soon as she couldn't do something or her now expert parents disagreed with the professional, he or she was replaced.

To keep her safe out hacking, we wedged her between Phoebe and myself and kept the pace as slow as possible. Chantelle didn't seem to mind or notice as she spent most of the ride tapping and snapping with her phone. I was yet to see evidence of the natural horsemanship her parents were convinced would propel her to the Olympics, but I had to give her credit for the balance she displayed. No matter how flamboyantly Zeus leapt and cavorted, spinning in pirouette style as he jogged between Treasure and either Flame or Skye, Chantelle stayed put. She seemed to be stuck to the saddle with some invisible super glue. Of course, she did nothing to correct the plunging and spinning. Her reins were long enough to hang a week of washing. I'm fairly sure that the combination of her tiny size and lack of contact, either from rein or leg, meant that her horse wasn't aware that he actually had a rider on board.

Today I had slipped out alone.

Izzy was busy schooling Eric and for once there was no one else around, so feeling like a naughty school child I had seized the opportunity to take Flame for a rare, solo ride.

I had taken the road towards the moor and turned off along a wide track which skirted an area of woodland. The early spring sunshine had woken nature from her sleepy winter slumber and the pressure from Flame's hooves released the earthy scent of the turf. Trotting down the track Flame adjusted her stride to avoid rutted puddles and shadows; leaning forward as the flat ground began to climb uphill, my weight invited her to slip into a gentle canter then with little encouragement into an exhilarating gallop. My eyes were streaming with the wind when I reluctantly sat up and brought my mare back to a more sedate pace. Leaving the wide springy track which the racehorses had used when my home had been a busy racing yard, we turned to follow a narrower track through the woods; the dappled sunshine pierced the gaps between the overhead branches. Eventually the trees thinned, and I found myself on the straighter track of a bridle path which hugged the boundary between farmland and the moor. Ahead I could see the roof tops of the houses and shops in the village.

As we turned from the soft muddy track into the village, we were passed by a small group leaving the Riding Academy. The instructor leading the group waved and called out a greeting as the chattering collection of ponies and children clattered down the road towards the bridle path.

A delicious aroma was drifting out of the new coffee shop Henry had enthused about. The windows were stacked high with tempting cakes and pastries. I made a mental note to come back later. The door opened and set an old -fashioned bell bouncing into life as I was riding past. Camilla came out, balancing a pale pink cake box in one hand and a tray of coffees in the other.

"Hi. They do take away! Isn't it great?"

I laughed, "Sounds dangerous; in terms of my waistline, anyway!"

"I'm glad I bumped into you; I was going to drive up later. I'm drumming up support for the Hunt Ball and wondered if I could flog you some tickets."

"Oh, but I haven't been hunting since I've lived here."

"That doesn't matter, as long as you aren't an anti or a saboteur!" Camilla laughed. "The closest half the people there will have been to a horse is watching Channel Four Racing on a Saturday afternoon."

"Okay then, that sounds like it might be fun." I ventured cautiously, "I haven't been to anything like that for ages."

"Do you think any of your liveries would be interested?"

"Maybe, I'll ask. When is it?"

"The weekend after the one- day event at Stonecross Hall. The ball is being held in the Hall."

Camilla delicately balanced the pink cake box on top of the coffee and dug a flyer out of her bag. "Here take this then give me a ring when you know how many tickets you want."

*****

I came out of Flame's stable and balanced my tack on the fence. As I turned back towards the stable, I saw a car on the road outside slowing down. It was maroon. My heart sank. Izzy had left and I was not in the mood to deal with Dominic, especially on my own, and I was sure it was his car. I led Flame out of the stable and towards the field. The car was still there, parked on the verge with the engine running but, as I took Flame's head collar off and she thundered away to join the other horses, another car came up the road. I was sure the maroon car flashed its headlights before pulling out and driving away.

I was certain it was Dominic's car, but I didn't have time to worry about what he was up to because the second car turned off the road and came through the gates. I left my saddle and went to meet the driver.

She was a young woman in about her mid to late twenties I estimated. Her long, highlighted hair was tucked into in a neat bun. She was wearing close fitting blue denim jeans over leather paddock books. Her black turtleneck was topped by a grey padded waistcoat.

"Hi, are you Abigail? I'm Hannah, I was told you might have a vacancy for a full livery."

"Yes. And yes," I smiled, "can I ask who recommended me?"

She looked past me towards the stables, "I can't remember their name, sorry. Someone in the pub a couple of nights ago."

"Ah, my friend works at the Dirt Dog. I wonder if it was her."

"Maybe. I'm not sure who it was, or which pub," she smiled sheepishly, "I confess we had all had quite a bit to drink."

"Don't worry, that doesn't make you bad person," I laughed, "come on, I'll show you around. Where are you keeping your horse at the moment?"

She closed the gate behind her, "Oh, he's new, so I'm not moving from anywhere."

"Okay, well come through and I'll show you around." I opened the gate into the stable yard. "Did you happen to see a car outside when you arrived?" I asked.

"No. I don't think so. I mean there might have been someone driving the other way, I wasn't taking much notice to be honest, why?"

"No reason. I just wondered."

"Who was that?" Phoebe asked as Hannah drove out of the yard.

"She's called Hannah. A new livery as of tomorrow!" I hugged Phoebe. "That makes eight paying liveries!"

40

"Well, this calls for a celebration! Come on let's go for lunch at the Dog."

The pub was quite busy given that it was a weekday. Small pockets of locals were scattered around the bar area; some sat at tables enjoying the home cooked food which helped to make the Dirty Dog so popular, Tom the builder and his son were finishing off a bowl of chips and a pint at the bar.

"You grab that table over by the fire and I'll get some menus from the bar," Phoebe directed me.

I settled into a deep, high backed chair and listened to the buzz of conversations around me punctuated by the crackle of logs splitting in the fire.

"Cheers! Here's to the success of Fellbeck Livery Stables!" I toasted. We clinked glasses before tucking into plates of steak and ale pie.

"I feel so decadent, drinking red wine in the middle of the day." I confessed, "will you be okay to drive?"

"Yeah. I'm just having a small one." Phoebe mumbled through a mouthful of pie and pointing from her glass to mine with her knife. "Tell me about this new livery."

"Not much to tell really." I balanced my own knife and fork on the edge of my plate and took a drink. "She's called Hannah, it's a new horse; a gelding, black, D.I.Y livery, at least to begin with. She's got some sort of phobia about people touching her stuff and is a bit particular… we'll see how she manages."

"She sounds a barrel of laughs," said Phoebe.

"She's paying me money, so I don't care."

"She looks familiar. Does she live round here?" Phoebe asked, chasing the last of her steak pie around her plate.

I pushed my own, empty plate away, "I can't remember. You can ask her tomorrow."

"Is that when she's coming?"

"Yep. Tomorrow morning, so as soon as we get back there's a stable to prepare."

"Not before dessert though, eh?" Phoebe grinned as she handed me a menu.

The following morning, I was awoken by the sound of a lorry outside. Forcing my eyes to open I concentrated hard, focussing on the clock, willing the blurry illuminated numbers to be clear enough to read.

Five thirty!

I scrambled out of bed and grabbed my dressing gown. What the hell was going on? I stared out of the window. A dark coloured horse box was outside on the grass verge. My heart was pounding. What if someone was trying to steal the horses? I must get a dog I decided.

I half ran, out half fell down the stairs. I pulled a pair of boots on, not easy barefoot I discovered, and tightened the chord belt around my robe. As I ran outside the security lights came on, illuminating the horsebox which was now having the ramp lowered by a man in a baseball cap and a woman with blonde hair.

"Hannah?"

The blonde woman turned and waved.

"Hi. The gate's locked!"

"Because it's only half past five!"

"Oh. Sorry." She looked at my stylish ensemble of pyjamas and wellies with renewed understanding. "The guys could only pick him up for me if we did it early. I guess I didn't realise how early it was." She giggled as I fumbled to undo the padlock. I swung the gate open and realised that while I had been busy with the lock the man had unloaded a very dark, possibly even black, coloured horse and handed the lead rope to Hannah. Without speaking he began to close the wing style gates from either side of the ramp.

"Here, I'll give you a hand," I offered.

"Oh, he's fine," Hannah interrupted, "why don't you show me where the stable is."

By the time I had escorted Hannah and her horse to the stable we had prepared the day before, the horsebox had driven away.

"Crikey, he was in a hurry! Who was it? Is he local?" I asked, amazed at the speed the guy had raised the ramp and driven off.

"Oh, just someone I saw advertising in the paper," Hannah said vaguely," I'm sorry I woke you up." She added grinning at my pyjamas. Before I could answer Phoebe drove into the yard.

"Hi, you're up early. Have you done morning feeds yet?"

She either didn't notice or was unconcerned about my choice of clothing.

"Not yet. Phoebe, meet Hannah, our new client. Hannah this is Phoebes, my right-hand woman."

"Pleased to meet you!" Hannah held out her hand.

"Hi. Yeah. Have we met before?" Phoebe held onto Hannah's hand and looked at her carefully.

Hannah smiled, "I don't think so."

"Do you live in the village?" Phoebe asked, "I'm sure we've met somewhere."

"No. I don't. And I'm certain we haven't met!" Hannah withdrew her hand and picking up an armful of rugs, set off towards the stables.

"Sorry, my mistake." Said Phoebe following her, "so, tell me about your horse. A gelding right? What's he called?"

Hannah paused for a moment, regaining her composure before answering.

"Erm, I've just got him, I haven't picked a name yet." She dropped the rugs by the stable door and took the grooming kit which I had carried.

"Oh, you shouldn't change a horse's name, it's unlucky," Phoebe told her.

"Or so some people think." I butted in. "What did the last people call him?"

"I err…" she stumbled before grinning, "Secret. His name's A Secret!"

"Secret. Hm. Cool name," I mused as I leaned on the half door with Phoebe. "Gosh he is really dark, black in fact. Does he have any white on him?"

"None at all." Hannah adjusted the horse's rug before carefully removing his travelling boots.

" I know, what about the pub? The Dirty Dog. Have you ever been in there?" Phoebe persisted.

"No. Never!" Hannah answered sharply.

"Like I said, my mistake, sorry."

Chapter 7

A small group were gathered around the table in the tea- room. Felicity was sitting down, and Henry was feeding tiny pieces of chicken to the little tabby cat who was sitting on her knee. Chantelle was updating her Instagram account and Phoebe was scrutinising the timetable on the small whiteboard where liveries booked time in the outdoor arena.

"I swear I had my name down for half two!" Phoebe grumbled, "that makes it three times I've thought I had booked the school but turns out Izzy is in there and I'm booked for an hour later."

"Getting forgetful in your old age sweetie," Henry joked.

"Ha, fucking ha!" She pulled a face at him. "I have a shift at the pub tonight and wanted to do some flat work with Treasure. I'll just have to go for a hack instead. Anyone else?"

"Sorry, I don't have time," said Felicity fussing the cat.

"Yeah, I'll come!" Chantelle unexpectedly looked up from her phone, "could someone help me tack up please?"

Felicity put the cat down, "Come on, I'll give you a hand."

"Where are they going?" I asked Felicity as Phoebe and Chantelle bounced out of the gateway.

"A quick hack." Felicity watched with me as they disappeared up the road towards the moor.

"Oh hell! I hope Phoebe takes it easy and brings that kid back in one piece," I worried.

"To be fair," said Felicity, "if she brings her home at all, I think we'll call it a win!"

I spent the next hour alternating between scanning the road, checking the time and watching Henry lunge first Solo then

Symphony. Eventually the sound of hooves clattering down the road alerted us that someone was home. I rushed from the arena around to the stables just as Phoebe and Chantelle came through the gate.

"Christ almighty!" Marc muttered, at my shoulder. He had followed me and stood, open mouthed by my side as we watched them return.

Zeus was normally dark bay, almost black and Treasure's bay coat was usually the colour of roasted coffee, today however, they were both flecked with white foam. Each horse was snorting from red nostrils and their tails were held high in excitement. Veins stood out all over their wet glistening bodies and as they finally came to a trembling standstill a gentle fog of steam began to rise around them.

Chantelle was grinning from ear to ear. "That was mint!" Her face was flushed with excitement and spattered with mud. She slid off Zeus and left him standing while she posed, with him behind her, to take a series of selfies for her social media post.

Phoebe sat in silence as her horse stood blowing as if he had just won the Derby. Her face was white, though the adjective falls short of describing the drained paleness of her countenance, highlighted by a liberal spraying of mud and several scratches. Her hair had escaped from its usual neat ponytail and she had lost her colourful silk hat cover. She was gripping her reins with white knuckled hands and stared blindly ahead through wide unblinking, yet unseeing eyes.

"Phoebe? Are you okay?" I asked.

She didn't answer.

Marc did a quick appraisal of both horse and rider. "Horse seems okay."

I put a hand on Treasure's bridle. He stopped fidgeting for a moment and tried to scrub his face on my arm. Still Phoebe sat motionless. Marc gently took her feet out of her stirrups and prised open her fingers to release the reins. Treasure snorted then shook from his head through to his tail. The powerful shake travelled through his entire body and through Phoebe, causing her to vibrate off the horse to the ground where she lay, frozen, still in a position which suggested she was riding an invisible horse, albeit rotated through ninety degrees.

I looked at Marc.

"You deal with the horse," he suggested, "I'll deal with her."

He bent over and lifted Phoebe from the ground before gently carrying her to sit on plastic mounting block while I led Treasure away to wash him down. Henry was showing Chantelle how to wash the sweat off Zeus, before scraping the water off his shining body and covering him with a rug.

"What happened?" I asked.

"Oh, it was great!" declared Chantelle, turning towards me and leaving Henry to deal with her horse. "We went up to the moor and onto the old gallop track. I've never gone so fast in all my life!"

I glanced at Henry. "Zeus is in his stable," he told us.

"Okay. Thanks. Anyway, we went around the track. Twice, no three times! Then through the woods 'cos Phoebe knew a short cut back home. I am totally ready to compete." She consulted her phone, "There's an unaffiliated One Day Event at Stonecross Hall coming up. I'm going to see if I can get an entry in."

"Oh my god!" said Henry and I in unison.

"I know!" Chantelle grinned.

Henry and I hurried over to where Marc was encouraging Phoebe to breath into a paper bag.

"And then I said, 'shall we trot?' and after that it was just a blur."

"It's okay, honey. Here breath." Marc handed her the paper bag again, "slowly."

"Twice round the old gallops!" she informed us in between breaths. "Fuck that horse is fast!"

Henry gently removed pieces of twig from her hair. "And the woods sweetheart?" he prompted, "Chantelle said you brought her home by a shortcut."

Phoebe paused from breathing into her bag and gave him a look that would have turned milk sour, "Seriously?"

Henry looked at me for confirmation. "That's what she said," I agreed.

"Hell's teeth! She. Is. Mental! She rides like you drive!" She pointed her bag at me, "after chasing her for two laps I didn't have the strength to handle a third, so I tried to block her path you know, make her stop; instead of slowing down she just cannoned straight into the back of Treasure, he bucked then pissed off, straight through the hedge into the woods. I don't know how she clung on!"

Henry took a white handkerchief from his pocket, used a nearby tap to wet it before gently wiping her cheek. Phoebe flinched.

"Here, this will take the sting out." He stroked some cream across the graze.

"What is it?" I asked.

"A mix of Calendula and Hypericum. We use it on the ponies," Marc explained, "now, how about a nice cup of tea Phoebes?"

*****

Hunts were now expected to follow a false scent, rather than hunt actual foxes, but they still clung to their traditions. Most Hunts celebrate with a ball at least once a year; popular times are around Christmas and New Year or as in this case, close to the end of the hunting season; sometime close to the end of March or mid-April.

The entire yard had signed up for tickets.

"What are you wearing for the Hunt Ball?" Phoebe asked. We were driving home from the feed merchant.

"Oh, I don't know. To be honest the closer it gets, the less I feel like going."

"Don't you dare bale on me! You might have decided that the entire male species are a bad lot, but I'm still optimistic that my Mr Right is out there somewhere."

"And you think that 'somewhere' is the ball?"

"Might be. At least it's worth a look," she grinned.

"I'm not saying all men are a, what was that expression? A bad lot?" I laughed, "it's just…"

Phoebe looked at me, "It's just what?"

"Well, I'm a bit out of practice. You know at dancing and… and … flirting."

"Okay. Simple solution. Dance with Marc and Henry and leave the flirting to me. Think of it as a girl's night out!"

"I'm not sure."

"I'm just saying it's a night out with friends, not a bloody orgy. Look, you're the one who said it would be fun in the first place."

"I suppose…"

"That's the spirit. Now come on let's get this feed unloaded, might be worth thinking about getting it delivered now there are so many horses here."

Chapter 8

A thin dusting of late snow had fallen overnight. Where the weak sunlight was able to warm the ground, it was already melting but large patches of ground were still treacherously slippery. I picked my way cautiously from the bungalow towards the stables. The cars in the carpark told me that Phoebe and Izzy were here along with Marc. I reached the stables and noted with relief that Phoebe had sprinkled some salt across some of the paths. Most of the horses had been turned out into the fields; their heavy quilted rugs created a colourful contrast to the winter snowscape. The sound of horses contentedly pulling hay from their nets suggested that Treasure and Eric were in their stables.

Marc peered out of the tack room and beckoned to me.

"You know I could listen to the sound of horses eating hay for hours; it's so relaxing. But people? Urgh. The sound of people eating could induce me to commit murder!"

"Shh!" Marc interrupted me and put a finger to his lips, "come here. Quietly." He held his hand out to help me over the ice. "Listen!" he whispered.

"What?" I hissed back.

In reply, Marc pointed through the wall which separated the tearoom and the tack room. We tiptoed across the stone floor. "Phoebe and Izzy. It's fucking hilarious!"

"What's going on?"

"They're arguing about the arena. Again."

There was no need to eavesdrop, their voices could be heard clearly through the breezeblock divide.

"Why do you even need the arena so often?" Phoebe's voice was loud.

"Because unlike some people, I take my riding seriously!"

"What is that supposed to mean?" demanded Phoebe.

"I would happily let you have the school whenever you wanted if I thought there was any chance it would help turn you into a half decent rider!"

"Why, you, nasty little gnome!" Phoebe snarled back.

"Name calling? How mature," laughed Izzy, revelling in the fact that she had got under Phoebe's skin.

"That poor horse must be bored out of his fucking mind!" snapped Phoebe, "round and round and round."

"Oo! I'm impressed you know what a circle is," Izzy taunted.

"It's all you do know and it's not like your hours of going around in ever decreasing circles ever make you any better?"

"Like you would even know a decent rider if one bit you!" hissed Izzy.

"I'll fucking bite you if you don't stop pissing about!"

"We'd better break them up," I whispered.

"Must we?"

"Yes! Come on!" I dragged Marc, semi-reluctantly out of the tack room and into the tearoom. Phoebe and Izzy were standing in front of the timetable used to schedule time in the ménage, glaring at each other. Fortunately, they were separated by a table, but Phoebe was gripping the wooden edge and was about to pull the table out of her way.

"Ladies, ladies what is going on?" Marc stepped in between them, standing like a referee at a boxing match. "Why are you fighting?"

They both began shouting at the same time before Phoebe decided to step things up a notch. She pulled the table to one side and lunged towards Izzy, making a grab for her hair.

Marc grasped Phoebe around the waist and lifted her off the ground and away from Izzy. Phoebe twisted and squirmed, but Marc was strong, and he held her tight. "If I wasn't gay, I'm sure there is the potential for this to be an incredible turn on, but as it is, you're just giving me a headache. Will you please keep still!"

Phoebe squirmed and twisted, screaming and swearing at Izzy and now also at Marc. He turned and carried her out of the tearoom.

"Izzy?"

She shrugged, "Your friend is crazy."

I considered the comment for a brief moment, "Okay, that's a difficult one to argue. But that's beside the point. What's going on?"

Izzy smiled, "There might have been a teeny-weeny mix up over who had the arena booked…"

"You have got to be kidding me. Two grown women fighting over who gets to use a sixty-metre patch of sand! For God's sake!"

"I know. I'm sorry. But she doesn't take her flat work seriously and …"

"I don't want to hear it. Quit messing with the time slots!" I turned on my heel and marched out of the room, hit a sheet of ice and fell over.

"Ouch! I bet that hurt."

I looked up and saw a strange man looking down at me. He held out his hand and helped me to stand up. As I was still standing on the same patch of ice that had already robbed me of my dignity, my legs shot straight out from under me; again. The stranger caught me this time before I hit the ground.

"Easy tiger. Here let me help you." My rescuer gently supported me and guided me carefully across the ice to the more secure footing of the gritted path. As he set me back onto my own feet, I couldn't help noticing the strength of his arms and a wave of Armani aftershave.

"Are you okay?" He asked.

I could feel the wet patch on my backside where I had hit the ice and was painfully aware of mud, filthy straw and the smell of horse pee which I had managed to acquire when I hit the ground. "I'm fine. A bruised dignity, but otherwise I'm okay. Thanks for helping me, can I return the favour?"

"My balance is good, thanks. And, no offence, but I'm not sure you could hold me up on the ice."

I smiled at his joke. Please let him be looking for livery.

Stop, rewind that wish please universe. Let him be single, have a weakness for women who smell of horse piss and can't walk on ice and be looking for livery!

Was that too much?

Am I being greedy?

"Hello? Did you bang your head when you fell?"

"What? Sorry, did you say something?"

"I think you should sit down for a minute."

"No, I'm fine. Sorry, you were saying...?"

I looked into his eyes. He had the most gorgeous eyes.

"I was saying that I was here to see Felicity?"

My confusion was clearly visible but before I could ask what he meant; Felicity interrupted us, "Hi Pierre, sorry I'm late they haven't gritted the side roads. I see you've met Abi."

"Yeah, she fell for me!"

It was Felicity's turn took confused. I pointed at my soaked backside, "The ice."

"Ah. I see, I think."

"I slipped, and ..." I searched for a name.

"Pierre," volunteered the stranger helpfully.

"... and Pierre picked me up."

"What's that smell?" Felicity wrinkled her nose.

"That would also be me. I'll leave you to it." I sighed. Just my luck. Mr Gorgeous was Felicity's latest mystery man.

Phoebe came out of Treasure's loose box, closely followed by Marc. He was grinning and she was giggling. I raised my eyebrows as she kissed him on the cheek. "Well, your mood's improved!"

"We had a chat." Marc smiled at me and winked at Phoebe.

She sighed. "I wish you weren't gay."

He laughed, "Oh but I am darling, I am. But, if it's any consolation, if anyone could have turned me, it would have been you."

"I'll take that as a compliment. But it's only fair to warn you, I won't stop trying."

"Okay this is a little bit creepy." I said. "Dare I ask what's happened to change your mood?"

"Make me a cup of tea, and feed me cake, Marc has just pointed out there's more than one way to peel an orange." Phoebe linked her arm through mine and escorted me gingerly back towards the bungalow.

"Lemon dwizzle?" Phoebe sprayed through a mouthful of cake, "nice. Haven't had Madeira for a while though."

"Oi. Beggars, choosers and all that jazz."

"Oh, don't get me wrong, this is lovely. I'm just saying, Madeira is a personal favourite." She cut herself another slice of lemon drizzle.

"Yeah. I'll make you one, soon. It's just that it reminds of that woman in my kitchen. You know, Susan?"

"Patricia."

"Whatever. Have you seen Felicity's new bloke?" I asked.

"Only from a distance. Why? Is he nice?"

"Mm. There's something about him?"

"Something nice or something creepy, like Dom?" Phoebe was curious.

"Nice. Definitely a nice something. Oo look there he is." I pointed out of the kitchen window.

We watched as Felicity walked with Pierre to his car.

"How does she do it? She was with a different bloke yesterday. Younger than him," Phoebe pointed with her cake out of the window towards Felicity and Pierre. They were laughing at some private joke.

"I've no idea. I mean she's pretty enough and she is a lovely person but ..." My voice trailed off.

"It just seems unfair. She seems to have so many and we can't find one!" Phoebe completed for me. "Here, have a slice of your cake. It's not bad."

A text message pinged Phoebe's phone into life.

"It's work," she explained looking at the screen, "they want me to cover a lunchtime shift, someone's called in sick."

"Are you going?" I asked as I used a cloth to clear away the cake crumbs.

"Yeah, I need the money. But, how do you fancy going dress shopping when I get finished? I need to find something gorgeous to wear at the hunt ball."

"I'm still not sure I'm going."

"But why? You're the one who said it sounded like fun."

I shrugged.

"Oh please. Look you'll change your mind once we're all dressed up and think how rubbish you'll feel if everyone goes except you. I wanted us to go dress shopping and I'll feel bad if you're not going..." She left the sentence hanging.

I thought about it for a moment. Outside Felicity was waving to Pierre as he drove out of the gates.

"Okay, you win. Call me when you're finished your shift, and I'll pick you up at The Dirty Dog." I agreed.

"Great, except, do you mind if I drive? I'll pick you up," Phoebe said.

Chapter 9

"Guess who I saw at the Dirty Dog when I started my shift?" Phoebe asked as I threw my bag onto the back seat and settled myself into the passenger seat of her car.

"No idea."

"Go on, guess."

"Was it someone famous?"

"Nope."

I began listing people, but Phoebe became frustrated with my inability to read her mind. "Hannah!"

"Where?" I looked around, expecting to see her car passing us or following behind.

"At the pub!"

"Oh." I couldn't understand why this was a big deal.

"Oh? Is that all you can say?"

"Well what do you want me to say? Breaking news, woman visits the pub!"

"She said that she had never been to the Dirty Dog!"

I started to laugh, "So? She obviously decided to give it a go. The place has quite a reputation for serving awesome food you know. Did she speak?"

"No, she didn't see me. But that's not the whole story." Here Phoebe paused for both dramatic effect and to switch lanes, "She wasn't alone!"

"Gasp! Don't say she was... with someone!"

"Oh, you may laugh. That someone was Dominic!"

"What?"

"That's got your attention!" she smirked.

"Are you sure? I wonder what she was doing with him of all people."

"I dunno. Looked like they might have been for lunch or something. Anyway, they both got into her car and drove off. And the more I think about it; I am certain it was her I saw in the pub the other night."

"Really?"

"Admittedly it was busy so there is a chance I was mistaken. But today absolutely one hundred percent it was her. And him. All cosy cuddly together."

"Yuk. No accounting for taste." I shuddered. "I mean, he doesn't exactly make your eyes bleed, but there's just something about him that makes me feel… Urgh."

This time Phoebe joined me in a dramatic shudder and we both laughed.

"There's a space," I pointed out of the window as we trawled through the carpark, "Over there beside the blue mini."

Wandering through the indoor shopping centre confirmed my hatred of shopping.

"I thought it would be quieter at this time of day." I moaned. "I might just look online."

"No, you need to try things on," Phoebe assured me, "but does that mean you are looking?"

"I might be."

"Excellent. I knew you'd change your mind."

"I haven't definitely decided."

"But?"

"Oh! If I give in will you stop nagging?"

Phoebe clapped her hands. "This is going to be so much fun! Let's go get us some spangly frocks before you change your mind again!" she said dragging me into a shop.

We spent the next couple of hours searching through rails of silk, satin and taffeta rainbows. We tried on dresses in so many different shops that eventually the myriad of changing rooms began to merge, each one becoming indistinguishable from the last or the next.

"This is depressing! I hate shopping!" I turned away from the dresses and slumped onto a seat near the changing rooms alongside a man who was resting his head on the wall behind the seats, with his eyes closed. Phoebe ignored me and continued to search.

"For what it's worth I share your pain," said the man without opening his eyes.

"I'm going to try this on," said Phoebe disappearing into the changing rooms.

"I'll wait here."

"What do you think?" I turned to see Phoebe standing in the doorway to the changing area wearing a long silver dress which seemed to cling in all the right places. "Well?" She turned around to show me the low back with thin criss-cross, shoe-string straps.

"Wow!" It was the man in the seat next to me.

Phoebe grinned, "That'll do for me."

"Yea, what he said. Phoebes you look like a gorgeous mermaid!"

"Then this is the one." She turned and found herself facing a woman who was wearing a long navy dress. The woman was frowning and looked more than slightly annoyed.

"Oops. Sorry. I didn't see you there. Excuse me."

The woman ignored Phoebe, who was forced to sashay around the woman as she went to get changed.

The man sitting next to me snapped to attention. "Wow. Like I said, wow. Th… that's the one sweet -heart." The angry woman continued to glare at the man as she stood with her hands on her hips. "Oh, wait, you didn't think the 'wow' was for that girl in the silver dress, did you? No, no I could see you standing behind her."

The woman looked slightly pacified, if not completely convinced, "Are you sure this is the one?"

"Absolutely darling." As he watched 'his darling' retreat into the changing area he whispered, "And that little lie is gonna cost me several more hours of my life searching for the perfect shoes." He sighed and closed his eyes again.

Phoebe emerged clutching the silver dress. "I'm going to pay for this then we absolutely need to find one for you."

I sighed and stood up. As I resumed my own search, flicking through the rails of dresses the slightly less angry lady came to collect her partner and his credit card to pay for the blue dress. "I need to find some shoes…" I heard her say as she walked past me. I glanced around and grinned at him; he stood up and followed her, as he did so he winked at me, "Try the red one." And then he was gone.

"What do you think?" I asked holding up a red dress for Phoebe's approval.

"Very nice. Go try it on. Take this one too, oh and this." She handed me a deep claret wine coloured dress and a black lace number. "Do you want me to come in?"

"No, you wait here, and you can give me your opinion if I like any of them enough to show you."

"Okay, but take this blue one, and this other black one and this one." She loaded my arms with a collection of dresses and sent me with a gentle shove towards the changing room.

Looking at the price tags I was determined not to like any of the dresses. Trying them on would stop Phoebe nagging and I surely had something at home that I could wear. My good intentions began to evaporate when I felt the caress of the silken fabric against my skin. The dress I loved was the claret coloured one which Phoebe had thrust into my arms. It was snug fitting until just past my hips where it fanned out like a fishtail. The dress had long, lace sleeves and just above the bust line the heavy fabric was replaced by the same lace as the sleeves; lace which skimmed my collarbone, leaving my shoulders bare. But the price!

"Any good?" Asked Phoebe when I finally emerged.
"Sadly no."

Her face dropped. "Oh, what was wrong with them?"

"Too tight, too plain, too fancy, too expensive and this one was just too slutty." I handed the dresses to the assistant.

"Now I feel bad that I got a dress and you haven't."

"Don't worry. I'll find something. There's a couple of weeks yet. But not now; can we please go for a coffee?"

We found a table in the window of a coffee shop and settled down to enjoy a caffeine boost and indulge in a spot of people watching. I cradled the oversized cup and relaxed, leaning back into the soft leather chair opposite Phoebe.

Suddenly Phoebe sat bolt upright. She slammed her cup down onto the table causing some of the coffee to spill into the saucer.

"There's Hannah! Look!"

"Where?" I followed her gaze.

"There! She's linked in with a man. I bet it's Dominic!"

"I can't see her. Are you sure?"

"Yes! There in front of that woman in the blue jumper! To the left of the couple with the pram." Phoebe pointed. "They're going into that shop!"

I leaned back into my chair again. "If you say so."

"Aren't you bothered?"

"Bothered? No. Curious? Mildly. Why is this such a big deal to you?" I asked.

"I don't know. There's just something about her. I can't put my finger on it. You know, like an itch you can't reach to scratch."

"Are you comparing Hannah to…" I searched for a way to complete the simile, "…a flea?"

"Well Dominic certainly makes my skin crawl."

I started to laugh and stood up, "I'm going to pay."

As I was stuffing the receipt and my loyalty card back into my purse, Phoebe grabbed my arm and dragged me to the doorway. "She is with Dominic! They've just come out of there," she pointed to an exclusive designer shop, "Then he kissed her, on the fucking lips. Urgh!"

"Well where is he now?" I asked.

60

"Dunno. He headed that way and she's gone into that nail-bar. Come on."

"Come on where?"

Phoebe didn't answer but charged off with the determination of Romeo (Felicity's horse, not the star-crossed lover), in the direction of the nail-bar. I followed.

Hannah was sitting with her back to the door, perched on a stool with one hand extended and receiving the attention of a skilled nail technician. She took a sip from the glass of champagne which was waiting next to her other hand. A large glossy bag was sitting under her stool. It bore the discreet, yet distinctive logo of the dress shop Phoebe had spotted her leaving and was tied with an expensive satin ribbon.

"Hi there!" Phoebe bounced up to Hannah making her jump. The technician scowled but continued without speaking, "I thought it was you."

"Oh, hi," Hannah quickly regained her composure.

"Bought anything nice?" I asked looking at the bag under her stool.

She smiled, "I might have picked up a little treat for myself."

"Expensive treat from that shop!" Phoebe said what I was thinking. How could she afford to shop in such an expensive place and pay these prices when she owed me livery!

"I confess I did rather push the boat out," Hannah glanced at the bag before giving the technician her other hand to work on. "I wouldn't normally spend that much on a dress, but I was talking to Izzy about the Hunt Ball and she told me this is where she buys her stuff, and Felicity said she shops here too, you know, for special occasions."

"Are you by yourself?" Phoebe asked.

"Yeah, why?"

"I thought I saw you with someone earlier," Phoebe persisted.

"No, not me."

"I could have sworn it was you. With a man. The same bloke you were in the pub with this afternoon," Phoebe smiled.

"The pub?" Hannah took her hand away from the technician, who was having difficulty hiding her irritation, and turned to look directly at us.

"What is this? Is there a problem that I'm not aware of?"

"I saw-," Phoebe began, but I cut her off.

"No, nothing's going on. Phoebes thought she saw you earlier at the Dirty Dog that's all."

"Well she didn't!"

"No, obviously she was mistaken," I continued attempting to soothe the situation, "Phoebe just meant we could have all come together. If you're on your own, and if it had been you in the pub. didn't you Phoebes?"

Oh. Well I am on my own," she relaxed, slightly, "and I've never been to your bloody pub!" she added turning to Phoebe.

"Hmph. Well you've got a doppelganger then!"

"It certainly seems so." Hannah smiled before turning her attention back to the technician.

"We'll leave you to it. See you later." I said smiling.

"I know it was her at the Dirty Dog! And she was with that bloody sleaze bag Dominic," Phoebe seethed.

"Are you sure?" I asked.

"It was her! One hundred percent it was her!"

"And you're certain she was with a bloke."

"Again, a million percent."

"Okay, but are you sure the mystery man was Dominic? I've never seen him without a hat on. I don't know if I'd recognise him without it, and you've seen him even less times than me."

We stopped walking.

"I'm al-mo-st certain it was him," she stretched the word out, "but she was with someone and that someone looked like Dom," she concluded with satisfaction.

62

I looked around, half expecting to see Dominic.

"I wonder why she lied?" continued Phoebe.

I shrugged, "Maybe she's just very private."

"Huh. You say private, I say she's hiding something!" Phoebe sniffed.

"Whatever it is, I wish she'd cough up the livery money she owes me."

Phoebe frowned, "I didn't realise she owed you money."

I sighed, "She asked to pay weekly rather than monthly, 'to make it easier to switch from D.I.Y to full livery if she needs help,' she said and like a fool I agreed. I mean she pays eventually but there's always a problem."

"Like what?" Phoebe asked.

"Oh, I don't know she's waiting for a cheque to clear, she's changed bank, the money's left her account but hasn't reached me so she'll chase it up…"

"You should have asked her for it. Do you want me to?" Phoebe offered.

"No. I'll see her at home."

We were standing outside of the designer shop where Hannah had bought her dress. The shop recommended by Izzy and Felicity. The dresses in the window were modelled by plastic androgynous figures. Cool and aloof, rather like Hannah I though wryly.

I peered into the depths of the shop, imagining Felicity and Hannah sipping sophisticated glasses of champagne as they tried on expensive dresses which would make them the belles of the ball. The Hunt Ball. My reflection stared back at me from the shop window. I wasn't impressed by what I saw. My roots were showing, and I couldn't think of a word to describe the remains of my hairstyle.

Everywhere I looked perfectly coiffured women with flawless make up seemed to be laughing at my slightly shiny face and practical, unfashionable clothes.

"Are you okay?" Phoebe asked.

"No."

"What's up?"

"Well look at me."

"I'm looking. What am I looking for, in particular?" she looked from actual me to reflection me then back again.

I turned and leaned my back against the shop window. "I'm a mess!" I wailed sliding down the glass until I was slumped on the floor of the shopping centre.

Phoebe slid down next to me. "What's brought this on?" she asked.

"I don't know."

She peeled open a packet of jelly sweets. "Want one?"

I accepted a small confectionary person and bit the head off savagely.

My friend ate several more members of the jelly family before standing up. She extended her sweet free hand and hauled me to my feet. "Okay, let's retrace the steps of this mini meltdown. We were standing here, discussing Hannah and Dominic. Oh, my shitty aunt! You fancy Dominic!"

"What? No!"

"Well what else was the trigger?"

In response I pointed to my reflection.

"I look so, so… frumpy." I leaned closer to the window, "and shiny."

Phoebe leaned forward with me and bit into another jelly baby, "Nope. You're feeling sorry for yourself because you didn't get a dress and fancy pants Hannah, who owes you money and who by the way is lying like a flat fish, did get a dress and is having a secret something with Dominic!"

"What? You are so far off the beam-," she stopped me talking by popping a jelly person into my open mouth.

"I haven't finished. You feel guilty because you fancy Dom; someone you know is a… a…" she searched for a word or phrase to describe Dominic, "a bad man! And don't ask me how I know he's a bad man, it's just something I can feel, in my water!" She finally declared.

My protests were blocked by both her hand being held up and several more jelly sweets being unceremoniously stuffed by Phoebe into my mouth.

"And," she continued, "you are projecting that guilt as a manifestation of self- loathing!"

I was speechless, mainly because I had a mouthful of sweets.

"You can speak now, I've finished," Phoebe smiled smugly and went to have another sweet. The bag was empty. "You've eaten all my sweets!" she announced accusingly.

"I truly don't know what to say."

"That's okay. You probably needed the sugar or something."

"I really hope your degree wasn't in psychology. I do not fancy Dominic! I'm sick of scrimping and saving that's all and I just feel…" I stopped speaking as a tall, very elegant woman, wearing heels that would probably be held as lethal weapons at airport security, came out of the shop. She was carrying several bags; all emblazoned with designer logos. "You're right. I'm probably just feeling sorry for myself,"

"Ah ha!"

"Not because of Dominic, I'm just out of my comfort zone in places like this. Sophie, the woman my ex was shagging, she loved shopping and she always wore designer stuff. I suppose everywhere I look I see Sophies."

"So, what are you saying? Do you want to get back with your ex?" she asked.

"No, of course not," I turned away from the shop. "Splitting up with him was a blessing in disguise. I'm not saying it wasn't hard at the time, but I've moved on."

"Looks like it." Phoebe snorted as we walked slowly towards the car park.

"I have! I've moved to a new house, sorted my own mortgage, started a business…" I listed my progress defensively.

"Yes, but have you moved on in here?" She tapped the side of my head. "Have you even had a flirtation since your divorce?"

"I've been on a couple of blind date type of things, people I was introduced to…"

"They don't count. Have you fancied anyone?"

"I've told you, once bitten, twice shy."

"Utter bullshit! You were fine earlier. I still think you fancy Dom and don't want to admit it."

"Bullshit back to you. I'm pissed that I have no money and didn't have the balls to confront Hannah."

"Mm." Phoebe didn't look convinced, "well in that case we need to find you someone, not all men are like your ex." Phoebe seemed happy to have found a solution.

"I've told you; he's put me off men."

"Well try a woman."

"No thanks."

"Are you sure? I have some very nice lesbian friends. I could fix you up."

"I'm certain! Thanks for the offer but I'm not a lesbian."

"There's nothing to be ashamed of if you are. Plenty of people don't recognise their true calling until later on." Phoebe continued.

"Oh, my life! I am not gay!"

"Shame. You and Helen would have made a cute couple."

"Who?"

"Never mind, she'll understand."

*****

"Good afternoon, ladies," Marc breezed.

I looked up from the tangle of leather in my lap, "Hi."

"Oo tack cleaning! I simply love the smell of saddle soap!" He inhaled deeply.

Phoebe threw a sponge across the tack room. "Here you go then, knock yourself out. I'd rather be sticking pins in my eyes than cleaning tack."

"Well that's a tad extreme, but I'll give you a hand 'til Henry gets here," he replied, catching the sponge. "How was yesterday's shopping trip?"

"Interesting," Phoebe loaded up her sponge with more of the yellow glycerine soap, "I got a dress and Abi decided not to be a lesbian, even though Helen is lovely."

"Who's Helen?" Marc asked.

"A woman who lives in the flat next door to me."

"I'm not gay," I interrupted.

"Yeah," he said looking at me, "my gaydar doesn't pick you up as being one of us. No offence."

"None taken."

"You however," he winked at Phoebe, "I think you could play for any team, or all of them if you wanted to."

"Shut up!" She threw another sponge at him.

Before the conversation could become anymore twisted Izzy burst through the door with her arms full of Eric's tack. Her face was glowing.

"You do realise the horse is supposed to work harder than you," Marc observed as she hauled the saddle onto its supportive rack.

Izzy laughed, "Oh, Eric worked hard, believe me."

Taking care not to let any of the water touch the leather of the bridle, she dipped Eric's complicated metal bit into a bucket of clean water.

"You know that I've been working with Klaus," she paused for a moment to ensure we all recognised her reference to her expensive German trainer, "and we've been focussing on lengthening stretching my lower leg."

"More focus on spreading than stretching if you ask me," muttered Phoebe.

Marc turned a laugh into snorting cough as Izzy spun around to confront Phoebe.

"Did you say something?"

"No, just cursing that my soap has turned all frothy," Phoebe smiled.

"Too much water," Izzy pointed out. "anyway, as I was saying, Klaus left me with some exercises to practice in between my training sessions and they are working so well. I've put my stirrups down and lengthened them by a hole twice this week already."

"Wow. You'll have to show me," I said.

"Happily," she breezed, "now I must be off, things to do, people to see."

"Sounds intriguing," Marc looked up from cleaning the bridle Phoebe had given him.

Izzy didn't answer. She simply smiled enigmatically and tapped the side of her nose before turning and walking away.

"She thinks she's someone," Phoebe squeezed the water out of her sponge. "Look at me, I have a German trainer," Phoebe tried to impersonate Izzy's voice. "Why can't she simply say she's having a lesson with her instructor!"

"I wonder what those exercises are?" I pondered as I began to buckle the pieces of a bridle back together.

"I don't think they're as amazing as you might think," Phoebe smiled across at Marc.

"What do you mean?"

"Nothing. I just think she's prone to exaggeration."

Marc grinned into the piece of leather he was cleaning.

"Is there something going on that I should know about?" I asked.

"'course not," Phoebe assured me, "Marc have you finished with that noseband yet?"

Chapter 10

The three weeks following the shopping trip were filled with preparations for the One Day Event. It wasn't an affiliated competition, but a lot of riders were planning to enter as a warm up event to ease themselves into the busy eventing calendar or like me and Skye, to give a young or new horse the chance to experience the three phases of competition without the expense, or pressure of affiliating. The event was organised by the local hunt as a fund raiser / social event and drew support from a wide band of loyal followers.

Phoebe was taking Treasure and despite our best efforts, Chantelle had also decided to enter. Izzy had helped Chantelle with some advice regarding the dressage test which formed the first element of the competition and her parents had arranged a couple of lessons with Klaus as well as some jumping lessons with their latest expert. I took Phoebe and Treasure with me and Skye to have some lessons away from home; both for flatwork, Phoebe's weakness and showjumping, my own Achilles heel.

The day before the event Phoebe and I decided to go and walk the cross -country course, rather than waiting until the day of the actual competition.

" Should we take baby Chantelle with us?" Phoebe asked. "If she goes with her mum and dad, poor kid will be left confused beyond belief." We were riding back towards the stables, having decided to let the horses have a gentle leg stretch rather than a demanding schooling session the day before the competition.

"We can ask her. I think she's starting to feel a tad nervous."

Phoebe laughed, "Her mother is certainly looking forward to it. I saw her in the village shop yesterday buying bottles of fizz for her al fresco luncheon party."

"Speak of the devil," I nodded my head in the direction of Margaret Thompson who was waiting for us as we turned off the road into the stables. She wasn't wearing her trademark furs today, instead she was dressed in a pair of fawn, moleskin trousers and a cream sweater with a tweed hacking jacket; her usual heeled shoes had been replaced by a pair of navy wellington boots decorated with the motif of a small white dog. The whole ensemble was topped off with a felt trilby which was decorated with the plumage of several pheasants. She waved and hurried to meet us.

"Abigail, I'm so glad you're back."

"Is everything okay?" I looked around for signs of trouble.

"Oh yes, everything's fine." She followed me to Skye's stable and hovered anxiously outside as I untacked.

"I just wanted to check a few things with you."

"Was there a specific something you wanted to check?" I asked as I flung Skye's rug over her back.

Margaret pulled a list and a short stubby pencil out of her pocket." Knots."

"Knots?"

"Yes, how many knots does Zeus need to have in his hair for tomorrow?"

" Knots?" I muttered to myself, racking my brain for a moment. "Knots? What the hell…? Oh! Plaits!" Realisation dawned, "It doesn't matter for tomorrow, as long as they're neat, and on the off -side."

"The what side?" Margaret paused from making notes on her list.

"Sorry, the right- hand side."

"But what did you call it?"

"The off -side. We call the side we lead a horse, get on or off from and so on the near side and the other side is the off-side," I explained.

"Oh," Margaret made another note, "why?"

I considered explaining the mix of equestrian tradition and historical cavalry necessity but decided against it. "We just do," I used a time saving cop out "was there anything else?"

Margaret consulted her list again, "Yes, the knots, how do you keep them from unravelling?"

I sighed, hoping her list wasn't too long, "That would be personal choice. Some people sew, others use bands."

"Oh," Margaret chewed the end of her pencil.

I left Skye for a moment and leaned on the stable door.

"Margaret, stop panicking. Why don't you go home and put your feet up, Chantelle can come and walk the course with me and Phoebes then later you can watch how we plait. I sew, Phoebe tends to use bands."

Margaret looked relieved, "Are you sure? About taking Chantelle. I mean, shouldn't we be there to check out the route with her?"

"She'll be fine," I reassured her.

Eventually, convinced that she would have the chance to walk around the course the following day and that Chantelle would be far better coming without her well- intentioned but inexperienced parents, Margaret agreed to stay at home. We later discovered that she had spent the time watching videos of Badminton and Burghley Horse Trials on- line.

As we were talking, Izzy led Eric across to the mounting block and after checking her girth, she swung her leg and settled into the saddle.

"Do my stirrups look level?" she called across.

I left Margaret and went to stand in front of her. "I think this one is longer," I pointed.

"Thanks." She frowned, sorted out her tack and rode around to the arena.

"What was that about?" Phoebe asked.

"Nothing just odd stirrups."

Phoebe grinned.

"What's tickled you?" I asked suspiciously.

71

"Nothing. Just looking forward to walking the course. Are you ready?"

"Room for a little one?" Henry asked as we were preparing to leave, "I love a good course walk!" Henry folded his long legs into the space behind Phoebe.

"Are you alright back there?" I asked before I started the engine.

"Well Phoebe could be a gem and swap places."

"Tough. I was here first. If you snooze you lose!" Phoebe snapped her seatbelt into place.

"Well at least move your seat forward," Henry grumbled digging his knees forcefully into the back of her seat. He and Phoebe spent the short journey squabbling good naturedly for the entire time.

*****

The competition was to be held in the grounds and parkland of Stonecross Hall; although this was an unaffiliated event, the organisers had gone to great lengths to ensure the day was as close to a British Eventing experience as possible. Several large tents, or small marquees, had been set up and a band of enthusiastic volunteers were busy marking out the dressage arenas with long measuring tapes and white boards.

"It looks proper posh like, doesn't it?" Chantelle immediately captured the scene and sent it to her various social media feeds.

"Wait until tomorrow when they dress the boards and the show- jumps with flower arrangements," Henry told her as we headed towards the cluster of tents. Most were empty, apart from tables and chairs, with the flaps secured against the weather; we followed a trickle of people coming and going from the one tent which was open.

Inside large boards stood in anticipation, ready to display results the following day. Each rider was listed in the section they would be competing in, along with the name of their horse. Chantelle found her name and snapped the evidence. "Over here," Phoebe called to her, "come and check what time you're on."

Chantelle slid her phone into her back pocket and joined us as we huddled around a smaller list which also showed each rider, their horse and the time they were expected to ride their dressage test, their showjumping round and when they would begin their cross country. Although the three phases of the competition replicated a three day event over the space of one day there were some subtle differences; most significantly, competitors were not required to present horses for a veterinary inspection, although eagle eyed stewards would report any concerns to the team of vets who would be on hand throughout the day, and the showjumping phase was held before the cross country, rather than after it.

"Make a note of your times," I told Chantelle, "We'll be here to help, but you'll be jumping while we are busy in the dressage arena."

"Dressage! More like fucking stressage!" mumbled Phoebe biting her nails.

"Don't worry chick," Henry put his arm around Chantelle's shoulders, "we're all coming to support you so there will be plenty of people to help. Both of you." He added extending his other arm to encompass Phoebe, "and you," he winked at me.

I smiled. Strictly speaking Chantelle wasn't my responsibility but I was relieved to hear that there would be people with some experience on hand to assist her if necessary. I took a quick photograph of the cross -country course map on my own phone.

"Okay Chantelle, your fences are purple and ours are orange," I added turning to Phoebe.

Chantelle looked puzzled.

"The numbers," Henry explained," sometimes the same fence is used for different classes, they might add a rail to add height or something, but usually each class has a fence of an appropriate size. We walk the course looking for fences with the number on a purple disc, they look for orange ones."

"Oh, yes of course," she giggled.

I pulled a small notebook out of my pocket and scribbled in the corner to check my pen was working. Phoebe raised an eyebrow, "Making a shopping list?"

"Laugh all you like but I can guarantee you will want to look at my notes before you ride this tomorrow."

"Oh, I was going to take a picture of each jump on my phone," she held up her mobile.

"Well… clever shite... I might also do that."

Phoebe laughed and linked her arm through mine as we left the tent and followed several other small groups who were making their way towards the start of the course.

There were 20 obstacles on the cross -country course which wound through quite a few fields and small patches of woodland. The jumps were made to look natural and rustic unlike the brightly coloured fences in the showjumping phase. The first jump was a simple log, or for Chantelle a telegraph pole. The course planners usually made the first jump look inviting and simple as this is where riders were encouraging their mounts to leave the safety and company of home and the other horses.

The track then wound away, heading slightly downhill to a log stack. Fence three was a wall of straw bales for Chantelle and a line of bales sitting on a mock -up of a wooden cart for myself and Phoebe. Fence four was a combination of three narrow arrow heads, one after the other. Chantelle's course required her to negotiate a zigzag of raised telegraph poles. She could bounce through the wide parts or stretch across the corners. Phoebe began to pace out the distances between the three elements we would be jumping. I followed her and made a scribbled note in my little book.

"What are they doing?" Chantelle asked Henry.

"They're working out the distance between the three parts of the obstacle, so they know where to push on and ask the horse to lengthen or shorten the stride."

Chantelle looked concerned, "Should I be doing that?"

Henry smiled, "Don't worry sweetheart, you just let Zeus make his own decisions. He knows his job better than you."

"Are you sure?"

"Positive. Don't let him go too fast, stay nice and balanced, take each fence straight and leave the rest to him," Henry assured her.

The next three jumps were made from telegraph poles: one raised off the ground on top of a mound or bank, creating a drop effect, another in a fan, spreading out from a fixed point and the third over a ditch. Fence eight was set into the fence line replicating a style into the woods where more logs of varying sizes were waiting. Fence ten was another log stack then out of the woods by jumping a trimmed section of hedge. A sloping fence known as a palisade was next, followed by a jump in the shape of a wooden house. Each class had a different height of 'house' and the more experienced horse and rider combinations, who were jumping much bigger versions of each jump marked with yellow and green numbers, had an obstacle which was a miniature version of Stonecross Hall. Chantelle and Henry spent several minutes posing for photographs in front of and on top of the replica hall.

As we approached fence fourteen the collection of other course walkers became more concentrated. This was the water, a man -made lake or pond with a variety of entry and exit points; some invited the horse and riders to drop down into or jump up and out of the water; as alternatives to jumping some classes were offered a selection of sloping banks, this provided a much longer, gentler method of traversing the aquatic obstacle. Several people had cautiously entered the water, checking the depth or ensuring they knew the exact line they would follow; others hovered anxiously on the bank, peering into the water, wondering if they would make it safely to the next jump the following day or if their plans would come to a wet and undignified end here, at number fourteen.

Chantelle and Zeus would ride into the element from one of the sloping banks, then splash through the water and jump up and out onto the structured step which formed the opposite bank. "Make sure you go through the right set of flags," Henry pointed out to her. "Look here, see how your number has a purple letter A here and," he splashed through the water, "B is here. Don't get lost."

Each class had a different route through the water, each with a varying degree of difficulty and the vast array of flags and colourful discs displaying numbers and letters was baffling.

"We drop into the water from here," Phoebe called to me. "How deep is it Henry?"

Henry waded boisterously through the murky water towards her, "I'd say about knee deep from where you'll land in."

"I meant to bring my wellies!" she moaned, "is it cold?"

Henry laughed and scooped a handful of water in her direction.

"You tell me."

I walked around the artificial lake. "And we jump out here," I called.

Chantelle followed Henry, giggling into the water and recorded a video of her legs splashing through the shallows at the edge. "I bet I fall off here!" she announced.

"I always bring spare clothes," I confided.

The sound of Phoebe squealing distracted us; Henry was giving her a piggy -back and following the line she would be riding the following day. Of course, being Henry, he couldn't simply carry her from A to B, he needed to do it in style. Chantelle watched through the screen of her phone as she videoed Henry cantering through the water, snorting and

76

tossing his head in his impersonation of Treasure. He spooked and shied before dropping a shoulder, almost sending Phoebe, who was both screaming and laughing hysterically, into the drink.

"You arse; you nearly dropped me!" she punched his shoulder good naturedly, still laughing.

"I just wanted you to enjoy the full experience," he teased, "Chantelle, send me that video will you sweetheart," he called over his shoulder as, still carrying Phoebe, he cantered away towards the next jump which was a stone wall leading into a second woodland copse. Here, the course designers had treated riders to a wide springy track through the woods where the wild garlic was just beginning to peep through the dappled earth between the trees. The track forked leading to a ditch under a pole for Chantelle while our number sixteen was a more complicated series of poles and a ditch known (unreassuringly) as a coffin.

After the ditches the two branches of the track re-united and sets of wooden rails designed to look like gates and ladders led out of the woods and back into the open fields. Once out of the trees the course led down a slope to a wide, solid fence called a table before climbing steadily uphill to number nineteen which was a decorative collection of tyres. From here the finish was insight and the ground became level once more. The final fence, number twenty, was built in the shape of a garden chair or bench.

Most of the fences were decorated with floral displays and theme related accessories such as flowers bursting out of picnic baskets at the side of the table jump.

"What a lush course!" announced Henry. He was standing on the giant chair belonging to the bigger class with his hands on his hips.

Chantelle was gasping for breath after the steep climb to number nineteen. "Christ, I hope I don't get lost!"

"Don't worry," Phoebe reassured her, "stay inside the white ropes and you'll be fine."

Chantelle didn't look convinced.

"There will be quite a worn track to follow," I reminded her.

"You can use that in your dressage as well," Phoebe chipped in, "the centre line gets worn in after the first couple of riders. I always try to use it to make sure I don't overshoot the middle."

"And the circles," Henry jumped down and we all walked back towards the car, "if you see a good- sized circle, with a decent shape, use it as a guide."

"Okay," said Chantelle, looking slightly overwhelmed.

Henry took her hand, "Do you know your dressage test?"

"Yes... I think so." Chantelle didn't look too certain.

"Come on." Henry dragged her away towards the white boards which had been painstakingly measured and set out in front of the backdrop of Stonecross Hall. "Do you have a copy of the test?"

A few taps of her phone brought up the test complete with diagrams. Chantelle handed it to Henry who proceed to drag a giggling Chantelle down the centre line of one of the empty arenas.

"Where does he get his energy?" I asked Phoebe as we stood and watched Henry and Chantelle walk, trot and canter their way through the test she would ride the following day.

"I know, I'm exhausted watching him. I wonder how a showing pro knows so much about eventing," she pondered.

"Dunno. But I'm glad he came along."

We both applauded as Chantelle saluted.

"I am sooo excited," she called over to us.

After a look at the showjumps, where once again I paced out distances with Phoebe and Henry gave advice to Chantelle, we headed back home where we found Marc waiting with Margaret in the tea- room.

"Oh hi!" He jumped up as we all came around the corner and kissed Henry on the cheek. "I wondered if you would be able to resist walking the course. Are you okay?"

"I'm fine."

Marc held him at arms -length and scrutinised his face for a moment, "Are you sure?"

"Certain. Stop worrying. Have you been waiting long?"

"A while, but I've been busy."

Henry raised an eyebrow, "Oh, what've you been up to?"

"He's been helping me!" Margaret announced, "he showed me how to knot Zeusy's hair. Come and see. He looks like the horses on the telly."

Chapter 11

The following morning, we left the yard in a small convoy. The sky was heavily laden with grey clouds and most of the inhabitants of Stonecroft village were still asleep as we drove through the empty streets. I was leading the way with Phoebe sitting next to me in the cab of my newly purchased small horsebox; the Thompson family were following me with Zeus tap dancing in their trailer and behind them came Marc and Henry in their car. Felicity and Izzy were going to come along later in the day.

A steward wearing a Hi-Viz tabard yawned and waved us through the gates of Stonecross Park. He pointed towards the makeshift car park for the competitors where lines of trailers and horseboxes were already beginning to form under the direction of another steward. Some horses had been unloaded and were standing tied to the side of trailers and horseboxes as riders and helpers unwrapped bandages and groomed already spotless coats. Buckets and muck scoops marked out territory between lorries along with brightly coloured garden chairs and mugs of coffee.

I could feel the excitement hanging in the air as we hurried through the parked vehicles towards the tents which housed the officials. After collecting our numbers and presenting the horses' passports for inspection, we took a final check of the show jumps before setting about preparing Skye and Treasure. Glancing along the line I was relieved to see Marc and Henry organising the Thompson family.

"I hope she'll be alright," I muttered to Phoebe, nodding my head towards Chantelle.

"She's not your responsibility. Stop fretting."

"I know, but after a potential customer popping her clogs in my kitchen, I'd hate to have another one killed off at her first competition."

"She'll be fine," said Phoebe, rolling her eyes, "she's come on quite a bit and let's be honest, she survived that crazy ride through the woods; in fact, I'd say she fared better than me!"

We tightened each other's numbers before Phoebe gave me a leg up onto Skye who was very excited and seemed to have springs in her feet. Treasure had helped to keep her calm while we travelled but her eyes were like huge organ stops as she stood trembling slightly, drinking in all the unfamiliar sights and smells. I waited until Phoebe had stretched from the high point of the lorry ramp onto Treasure's back before setting off towards the collecting ring to warm up before riding our dressage tests.

Chantelle and Zeus were in the far corner. Henry was with her and had obviously told her to keep a distance from other horses. Margaret and James were standing with Marc near the dressage arenas where some competitors had started their tests. Marc waved when he saw us. We waved back. He turned and said something before leaving the Thompsons and hurrying over towards us.

"Is everything okay?" I asked.

"Yes. I mean nothing to worry about, but we thought it would be best to keep Ma and Pa Thompson away from the collecting ring."

"Good idea." Phoebe agreed.

"I told them only riders and trainers are allowed in due to health and safety. Henry took Chantelle away from the busy end." Marc pointed to where Zeus was rocking around the figure we recognised as Henry.

"We saw them when we came over," I said, "how is she doing?"

Marc paused, choosing his words carefully, "Her test sheet will be interesting to read," he finally said.

"As long as she doesn't fall off, I think we'll all be happy!" I said watching Chantelle and Zeus continued to circle Henry in a manner which appeared more menacing than educational.

Marc laughed, "Good luck. I'd better get back to my babysitting duties."

*****

Skye settled down and began to relax as I found an area to claim as my own and we both started to concentrate. I was vaguely aware of Phoebe not too far away with Treasure. Out of the corner of my eye I saw the collecting ring steward wave her clip board and beckon Chantelle. Henry, dodging to avoid Zeus' swinging hind quarters accompanied her and pointed to the arena where she was to ride her test.

"Remember, stay outside the boards until the judge gives you the signal to start. This judge is using a small bell. Good luck!"

He stepped back and joined Marc and Chantelle's parents to watch the test. Chantelle and Zeus bounced down the centre line towards the judge's car. They managed to complete most of the movements where they were required to trot. Zeus was far from being on the bit; his head was so high that his ears were almost lodged in Chantelle's nose. He was more interested in the horses in the nearby collecting ring, other dressage arenas, horses in the lorry park; in fact, he was interested in just about anything other than his rider.

"Oh, he's talking to his friends," Margaret crooned as Zeus let out a shrill whinny which was answered by several horses who were warming up nearby. Margaret, who was again wearing her tweed ensemble and her feather decorated trilby hat, extracted a camera from the depths of a large handbag and snapped several photographs as Chantelle and Zeus exploded into canter. The pair steadily gained speed as they thundered around the arena before Chantelle was able to steer her horse into what was almost a circle, while somehow managing to remain inside the white boards.

Standing beside the proud parents, Marc closed his eyes for a moment and whispered to Henry, "I can't bear to watch!"

"I know," Henry clutched Marc's arm, "but it's nearly over, look, she's just finished the second canter and she's sort of got him back into trot."

"Does that count as a halt?" Marc asked as Chantelle and Zeus stormed down the centre line towards the judge in his car. There was a brief moment when Chantelle managed to haul the horse almost to a standstill. She flashed a quick salute which the judge didn't have time to respond to before they were off again heading towards the gap in the boards between two brightly coloured floral displays where the riders entered and left the competition area.

As Chantelle re-joined her small group of supporters Marc and Henry leapt into action, in a pre-arranged operation to grab Zeus and lead him and his red faced, grinning rider back to their trailer.

Once there, they sent Chantelle's parents to grab a place where they could watch the showjumping while they did their best to calm down the super charged Zeus and his rider.

My own test was uneventful which I took as a personal win. It was Skye's first one day event and a dressage test at a dressage competition where everyone seems to speak in whispers and the tests are held in quiet spaces treated with almost religious reverence are very different to competitions surrounded by wide open spaces and brightly coloured show jumps.

There wasn't much time between my dressage and showjumping, so I headed straight to the horsebox to change Skye's saddle. On my way I passed Izzy and, rather unexpectedly, Hannah, hurrying in the opposite direction towards the dressage arenas.

"How did it go?" asked Izzy.

"Not too bad," I stopped for a moment and Hannah stroked Skye's nose. "She was a bit tense to start with, but she was obedient and there were some nice moments. Did Felicity come with you?"

"Yeah she's with the Thompsons. Do you need a hand with anything?" Hannah asked politely, though her eyes were scanning the area behind me.

"I'm fine thanks, but I'd better get a move on."

Felicity was waiting at my horsebox.

"I thought you might need someone to help with your tack change. Chantelle has Marc and Henry." I glanced across towards the Thompson's trailer just in time to see Chantelle being led towards the showjumping arena.

"Good luck!" I called.

Each of her escorts gave a thumbs up in response as they continued on their way, but they didn't turn around.

"I'm furious I missed your dressage," Felicity grumbled.

"That's okay," I laughed, "it was nothing to get excited about."

"All the same. I wanted to be here earlier." She slid Skye's saddle off and I replaced it with a jumping saddle.

"So, what happened to hold you up?" I asked, passing the girth to her under Skye's belly.

"Well, Izzy wanted to ride before we left, and that was okay. I mucked out while we were waiting for Hannah, but Izzy took bloody ages. She spent as much time faffing about with her stirrups as actually riding!"

"Who was faffing?"

We both looked up to see Phoebe sitting on a very relaxed Treasure. I threw a pair of protective boots towards Felicity who caught them and bent down to fasten them onto Skye's front legs.

"Izzy," I said as I began to fit the boots to my horse's back legs.

Phoebe dismounted and rolled her eyes, "I thought I saw her near the dressage." She listened as Felicity moved from

Skye to help with Treasure while she recounted the story to explain her lateness to Phoebe.

"I mean, my stirrups stay the same, don't yours?" Felicity asked as she finished her tale.

I chose not to point out that her stirrups had probably welded themselves into position under a layer of dust because I had never seen her saddle move from the tack room.

"Yeah. I mean I alter them sometimes, but not on a daily basis like she seems to", I said.

"Must be those lengthening exercises," said Phoebe as she fastened her hat. "Come on then, let's go jump some fences!"

We thanked Felicity and headed towards the collecting ring assigned to the jumping sections; Felicity set off to find the others at the ringside.

Somehow Chantelle made it to through the showjumping without being eliminated. She had a few poles down and her speed would have landed her in trouble if the ground had been slippery, but she remembered Henry's advice and simply steered Zeus around the jumps, sitting up in an attempt to slow him down between fences. After her round, Marc and Henry again snapped into action with the speed and precision of a formula one pit stop team and managed to safely return the pair to the trailer in order to prepare for the cross- country section.

Izzy and Hannah were standing at the ringside, Felicity was close by, watching from the doorway of the beer tent. Camilla from the riding school was there with two men; one I recognised as Steve, her husband, the other was Dom.

Phoebe rode a beautiful clear round and left the arena grinning to a rapturous round of applause.

Skye was slightly overwhelmed by the floral displays and clapping of the crowds and twice rolled a pole when she became distracted. However, I was still thrilled with her behaviour and made a huge fuss as I rode out of the arena to the shouts and cheers of our band of supporters who were steadily becoming more enthusiastic with the help of the beer tent. I gave them a wave to acknowledge their support and spotted Felicity standing to one side of the officials' tent, a plastic glass of something in her hand, laughing and chatting to a very sexy looking man. Pierre.

I rode away from the crowds, not wanting to watch Pierre and Felicity. Not wanting to admit, even to myself, (especially to myself) that seeing the two of them together bothered me.

The Thompson's had a picnic table, complete with tablecloth and chairs set up next to their trailer. An ice bucket was skewered into the grass and the table was groaning under the weight of assorted pies, sandwiches, cakes, nibbles and sausage rolls.

"Can we tempt you Abi?" James called out, waving a pork pie as I rode past.

"I'd love to, but after I've ridden the cross country," I thanked him.

Margaret pushed him to one side, sloshing champagne down her tweed bosom. "Our Chantelle has done so well!" She gushed.

I asked Skye to stand, "Oh?"

"Yes, yes she has the best score in her class for the dancing!" she boasted.

"She has?"

"Yes. And she looked very fast in the showjumps," she confirmed.

Before I could speak Marc bustled forward, "Come along Mrs T. Let's get you a nice spot where you can watch the cross country. And we'll bring this with us shall we." He swept the champagne bottle out of the ice bucket and propelled her away. James selected a can of alcohol free larger and was about to follow them when Margaret halted his progress. "Glass James!" she called without even turning around.

He returned to the table muttering about eyes in the back of heads and poured the contents of the can into a glass with a sigh before following in the wake of his giddy wife and her guide.

Henry appeared by my side. "We didn't have the heart to tell her that in eventing the score shows penalties, so it is the lowest score that is the best."

"Ah. I see." Margaret's comments began to make sense.

"Do you need a hand with anything?" he asked.

"No, I'm fine. You get back to Chantelle."

He grinned and took a large swig from a hip flask. "Two phases down and one to go!"

"Do you think she'll be alright?" I worried accepting a swig. "I mean what if she can't stop and gallops straight through the finish towards the lorries and … and …. well…someone could be killed!"

Henry had another mouthful before answering, "We're working on the theory that Zeus isn't actually that fit so hopefully if she can stay on and steer, the final hill should tire him out a bit."

"Good luck!"

"And you!" Henry had a last draw from the flask before separating Chantelle from her phone and skilfully throwing her onto her horse. I watched them leave, Henry delivering last minute advice to the figure bouncing along beside him. Actually, bouncing around and crashing into him would be a more accurate picture. "Remember, white flag to the left, red to the right and…" His voice faded as they disappeared towards the starting area.

Phoebe had already changed into her brightly coloured cross -country top and exchanged her dark blue hat cover for a red and yellow one to match her top when I joined her at the horsebox. She was using the ramp as a mounting block again. I wished her luck and assured her that I was quite certain she wouldn't fall off at the water jump and even if she did, there was no chance she would drown as one of the many spectators would surely drag her out. She rode away, giggling.

It wasn't long before I had altered Skye's tack, added an over-girth for safety and changed into my own coloured cross -country shirt. I headed away from the parked vehicles, following the same route that Phoebe, and Chantelle before her, had taken towards the start of the cross- country phase.

The warm up area was close to the start but the undulation of the ground and surrounding trees meant that most of the course was hidden from view so I didn't see any of Chantelle's round but there were no ambulances in action, so I took that as a good sign. The clouds had finally parted, and the sun was casting a warm glow across the parkland. Skye had begun to grow accustomed to the hustle and bustle and had settled down. I could see Phoebe in the distance, heading in the opposite direction, leading Treasure. The former was grinning from ear to ear and the latter also appeared to be very pleased with himself, ears pricked veins standing out on his body; both spattered with mud. She spotted me and waved.

"That was bloody amazing!" she called.

I waved back, "Clear?"

She answered by giving me a thumbs up.

"See you soon!" I called.

We popped over a couple of logs and a combination of poles as a warm- up before the steward waved in my direction and beckoned me towards the start.

"Are you ready?" The steward asked, "Girth tight enough?"

"Yeah. All good thanks."

"Okay, you can go through to the starting box."

I thanked her and shortened my reins as we passed from the collecting ring through the string gateway and onto the course. We circled the area just behind the flags marking the start. The starting judge checked his stopwatch, "On my word then in three, two, one. Off you go!"

And go we did.

Skye leapt forward the moment I touched her with my leg; she barely noticed the first jump; a simple log. I leaned back slightly, altering my weight to steady her speed as we headed downhill to the stack of logs. A flutter of straw flew into the air like confetti as we flew over number three. The speed was exhilarating as her stride ate up the ground between each obstacle. The ground through, and around, the combination of arrow heads was churned and rutted. I slowed Skye to a steady canter. A mistake here would mean repeating all three parts of the jump. Skye cleared the first arrow easily and the second didn't present a problem, but she wavered before the third; surprised to see another jump so close. I gritted my teeth and tried to look through the arrow, visualising where I wanted her to go, and rested my whip against her shoulder to remind her I was there.

She jumped slightly to the right and I clipped the red flag with my boot, but we were through. Just.

The raised pole was a simple jump after such a complicated combination and the drop created by the mound made me feel that I was flying. The brief moment of airborne suspension seemed never ending. I made sure that as we continued down the hill, we avoided the uneven track created by the horses who had gone before us and I made sure we swung wide enough to give Skye time to see the fan of telegraph poles. The ditch disappeared without a problem along with the simple style into the woods. The sun, which had broken through the clouds as we began our round, was blocked out by the trees. The ground here was damp, and I welcomed the cool air against my flushed cheeks. We negotiated the next two jumps before heading for the trimmed hedge back into the now brilliant sunshine. As the ground became level and bouncy Skye took a strong pull and it was all I could do to keep her balanced for the palisade and model house.

Ahead I could see the crowds gathered around number fourteen. Everyone loved to see someone get a dunking; I prayed it wouldn't be me. The water sprayed around us as we leapt into the artificial lake. This slowed Skye down and we trotted towards the opposite side. She lifted her knees high, sending cascades of water droplets into the air. A cheer and a small ripple of applause from the spectators sent us on our way towards the last part of the course.

Refreshed by the water, Skye took advantage of my now very slippery reins and she took charge as we galloped through the second area of woodland, over the table and on towards the final hill, the line of decorated tyres and last of all, the chair. Once through the flags marking the finish, I slowed Skye to a canter, and we circled gently until I was able to bring her back to a walk. I was out of breath and my legs felt weak, but I slid off her back and led her towards the horseboxes.

Phoebe was waiting for me with buckets of lukewarm water and sponges set out, ready to wash down my sweating horse. Treasure was already washed and wearing a rug. As the horse grazed Phoebe was turning the neatly plaited mane into a wild frizz as she removed the restraining bands. Tying Treasure to a bulging net of hay, she helped me to remove Skye's tack before we swiftly washed her down and covered her with a dark green rug.

"I'll take her for a walk with Treasure to help her dry off while you get changed." Phoebe untied her horse and took Skye and Treasure for a wander.

Getting out of my cross-country top was a lot more difficult than getting into it. The combination of nervous adrenalin fuelled sweat, heat from the sun and splash from the water jump had managed to form a bonding agent between my blue and white top and the tee-shirt I was wearing underneath which in turn was clinging to my bare skin.

My arms were already aching from Skye's enthusiastic cross-country round. I winced as I reached behind and tried to drag my top over my head.

I gave up and tried a different approach; I crossed my arms in front of me and grasped the left side in my right hand and the right side in my left hand, took a deep breath and lifted. This method was more successful.

Or would have been if I had remembered to unfasten the top enough to get my head through the hole. I twisted and turned, trapped in my homemade straight jacket and blindfold combination. Unable to see where I was stumbling, and becoming increasingly dizzy and hot, I tried to extricate myself back to my starting position, however, I was by now so entwined it was impossible to break free and my contortions only seemed to make things worse.

"Need some help?"

I stopped wrestling with my invisible assailant and tried to locate the speaker, both in terms of direction and identity.

"Who is it?" I mumbled through the layers.

The voice laughed and I spun around, tripped over a bucket and caught my boot neatly in the handle. Down I went like a solo skittle in a bowling alley.

The laughing grew louder. "Keep still before you damage yourself."

I froze, still trying to locate the speaker. I sensed a shadow fall over me a second before I felt a pair of strong hands grasp my arms. I wriggled and squirmed in panic.

"Who is it? Who are you?" I demanded or tried to.

"Okay, stop wriggling and I'll get you out of there!" The voice ordered. It sounded vaguely familiar but was too muffled by the layers of clothing for me to identify the speaker.

The hands were busy pushing, pulling and rearranging the knotted tangle which had been created by my struggles when a second voice caused a momentary lull in the proceedings.

"Good grief, who do you have in there?"

It was a woman's voice.

I froze, straining to hear who was speaking.

My 'rescuer' laughed. "It's Abi. At least I think it's her!"

"Oh," said the woman, "I didn't realise you two knew each other!"

"Really? We're great pals, aren't we Abs?"

I felt an extra strong wrench which simultaneously propelled me to freedom and almost ripped off my left ear. I was catapulted backwards onto the cool grass where I lay for a moment, enjoying the caress of the damp ground on my hot skin.

Opening my eyes, I found myself gazing up at the blue sky and three people.

Dom.

Camilla.

And Pierre.

At about the same time I became aware of how much of my skin was enjoying the cool grass. Too much, was how much.

My tee-shirt had remained attached to my cross -country shirt, leaving me in my harvest festival under wear; not even slightly sexy but keeping everything safely gathered in.

Pierre grinned and was about to speak when his mobile trilled into life. Answering the call, he listened intently for a few moments, punctuating the conversation occasionally with affirmations such as, "I see," or "yes, okay." Finally, he ended the call. "Sorry I have to dash. I'll catch you all later." And with that he was gone.

Dominic stretched out a hand and hauled me to my feet. Thanking him and taking my clothes from him I scrambled into the back of the horsebox and pulled a clean tee-shirt out of my kit bag. When I re-joined them, Camilla and Dom were chatting together like the good friends they obviously were.

"That's better." I said smoothing down my shirt. "I didn't realise you two knew each other."

Camilla laughed, "Not as well as you two know each other it seems!"

I blushed. "Oh, no we- "

Camilla waved her hand dismissively. "Hey, I'm not judging you."

"You've got grass in your hair." Dom removed various pieces of thatch.

"What's going on?" It was Phoebe.

"Oh, thank goodness you're back!" Camilla grinned, "I was beginning to feel very much like the spare wheel around here."

"Third wheel." Dom corrected her as he continued to pick dry grass and hay out of my hair.

"Camilla! Behave!" I pushed Dom away and took Skye from Phoebe. "Thanks Dom, I can manage now."

"Okay. I'll see you later for a drink."

Before I could respond he had gone, taking Camilla with him.

Phoebe watched them go then turned to look at me, "Again, what's going on?"

"You truly wouldn't believe me!"

After settling the horses, we wandered away from the horseboxes towards the collection of tents and marquees. The heat inside the canvass shelters was stifling and the air was filled with the sickly, sweet smell of crushed grass. We checked the score board. The class wasn't finished yet but currently Phoebe had finished on her dressage score and was in third place; I was lying just outside of the placings, but I was thrilled with how Skye had performed at her first one day event and was delighted with our clear cross country.

We joined the crowd jostling to be served in the beer tent before taking our drinks back out into the fresh air.

Small pockets of people were gathered around the showjumping arena to spectate, others were wandering around the cross-country course, re-living earlier rounds or watching riders tackle the large obstacles of the later classes.

"Abi! Phoebe!" Marc was waving at us both from an area near the showjumping, "over here!" he beckoned. He was with Henry, the Thompsons and Hannah.

We both waved back and were on our way to join them when we bumped into Camilla and Dom.

"Congratulations sweetie!" Camilla air kissed Phoebe on both cheeks before clinking her glass of champagne against Phoebe's cider. "We've just seen the results."

Phoebe grinned.

"And I see you have managed to find some clothes darling," she winked at me.

Dom began to laugh as I blushed.

"Are you riding?" Phoebe asked him.

"Not horses!" Camilla shrieked as she nudged him and looked at me, before descending into giggles.

"I've been watching some horses who are the progeny of my stallion." Dominic explained.

"Actually," said Camilla composing herself, "that's why I was looking for you earlier and why I was going to introduce you to Dom, before I realised how well you were already acquainted."

I sighed and was about to explain, yet again, that I had only met Dom a couple of times and was not (and had no desire to be) 'well acquainted' with him. Before I could speak, Camilla continued, "I remember you said once that you were thinking about taking a foal off that pretty chestnut mare of yours and I wondered if you had considered Dom's stallion."

"Ah," said Phoebe and I together.

Camilla took a sip from her glass, "Oh, it's all gone!" She tipped the empty glass upside down and gave it a shake.

"Come on then, let's go fill it up!" Phoebe took Camilla by the arm and prepared to steer her through the crowd towards the well- stocked table which our friends were using as base camp. "Are you coming?" she asked, looking from me to Dom.

"I'll follow in a second," I assured her.

"Okay, don't be too long!"

And they were gone.

94

Dom spent the next ten minutes or so telling me about his stallion and listing the reasons why the horse would make the perfect breeding partner for Flame. As he described the successful eventing careers of some of the young horses which were the offspring of his stallion, he illustrated his commentary with photographs from his mobile.

"Here's the boy himself," Dom handed me his phone, "Silverwood Brightstar, or Star to his friends." On the screen was a photograph of a dark chestnut horse with a white marking on his broad forehead. His bridle was festooned with rosettes.

"He's gorgeous," I handed the phone back to him.

"Thank you. You should come over and see him sometime."

"Actually, that's not a bad idea."

A shadow blocked out the sun for a moment as someone squeezed through the gap between us and a small group hovering near the entrance to the beer tent.

"Excuse me… Thanks… Sorry… Excuse me."

Dom stepped back and took my arm, inviting me to step into the space he had just vacated in order to allow the stranger, who was behind me, the opportunity to pass, or at least shuffle, by.

"Thanks. Oh hi, I didn't realise it was you guys!"

The shuffling stranger was Pierre.

"Probably because I'm upright." I tried to make a clumsy joke and reference the fact that the first time I had met Pierre I had been flat on my back due to the ice and this, the second time I had fallen over blind folded and trapped in my cross country top.

In reply Pierre raised his eyebrows and he was about to speak when Dominic slid an arm around my waist and interrupted him, "We were just discussing the beautiful children we could make."

"Oh. Well I'd better leave you to it." Pierre said coldly. He turned to go and walked straight into Felicity.

"Pierre, darling!" She kissed his cheek and slipped her arm through his, "I thought it was you! Come and have a drink. Have you walked the course?" Her voice drifted away as the two of them disappeared into the crowd.

"For God's sake, Dominic!" I pushed him away.

Chapter 12

The days following the one-day event were something of an anti-climax after the flurry of preparation and the excitement of the build- up. The only moment of raised adrenalin came from another cat fight between Phoebe and Izzy.

I returned from a shopping trip to the sound of raised voices in the tack room.

"I'm only saying you might have been placed but you didn't actually win!" Izzy was screaming.

"Oh, stop flapping your gums grandma!" Phoebe screamed back.

Before I could reach them to intervene Izzy came out of the tack room carrying Eric's tack. Unable to face the drama I turned my back on the stables and hurried into the house with my bags of shopping. After a quick cup of tea and a slice of cake I braced myself for whatever was kicking off between Phoebe and Izzy. The latter had just mounted Eric and was fiddling with her stirrups.

A black four -wheel drive with tinted windows and a private number plate purred into the yard.

Klaus stretched as he got out of his car. He reminded me of a cat with his long, perfectly sculpted limbs. He was wearing a pair of highly polished, long black leather boots and a pair of tight pale breeches. His black bomber jacket was emblazoned with familiar equestrian logos, many of whom were his personal sponsors. I stopped for a moment to appreciate the sheer beauty of the human standing a few feet away from me. His strong jawline was balanced by perfectly chiselled cheek bones. He could have made a fortune as a model I thought as I watched him adjust a baseball cap over his short brown hair.

"Good evening Abigail." Klaus seemed to pronounce each syllable separately.

"Evening Klaus. Do you have a lesson with Izzy?"

"Yah. That is correct," he looked at his watch, "vee haf approximately fifty- three minutes before darkness arrives." He nodded as if to signify the end of our conversation and walked across the yard towards Izzy.

"Darling, put down ze stirrups at least by two holes. You look like za fucking jockey in za donkey derby."

Izzy fluttered like a school- girl under his rebuke. "Oh Klaus, could you help?"

"Ya, be giving me the leg." He lifted her leather- bound foot out of the stirrup and ran his hand up the length of her leg, resting his fingers against the crease between her crotch and her leg before pulling at the buckle and adjusting the length of the leather.

Izzy gasped as he repeated the movement on her other leg.

Klaus helped to guide her feet back into the irons one by one.

"There, dat looks so much improved."

He retained his hold on her foot and pressed his crotch against her toe. Izzy flushed and looked down towards him.

"Thank you. That feels perfect." She moved her toe up and down against him for a few minutes before they both seemed to remember where they were. After a momentary pause they headed towards the arena.

"Shit the bed!"

I jumped, startled by Henry's comment. He laughed, "Sorry love, I didn't mean to startle you, but holy fuck did you see the size of his hard on?"

"Uh huh." I nodded.

"I mean she was totally rubbing his dick with her boot!" he continued.

"I think I feel a bit sick."

Henry laughed and hurried away from me towards the tack room; by the time I caught up with him he was giving a detailed recount, complete with actions, to Marc and Phoebe.

"Well she did say the exercises he gave her were lengthening exercises!" Phoebe said.

"Something was certainly stretching!" exclaimed Henry and the three of them burst into more peals of laughter.

"Enough!" cried Marc, holding up his hands in surrender and gasping for breath as Henry, encouraged by Phoebe, continued to both re-enact and exaggerate what he had seen.

"I've laughed so much I think I've done a little wee!" Phoebe declared.

"What's going on?" asked Hannah as she walked into the chaos.

"Absolutely nothing!" I didn't want to add to the growing tension between Phoebe and Izzy. Hannah seemed to be quite friendly with Izzy and would almost certainly tell her that Phoebe and the boys and had been making fun of her. "Just this lot making filthy jokes, as usual," I added when it was clear that something was causing the loud hilarity.

"Oh?" She looked unconvinced.

"Yes," said Phoebe, "just discussing how I could learn to improve an outline in dressage by using my lower leg in a different way."

This set the three of them off again.

Hannah looked at me for clarification.

"Ignore them," I said. "they're making a mountain out of a molehill."

My comment was the unintended catalyst for more shrieks of laughter.

Hannah shrugged as the laughter again reached crescendo levels, "Okay then. I just wanted a quick word about my bill."

I sighed in relief. I hated asking people for money, but Hannah was a few weeks behind with her payments and I had been trying to find the right time, and words, to tackle her since seeing her out shopping.

"Is something wrong?" I led Hannah out of the tack room and closed the door.

"Oh, it's fine, nothing to worry about." Hannah assured me, "I'm changing banks, again and despite what they say on the telly it is proving a tad complicated with money in and money out." She paused for a moment, "I have a feeling the electronic payment to you hasn't come out."

"You can just give me cash or a cheque if it's easier."

"Thanks. "Hannah breathed a sigh of relief, "I'll bring the money up tomorrow."

*****

The following day Izzy was standing close to Eric's stable, holding him for her farrier. Most of my customers used my blacksmith to shoe their horses but Izzy and Hannah preferred to make their own arrangements. Izzy liked her horse to be shod by a farrier called Brad.

While not being fat, Brad was certainly stocky. His muscular arms bore several tattoos; a flock of birds flew from his collar bone and he had an artistic combination of decorative horseshoes on his left forearm, while a Celtic pattern formed a band around the top of his right arm before extending across his back and shoulders.

I waved but didn't stop to chat as they were deep in conversation. I headed straight to the tack room.

It was a bright day and it took a moment for my eyes to adjust to the gloom. When they did, I realised that I was not alone. Phoebe was standing in front of a saddle, fiddling with the stirrup leathers.

"What are you doing?"

"Aargh!" she screamed in reply.

Her sudden scream gave me such a shock, I screamed right back at her.

100

"Shush! What the fuck are you doing creeping up on people? You frightened seven years of growth out of me!" She left the saddle and closed the door.

"What am I doing? My heart is pounding!" I put my hand to my chest.

Phoebe giggled but didn't answer my question.

"That's Izzy's saddle. What are you up to?" I asked.

"Nothing dangerous."

"But you are up to something?" I insisted.

"Might be."

"Are you going to tell me?"

Phoebe tilted her head and considered the question. "Maybe. But not now. Are you riding?"

I saw no point in pushing her. I'd find out, eventually.

"Have it your way. But to answer your question, yes, I thought I'd do something with Skye. You?"

"Wish I could. I'm working. See you later though."

And off she went.

I had a quick look at Izzy's saddle. I couldn't see anything obviously wrong; no unpicked lines of critical stitching, scratches or attempts to cut through the girth tabs. I shrugged and collected a headcollar before setting off to catch my horse. Izzy was still deep in conversation with her farrier.

Leading Skye back from the field towards the stables my heart sank at the sound of the unmistakable pattern of 'clip, clop, thud, clip'. Izzy was speaking to someone on her mobile. She waved as I drew closer, said something to the farrier, then hurried across towards me.

"Abi! Abi could you possibly-oh, is something wrong?"

I sighed, "More irritating than anything. Skye has pulled off a shoe."

"Well, why don't you ask Brad to knock one on for you."

"That would be amazing. Do you think he would?" I glanced over to where he had Eric's hind leg balanced on a metal tripod as he used a clincher to flatten the new nails painlessly against the hoof wall.

"I don't see why not. I'll ask him for you. I was going to ask a quick favour."

"Go on…"

"Brad has nearly finished but I need to dash away. Would you mind putting Eric back into his stable and feeding him when you feed the others? I've left everything ready."

"Of course. No problem."

She thanked me before hurrying back to Brad and Eric. I heard her ask him to replace Skye's shoe as her phone burst into life again. "Get yourself away, I can manage. We can settle up payment next time," Brad assured her.

"Thank you!" She gave him a peck on the cheek, before waving to me and hurrying across the carpark. She disappeared in a cloud of dust.

"Crikey!" I exclaimed to Brad as he lifted Eric's hoof off the tripod, "She's in a hurry."

Brad grinned and tapped he side of his nose, "Solicitor called her. She has some papers for Izzy to sign."

"Oh, sounds like a good day for her and a not so good day for her ex." I laughed. "What was his name? … Michael?"

Brad laughed with me, "No I think he was the one before last. The latest divorce victim was a bloke called Ryan."

Brad stood back and scrutinised his work. He gave Eric's hoof a final tap. "There we go, all done." Satisfied that he had finished with Eric, Brad turned to me, "Izzy said you need a shoe putting on your little mare."

"That's right," I nodded, "she's pulled it off in the field."

"I don't suppose you have the shoe?"

"I do actually." I smiled and proudly handed over the troublesome horseshoe which I had found in the mud close to the field trough.

"Excellent, in that case lead the way."

He scooped up his tools and followed me to Skye's stable. I tied her up by the open door and left Brad cleaning the mud from the shoe while I dealt with Eric. By the time I returned

Brad had cleaned the shoe and had almost finished nailing it back in place.

"There you go, all done," said Brad, giving the hoof wall a final tap as he had with Eric.

I untied Skye and led her back into the stable, "Thanks. I really appreciate this. How much do I owe you?"

"Not much, it was just a case of nailing a shoe back on. Do you want to pay the same way as Izzy?"

I patted Skye who, now that her headcollar had been removed, had turned her attention to the haynet. "Yeah. I suppose."

"Great."

Brad stepped into the stable.

" Does she use cash or a che-! Oh, my Christ! What are you doing?" As I turned from the horse to the man in the doorway, he swiftly dropped his trousers to reveal an enormous erection.

"It was only a refit, so just a blow job will be fine." He said matter of factly, as he adjusted his stance.

"You have got to be kidding!"

He shrugged, "Ok, a quick hand job then. I suppose you did have the shoe." He took hold of his erect penis and stroked it while admiring himself in a similar way to how he had admired his handiwork shoeing the horses.

"You seriously want me to…" words failed me.

Brad yawned and checked his watch, "Yeah, just a quick wank 'll be fine."

"Oh. My. God! It most certainly will not be fine! What kind of person do you take me for?"

"What?" Brad's erection began to lose some enthusiasm, "You said you wanted to pay the same way Izzy does!"

"And this is how she pays you?" I couldn't believe what I was hearing.

Suddenly Brad's hard on wasn't anymore, and he shuffled about as he tucked his now flaccid and rapidly shrinking penis out of sight.

"Hell, I'm sorry Abi. I just thought…"

"Well, you know what 'thought did'." I bristled in indignation, using a time -honoured expression which I had learnt from my grandmother, "when thought looked, he hadn't!"

Brad's puzzled expression showed that he didn't know 'what thought had or had not done' so I continued, "I meant do you want paying with cash, cheque or electronic transfer!"

"Oh," Brad answered slowly. "I thought you meant-,"

"I know exactly what you thought!" I interrupted, "though how you translated 'paying like Izzy' into an offer for a shag-,"

"I said a quick wank would be fine, not full on sex!"

"Stop!" I held up my hand. "How much, in money? Pounds, pence, for the shoe?"

"Don't worry. Have it on the house." Brad grinned before he turned and left the stable.

I followed him. "Oh no, I insist."

"No, honestly Abi." He started to laugh, "your reaction was payment enough!"

I was confused. "So, Izzy doesn't really pay you…"

"In kind?" He completed my thought for me, "oh yeah, she does. Sometimes a shag in her horsebox, sometimes just a blow job. Just depends really."

I gasped, "Do all your customers…?"

"No," he laughed, "how would I pay the rent?" He was very matter of fact about the whole thing.

"Anyway. I'll be off." He threw his tools into the back of his van which doubled as a portable forge, complete with mini furnace to heat up the metal horseshoes. "Are you going to the ball at the weekend?"

"Uh hu," I nodded weakly.

"Great see you there. Bye."

And with that, he drove out of the yard.

Phoebe shrieked with laughter when I told her about Brad.

"You mean he just dropped his pants and expected you to blow his trumpet? Out there? Just because he put a shoe on Skye?"

I nodded and pushed the plate of cake across the kitchen table towards Phoebe.

"Bloody hell! What did you do?" she asked, helping herself to a large slice.

"What do you think I did?" I paused for moment before placing a mug of tea next to her cake.

"Did you kneel on a towel or something?" Phoebe asked, "nice cake by the way," she continued, "glad the madeira is back!"

"What?" I choked on my tea, "no! I didn't kneel on a towel! I didn't kneel on anything!"

"Oh. 'cos those shavings can cause nasty stains on your jodhpurs," she said.

"I didn't kneel-,"

"Oh," Phoebe raised an eyebrow, "interesting…"

"What? Urgh no! I didn't do anything!" I exclaimed.

"Ah. I just thought… I mean he is good looking in a rugged sort of way."

I shuddered. "Urgh. He's not that good looking. I mean, urgh." I put down my tea and looked at Phoebe carefully, "Would you have…?"

"Oh, hell no! Well … probably not," she grinned, "do you think Izzy really pays him…?"

"At first, I thought absolutely not, but now I think about it… possibly yes."

Phoebe snorted, "More like probably!"

Chapter 13

"Do you guys want to share a taxi tonight?" Marc asked.

We were leaning against the gate watching Phoebe as she schooled Treasure in the arena.

"Thanks, but isn't it out of your way?"

"That doesn't matter, we're coming into the village to pick up Felicity, so it's just a quick dash up here," said Henry.

"To be honest, I'll probably just drive."

"You can't do that," Mark insisted, "you won't be able to have a drink!"

"That doesn't matter. I need to be up really early tomorrow, so I won't be drinking much anyway."

"But-," Mark tried to interrupt.

"And I'm only half- way through a course of anti-biotics so I really shouldn't drink. Having the car will give me an excuse to be good."

"Phoebe?" Henry called across the arena, "how are you getting there tonight? Do you want a lift?"

Phoebe looked up and brought Treasure to a standstill. "I'm good thanks! I'm going with Abi, then staying here tonight."

"Are you finished? You should have vacated the arena almost five minutes ago!" Izzy's voice cut across the conversation.

"Okay, don't get your knickers in a knot, if you're wearing any that is!" Phoebe snapped back.

"Good morning Klaus," Henry did his best to break the building tension.

Klaus smiled and nodded in acknowledgement. "Henry. Marc. Ladies." He turned and watched as Phoebe dismounted. "Nice horse. Yours?"

"Thanks, and yes."

Izzy coughed. Loudly and dramatically. Everyone ignored her and focussed on Klaus and Phoebe. "I wish she would stretch that little bit more when she is offered the rein."

"Mm. I vas vatching for several moments vis Isabella." He glanced at Izzy who was struggling to hide her impatience. "Call me if you vant to book a session. I am happy to be of help to you."

"Again, thank you." Phoebe smiled and accepted the small black card from Klaus which, when she turned it over, was emblazoned with the embossed silhouette of a dressage horse and contact details for Klaus.

Izzy snorted as she rode through the gateway, "Darling don't waste your time."

"Mind your own business granny!" Phoebe snapped back at her.

Klaus smiled at Phoebe and said quietly, "Call me if you vant a lesson." He then strode into the centre of the arena and told Izzy to shorten her stirrups. "Always they are needing the attention! Too long, too short…"

"Or in today's case right up and left down," Phoebe giggled as she walked away.

I watched carefully as Izzy once again fiddled to adjust her stirrups; sure, enough from where I was standing at least one appeared to be too long while the other was too short. I hurried after Phoebe and caught up with her and Marc in Treasure's stable.

"Okay what are you up to?" I demanded.

They looked at each other before answering.

"What do you mean?" Marc struggled to keep a straight face as he spoke.

I let myself into the stable and carefully bolted the door behind me. Glancing furtively over my shoulder I lowered my voice, "I know that the pair of you are up to something." I stared at each of them with what I hoped was a piercing and demanding glare that would project an aura of authority, and thus force them to spill the beans.

They stared back. Looked at each other again and then burst out laughing.

"Stop it!" I yelled.

Treasure snorted.

"It's alright, calm down," Marc soothed. I wasn't sure if he was talking to me or the horse.

"It is not alright," I hissed, lowering my voice, "you two are up to something and it involves Izzy. This is my livelihood and if you are both fucking about with something dangerous or, or…" My voice trailed off.

"Sweetie," Marc put his arm around my shoulders, "calm…"

I shook his arm off, "Do not tell me to calm down!"

"Okay," Phoebe pulled me further into the stable, "but please stop shouting."

"I'm not shouting," I shouted. I took a breath and lowered my voice, "well, okay, maybe I'm a little bit shouty. But," I concluded, my voice starting to rise again, "what are you doing to Izzy?"

They both began to giggle again.

"It honestly is nothing dangerous." Phoebe tried to reassure me as she un-buckled Treasure's girth and slid off her saddle.

"You either tell me or-,"

Fortunately, Marc interrupted because I had no idea what word or phrase would follow the word 'or'.

"We simply found a way to head fuck with Izzy."

"Explain."

"Well," Marc glanced at Phoebe before continuing, "Izzy is always looking for ways to wind up Phoebes, flaunting her dressage diva status…"

"And…" I prompted impatiently.

"And generally being a nasty bitch. She is always changing the board when I book the school," Phoebe added.

"Not this again," I sighed.

"So," Marc took control of the conversation again, "I suggested that rather than reacting in such an obviously volatile manner, it would be more fun for Phoebe to do a spot of altering herself." He winked at Phoebe and they once again dissolved into fits of infuriating giggles.

"What are you altering?" Clearly, my death stare was improving because they both stopped laughing and pulled themselves together.

"Her stirrups," Phoebe whispered.

"Eh?"

"You heard," Marc drew me away from the doorway into a close, conspiratorial huddle, "her stirrups!"

"Every time I am in the tack room, I alter her stirrups by a hole or two," Phoebe confided.

"Sometimes up. Sometimes down." Marc chimed in.

"Sometimes a combination," Phoebe giggled.

"Oh…OH! So that's why she is constantly having to faff about with her leathers each time she rides."

The conspirators grinned.

"Exactly," confirmed Marc.

"So, the leg exercises…" I began to ask weakly.

"Completely fucking useless!" laughed Phoebe.

"Not that Klaus isn't a fabulous trainer," Marc added hurriedly, "just not quite as fabulous as Izzy seems to think at the moment."

"But why?"

"Because it gives me a sense of satisfaction to know I am messing with her head," Phoebe said emphatically.

"I see. At least I think I see." I looked at the pair of them. Phoebe was cradling her saddle defensively and Marc was nervously twisting the leather of Treasure's bridle. Together, they looked like a pair of naughty school children.

"Who else knows?"

"No-one!" They both answered at once.

"Please don't say anything," Phoebe begged.

"What about Henry, does he know?" I asked.

"He hasn't a clue," said Phoebe.

"He has no idea," Marc added, "it doesn't cause any actual harm," Marc continued, "and it has stopped the screaming matches."

In response I raised my eyebrows.

"Okay," he conceded, "most of the screaming matches."

I sighed, "Keep me out of it. If she finds out I shall deny all knowledge. But please don't do anything else to piss her off, I really need her money."

"Promise." They both breathed in relief.

As I turned to go, I saw Hannah getting into her car.

"Speaking of money," I muttered, "Hannah! Hannah!"

Hearing me call she glanced over, "Hi," she called, "I'll see you tonight. Bye!" Without another word she hopped into her car and left.

Chapter 14

Getting ready for the ball with Phoebe reminded me of preparing for a night out with the girls when I was a teenager. Money was tight for both of us, so rather than a trip to the salon, in the style of Felicity and Izzy, we applied false tan to each other's backs and hard to reach bits; applied false nails to each other from a pack bought in the local chemist.

Phoebe whistled as I stepped back to check my reflection in the full- length mirror in my bedroom. "Wow, nice dress. When did you get that?"

I smiled sheepishly, "I decided to treat myself."

Unable to justify the cost of a dress from the shops in town, I had taken a gamble and ordered a dress online. Fortunately, the gamble had paid off. I had bought a dark red dress; the straps sat just off my shoulders and the long skirt was gathered in a waterfall of folds down my right leg.

"You look gorgeous!" Phoebe stood back and invited me to twirl in order to show off the full effect of the dress. Linking her arm through mine, Phoebe stood next to me in front of the mirror and adjusted her own silver dress which clung to her like a second skin; actually, there was no room for a second skin, it just clung, like skin!

Phoebe's blonde hair had been pulled back from her face with delicate tendrils left to frame her face. Her trademark ponytail had been plaited and twisted, up off her neck and shoulders, all held in place with tiny crystals.

My own dark hair had been styled by Phoebe and gave the impression of being worn up if viewed from the front, while the view as I walked away showed a cascade of curls falling towards my bare shoulders.

"If I dare say so," Phoebe said, "we're gonna knock them dead!"

I grinned back at her in the mirror. "I don't know about we, but if you're ready, let's go!"

*****

The ball was being held at Stonecross Manor. The flags and tents from the previous week's horse trials had gone and already the churned ground and yellow grass was beginning to show signs of natural regrowth and repair. The light was beginning to fade, and the parkland was bathed in a golden light as we followed the neatly painted signs towards the temporary carpark behind the Manor House.

Fairy lights twinkled in the trees and the sound of laughter and music drifted out of the double doors which stood open and welcoming at the top of a small flight of three wide, shallow stone steps.

Two waiters, wearing red tailcoats, greeted guests as they arrived at the top of the steps. Each waiter balanced a silver tray, laden with crystal glasses of champagne. Phoebe and I each accepted a glass as we passed between the doors. Inside, floral displays of pungent lilies, brilliant tulips, heavily scented roses and statuesque delphiniums provided both a visual and aromatic display to seduce the senses. Discretely positioned lighting reflected off polished surfaces, mirrors and crystal chandeliers, continuing the magical ambiance created by the earlier trail of twinkling fairy lights.

"I feel as if I've just stepped into the middle of *A Midsummer Night's Dream*!" Phoebe remarked as we took a moment to admire our surroundings before we followed the small groups of glittering guests from the entrance hall into a large lounge room. The furniture had been cleared and a bar had been set up in front of the double bay windows which were hidden behind heavy brocade curtains.

Several familiar faces were dotted throughout the crowd. At the end of the bar Felicity and Hannah were doing some serious damage to a tray of champagne cocktails, aided and abetted by Marc and Henry. Margaret and James Thompson were standing awkwardly at the side of the room. James was wearing a tuxedo and each time his wife wasn't watching, he fiddled with the unfamiliar bow tie. Margaret was wearing a long black dress with chiffon sleeves. Small crystals picked out the details around her cuffs and neckline and along with the diamanté drop earrings and choker, reflected the light from the thousands of fairy lights which twinkled around the room. They waited with their daughter who, with the aid of much make-up, an industrial coating of spray tan and a tiny pale pink dress she had poured herself into, looked at least ten years older than she actually was.

"How old is Chantelle?" I asked Phoebe.

She followed the direction of my gaze, "Not sure. Sixteen, maybe seventeen."

"She looks like jailbait in that outfit."

"Perhaps that's why Pa Thompson looks so nervous!" Phoebe laughed.

"Good evening ladies," Dominic slid an arm around each of our waists and kissed us both on the cheek, "can I get you a refill?"

"I'm fine thanks." I gave my champagne glass a jiggle, reviving the bubbles as I side stepped out of his embrace.

Phoebe mirrored my sidestep but accepted the drink as she drained her glass. Dom headed towards the bar and his place was filled by Camilla and Steve.

Camilla greeted us both with air kisses and Steve offered to replenish our drinks before disappearing into the glittering melee after Dom.

"Gosh, there are so many people!" I said looking around, "Where did they all come from?"

"Well," Camilla said scanning the crowd. "That group over by the door are clients from the Academy; the tall man near

113

the fireplace, he's the Master of Foxhounds, the lady next to him is his wife…" She spent the next few minutes pointing out supporters and employees of the hunt as well as vets, farriers and members of the local farming and equestrian communities. Camilla appeared to know everyone. "…and the blonde lady in the navy dress and the grey -haired chap talking to the Master are Timothy and Elizabeth Coleman. Very good of them to turn over their house for the night," Camilla concluded.

"Goodness, I thought she was his daughter, grand-daughter even!" I gasped.

"What? They live here?" Phoebe gazed around at the opulent surroundings, "it must be like living in a hotel!"

"Plenty of rooms if you want to avoid someone after an argument," I said.

"Seventeen," Camilla said before lowering her voice, "between you and me it almost is a hotel. If rumours are to be believed Mrs C often has erm…" she coughed dramatically, "'friends' staying overnight, if you see what I mean," she winked.

Dom and Steve returned with drinks for everyone. Rather than make a fuss I simply thanked them and accepted the drinks; Phoebe drank mine, as well as her own, without anyone appearing to notice.

"What are you three gossiping about?" Steve looked accusingly at his wife.

"The girls were asking about the house."

"Lovely isn't it," said Steve.

"Seventeen bedrooms," Dom added.

It was a simple statement, but I couldn't believe how he could make two words sound so salacious.

Camilla giggled.

"Mind you," Steve continued, "I think it is more like a hotel than a home. Tim and his missus live mainly in the East wing and keep most of the bedrooms for guests. They hire out some of the reception rooms for conferences. You can even get married here if you want!"

"Have you checked your table yet? Where are you sitting?" asked Dom changing the subject.

"We haven't looked yet." said Phoebe, "come on Abi, let's go and check out the seating plan. Thanks for the drinks."

"I'll catch you all later," I said as I followed Phoebe.

The doors to the dining room were closed. To the side of the doors a large diagram of the table plans, and a list of the guests showed where everyone would sit for dinner. I was sitting with Phoebe, Marc, Henry, Steve, Camilla and a couple who rode at the Academy.

"I'm glad Dom isn't on our table," said Phoebe.

I agreed, and also silently thanked the gods of table planning that Phoebe and Izzy were sitting at different tables. A lady from the hunt fundraising committee was circulating and selling raffle tickets. "The prizes are on display on the table over there," she indicated with a nod of her head as she tore a strip of tickets from her book.

As we examined the prizes on offer, which ranged from bottles of whiskey and vouchers for riding lessons, to a television set and a ride in a hot air balloon, a sharp double blast of a hunting horn silenced the conversation. All eyes focused on the tall man Camilla had identified as the Master.

This call on the horn was usually the signal blown to indicate that the huntsman and hounds were moving off from the meet to begin the day's hunting; this evening it was the signal to move from pre-dinner cocktails into the dining room.

The double doors were opened, and the crowded bar area began to empty. The circular tables were arranged down the two long sides and across one short side of the room in the approximate shape of a horseshoe. A panel of folding doors which led to the ballroom had been folded back to create one huge space.

There was a stage at the far end opposite the doors, some dining tables flowed from the dining room into the extra space creating the illusion of one room, leaving a large dance floor in the centre. A collection of instruments were waiting on the stage, indicating that there would be live music after dinner to replace the gentle music which was currently playing in the background.

Crystal tealight holders flickered on each table and yet more fairy lights and hidden lamps continued to build the magical atmosphere. Glitter and tiny crystals were scattered across the heavy white tablecloths, casting miniature prisms of light towards the place settings. Bottles of red and white wine as well as decanters of water were already on the tables along with a selection of artisan bread with small dipping bowls of balsamic vinegar and olive oil to keep the guests occupied while waiting for dinner to be served.

I helped myself to a piece of bread and scanned the room, watching as the tables around the room filled up. I could see Izzy, sitting with her back to me on a table close to the stage; Klaus was sitting by her side. Hannah and Felicity were on the same table with three people I didn't know. There was an empty seat between Felicity and one of the strangers.

"Who's the girl next to Felicity?" Camilla asked.

"That would be Hannah," Phoebe told her.

"Don't think I know her. Where is she from?"

"Not sure to be honest," Phoebe continued, "she's quite pally with Izzy but I don't think they knew each other before she came to Abi's place."

"She reminds me of someone," Camilla wasn't used to not knowing people. "Steve, have you seen that girl before?"

Steve was deep in conversation with Henry.

"What's that Cam?"

Camilla waved her bread towards Hannah, "The girl sitting with Felicity. Do you know her?"

Steve peered across the room, "I think we met her briefly at the one-day event. Why?"

116

His wife patted his arm, "No reason darling, just wondered. I love her dress." She added, "I bet that cost a few quid."

"About five weeks' worth of livery." I muttered.

On the other side of the room Dom was holding court and entertaining everyone on his table, including the Thompson family and Brad who was appreciating Chantelle's dress and spray tan.

The first course of beetroot and gin cured salmon arrived.

"This is delicious!" Phoebe announced, "Oh, what's that?" she asked watching a waiter who was carrying plates towards the Thompson's table.

Marc consulted the menu which was displayed in the centre of the table, "That would be the veggie option; baked goat's cheese with orange and walnut dressing."

Henry looked over his shoulder to confirm the delivery of the dish. "Yeah, Chantelle is a vegetarian."

"Well, her cheese thing looks nice," said Phoebe, "but she's missing a treat with this salmon."

"I completely agree! What's next?" Steve asked as he wiped a piece of bread across his plate.

"Roast beef," his wife coughed and frowned at him, "and the vegetarians get some mushroom thingy," Camilla told Phoebe.

Steve took a moment to interpret the frown before he pushed his empty plate to one side.

As the waiting staff leapt into action, clearing plates and cutlery, the sudden popping of a champagne cork followed by a loud cheer and clapping caused us to twist in our chairs to see what was causing the commotion. The excitement, it seemed, was coming from Izzy's table.

I could see glasses clinking across their table.

"I wonder what that's all about?" I mused.

Henry leaned back as our roast beef and dishes of vegetables arrived, "Izzy and Klaus have probably just announced their engagement."

"Their what?" I gasped.

117

Camilla slapped Phoebe on the back as she coughed and spluttered in shock at the news.

"Bloody hell's bells!" Phoebe glared at Marc and Henry, "I can't believe you knew and didn't say anything!"

Henry laughed as he cut into his beef, "We thought you already knew. I mean it's hard to miss the rock she is wearing on her left hand!"

"But the expression on your face…" Marc chuckled as he helped himself to vegetables.

"I can't believe how quickly it's happened," I glanced across to Izzy's table, "I mean only the other day she was sorting out paperwork for her last divorce."

"Nah, her divorce was done and dusted a couple of months ago."

"Well that's still quite quick," Camilla agreed with me.

"Oh. I see. I just… I mean she dashed off to a meeting with her solicitor the other day. I thought… well, never mind," I said, "I shouldn't have jumped to conclusions."

"That wasn't connected to her divorce, that was so she could proof -read the pre-nuptial." Marc lowered his voice conspiratorially, "she always makes them sign one!"

"Well," said Camilla, "I can't wait to see the ring!"

The conversation during the rest of the meal was mainly centred around horses; the good, the crazy and newly acquired and those potentially for sale; the high spots and dramas of the hunting season which had just drawn to a close and most importantly, who was shagging whom.

We all agreed that the deconstructed cheesecake with a gingerbread crumb base was the highlight of the meal and we expressed a private vote of sympathy for those who had selected the fruit salad for dessert.

As the tables were cleared the wine continued to flow and the music stepped up a beat; some of the younger guests took to the dance floor rather than sample the Northumbrian cheese boards and coffee.

"I must be getting old," I groaned, "I need at least half an hour to digest that meal before dancing."

"Nonsense," Phoebe leapt to her feet and tried to drag me to mine, "it's because you're sober," she plucked some grapes from the cheese board and threw them at me, "come on!"

"In a minute. Honestly."

I watched as Phoebe bounced away from the table with Marc and Henry. Before long the dancefloor was packed, and I was unable to resist the draw of the music. I joined Phoebe and we twirled and spun under the flashing lights, following the beat of the music with our bodies. Eventually, feeling dizzy and breathless I left Phoebe dancing and pushed my way towards the bar. As I threaded my way through the crowds, I saw a familiar figure standing in the doorway.

Pierre.

I stopped and stared, aware that my heart was racing and determined not to acknowledge the reason why. As I watched Pierre raised a hand and waved. I waved back, grinning then realised that he wasn't waving at me. In fact, I don't think he had even noticed me.

I followed the direction of his gaze and watched as he made his way from the doorway, through the tables. He paused occasionally to greet someone and share a joke, but eventually, inevitably, he ended up at Felicity's table where he immediately shook hands with Klaus before kissing Izzy.

For a moment I considered going over. I did want to congratulate Izzy. However, before I could act, I felt an arm around my waist, and I was guided away from the edge of the dance floor towards the bar.

"What are you drinking?" Dom asked.

"Oh, I'm fine thanks."

"Rubbish," he signalled to the bar man, "come on, let me buy you a drink."

Glancing at Felicity chatting to Pierre as the waiting staff fluttered around bringing him a main course which had been reserved under the protection of a silver looking cover, I sighed.

"Go on then. But just a softie. I'm driving."

"Me too."

I wrinkled my brow at the large gin and tonic being placed in front of him. Dom laughed.

"It's what I call a virgin G and T. All tonic with the trimmings but no gin. It stops people trying to force drinks on me."

"Good idea," I smiled, "I'll have the same."

"Cheers! Here's to a good night with clear heads! Dom clinked glasses with me, "So, when are you going to come and see my stallion?"

"Soon."

"Really? Or are you just trying to shut me up and get rid of me?"

I blushed.

"No, honestly I am interested."

I couldn't quite fathom this guy. He seemed to swing from creepy to charming in a heartbeat. We chatted about horses, the difficulties of running a small business and life in general for a while until he suddenly put down his glass, leapt off his stool and grabbed my hand.

"Where are we going?"

"Come on, the spotty child in charge of the disco has been replaced."

"What do you mean?" I managed to safely put my own glass down as Dom dragged me through the maze of tables and abandoned dining chairs.

"Decent music at last! The band are on. Come on!"

Dom turned out to be an amazing dancer. I wasn't.

He spun me around, flinging me into spaces, and other dancers before sweeping me back into his embrace. I felt rather like a rag doll as I bounced uncontrollably and without any semblance of co-ordination around the dancefloor.

"Oh, there you are darling," Camilla grinned as I ricocheted off her and Steve, "we wondered where you had disappeared to." She winked as Dom reeled me back into his arms.

The band paused for a moment at the end of the song and everyone applauded. Before I was able to escape from Dom, the musicians struck up again. This time the music wasn't quite so lively, and my partner chose to keep me closer but at least I was able to avoid crashing unceremoniously into other dancers. I could see Phoebe gyrating with Marc, Henry and Felicity; Hannah was dancing with James, Margaret was proving to be surprisingly nimble as Pierre navigated her around the floor and Izzy was moulded to Klaus playing tonsil tennis in the middle of the dance floor.

After another couple of dances, I managed to ingratiate Dom and myself into the larger group of dancers with Phoebe. Eventually, I managed to slip away from the group, and I set off the find the loo.

*****

The powder room was busy with women jostling for a space in front of the mirror; I joined them and did my best to repair the glossy, shining reflection which gazed back at me. A group of teenagers emerged from a cubicle. I couldn't decide what constituted the greatest act of wonder; the number of girls emerging from the same cubicle or the gravity defying tiny scraps of material masquerading as their dresses which appeared to be held in place by nothing more than good luck and will power.

I watched in the mirror as they extracted hip flasks from bags and cleavages. One girl, clearly an expert at alcohol smuggling, even had a bangle which upon closer inspection was in fact a form of flask. Another girl with less finesse but clearly more determination simply had a small bottle of vodka under her skirt. I shuddered to think of exactly how and where!

121

They tipped liberal amounts of booze into glasses of cola and lemonade as well as fortifying themselves with slugs directly from their various containers of contraband.

"Do you want some?" one of the girls noticed me watching and offered me her pink sparkly hip flask.

"No thanks," I smiled, "I'm driving."

"Bummer."

I agreed, it was indeed 'a bummer' as my new friend secured her flask in the depths of her ample, and well displayed cleavage.

"You'll save some money though," the girl with the bottle confided, "Jesus, the prices on the bar! They take your eyeballs out, places like this."

"My dad says it's to cover the cost of the free bar when you first come in," one of her friends explained.

Again, I agreed.

Another member of the group began to share out condoms as they discussed strategies and experiences.

"Have a good night, girls," I said as I packed up my things and prepared to leave them to it.

"Do you want one?" the girl with the bottle asked, "it won't affect your driving," she added winking.

"That depends," one of her friends quipped, "she might have trouble sitting if her bloke has a really big co-,"

I didn't wait to hear the rest and left with their shrieks of drunken laughter ringing in my ears.

I decided to get some fresh air before re-joining the party. It really was quite stifling in the ballroom and the air in the powder room seemed to be more perfume and hairspray than oxygen. There should be a sign on the door warning asthmatics I decided.

I negotiated my way through a maze of corridors; if I returned to the front door via the bar there was a chance I would be dragged back to the dancefloor by a well-meaning but drunken friend, or a sober Dom and I wasn't entirely sure his intentions were well meaning or honourable. I just wanted a moment of peace to enjoy the cool air.

Eventually I turned a corner and found myself in a kitchen. It was nothing like the huge, industrial kitchen filled with stainless steel and catering ovens which had been set up in a marquee in the garden and used to prepare dinner; this was a small quite private space which I suspected was the one used by my hosts.

A scrubbed table stood in the centre of the room and an aga, which upon closer inspection turned out to be a combination of gas hob and electric oven, hinting at a desire for nostalgia or country house appearance being over- ridden by practicality. Photographs of horses and dogs covered the walls along with a collection of faded rosettes and some dusty bunches of lavender which had been hung up to dry last summer and forgotten about. A black and white cat watched me from a mantlepiece which framed a woodburning stove; like the aga, the stove was fuelled by gas. A large clock on the mantelpiece, doubled as a letter rack with bundles of papers stuffed behind it.

Feeling suddenly that I was intruding, I was about to turn and retrace my steps when I heard voices in the passageway behind me, I didn't want people to think I was snooping so I tried the back door.

Surprisingly it was unlocked. I slipped out and pulled the door behind me.

Chapter 15

Outside it was dark.

There were no fairy lights in the trees at this side of the house and the only form of illumination came from the moon, which was shrouded in clouds, and from the electric light in the kitchen which shone out through the window. I shivered; it was colder than I had expected.

I could hear a girl, she was giggling. As I waited by the door, trying to decide what to do, the sound of the girl's high heels click clacked across the stone floor towards the door. I held my breath and tried to think of an excuse which would explain why I was hovering outside. Before I could think of anything, I heard the unmistakable sound of a key grating in the lock as it was turned from within.

Bugger!

Now I was locked outside, in the dark and it was freezing cold. There was nothing for it; I could either knock on the door and ask them to let me in or make my way around the building to the main entrance.

I could hear a man's voice.

Carefully, I crept from the doorway to the kitchen window. The light was on and there was a gap between the curtains; someone had closed slightly but hadn't managed to pull them completely together. I peeped through the gap.

Inside, a man was lying on his back across the table. His trousers were around his ankles and his shirt was open; his eyes were closed, and he was groaning, loudly in pleasure because sitting on top of his erection was a young woman. Her dress was both hitched up to her hips and pulled down to her waist, giving the impression of a rather unnecessary belt. There was no sign of her underwear and her partner was

124

fondling her naked breasts. She leaned forward for a moment and whispered something before tucking her heels under his naked backside. Then she closed her eyes, arched her back and rode him with the kind of deep seat any dressage trainer would be proud of.

I gasped and felt sick.

The man was Brad.

The almost naked girl was Chantelle.

Knocking on the door was quite obviously not an option. I tip- toed away from the window before pulling my phone out of my bag and using it as a torch.

I made it back to the main entrance without incident and was able to slip quietly back inside with a small group who had been outside to enjoy a cigarette.

Using the smokers as shield I scanned the entrance hall looking for someone I knew, while hoping to avoid Margaret and James. I needed a moment to get over my unintentional moment of voyeurism before anyone asked if I had seen Chantelle recently.

The smoking group paused in the hallway and I waited with them, smiling casually as if I too had been out for a quick cigarette. To the left a large display of foliage and fairy lights was providing cover for another couple. Unlike Brad and Chantelle, this couple were arguing furiously.

I couldn't see them, nor could I discern what was being said but the violence of their row was obvious.

"Oi," one of the men from the smoking group shouted at the couple, "that's enough!" He stepped forward as the man behind the display grabbed the woman above the elbows and shook her violently.

"Stop it, you're hurting me!" she screamed.

It was Hannah!

Two men broke away from the group. "I said that's enough!" the first man spoke" let her go!"

I still couldn't see who Hannah was with, but I recognised his voice as he snarled back, "You keep out of this. It's none of your business!"

"Really? Well how about I make it my fucking business!" The man from the group began to take off his jacket.

Hannah shrugged out of the man's grip and turned to the strangers, "It's alright honestly. I'm okay."

"Are you sure?" The two men seemed disappointed that there wasn't going to be a fight.

"Yes. It was just a misunderstanding." Hannah implored the men not to make a fuss.

"Well," said the first man reluctantly, "if you're sure."

"I'm certain. But thanks. I think we've all had a bit too much to drink." Hannah regained her composure and walked away in the direction of the ladies' powder room.

Dom stepped out from behind the flowers and headed in the opposite direction into the bar.

"Fucking prick!" the man who had been preparing for a fight called after him. I pushed myself into the centre of the group to avoid being seen.

Crikey. What a night this was turning out to be.

*****

Noticing that my shield of strangers was rapidly disappearing as people made their way to the bar or ballroom, I decided to search for Phoebe.

I slipped into the bar; a quick look around revealed no sign of my friend, but Dom had his back to the door. I watched as he downed a drink. It certainly wasn't a tonic water; it looked more like a brandy if the colour and glass shape were anything to go by. I hurried on into the ballroom as Dom ordered another drink. Circling the room, I could see no sign of Phoebe. A quick check in the powder room also drew a blank.

Finding myself back in the bar I began to regret my decision to drive. Dom was still sitting with his back to me, apparently deep in thought. Suddenly he appeared to reach a decision; he stood up, drained his glass and smoothed his hair before adjusting his cuffs. Without turning in my direction, he left the bar and went purposefully into the ballroom.

"What can I get you?" the barman asked.

"I'm not sure, I'm driving but I really wish I could have a proper drink."

"Okay, we have a range of softies…"

"Have you something with a bit of a kick?"

"Coming up." He poured a small bottle of ginger ale over some crushed ice, added a dash of lime and gave it a stir before running a wedge of lime around the rim of the glass.

"Delicious!"

I climbed onto one of the tall stools to enjoy my drink. "Nice dress," a voice spoke next to me, "I though you would suit red."

"I beg your pardon?"

I looked at the speaker. I was certain I didn't know him.

"Your friend bought the silver number."

Realisation dawned; this was the man from the dress shop.

"Have you seen her by the way?" I asked.

He looked puzzled for a moment. "Oh, your silver friend?"

I nodded.

"Yes, she was chatting to some bloke in the ballroom. Lucky bugger."

Perhaps Phoebe was looking for me and we were actually following each other in circles.

"Can I get you a drink?" my new friend asked.

"I'm fine, but thanks for asking." I held up my glass of lime and ginger. Before our conversation could continue Marc bounded across.

"There you are!" Marc greeted me. "Where did you get to?"

127

"I was thirsty." I told him. "Have you seen Phoebe?"

"Yeah, she's over there." He pointed across the room and I was just in time to see Phoebe's silver form vanishing though the door.

"Are you coming to dance?" Marc continued.

I shrugged; Phoebe would be back. "See you later," I called over my shoulder as I allowed Marc to lead me towards the dancefloor.

After several more up- tempo numbers the band left the stage for a short break. The dancefloor emptied and the band were replaced by a lady from the hunt committee announcing the raffle draw. Some people returned to their tables, searching bags and pockets for raffle tickets; other people made for the bar.

The bar was busy, but Marc managed to attract the attention of the bartender by waving the cocktail menu. "Let's see, we'll have a Shirley Temple for the driver here and I will have an orgasm please."

"A what now?" the barman looked confused as he searched the menu.

"A Shirley Temp-," Marc began.

"Yea I got that. What was the other one?"

"An orgasm darling. Equal parts peach schnapps and Cointreau poured over crushed ice." He smiled as the barman offered a selection of glasses for his approval. As we waited for our drinks we were joined by Henry.

"Hello sweetheart," he kissed me on the cheek and Marc on the lips, "have you ordered?"

"In the process of," Marc smiled, "orgasm?"

"Always!"

They both laughed as the barman placed our drinks on coasters and Marc ordered another round, "Oh what about Felicity?" He scanned the room.

"She's organising her own orgasm. Get her a mother fucker."

The barman looked amused, "Are you making these up?"

"I don't think so," Marc said, becoming serious for a moment, "Henry, did we invent these?"

"No, orgasms and mother fuckers have been around for years." Henry confirmed.

"Okay, how do I make a mother fucker?" the barman sighed.

Henry leaned across the bar. "Whiskey glass, ice, cubes not crushed, shot of Irish whiskey then carefully pour in a double shot of that cream whiskey liqueur stuff." He supervised the mixing of the cocktail before deciding that a third round plus one of each cocktail for Phoebe would save time. He loaded up a tray and led the way back to our table in the ballroom.

There was no sign of Phoebe.

Across the room Dom was deep in conversation with James, Camilla was admiring Izzy's engagement ring and Felicity was snogging someone at the side of the room. Steve joined us as the band returned to the stage; he helped himself to the drinks we had brought for Phoebe. Felicity and her friend broke apart. She headed towards our table and he took up his position as saxophonist on stage.

"Where's Pierre?" I asked as she accepted her drink from Marc.

Felicity shrugged, "Not sure."

"We seem to have lost a few people," Marc observed.

"Probs in the bar," said Felicity finishing her drink.

"Another?" asked Marc looking at the collection of empty glasses.

"Mm. That was nice." Felicity ran her tongue around the inside of her glass.

Marc took it from her and laughed, "Okay, one more mother fucker coming up."

"I'll come with you," I said following Marc.

Now that the band had resumed playing, the dancefloor was filling up and there were less people in the bar. As we waited to be served, Izzy appeared.

"Congratulations!" I gave her a tentative hug and kissed her cheek before admiring the enormous engagement ring she was happily showing off.

Marc handed her a glass of champagne. "Where's your fiancé?" he asked.

Izzy wrinkled her brow, "Actually, I'm not sure. I expected to find him in the bar with Steve." She looked around.

"Steve's chatting with Henry at our table," Marc assured her.

"Oh. I wonder where he can be?" Izzy began to look concerned.

"Don't worry, he'll turn up," said Marc.

"Who'll turn up?" asked Hannah. She had the beginning of a bruise showing through her expensive false tan on her upper arms where I had seen Dom grab and shake her earlier.

"Klaus." Izzy said, "have you seen him?"

"Never mind him," Marc interrupted, "what's happened to your arm?"

Hannah laughed, "I was dancing with someone who could do those proper jive swings and lifts, I guess we got a bit carried away."

"Christ it looks really sore, you should take some arnica." Marc looked closely at the bruise.

Before we could discuss Hannah's injury, Phoebe swept across the room and joined us. She had a huge grin on her face.

"Where have you been?" I asked looking at her carefully. She grinned in reply.

"Yes, where have you been?" Izzy looked at Phoebe carefully.

"Around," Phoebe answered breezily.

"Have you seen Klaus?" Izzy asked.

Phoebe accepted a drink from Marc and took a sip before answering, "Oh dear, have you lost him already? That was careless."

Izzy took a step towards Phoebe and narrowed her eyes. Phoebe laughed and pointed with her drink, "Don't get your dentures in a tangle grandma, he's over there."

All heads turned to look.

Klaus was in the hallway. His shirt was undone at the neck and the buttons which were fastened, appeared to have been done quickly and not correctly. He looked, unusually for him, quite dishevelled. The most intriguing thing about his appearance wasn't his escaping shirt tails, it was a strange green slime or stain which clung to his trousers, shirt front and jacket; his shoes were scuffed and wet and his hands were filthy.

"What have you done?" Izzy was torn between wanting to grill Phoebe and wanting to go to Klaus.

"Me?" Phoebe laughed, "what on earth makes you think I've done," she paused and looked at Klaus and his green slimy shroud before continuing, "anything!"

"Yeah, steady on Izzy," Marc intervened, "I saw Phoebe coming down the stairs on her own and Klaus has clearly just come through the main doors. Obviously, they weren't together."

Izzy snorted but said no more. She stormed away to confront her fiancé.

"What do you think happened?" Hannah asked, watching Izzy's retreating back.

I looked at Phoebe; she said nothing, but I had a feeling Izzy was right, whatever had happened to Klaus, Phoebe was involved somehow.

"I don't know, perhaps he went outside for a cigarette and tripped over," said Marc.

"Does he smoke?" Hannah asked dubiously.

Before we could debate what may or may not have befallen Klaus, a drunken Margaret and James joined the group along with their new best friend; Dom.

James waved to the bartender. "Brilliant night! Absolutely top dollar!" James gushed, "do you all know this chap? Top

131

bloke, top bloke!" James patted Dom on the back before resting his arm around Dom's shoulders.

Margaret was very flushed, "I haven't seen Chantelle for ages. Do you think I should go and look for her?"

"She was with Brad last time I saw her," Marc volunteered.

Margaret looked around, "Oh, I wonder where they are."

"Probably dancing, stop worrying," Marc reassured her.

"Horizontal dancing," I muttered under my breath.

Phoebe looked at me and wrinkled her brow. "Not now, I'll tell you later," I whispered.

James meanwhile was introducing Dom to everyone.

"Dom this is Marc and his partner Henry. Henry?" James spun around unsteadily, looking for Henry. Marc caught him and held him by the elbows for a moment.

"Yes, Henry and I met Dom at the one- day event," Marc reassured James.

"But where is he? Where's Henry? HENRY?" James shouted.

" It's alright, Henry's through there," Marc pointed, "he's talking to Steve."

James relaxed, "that's a relief! Oh Steve! Do you know Steve? Top bloke!"

"Yes," Dom grinned, "I've known Steve and his wife for years."

"Ah, good, good." James looked around the group. "Dom, this is Abigail and Phoebe."

"We've met," Phoebe told James.

"Oh." James looked slightly deflated until he remembered Hannah.

"Hannah! Hannah this is my good friend Dom, a top bloke. Dom this is Hannah, have you met?"

"No," Dom held out his hand, "I haven't had the pleasure."

I watched them closely. Now I was confused; neither gave any indication of having met before, yet I could clearly see the bruise where Dom had gripped Hannah's arm earlier in the evening.

"So how do you know this shady lot?" Dom asked, smiling at Hannah.

"Hannah is another livery. She keeps her horse on the yard," James explained before Hannah could speak.

"Is that right?" Dom was still holding Hannah's hand when a riotous group came charging through the doors shrieking with laughter.

The group was mainly comprised of the girls I had met in the powder room earlier, plus a few others; each girl was riding on the back of a young man piggy- back style. Chantelle and Brad were at the head of the group leading the way, she was using his tie as a whip as they galloped into the bar.

"We won!" shrieked Chantelle waving the tie above her head, as Brad sat her on top of the counter. The rest of the 'field' joined them and began ordering bottles of champagne to toast the winners.

Chantelle and Brad, it seemed, were the winners of a 'steeplechase' around the perimeter of the house. As the runners and riders became part of our group, I drew Phoebe away to one side.

"What have you been up to?"

She smiled, "I don't know what you mean."

She looked across the room to where Klaus was desperately trying to placate a furious Izzy, while at the same time he appeared to be searching the pockets of his moss stained tuxedo.

Phoebe carefully lifted her dress to reveal a bow tie, wrapped and tied around her thigh like a garter. Slowly and seductively she gently tugged the black ribbon and looked across the room towards Klaus as the fabric unwound.

From the other side of the room Klaus saw what she was doing. He began to smile, then remembering his furious fiancée the smile tuned to a look of terror. Glancing between the two of them I felt a cold dread creeping over me.

"Phoebe, please stop mucking about and tell me why Klaus is covered in green crap."

"Simple really. I took Klaus and showed him that I am a much better rider than Izzy. He said so himself. You can ask him if you like," Phoebe giggled.

"Oh my God. Did you have sex with Klaus?"

"Isn't that what I've just said? Honestly Abi, keep up."

"But where? Look at the state of him, did you do it in the shrubbery?"

"What? No. Don't be ridiculous. Upstairs, in one of those conference rooms."

I shuddered, "Christ Phoebes. I don't know much about him, but he's definitely been with her," I nodded my head towards Izzy, "and she's been with, well loads of people, including him!" I looked across towards Brad who was carrying Chantelle over his shoulder towards the ballroom. "Please tell me you took precautions."

"Of course, I did; I locked the door. I'm not stupid!"

I sighed, "and the green slimy stuff?"

"From the ivy I suppose," Phoebe shrugged.

"The ivy?"

"Yes, I presume he used it to help him climb down the wall rather than relying just on the drainpipe."

"What the hell are you talking about?"

"I didn't want people to see us coming downstairs together, so I locked him in when I left. I was going to give the key to someone but obviously he decided to take the alternative route."

As she was speaking, Phoebe had been fiddling with the black ribbon, which I now realised was Klaus' tie. Smiling, and knowing that he was still watching she took the tie and dangled it for him to see from her fingertips. Suspended from the fabric was a small key.

Klaus began to laugh, and a furious Izzy spun around. However, always one step ahead, by the time Izzy had turned to see what her fiancé was looking at, Phoebe had dropped the tie and was standing with her back towards Izzy and Klaus, apparently deep in conversation with me.

"Shit the bed, Phoebe. If Izzy finds out, she'll kill you!"

Phoebe glanced over her shoulder at Izzy. "She does look a tad cross," Phoebe giggled.

"I think he's talking her round, she looks calmer," I observed, "he must have a silver tongue to have calmed her down."

"Oh, I can vouch for his tongue credentials."

Before I could comment, Izzy led, or dragged, Klaus past us towards the dancefloor. She paused, "I'm watching you!" she hissed at Phoebe.

"You do that grandma; you might learn some new moves."

"Why you –, "

"Come on." Klaus steered Izzy past and on towards the dancefloor.

Phoebe grinned and hung his tie with the key around her neck like a trophy. We followed them into the ballroom. Brad and Chantelle were snogging behind a speaker and Felicity was giving someone a lap dance at the edge of the dancefloor. I couldn't see who the man was because he had his back to me; probably Pierre I thought and wondered if he knew she had been snogging the saxophonist earlier.

Before long we joined on the dancefloor by James and Margaret, Marc and Henry were trying to recreate some moments from Dirty Dancing and Hannah was dancing in a small group with Camilla, Steve and the two people from the Riding Academy who had been on our dining table.

"Oh good, the band's coming back on!" said Dom looking towards the stage. He had joined Phoebe and me as we danced. We looked towards the stage. Felicity's mystery man withdrew his hand from inside her dress and gave her another long, deep throated kiss before taking his place behind the drum kit on the stage.

"Oo, the drummer!" Phoebe declared, "Good old Felicity, he can probably do something different with each hand while maintaining a steady rhythm!"

Dom threw back his head and laughed.

"I wonder what happened to the sax player," I said.

"The who?" Dom asked cupping a hand behind his ear to indicate he couldn't hear over the music.

I leaned closer to him and spoke into his ear, "The sax player. She was snogging him earlier."

As I pulled away, I saw Pierre standing, glowering in the doorway between the bar and the ballroom. He had obviously just watched his date removing her hand from the musician's drumstick too.

Dom glanced at his watch, "I wish they'd hurry up with the bacon sarnies."

"The what?" It was my turn to be deafened by the band.

"Breakfast is served at one then carriages, polite for piss off home the party is over, at two," he said into my ear.

"What?" Phoebe asked.

I relayed the message.

"Not sure I'll make it 'til carriages!" Phoebe said.

I nodded. Pierre had gone from the doorway.

There was a slight pause in the music; the singer appeared to have been distracted and was helping someone up onto the stage. That someone was Felicity. She waved and danced as the band continued to play. Someone gave her a tambourine and she continued to accompany the musicians.

Dom left me dancing with Phoebe and he went to see if there was any chance of an early bacon buttie.

"And I, ee I, ee I wi- ill all ways lurve yoooooooooooooooooooo," Felicity warbled from the stage where she had taken control of the microphone; the actual singer was gazing into her eyes.

"Do you think she uses some sort of drug?" Phoebe asked as we watched the man drool over Felicity.

136

"Not sure, but I think this might be one step too far for me!" I said grimacing as Felicity continued to murder the song.

Phoebe nodded in agreement. We looked around to say our goodbyes only to discover that the dancefloor was packed with couples, slow dancing, apparently oblivious to Felicity's lack of talent. Shrugging we decided not to break the mood for any of them and we slipped away.

Chapter 16

"That was a bloody good night!" Phoebe declared sinking back into her seat and clipping her seat belt into place with a clunk.

"It certainly was," I agreed, "I can't believe you shagged Klaus just to get your own back with Izzy!"

Phoebe grinned, "And I got me a trophy!" She opened her bag and took out the black ribbon, which was Klaus' unfastened bow tie, complete with the room key still attached.

"What are you going to do with that?"

"Not sure," she shrugged, "I'll think of something. Oh bugger, they've closed the road off for over- night works. I bet the diversion takes us miles out of our way." Phoebe yawned.

"Don't worry, I'll take the back route, it's a bit swirly and bendy but I think it'll be quicker in the long run."

"Okay, if you're sure, but take the bends slowly."

As we drove, I told Phoebe about Chantelle and Brad in the kitchen, this made her giggle. Then I told her about the strange encounter with Dom and Felicity and the argument I had witnessed them having. This made her sit up and pay attention. "Are you sure it was him?"

"Certain!" I confirmed, "I'm stone cold sober remember. And then she lied to Marc about the bruise on her arm."

"Mm. Perhaps she was embarrassed," Phoebe suggested.

"Maybe," I conceded, "but then later they both-,"

Suddenly a deer leapt over the hedge directly into our path.

I screamed and instinctively hauled on the wheel to avoid hitting the creature. The sudden, violent turn was too much for the car and we skidded towards the hedge; I tried to correct the turn, but we careered onto the opposite side of the road. The previous winter's weather had eroded the side of the tarmac and there was a loud hiss as at least two of the wheels sliced along the jagged edge of the road. We came to an unceremonious halt, lying on our side with the car wedged against the ditch half -way through the hedge.

"Jesus! Are you all right?" I looked across, or rather up to where Phoebe was still trapped in the passenger seat, dangling by her safety belt.

"Yeah. I don't think there's any major bleeding. You?"

"I've been better, but don't think anything's broken." I wriggled to release the seatbelt from my crushed position against my door.

Phoebe managed to push her door open and we both scrambled out of the car and assessed the damage; both to each other and the vehicle.

We were bruised and sore but otherwise seemed to be remarkably unscathed. The same could not be said of the car.

"What'll we do?" I wailed, "it's so dark and I don't know where we are and I'm cold and… and…"

"You don't do well in a crisis do you Abigail," Phoebe took control of the situation, "I wonder if it's because you're quite highly strung. That'll be why you're such a shit driver."

I decided to let the insult pass, given that I had been driving. And the car was now on its side and stuck in a hedge. Phoebe clambered back into the wreckage and emerged with our bags and an old travel rug.

She handed me the rug, "I didn't bring a jacket, did you?"

"No," I snivelled, "I didn't think I'd need one."

Phoebe used the torch on her phone to have a closer look at the car. "Well there's no way we can get that out."

I agreed. The car was firmly wedged, albeit on a rather precarious angle, in the hawthorn hedge, two wheels were completely mangled, hinting at damage more serious than burst tyres; steam was hissing out from somewhere towards the front of the car and both airbags had been deployed.

Phoebe started to wander around in the middle of the road, holding her phone to the sky. The moonlight caught the shimmer of her silver dress.

"I don't have any signal. You?"

"No." I answered dismally, wrapping myself in the travel rug, "oh, Phoebe, what'll we do?"

"Stop whining for one thing." She gave up trying to capture a signal. "Come on, we'll have to walk."

I checked my phone, no hint of a signal and a worryingly low battery. We linked arms and spread the rug across both of our shoulders as we set off walking in the middle of the road.

"Shouldn't we walk at the side?" I worried, twisting the fringe of the travel rug between my fingers, "I mean we could get run over."

"Who's gonna run us over? A squirrel?" Phoebe laughed looking around at the emptiness which surrounded us.

Our eyes soon became accustomed to the dark and the light from the moon provided enough illumination for us to negotiate our way without too much difficulty. We followed the road for about a mile, periodically checking to see if we could get a phone signal.

Suddenly Phoebe stopped. "Did you see that?"

"See what?"

"There!" She pointed ahead of where we were standing, "like a torch or something."

We waited, peering into the darkness, trying to locate the distant lights again.

"Oh, I see it!" I gasped, "I wonder why someone is wandering around out here at this time of night."

"Maybe they've broken down, like us. Come on!"

"Could be, but let's be careful, it could be poachers or someone up to no good." I said, dropping my voice to a whisper.

Phoebe paused, "Mm. Poachers are a possibility. But it might be someone who can help, so come on."

I stayed where I was in the middle of the road.

Phoebe came back and took hold of my wrist, "We can't stay here all night."

"I know, but…" I resisted her attempts to drag me onwards.

"But what? They're miles away, they'll probably be gone by the time we get there! But we'll be careful. I promise! Now come on."

Sighing in resignation I gave in and once again we linked arms, adjusted the travel rug and set off following the road towards the torchlight ahead.

The lights, it turned out, were not miles away. Two very tight bends in the road had caused a false perspective in the darkness and after about five minutes of walking we suddenly found ourselves within a few metres of the torches; and the men holding them.

Chapter 17

A large horsebox, with the ramp down and the lights turned off, was parked on the grass verge by a field gate. The voices of two men could be heard, muttering and cursing in the field; this coupled with the erratic movement of their torches suggested they were trying, with limited success, to catch a horse.

"Oh my God! They're horse thieves!" I gasped.

"Crikey, that's certainly what it looks like," Phoebe agreed.

"What'll we do?" I grasped her arm and looked wildly around.

"Well I think it would be a good idea to get out of sight to start with!" she said. Looking at the moonlight reflecting off Phoebe's silver dress, I more than readily agreed to follow her off the road and into the hedgerow.

"Ouch! Watch out for those nettles," Phoebe whispered.

"Too late," I muttered back as we scrambled across the muddy verge and pressed ourselves as close to the prickly hawthorn hedge as possible.

"Can you see them?" I hissed, "what are they doing."

"Shh." Phoebe hissed back, "I'm going to get closer."

Before I could stop her, she began to creep closer to the horsebox and the gateway.

"Wait for me. Oh, these damn nettles!"

"Shh!" Phoebe warned as I crashed into her, "look!"

Carefully, she pulled the lower branches of the hedge to one side and we both peeped though into the field. The torches were bouncing randomly into the air, onto the ground and highlighting a horse as the men fumbled to fasten a lead rope onto the head collar being worn by one of the horses before it was able to break free. We watched as eventually, after much cursing and several failed attempts, they successfully caught the horse.

One of the men, a heavy-set individual, led the horse, a mare, towards the gate while his companion, a much slimmer, possibly younger man, tried to chase a second horse away; back into the field.

Both horses were excited. The mare was dancing around the man who was desperately hanging onto the rope. Her tail was high, and her red nostrils flared in the torch light as she squealed and kicked out. The cause of her excitement was clear to see; the second horse was a stallion.

"Do you have a signal on your phone yet?" Phoebe whispered.

I checked. "No. And I don't have a huge amount of battery."

"I'm going to see if I can get close enough to see the registration on the lorry."

"What? Why? They'll see you!" I hissed.

"They won't, I'll be fine, "she tried to reassure me. "We'll need to be able to give the police a description of the men and details about the horsebox. Wait here!" Before I could stop her, Phoebe crawled out of our hiding place and ran towards the waiting vehicle. I watched and marvelled that she could run in such high heels. She crouched by the back wheel and peered under the ramp.

Suddenly the man leading the horse was out of the field. His partner was preoccupied and struggling with the gate as the stallion whinnied after the mare, leaping and plunging in the darkness, furious that she had been taken way. I held my breath as Phoebe crawled into the space under the ramp to hide and the first man hurried the horse into the back of the open horsebox.

My heart was pounding.

Surely Phoebe would be discovered any minute now when he lifted the ramp. I strained to see what he was doing. The light from his torch bounced around the inside of the horsebox as he hurried to tie up the excited mare.

Before he could secure the partition into place the other man called to him.

"Give us a hand wi' this!" He was still struggling with the gate.

Leaving the ramp, the larger of the two men hurried to help and together the two of them wrestled with the gate which they seemed to be lifting into place. There was no time to wonder any more about the men as while I was watching them, Phoebe crawled out of her hiding place and disappeared in a flash of silver up the ramp and into the lorry. I could just see the glimmer of her dress in the moonlight as she squeezed into the space next to the horse.

What the hell was she doing? Surely, she didn't intend to release the horse and confront the men. What was I supposed to do? I didn't have long to ponder because before she could get out of the lorry both men returned and flung the ramp into place before leaping into the cab and driving off.

"Shit!" I shouted into the darkness.

Now what was I supposed to do? Shivering, both from cold and fear, I pulled the rug around my shoulders and stared dismally into the empty night. The lights from the horsebox were disappearing rapidly into the distance, and with them the stolen horse and my friend.

I stood, dithering in the middle of the road for a moment and checked my phone; still no signal and the battery was flashing a critical red. Even if I had a signal, who would I phone? The police?

The police!

Did you need a signal to phone the emergency services? Before I could find out the screen went black as the final trace of power drained out of the battery.

Now what!

I had two choices: either A, turn around and retrace my steps until I found the wreck of my car and wait there;

144

perhaps I could restart the engine and plug my phone in, or B, I could continue following the road. Remembering the state of the car I wasn't sure how likely it was that the engine would restart. Plan B it was then.

*****

Clinging onto my travel blanket I told myself that there was nothing to be afraid of; no one was following me and there were no dark monsters lurking in the hedge. Walking in heels down a country road in the dark was a lot more difficult without Phoebe to link arms with and without the extra light created by the moon reflecting off the millions of silver sequins which made up her dress.

After a few minutes, (or half an hour, I could no longer tell,) of hobbling down the road, I heard a sound that both terrified me and ignited a flicker of hope; a car.

Two spots of light from the car's headlights danced through the darkness towards me. Before I could decide whether to flag down the car and risk being abducted or raped or murdered, the car appeared around the corner and suddenly I found myself dazzled by the full beam of the lights.

I screamed as the vehicle hurtled towards me.

There was a squeal of brakes as the driver swerved to avoid me and bring the car to a standstill.

"What the fuck? Are you trying to get yourself killed?" The driver leapt out of the car and yelled at me. "Oh my God, Abi? Abi? Stop fucking screaming Abigail!"

The sound of my name being shouted by a stranger, in the darkness, shocked me out of my panic. I opened my eyes, which until this moment I didn't realise I had closed and looked at the driver who was standing in front of me with his hands on my shoulders.

"Abi! Are you hurt? What's happened?"

And then a wave of utter relief.

The stranger, the driver, was Pierre.

145

"Christ is that wreck back there your car?" He held me at arm's length looking for signs of injury, "hell, you're shaking. Where's Phoebe? I thought you guys left together."

The taste of salt reached my lips and I realised that I was crying.

"Abigail, you're frightening me. What's happened?" Without letting go of me, Pierre looked over his shoulder in the direction of our crashed car, "Oh no, she isn't..."

I shook my head, "No, no. She's been kidnapped!"

"What?"

"There's no time to explain," I gulped in between the sobs which were gradually becoming stronger, "we need to follow the horsebox and phone the police."

"Are you sure you didn't bang your head? That looks like a pretty bad smash back there. Let me take you to get checked out at A and E and then you can tell me where Phoebe is." Pierre spoke slowly and began to guide me gently towards his car.

Taking a deep breath, I struggled to compose myself, "Listen, I really do need your help, but I am not concussed or hallucinating, I wish I was."

"Okay," Pierre opened the passenger door of his car, "what's happened?"

"We, I, crashed the car then we couldn't get a phone signal, so we started to walk."

"I thought it was your car. Hell, what a mess. Are you sure...?"

"Stop wasting time!" I interrupted. Pierre looked taken aback for a moment, but he did stop talking.

"So, we started walking," I continued, "then we saw the men stealing the horse, Phoebe climbed into the horsebox and they drove off and if we don't hurry up we'll never know where they've taken her and she will be murdered and buried in a shallow ditch or sold by people smugglers or..."

"And breath," Pierre held up a hand.

"We've got to hurry. Please! They went that way. Come on!"

"She's in the back of a horsebox?"

"Yes, weren't you listening?"

"And the people driving the box don't know she's there?"

"I don't know they might have found her by now. They could be doing anything to her!"

"How long ago did this happen?"

"I don't know!" I wailed.

"Okay, I still think I should take you to get checked out, you're shaking like a leaf."

"I'm just cold."

"Mm and in shock." Pierre appeared to consider the situation for a moment. "Right then, here put this on." He handed me a thick Puffa jacket from the back seat," I hope it doesn't smell too badly of sheep or dogs," he apologised as I wrapped myself into the downy warmth, "and have a swig of this." He reached across and I clipped my seatbelt into place as he handed me a hip flask from the glove box in front of my knees.

The spicy, musky smell of his aftershave (and of him) caused my senses to tingle. I shook my head to physically rid myself of the feeling. This was not the time.

"Are you sure you don't want to go to hospital?"

"Absolutely. Come on, we're wasting time."

Pierre started the engine and we set off into the night. The headlights lit up the road and the tall hedges at either side. As we sped down the country lane, I tried to tell Pierre about the men and the mare they had taken out of the field.

"And you're sure they were stealing the horse?" Pierre asked.

"I'm sure. I mean who loads a horse in the middle of the night? And why else were they doing everything by torch light, rather than use the lights from the lorry?"

"Yeah, I see what you mean." Pierre acknowledged but he still didn't sound convinced.

147

We continued to travel in silence for about ten minutes; Pierre drove quickly and we both scanned the road ahead, looking for the horsebox, and Phoebe.

"Oh, where are they?" I leaned forward, peering into the darkness.

"Are you sure they came this way?" Pierre asked.

"Certain. Do you think they've turned off somewhere?" I asked.

"We haven't passed any side roads or junctions, but I suppose they might have turned into a farm," Pierre answered, "oh, hang on. What's that?"

Pierre slowed the car down. The darkness ahead was punctuated by the red lights of a large vehicle.

"That must be them! Quick!" I urged Pierre, "don't lose them!"

It didn't take long for us to catch up with the horse box, now that we had found it. "Is that the box?" Pierre asked.

"I think so." I said, "I mean it was pitch black, but how many dark coloured horse boxes are likely to be travelling down this road at this time of night? It must be them!"

As we caught up with the lorry, it began to slow down. "Do you think it's getting ready to turn off?" I asked.

"I don't think so," Pierre slowed down, looking for a gap in the hedge line which might indicate a track or gateway for the lorry to turn into, "I think it wants us to overtake."

"No, we can't, if we pass, we won't see where it goes!"

"Don't worry, I'll drive slowly, and we'll see them in the mirror." Pierre prepared to pull out in order to pass the horsebox which by now had slowed down even more. "As we drive past, have a good look, you know for identifying marks or anything," he said.

"Okay!"

I craned my neck as Pierre steered our car past the lorry; even though we were going really slowly, there still wasn't time to see anything worthwhile. I had hoped to see Phoebe

148

or at least be able to describe the two men, but it was too dark.

"Did you see anything? Are they the men?" Pierre asked.

"I don't know it was too dark!"

For a few minutes we could see the lights of the horsebox following us, then without warning, they simply vanished.

"Shit! Where did they go?" I twisted in my seat.

"I think they've turned their lights off!" Pierre said.

"Why? I mean are you sure?" I turned to look at Pierre.

Pierre slowed the car down and pulled up on the edge of the grass verge. He checked the mirrors before turning around to look out of the back window. "Look, I'll be honest Abi, to begin with, I was a bit sceptical about horse thieves in the middle of the night, but there is definitely something odd about that horsebox."

"Hmph," I snorted in what I hoped sounded like a snort of indignation and not wind.

Pierre continued, "They were determined to make me pass, and if they had turned off, I would have seen their lights swing off the road, but they just vanished. And anyway, did you see any driveways or openings?"

"But why? I mean why would you risk driving down a road like this without any lights?"

Pierre got out of the car and stood for a moment listening.

"What are you doing?" I asked.

"Shh, I'm listening for the horsebox." He cocked his head for a moment before jumping back into the car. He turned on the engine but dipped the lights as he pulled off.

"Pierre, what are you doing?"

"I think there's a turning coming up and they don't want us to see where they go." We drove carefully down the lane looking for a break in the hedge.

"There!" I shouted pointing.

"Okay. I see it."

"Then why are you driving past it?"

"I'm not going far, but if I'm right, we don't want them to see us parked at the end of their driveway like an unwanted welcoming committee, do we?"

We drove a little way past the opening, around a slight bend, before Pierre pulled off the road, he manoeuvred the car as close to the hedge as possible then he turned off the lights and the engine.

"Wait here." He instructed, getting out of the car.

"What? Oh no, you're not leaving me!" I scrambled out of the car and stumbled after him.

"Okay but be careful," Pierre waited for me, "here, take my hand."

Together we crept closer to the opening which turned out to be a track leading off the road. The remains of a wooden gate lay in a tangle of brambles at one side of the track with a couple of wheelie bins and a rusted mailbox was nailed to a post at the other side.

"Listen," Pierre tensed, "can you hear anything?"

I gripped his hand as the distinct rumble of a large vehicle became clear.

"Come on, quickly, hide!" Pierre pulled me into the long grass behind the broken gate. We huddled together behind the bins as the sound of the lorry drew closer.

As we watched, the horsebox slowly turned off the road and through the gateway. Its' lights were still turned off but after driving a short distance along the track, they were turned on and the lorry sped up slightly.

"Well if nothing else, that proves they didn't want us to see where they were going!" Pierre stood up.

"Now what?" I asked, "should we phone the police? What about Phoebe?"

"I think we should try to get closer." Pierre said, "or at least I should get closer. You should wait in the car, maybe call the police from there. I'll see if I can find Phoebe."

"I'm not waiting here on my own!" I said adamantly, "I've already lost Phoebe, what if they get you?"

"I'll be fine," Pierre assured me, "I don't want you to get hurt."

"Hurt? What do you think's gonna happen?"

"Nothing! I don't know! Look just wait in the car!"

"No! I have no battery left on my phone, and even if I did what could I say to the police? That I'm somewhere on a country road and a horsebox I can't describe has turned off the road I don't know?"

"Well when you put it like that…" Pierre hesitated.

"Good, so now we've agreed that point, what next?"

"I suppose the only thing to do is follow the horsebox, try to help Phoebe and gather some evidence so the police can find this place later."

"Should we walk or take the car?" I asked.

"There's less chance of them seeing us if we go on foot, but will you manage?" He looked down at my shoes.

"I'll be fine. Come on."

Pierre held my hand and I hitched up my long dress with my other hand. Together we followed the track, looking for the horsebox. A ditch ran along both sides of the track which had been tarmacked at some point but hadn't been maintained in recent years, so it was rutted and full of potholes; a tall hedge ran behind the ditches.

After walking for about five minutes we came to a gate on our left and the remnants of a small, derelict stone building on the right. The track curved around the ramshackle remains to reveal a building which looked like a barn a short distance away. Beside the barn we could make out the silhouette outline of some run -down stables and a collection of rusting vehicles and farm machinery. The lights from a small house were shining through some trees and parked in front of the barn was the horsebox.

The ramp was down.

We pressed ourselves into the shadows close to the crumbling stone walls of the ruinous building at the corner of the track. Glancing around to check there was no one in sight

151

Pierre whispered, "I'm going to check the box. Wait here 'til I know where those blokes are."

"But…" I began to protest.

"Abi, listen to me, if those men are about, I don't want to be worrying about you."

"But…"

"No buts. You couldn't make a run for it, and…"

I tried to interrupt but he continued, "…if something does happen, I need to know that you'll be able to slip away and get help. Now wait here and keep watch. If you see someone coming…"

"What? What do I do if I see someone?"

My heart was pounding, mainly because we had found the lorry and I had to confess partly because Pierre was still holding my hand.

"Erm. Make a noise, you know, hoot like an owl or something."

Before I could decide whether or not I could hoot like an owl, Pierre squeezed my hand before slipping something into the pocket of the jacket he had given me. "Car keys. Just in case."

If this had been a film, this would have been the moment when he would have looked deep into my eyes before kissing me.

This wasn't a film.

He didn't kiss me. But he did look deep into my eyes as he zipped up the pocket, "Don't lose them!"

Quietly, and looking around, Pierre ran across the space towards the horsebox. I held my breath as I strained to listen for the sound of anyone coming. Pierre pressed himself against the side of the lorry and waited for a second. He peeped into the open end of the vehicle. It was empty. The wooden partition was fastened back, and a pile of fresh droppings showed that a horse had recently been inside.

Pierre cautiously circled the lorry. Satisfied that the cab was empty he tried the doors, they were locked. Next, he tried the small door set into the outer wall of the lorry which led to the living section between the cab and the horse area; it too was locked. Looking around to be sure there was still no one coming, he hurried up the ramp and looked inside.

Somewhere close by a dog began barking. Pierre came back down the ramp. He looked across to me and held out his arms. As I prepared to run into them, I realised he was shrugging and the arm gesture was to show he wasn't sure where to look next, not a romantic invitation.

Too late, I was already dashing towards him.

"I told you to wait," he hissed.

"I know but…" I wasn't sure what to say next. Fortunately, Pierre didn't seem bothered.

"The lorry's empty!" Pierre whispered.

"What about Phoebe?" I whispered back.

"I'm telling you, there's no one in there."

"But she has to be there!" I turned and hitched up my long dress again before I scrambled up the ramp into horsebox. Pierre followed me.

"See, there's no one here."

"Have you checked through here?" I whispered as I took hold of the handle on the small internal door which connected the horse area to the living.

"Yes. Now come on, we need to get out of here."

"We can't go until we find Phoebe!" I opened the door and looked into the small living area. I pulled the cushions off the bench seats, checked the wardrobe and even looked under the sink. I stuck my head through the cut out into the cab. There was no sign of my friend.

"I don't understand. She must be here somewhere. Unless…"

"Unless…?" Pierre ran a hand through his hair.

"Unless they found her! Oh my God! What if they've found her?"

I looked around frantically. Desperate to find some clue which would explain what had happened to Phoebe. My eyes rested on the luton, the area which extended above the cab. "Give me a leg up."

Pierre held my leg and boosted me up to the space. "Give me your phone."

"Why? Who're you gonna to call?"

I resisted the urge to say 'Ghost Busters'. This was not the time for sarcasm. "No. It's dark, I need the torch."

"Abi, if Phoebe was there don't you think she would have made herself known and come out of hiding!" Pierre muttered, but he handed me his phone.

"She couldn't do that if she was tied up, unconscious. Or dead!" I hissed back.

I flicked up the bottom of the phone screen and turned on the torch. I gasped. "Oh my God!"

"What? What have you found? Is she…" Pierre gulped, "is she …dead?" He grasped the edge of the luton and tried to climb into the space next to me.

"No, but she's definitely been here. Look!" I held up a length of black fabric.

"What's that?"

"A bow tie."

"That could belong to anyone. How does it prove Phoebe was here?" Pierre asked, dropping back down.

"Because this is Klaus' tie."

Pierre raised his eyebrows in the darkness. "Really? How do you know? And again, what does it have to do with Phoebe?"

I opened my hand and showed him the entire length of the tie, complete with the small gold key.

"Clearly this is part of another story," he said.

Pierre helped me down from the luton.

"I'll tell you later, but for now just accept this proves she was here. This is the right horsebox."

"Well, where the hell, is she now?" Pierre looked around as I had done previously.

"I don't know, but you're right, she isn't in here any longer. Let's go before someone finds us."

"Agreed. I don't like the sound of that dog." Pierre said.

I tucked the ribbon into the pocket of my borrowed jacket with the car keys and followed Pierre back down the ramp.

"Since we've come this far, let's check that building." Pierre pointed to the barn.

Suddenly we heard a bolt.

We both froze. Pierre put his fingers to his lips and drew me after him into the shadows at the side of the lorry.

One of the stable doors began to open.

Pierre edged closer to the corner of the vehicle and peeped around. "I can't see anything, but there's definitely someone out there."

The dog started to bark again.

We both looked at each other as we heard the much closer sound of the stable door closing and being bolted. Whoever it was out there, they were being careful; closing rather than slamming the door and gently sliding the bolt into place.

Pierre looked at me and mouthed, "Did you hear that?"

I nodded and gripped his arm, "Perhaps they're stealing another horse."

"I think someone is coming this way!" Pierre whispered.

We pressed ourselves against the high side of the lorry. Suddenly there was movement. A shadow creeping from the stables towards the barn.

"Get ready to make a run for it, back towards that old building on the corner of the track, as soon as they go inside!" Pierre took my hand.

Whoever was in the shadows, was trying to open the door to the barn.

"Are you ready?" Pierre checked as he looked towards the building.

I nodded, "Uh huh."

"Okay, run!"

Pierre set off, away from the shelter of the horsebox towards the derelict stone building. He half supported and half dragged me after him. As we ran, I glanced over my shoulder. The moon light broke through a cloud and for a split second I saw a flash of silver. "Phoebe!"

"What?"

I pulled my hand free. "There! Going into that barn. It's Phoebe!"

"Are you sure?"

"Yes, come on!" This time I led the way, running as quickly as my heels and long dress would allow. Pierre followed as we crossed the open space before reaching the shadows of the barn. The sliding door was open slightly and without hesitation I slipped inside.

"Phoebe?" I hissed as loudly as I dared, "Phoebe! Where are you?"

"Shh." Pierre pulled me away from the open doorway.

A glint of silver from the corner caught my eye. "Phoebe, it's me!"

"Abi?"

The silver figure came out of the corner. "Abi? Is that you? Oh, my life!"

Phoebe hurried down the barn towards me. "Thank God, you're alright!" I hugged her, "You are alright, aren't you?"

"Yes, all the better for seeing you though! How did you find me?"

"It was Pierre really."

"Pierre? Is he here?" Phoebe peered over my shoulder.

"Yes, he found me after you had been kidnapped."

"That was lucky! Is this his jacket?"

"Yes." Even in the darkness and obvious danger of our situation, I felt myself blushing at the pleasure I had in wearing his coat. I was like a hormonal teenager.

"Nice. Is it a Puffa? I like those, they wash well and have plenty of pockets."

"Ladies!" Pierre cut through our reunion, "I hate to spoil your catch up, but do you think it could wait until we're out of here, wherever here is!"

The dog in the distance was barking again. It sounded closer.

We were just about to make a dash for it when Pierre signalled for us to be quiet. Someone, a man, had returned to the horsebox. He flung the ramp into place and then jumped into the cab and started the engine. More worryingly the dog we had heard barking was with him.

It was a skinny mongrel of indeterminate breed and it raced straight towards the barn, growling and barking furiously. Pierre slid the door until it was almost closed, and we prayed that the man outside had been too preoccupied with closing the ramp and getting into the cab, to have noticed the door moving.

The dog snarled at the doorway, scratching and clawing at the small gap.

"Dog!" The driver of the horsebox opened his door and shouted, "What's the matter with you?"

He climbed out of the vehicle and began walking towards the barn.

Suddenly I was aware of Pierre sliding his hand into one of the pockets of my jacket. I gasped as his fingers probed and fondled my thigh for a moment. Before I was able to react, he withdrew his hand and dropped something into the space where the dog was trying to force its way through the door. It stopped barking and sniffed the ground before swallowing the small handful of dog treats Pierre had taken from the pocket.

The man shouted for the dog again and this time it responded and trotted over to him. Suddenly another voice cut through the night air. "What the fuck are you doing? Get a move on!"

The driver began to grumble, "Bloody dog was going mad. I think someone's in the barn. I'm gonna have a look."

"Doesn't look like it's gannin' mad now!" The second man shouted, "Leave it and get this shifted before he comes back."

"But..." The driver protested as the dog came back and began to whine and scratch at the door.

Pierre dropped a single treat into the space. We held our breath. I was certain the man, who by now had his hand on the door, would be able to hear my heart pounding.

The dog licked up the treat.

"It'll be a rat!" The second man headed towards us. I was desperate to peep out of the gap to see their faces but didn't dare move.

Suddenly the two halves of the sliding door were slammed shut. We heard the engine of the horsebox, followed by the sound of the vehicle being driven slowly away. The dog stayed outside, snuffling and searching for treats until one of the men whistled and it trotted away into the darkness.

"Have they gone?" Phoebe whispered.

"I think so," Pierre inched the door open a fraction and we all listened for signs of the men, the dog or the lorry.

"I think they've moved the horsebox, possibly to behind this barn." Pierre slid the door open another inch. He looked outside. "I think they've gone. Come on let's get out of here!"

The three of us slipped silently out of the narrow space and hurried towards the track, keeping close to the shadowy protection of the buildings before making a heart pounding dash across the open space towards the derelict building which marked the corner of the track or driveway.

"I wonder who 'he' is?" Phoebe pondered.

"He?" I wrinkled my brow.

"Yes, one of those men said to hurry before 'he' got back. I'm curious to know who 'he' is."

"There's a good few questions I'd like to have answered about tonight," said Pierre," but we need to get back to the car before whoever 'he' is, gets back. I have a feeling we wouldn't be made very welcome."

We made our way back to Pierre's car and we were just about to climb in when the sound of an engine told us someone was coming along the road in a car.

"Quick hide," Phoebe instructed, "if we open the car doors the inside light will give us away."

"But it might be someone just driving along the road," I moaned, desperate to get into the car.

"Maybe, but I'd rather not take the chance." Phoebe insisted.

"I agree. There's something odd going on up there and I'd be happier if no one knew that we were here," Pierre said.

We crouched in the long grass of the ditch as a car with full headlights hurtled down the narrow lane towards us. It slowed down slightly as it approached the gateway and turned off the road, following the track with the speed of someone familiar with the route. The dazzling lights coupled with the darkness of the night made it impossible to determine any details about the car or the driver.

Chapter 18

Pierre drove us back to my cottage. On the way, Phoebe briefly explained that she had climbed into the horsebox in order to get a closer look at the stolen mare, but the ramp had been lifted before she had a chance to get back out. She had managed to slip through the internal door into the living but hadn't been able to get out of the horsebox before it had driven off. Knowing that all that separated her from the thieves was a curtain, she had climbed up onto the luton where she had remained hidden until the lorry stopped for the men to unload the horse.

"Weren't you afraid they would hear you climbing up there?" I asked.

"Terrified, but the engine was really noisy, and I was even more afraid of one of them sticking his head through the curtain and seeing me. When we stopped, I could see through the window that they were taking the horse to one of the stables. I waited until I thought they had gone then I climbed down and got out through the horse area and down the ramp, which they had left down."

"So why didn't you just get out of there? Why go poking about in the stables?" Pierre asked.

"I wanted to get a good look at the horse and work out how to get away. It was pitch dark and I had no idea where I was."

"Well, you're both safe now," Pierre pulled up and the three of us trooped into my kitchen.

"Ahh. That feels good." I kicked my shoes into the corner, "my feet are killing me."

"I'm putting mine in the bin!" Phoebe announced inspecting the scuffed, filthy shoes in her hand.

"Better hang on to them, the police might want them for evidence," I said.

Pierre and Phoebe exchanged glances.

"Explain." Phoebe sighed.

"You know, DNA and the like. Forensics."

"Ah," Phoebe replied, dropping her shoes into the bin.

"She watches too much crime drama," Phoebe explained to Pierre.

"And I think she banged her head in the crash," Pierre dropped his voice, "when we were looking for you, she kept spacing out, just … gazing. I think she might be concussed."

"Should we phone the police?" I asked.

"I'll do it," Pierre offered, "you two get something warm on."

Our dresses were ruined. They were covered in mud and dirt from the filthy puddles we had encountered; climbing through prickly hedges and ditches had snagged the fabric and caused a variety of stains.

Under the harsh scrutiny of the electric light in the bathroom I was also dismayed to see the state of my hair which did in fact prove I had literally been dragged through a hedge. My make- up was smudged and smeared across my face; I looked like an extra from a low budget horror movie.

By the time I had washed my face and changed into a fleece jumper and pair of jogging trousers, Phoebe had made a pot of tea and Pierre had spoken to the police and arranged with a twenty four hour recovery garage, to have my car collected the following day.

"The police are sending someone round tomorrow," Pierre looked at the clock," Well later this morning! And the garage will be in touch when they've pulled your car out of the ditch and you've spoken to your insurance."

He drained his mug of tea.

"Now are you sure neither of you wants a lift to A and E?"

*****

161

Getting dressed the next morning was painful. Although we had both escaped the crash without serious injury, Phoebe and I were both suffering from pulled muscles and a rainbow of colourful bruises were beginning to show.

"How did we manage to do what we did last night? Phoebe asked as she hobbled across the kitchen.

"Probably adrenalin," I swallowed a couple of painkillers.

Our grumbling was interrupted by someone knocking on the back door. "Hi, is it okay to come in?" The visitors didn't wait for an answer and Marc, Henry, James and Margaret flowed into the kitchen.

"Oh, my poor darlings!" gushed Henry as he swept both Phoebe and me into his arms.

We both winced.

"Are you badly hurt?" asked Marc.

"What did the police say? Margaret asked as she began to unpack several Tupperware containers of food into the fridge and deep freezer, "have they been yet?"

I looked at Phoebe. "Not yet, but how do you know?" I asked.

"It's all over the village," Marc explained, "jungle telegraph."

Henry placed a box from the deli on the kitchen table.

"Angus told his mother, and from there…well," Marc made a gesture to suggest that no further explanation was required.

"Angus?" Phoebe asked, "who the hell is Angus?"

"Angus! You know Angus!" said Marc.

We shook our heads.

"Angus works for Ron," Marc explained.

I lowered myself into onto a seat and accepted a cup of tea from Margaret.

"Ron?" I asked weakly.

"Recovery Ron. He went to get your car," Marc continued, "and this morning he told Angus, and Angus told his mum…and she told… well… everyone!" Marc concluded.

162

"Oh." I looked across at Phoebe hoping she could add some clarity to what was a clearer, but still rather muddy, picture. However, Phoebe appeared to be oblivious to my confusion.

"And she sent these with her best wishes," Henry added as he opened the cake box.

I pieced the trail of information together and decided that the lady who ran the deli, Louisa, must be the mother of Angus, who apparently worked for Recovery Ron, the man who had seemingly taken my car to the garage.

A few minutes later the party was broken up by the arrival of the police.

Chapter 19

"I thought I recognised the address," the police officer sighed.

"Oh, you were the man who came when Susan died!" Phoebe exclaimed.

"Patricia," I corrected her.

"Yes," he sighed again.

He was a nice chap but seemed as confused about our ordeal as he had been about poor Patricia.

"Let me make sure I've got this right," he glanced at his notes, "you were kidnapped," he looked at Phoebe.

"Yes. By the horse thieves."

"Okay," he said slowly, "were you restrained, tied up...?"

"No, nothing like that, I was locked in the horsebox," Phoebe explained.

"And how did they get you into the horsebox?"

"Sorry?"

"Did they carry you, drag you in..."

"Oh, I see what you mean. I climbed in."

The policeman made a note in his little book. "And tell me again what they did to make you climb into the horsebox."

"What do you mean? Did to me?"

"Did they threaten you or-,"

"Oh no. Nothing. They didn't do anything. They didn't see me," said Phoebe.

"So, you got in of your own free will?"

"Yes."

"Why?"

"I've told you, so that I could see the horse," Phoebe explained, speaking slowly.

"Did the men-,"

"Thieves!" I corrected.

"Did anyone know you were in the back of the horsebox when the ramp was raised?"

"Obviously," Phoebe rolled her eyes, "Abigail knew."

"Yes, I knew she was locked in."

The policeman sighed, "But the men driving the horsebox, did they know you were in there?"

"Of course not! I hid in the living part."

"So, to clarify, you climbed into the back of an open horsebox of your own free will, to look at a horse. You hid from the driver and the man with him-,"

"The horse thieves," I reminded him.

The policeman ignored me and continued, "You remained hidden until the horse had been led to a stable, then you walked out of the horsebox and went to have a look around."

"Yes," Phoebe said, "how many times do I need to tell you, I needed to see the stolen horse so I could identify her then the thieves kidnapped me, and I escaped when they parked the lorry!"

"To be fair miss, hiding in the back of other people's vehicles without their knowledge, usually falls into the category of 'stowaway' rather than kidnapping."

"But what about the stolen horse?" I asked.

"Again, there is nothing to suggest any horses have been stolen. There have been no thefts reported in this area for a couple of months."

"Are you sure? I think you should check!" I insisted.

The policeman sighed. He did that a lot I thought.

"But we saw it happen." Phoebe protested, "We're eye-witnesses!"

The policeman stood up. "Look, I saw the state of your car. I'm sure you thought you witnessed something untoward, and I absolutely believe that you climbed into someone's horsebox without their knowledge where you became trapped. But there is no evidence at all of a crime being committed, except perhaps your act of trespass, but that is a civil matter not criminal, unless of course you caused any damage."

We watched the policeman drive away.

"Well that was a waste of time!" I snorted.

"I know I can't believe they aren't going to follow this up! Oh look, there's Pierre!" Phoebe pointed out of the window.

"I expect he's come to pick up his jacket," I said, trying to sound nonchalant.

"Either that or he's arranged to meet Felicity," said Phoebe watching the two of them chatting outside.

"What? I mean, oh, that could be awkward, you know after last night. They must be breaking up. Unless they broke up last night. You know? I mean they didn't leave together, did they?" I pointed out.

"Well, whatever they're talking about, he seems to be taking it well," Phoebe observed.

I joined her at the window. Pierre and Felicity were laughing by her car. As we watched they walked to the stables together. There didn't appear to be any tension between them at all.

"Well that's odd!" I turned away from the window.

"Do you think he knows about all the blokes she was with last night?" Phoebe asked.

"He must. She wasn't exactly discreet!"

"Oh, he's heading this way. Act natural!" Phoebe cried, "we don't want him to think we were talking about him."

"Knock, knock," Pierre called as he opened the door, "is it alright to come in?"

"Yeah, we're in the kitchen!" I shouted back.

"Hi, how are you both feeling today?"

"Sore, but okay," I said.

"Bloody furious! That's how we're feeling!" Phoebe exploded.

"Excuse me?" Pierre took a step backwards, "what's going on?"

"The police aren't going to do anything," I explained.

166

"Oh."

"Oh? That's all you have to say. Can you remember what happened last night?" I asked.

"I remember, but you have to see it from the point of view of the police," said Pierre.

"Have you spoken to them?" Phoebe asked him.

"Yeah. Someone came around just after lunch. They said there was no evidence of a crime."

"Did you tell them what happened? Did you?" I asked.

"About me being kidnapped and the lorry…"

"The lorry driving without any lights?" I interrupted

"Now that is a crime!" Pierre declared triumphantly, "unfortunately," he continued," they only have my word for it-,"

"And mine!" I cried, "I was there, I saw it! Or didn't see it depending on your perspective."

"Even so…" his voice trailed off.

"But the horse and the dog and…" I began.

"As far as the police are concerned a horse was driven to a farm and put in a stable. We entered the farm and hid in the buildings without the owner's knowledge and fed treats to their dog, again without their knowledge or permission."

I sighed. "So that's it then."

"No!" Phoebe thumped the table, "I know what we saw!"

"Well I'm afraid as far as the police are concerned that is an end to it," said Pierre, picking up his jacket from the back of a chair, "no horses have been reported stolen within the last twenty-four hours so … I'm glad you're both okay. I'll see you soon."

"I'll see you out," I offered.

"Thanks again for all your help last night," I said as we reached the door.

"No problem."

"And I'm sorry about Felicity."

"What do you mean?" he looked puzzled.

I shuffled awkwardly, "You know last night with the drummer and the other blokes from the band."

"Oh, that. Yeah, she's quite a gal when the vino is flowing it seems," he laughed, "but hey, there's no need for you to apologise. What your liveries get up to doesn't reflect on you. I'll see you later."

"They must have one of those open relationships," said Phoebe when I told her later, "I could see her doing that sort of thing but wouldn't have thought of him in that way."

I sat down and picked at the remains of the cake Henry had brought earlier, "Well either way it doesn't matter does it," I muttered.

"Did you say something?" Phoebe asked.

"No, no. Just thinking about last night."

"Good, because I don't think we should let it drop," she declared.

"What do you mean?"

"We know what we saw last night! I know that the police and possibly Pierre, think we were confused about the horse being stolen because we maybe banged our heads in the crash, but that's because we couldn't give them any details."

"What's your point?" I asked.

"I think we should do some investigating ourselves," Phoebe said.

"Go back to the farm? We don't know where it is. Even if we did what would that prove?"

"No, not the farm, the field!"

"Why the field?" I was confused. Perhaps I had banged my head harder than I had realised. "The police said no thefts had been reported, but maybe the person doesn't realise their horse has gone!" Phoebe explained, "perhaps, they only check their horse once a day."

"That is a good point! Do you have a plan?"

Chapter 20

We drove in Phoebe's car back to Stonecross Hall. We weren't sure where we had crashed or the location of the field where the horse had been taken from, so the best plan seemed to involve retracing our steps.

"This is where the road works diverted the traffic," I said.

"So, we must have turned off down there!" Phoebe pointed.

The road looked different in daylight and we were beginning to think we had taken the wrong turning when we spotted some broken glass at the side of the road. Phoebe pulled over and we got out to inspect the hedge. "This looks like the spot where we crashed," I said poking at the broken glass with my toe.

Phoebe was standing in the ditch inspecting the hole in the hedge, "Yeah which means the field where they took the horse from can't be too far away."

We continued to drive down the lane, stopping to inspect every gateway.

"This is hopeless," I said leaning against yet another gate, "how can we possibly tell which gate is *the* gate?"

"Mm. I know what you mean. We need to think logically," Phoebe leaned on the gate next to me, "what do we know about the gateway and the field?"

"It was dark!" I reminded her.

"Don't be a defeatist. Come on think."

"Well," I began slowly, "we know which side of the road the gate was on, and there was no ditch immediately after it, there was a grass verge right up to the gate."

"Excellent," Phoebe beamed, "how can you be sure?"

"The side of the road is easy, but as for the verge, the lorry was pulled off the road so it must have been parked on something that wasn't a ditch!" I declared proudly.

"There we go! Anything else?" Phoebe asked making a note of my comments on her phone.

"The ground was quite soft so there might be tyre tracks where the box was parked."

"Oh, and hoof prints," Phoebe added, "there might be hoof prints from where the horse was led out."

"That's right. There were two horses remember so there could be several prints."

"Oh, we are on fire! Come on," said Phoebe leading the way back to her car, "and I'm pretty sure it was a wooden gate!"

We set off, once again, driving slowly to account for the fact that last night we had been walking. After two false alarms we came to a wooden gate set in the hedge. A ditch ran along the side of the road up to the gate but on the other side there was no ditch, only a verge. The grass had been flattened and there were deep tracks where a large vehicle had been parked. Phoebe drove until the grass was no longer damaged before she pulled over and we got out to inspect the tracks more closely. She took out her phone and took photographs of the scene.

"I'm sure this is the gateway," I said looking at the hoofprints and churned up ground on both sides of the gate.

"I agree," Phoebe extended her photographing to record the hoof prints, "they seemed to be struggling to close the gate, I wonder why."

We inspected the gate.

"There's a chain and padlock at this end," I pointed out, "perhaps the owner of the horse has realised and put a chain on."

"Or," said Phoebe, looking at the hinges, "perhaps the gate was already chained and locked and they had to lift the gate off its hinges at this end because they couldn't open it at that end!"

She took more photographs.

"I think you're right," I agreed.

"There were two horses, right?"

Again, I agreed.

"I wonder why they only took one." Phoebe pondered.

"That's a good point. I'm sure the other one was a stallion. Surely that's the one you would take; a stallion would be worth more than a mare, wouldn't it?" I said leaning over the gate into the field.

"Maybe they couldn't catch the second one," said Phoebe, "it did look like they were struggling."

"I wonder where he is?"

"Where who is?" a voice behind us asked.

"Oh my God!" I screamed, falling off the gate, "you frightened the crap out of me!"

Phoebe helped me up. "We were just wondering about the horses. And you really shouldn't creep up on people like that!"

"What the hell has my horse got to do with you?" The speaker was a woman in her mid- sixties. As she spoke, she took off a cycle helmet and threw it onto the grass verge next to where a bicycle was propped against the hedge; the bicycle explained her silent arrival. She was about my height with grey spikey hair.

"Do you own these horses?" Phoebe asked.

"Horse singular, and again what has it got to do with you?"

"I know this looks weird," I joined in the conversation, "but we had an accident further up this road last night, and we saw a horsebox parked here. It looked as if someone was taking a horse out of the field."

"This field? I don't think so." She took a key out of her pocket and unlocked the padlock. She let herself into the field and closed the gate firmly with Phoebe and I on the outside. She whistled and looked down the field.

"Yes," Phoebe insisted, "this field."

"Is this your first visit to check them today?" I asked.

"No! Not that it's any of your business. I was here first thing." She whistled again and I leaned over the gate to look down the field.

At the far end of the paddock a large chestnut horse was grazing. "Can you pass me that bucket?" She pointed to the bicycle and I noticed a purple bucket hanging from the handlebars.

Phoebe handed her the bucket and the woman rattled it after peeling off a nylon cover. The horse lifted its head and began to trot towards us. The trot became a canter and soon a gallop. We all took a step back as the horse skidded to a halt sending mud and a scattering of small stones in all directions. The woman moved the bucket away from the gate.

"He's gorgeous," I said.

"Thanks. He's called Charlie. He was a brilliant eventer 'til he damaged his tendon."

"Ah that's a shame. He looked sound just now," Phoebe said.

"Yeah, he's just about right. We have painkillers for bad days but as long as I'm careful he's sound enough to hack but his eventing days are over. Fortunately, he's entire so he can still earn his keep and enjoy his retirement."

"What about the other one?" I asked.

"Other what?" the woman asked.

"Other horse," said Phoebe, "the mare."

"There is no other horse. I've already told you!" the woman exclaimed, "and even if there was, what sort of idiot would keep a mare in the same field as a stallion?"

"But there was a mare in this field, and we saw her being stolen!" Phoebe was adamant.

"Look, for the last time, there is no other horse and you are starting to annoy me."

"But..." Phoebe began.

"I'm sorry," I interrupted, "You're right. We've obviously made a mistake. Sorry to bother you."

"What are you doing? You were there!" Phoebe insisted as I dragged her away.

"Again, sorry for the mix up!" I called.

"Yeah. Okay then. You probably banged your heads in that crash you mentioned." The woman shouted as we got into Phoebe's car.

"I cannot believe you did that!" Phoebe exclaimed as she started the car.

"I'll explain but let's get away from the field."

Phoebe continued to mutter and mumble under her breath as we drove away from the woman in the field and her stallion.

"Okay, this is far enough," I said, "pull over here."

"This better be good, because ..." Phoebe began.

"I know, I know, but she was starting to get all worked up and was never going to admit that there was ever a second horse in that field," I explained.

"Your point?" she asked.

"Maybe she's involved in some way."

"How?"

"I'm not sure, yet." I said slowly, "but she was adamant there was no other horse, and never had been. She might have come to help them catch the horse we've just seen so he can be stolen too, for all we know."

"That's a point," Phoebe agreed, "we only have her word that she owns the horse."

"Regardless of whether or not she is involved I think the next thing is to find the mare."

"Oo, good idea. How?" Phoebe asked.

"Again, I'm not sure; yet!"

Phoebe started the car and we set off driving down the lane once more. We decided that finding the mare, meant finding the yard and the stables where the horsebox had taken her. "That's not going to be as simple as finding the field,"

Phoebe pointed out, "neither of us know how far the box travelled before turning off this road."

"But we do know it was off this road, so that's a start," I said.

The light was beginning to fade and we both agreed that finding the track and the stable yard was a task best carried out in daylight. "Perhaps Pierre could help us look." I suggested.

Chapter 21

The following few days offered no opportunity for serious searching. My car was still being repaired so we could only go when Phoebe was free to drive and only in daylight. We identified a couple of possibilities using Google maps; we were determined to investigate at the earliest opportunity.

The police refused to consider helping and seemed to think our idea for them to send some officers to visit the properties along the lane, asking for proof of ownership of any horses, was a waste of resources; especially, they reminded us, as no horses had been reported stolen in the area. We were also warned that a lady who owned a field along the lane in question had reported several suspicious sightings of a vehicle snooping around properties in the area; the description and number plate of the vehicle matched Phoebe's car.

Phoebe had spoken to Pierre when he had called into the Dirty Dog for a pint while she was at work. He didn't think our decision to take over the investigation was a good one, "'Just leave well alone!' is what he said," Phoebe explained as we hung headcollars on the post next to the gate into the paddock. We watched the horses we had just turned out for a few minutes before walking slowly back to the stables.

"I can't believe it; I was certain he would help," I said.

"I know!" Phoebe agreed, "but he was really dead set against us looking for the horse or the stables."

"Well, we'll just do it without him!"

Before we could discuss searching for the horse the Thompson family arrived in a flurry of excitement. "Hi, Abi!

Yoo- hoo! Abi!" Margaret waved excitedly as James helped her out of the car.

"Looks like someone has had too much coffee," Phoebe giggled.

"Do you have a minute, for a quick chat?" James asked.

"Of course. Is everything alright?" I asked.

"Everything's perfect dear," Margaret patted my arm and grinned.

"We were just hoping you might have another stable we could have." James stood by Margaret with the same wide grin on his face as his wife.

"Erm. I suppose. Is there a problem with Zeus' box?" I asked.

"Oh no. You misunderstand, we're thinking about getting a second horse for our Chantelle."

"Really? What's brought this on?" Phoebe asked.

"Well," Margaret began," Zeus is great and is obviously a very talented jumper."

"Obviously," Phoebe agreed. She appeared to be wearing the same grin as the Thompson family.

"But his floorwork,"

"Flatwork mother," Chantelle corrected.

"His flat work," Margaret accepted the correction, "needs time to improve and we think it would help her career, if she had a second mount."

"Career?" I asked.

"Competition career," James explained, "she is very talented."

"It would help," Margaret interrupted, she was determined to continue with her story, "if our Chantelle had a dressage schoolteacher to compete on while she trains Zeus."

"School master," Chantelle corrected for a second time.

"Okay," I said slowly, "have you seen any horses advertised?"

"Better than that," Margaret beamed.

"We've just been to try one and he's perfect," said James.

176

"Crikey, that was quick!" I exclaimed.

"We've been thinking about it since the event at Stonecross," James said.

"We got chatting to that lovely man, Dom," Margaret explained, "and he pointed out that all the professional riders have more than one competition horse. So, if Chantelle is going to compete in the big league with other professionals, she needs a second mount!"

"Big league?" I wasn't sure I had heard correctly.

"Professional?" Phoebe asked.

"Yes," James turned towards her, "Chantelle is going to focus on becoming a professional event rider once her exams are over."

"Exams?" I remembered Chantelle and Brad at the Ball, "A-Levels?" I asked hopefully.

"GCSEs." Chantelle spoke up. "I have a place at Kirkley College from September, but I can work that around my riding."

"Anyway, this horse," Phoebe prompted, "did you say you had been to see one already?"

"Yes, can you believe we just mentioned to Dom, the other night, that we had given some thought to his suggestion that Chantelle needs a second horse and he actually knew of the perfect one." James explained.

"Can you believe it?" Margaret looked between Phoebe and me.

"Barely," Phoebe replied.

Her sarcasm was lost on the family, but I assured them that a second stable would not be a problem. They were not planning to have the new horse checked by a vet because Chantelle was happy with what she had seen and after all, they were buying it from Dom; a top bloke. They had arranged to collect the new boy themselves the following day so there was nothing else to be said. I left them to tell Phoebe all about the new horse while I hurried across the yard to catch Hannah. She owed several weeks of livery now and I was running out of patience, especially given the expensive dress she had been wearing at the ball, along with the cash she had been splashing at the bar all night. The problem was catching her. She seemed to ride really early and had usually left the yard before most of the other liveries had even arrived.

"I am so sorry," She apologised when I tackled her about the money. "Here, I have some cash, will this cover my bill until I get my bank problems sorted." Hannah smiled and handed me a roll of fifty-pound notes from the glovebox in her car.

"Gosh, aren't you worried about having that amount of money in your car?" I asked.

Hannah smiled and shrugged her shoulders before getting into her car and driving away.

*****

Phoebe was working when the Thompsons drove into the yard with their new horse the following day but there were plenty of people hanging around to help. Izzy and Felicity were both there, along with Marc. As usual Hannah had been and gone before anyone else was up and about.

James drove carefully into the yard and was closely followed by Dom. Once the trailer was parked and the ramp lowered, a bay head looked out and calmly took stock of his new surroundings.

"Different type to Zeus," I muttered to Marc.

He smiled and answered through gritted teeth like a ventriloquist, "Thank God!"

"Aw, he's lovely," Felicity stepped forward, "so calm. I love his funny little squiggly star thing. It's hard to see under this long forelock isn't it baby?" She scratched the new horse affectionately on his forehead.

"Hope the bugger isn't doped," Marc whispered to me.

Margaret fussed around in her usual way, swathed in furs and clicking to make the new horse look towards her camera lens. Chantelle led the gelding down the ramp. It was a different scene to the chaotic arrival of Zeus, and she was able to record the event and upload several pictures and short videos directly to her social media.

Dom stood close to me and watched the family, "He's a lovely horse. He'll teach her and they'll grow in experience together."

"How old is he?" I asked.

"Twelve."

"Is it doped?" Marc asked.

"Cheeky sod!" Dom laughed.

"What's he done?" Marc continued.

"Bit of everything really. Dressage, jumped a bit, some eventing…"

Before Marc could continue his questioning, Dom walked away to advise the Thompsons regarding which rugs the horse should be wearing after his journey. Izzy and Felicity followed him.

Marc checked his phone.

"Is everything alright?" I asked as he frowned and slid the device back into his pocket.

"Yeah. Just wondering where Henry's got to."

"Probably waiting 'til you've mucked out," I joked.

"That'd be right!" he laughed, "I'd better crack on then."

As Marc headed towards the stables, balancing a pitch- fork and broom on a wheelbarrow, Dom came to stand next to me again. "What do you think?"

"Looks like a nice horse. Where did you say he came from?"

"He is nice, and I didn't." Dom grinned and his eyes twinkled.

"Have you had him long?" I persisted.

"Not really. Long enough."

"Oh, talking to you is like trying to nail fog to a black board!" I declared in exasperation. I picked up the buckets I had been rinsing and went into the feed room. Dom followed, laughing.

"I'm sorry, but you are so easy to wind up. The horse belonged to a livery, but she had an unfortunate change in personal circumstances, so I bought the horse, to help her out."

"Oh, divorce?"

Dom gave a sort of half smile which I took to mean yes.

"I didn't realise you had a livery yard. How come you were after stables here a few months back?" I asked.

Dom helped me to lift a bag of feed into the metal feed bin, "I don't run a livery yard, she was a one off, she was useful to have around to help with mucking out and if I wanted to go away she'd keep an eye on things. I mainly breed event horses. I was interested in stables here because I could have made use of your facilities, you know, the arena and stuff."

"Oh, okay; how many horses do you have?" I asked, lifting another bag of feed.

"Here, let me help you." He took the bag out of my arms and waited while I opened the lid of the next feed bin. "I have a few brood mares and my stallion, a couple of youngsters, one really promising little horse just turned five and some visiting mares."

He dropped the sack of feed into the storage bin. "Actually, I wondered if you'd like to come and have a look at my stallion, just to see if you like the look of him for your mare."

I folded up the empty feed sacks, "I would love to see him, but until my car gets fixed, I'm pretty much grounded." I didn't mention my attempt to visit the supermarket using the horsebox. Parking had not been easy!

"Didn't the garage give you a courtesy car?"

"I could have taken one, but it was a tiny little 'mook' mobile and after the incident with the deer, I felt quite vulnerable, so I chose to just manage."

"That's understandable." Dom side stepped around me as I swept the floor.

"It shouldn't be long before mine is sorted and Phoebe is great for lifts and stuff."

"Well, if you want, I could drive you to my place and then drop you back home," Dom offered.

"Oh, that seems like such an inconvenience, not to mention lots of driving, for you," I stopped sweeping and leaned on the broom.

Dom smiled his twinkly smile, "Not a problem. But if you want, you can buy me a late lunch at the pub on the way back."

"We'll see. Another time perhaps."

"Come on," Dom teased, "You know you want to!"

Chapter 22

I was curious about Dom; he was quite mysterious and gave little away about himself. I tried to look for landmarks or clues to where he must live as we travelled through a maze of country lanes and back roads but he drove quickly, and his car was so low that it was almost impossible to see over the top of the hedgerows which bordered most of the twisting lanes.

Dom chatted for most of the journey about the eventing successes of his stallion and the progeny the horse had sired. Dom had used several of his own mares and the offspring had all done well, being placed in the top three at the Burghley Young Event Horse Championships over the last few years, to name but one prestigious accolade.

Suddenly he swung the car off the road and through a gateway. He slowed down slightly and steered around the pot- holes with ease. "I must get these filled in. I got some gravel, but the heavy rain just washed it out again."

"Uh, huh," I muttered in agreement, hanging onto my seat as the car bounced along the track. There was something about the track that seemed familiar. Dom slowed the car as we curved around a tumbledown stone building. Suddenly I realised why the track was familiar. Dom steered to avoid the skinny dog who came bounding out of the barn to greet the car. He parked in same spot the horsebox had been the night of the ball.

"This way." Dom pushed the dog away as it bounced around him. It trotted around the car and stopped when it reached me, sniffing my boots. "Don't worry about him, he makes a lot of noise but that's about it. Go on dog, get away."

The dog stopped sniffing and wandered off. The yard looked more rundown in daylight; the tufts of weeds were visible; a pile of rotting pallets was slowly disappearing into a profusion of dock and nettles and a collection of rusting pieces of farm machinery was stacked to one side of the barn.

Several bales of green wrapped haylage were stacked close to the pallets and an open bale was spilling its contents onto the ground. The stables were white with doors which were painted black and as we approached some of the horses put their heads over to watch us through the gaps in the anti-weave grills. "Are these all yours?" I asked looking at the horses; a chestnut with a white star on its forehead, a grey, two bays, one with a narrow blaze and a brown and white coloured horse who had its ears flat back and was furiously trying to bite its neighbour.

"All except one."

"Oh, which one?" I asked, looking at the bay heads.

"The grey on the end. She's here for a couple of days to be covered by Star. He's 'round here"

I followed Dom past the stables and behind the barn. Here, a row of three stables, wooden this time were set in a surprisingly neat hemmel. A shaggy haired grey pony was reaching under the fence to nibble the grass on the other side. One of the stable doors (the middle one) was open, I presumed this was the pony's stable; the stable closest was bolted top and bottom and a dark chestnut horse was looking over the last door.

"Here he is!" Dom announced proudly, "Oh and this chap is his best buddy. You keep the sexy one calm don't you mate?"

I laughed nervously and admired the stallion when Dom brought him out of his stable to show him off. To be fair, he was a gorgeous horse, but all I could think about was that this was the yard, where we had followed the horsebox to on the night of the ball.; the yard where the stolen horse had been taken.

"Can we look at the other horses?" I asked when Star had been settled back in his stable and was calmly pulling haylage from his net.

"The mares and youngsters? Sure."

"Last year's youngsters are in the field, just there," he pointed through the trees to a group of three horses, "Just to the left of the house the group in the field near the silver birch trees are a mix of two and three-year olds and behind the barn here, a handful of four-year olds. All for sale if any of them catch your eye," he added with a wink.

I followed his gaze as he pointed out the different groups. Two horses looked out over their half doors of another block of very old stone stables as we walked towards the paddock behind the barn. I hadn't noticed these stables earlier as they were virtually hidden from sight by a combination of birch trees, long grass and the stack of haylage. "Who are they?" I asked.

"The very dark gelding is a five- year old I bred. He doesn't have a spot of white anywhere," Dom said proudly, "I wish I'd kept him entire to be honest." Dom nodded his head in the direction of the gelding, "I've started to event him, fabulous horse, very talented. I want to get some points on his card and let him get some experience under his belt, then he'll be for sale."

"And what about the chestnut in the next stable?"

"Similar story, homebred but not as flashy, or brave. He's a great jumper and a really honest little horse, but I don't think he has the dressage ability of the other one. Still make a nice horse for someone doing riding club levels or he might make a showjumper...why? Are you interested?" Dom raised his eyebrows.

"I've got enough thanks." I laughed. "So, is that what you do? Sell horses? Are you a dealer?"

"I'm a breeder, not a dealer." Dom emphasised the difference before leading me back to the white brick stables. The horses had disappeared back inside, and we could hear them contentedly chewing their haylage. As we approached each half door, the horses left their nets and came to snuffle our hands and pockets for treats. Dom introduced each mare, gave each one a mint and fussed with them in turn. Of the five mares one was in foal, the coloured was yet to be covered and the others were due to be checked to see if their covering had been successful.

"You start early," I commented, "most people don't think about breeding from their horses until closer to May."

"We're quite exposed up here, despite the shelter from the woods, it's deceptively high so we get hit pretty hard by the harsh Northumbrian winters. I like to get my foals out early, so they have a chance to build up some strength before the bad weather hits," he explained as he bolted the last stable door.

Driving home, my mind was racing. Dom had calmly shown me all of the horses including two bay mares. Could one of the mares be the horse we had seen being taken from the field? This was certainly the yard where the horsebox had brought her.

"You're quiet? Is everything okay?" Dom asked.

"Oh, what? Yes, I'm fine just trying to work out if I can afford to breed from my mare this year or whether I should wait until next spring."

"If it's the stud fee, I'm sure we could come to some arrangement…"

I decided to ignore the inuendo. "There are the extra vet costs. But he is a lovely horse. I just want to think about it."

"No problem, but don't think on it too long, you don't want a late foal. If it's a bad winter, you want the little 'un to have some flesh on its bones and to have some type of immune system developed."

185

I agreed to have a late lunch with Dom at the Dirty Dog, mainly because I wanted to see Phoebe and by having lunch at the pub, I could go home with her and avoid the awkwardness of Dom hanging around. We sat at a table close to the window. I insisted that as Dom had acted as chauffer for the morning lunch was on me.

"New friend?" Phoebe raised her eyebrows and nodded towards Dom who was sitting with his back to where we were talking at the bar.

"Phoebe, believe me, it seemed easier to agree to have lunch. Can I hang around and get a ride home with you?"

"Of course. Are you okay?" she asked.

"Yeah, just trust me. I can't talk about it now," I glanced over my shoulder before giving her what I hoped was a meaningful look.

Phoebe paused before filling two glasses with lemonade, "I'll bring your food over when it's ready."

*****

"Are you sure?" Phoebe gasped later that afternoon.

"I'm certain! I didn't immediately recognise the gateway because we arrived from the opposite direction and it was daylight."

"What about the mare? Is she one of the bay horses you saw? she asked.

"To be honest, I'm not sure. I only saw the stolen horse from a distance when she was being led into the horsebox, and it was dark remember. Would you recognise her again?" I asked.

"Absolutely!" Phoebe said with certainty, "She had no white markings on her face or legs but had a distinctive white mark, just behind her wither where a saddle must have rubbed in the past."

"She had a rug on."

"Then we need to go back," said Phoebe," and have a closer look."

When we arrived home, Felicity had tied Jasper outside in the yard and was combing tangles out of his tail; Izzy was riding in the arena and Henry was standing with Marc close to his car. "Looks like those two have had a row," Phoebe observed as Marc turned away and left Henry standing, staring after him. A few moments later, Henry followed Marc and we could see them walking towards the field in silence.

"Marc was pissed this morning because Henry was late and hadn't texted or something," I explained, "come and see Chantelle's new horse."

Chantelle was in the stable brushing the new arrival. She happily peeled off his rug and showed him to Phoebe.

"He is lovely." We both agreed.

"How old is he?" Phoebe asked, looking carefully at the horse.

"Twelve," Chantelle answered.

"Twelve eh?" Phoebe glanced at me as she looked at the horse's teeth.

"Yeah. Why?"

"Nothing, nothing. I just wondered. I thought he looked familiar," Phoebe patted the gelding's neck, "you are a lovely boy. Have you got his passport? I love looking at where they've been, what they've done, how they're bred…"

"Dad has it," Chantelle explained, "but he is a dressage schoolmaster, plus he has some eventing experience."

"Well," said Phoebe helping to replace the rug, "he is lovely. What's his name?"

"Fly by Night Moonlight Shadow," recited Chantelle, struggling with the ridiculous name.

"Crikey. That's a lot to shout down the field," Phoebe smiled at me.

"But his stable name is Shadow, because of the white mark on his forehead, it looks like the moon during an Eclipse, when it's in shadow," said Chantelle proudly, fiddling with the horse's silky forelock. "It's so high up you can only see it when his forelock's plaited!"

Chapter 23

"That new horse is so familiar," Phoebe mused as we drove towards Dom's house, "I'm sure I've seen him before."

"What do you mean, at a show or something?" I asked.

"I dunno, but it's really bugging me."

"I know what you mean, but I think he's just one of those horses, you know, bay gelding, hard to see white bits or no noticeable features at all. Quite common really."

" I suppose. Either way it's a dam sight older than twelve!"

"Yeah, that's what I thought," I agreed with her, "did you notice the angle of his teeth, not to mention the length of them?"

"Oh yes and the Galvayne's Groove mark has almost disappeared, you can just see it close to the gum line on his lower incisor," Phoebe pointed out, "so that would make him what…twenty…ish?"

"'fraid so. Do you think I should tell James and Margaret?" I worried.

"To be honest I wouldn't. They chose not to have the horse checked by a vet and he won't have a hard life with them."

"I suppose so. Makes you wonder about Dom; do you think he knows the horse isn't twelve?"

Phoebe snorted, "I think he absolutely knows how old that horse is. Tell you what, I'd love to see its passport!"

We parked Phoebe's car on the side of the road close to the spot where Pierre had parked. We could only hope that if Dom drove down the lane, he would either approach from the opposite direction, or not realise the car belonged to Phoebe and perhaps think it was owned by a dog walker. We retraced our footsteps from the night of the ball. The track

189

seemed to be very exposed and we both felt vulnerable as we hurried towards the tumbledown building. It was much easier to walk over the rough surface and avoid the potholes wearing boots in daylight, than it had been when wearing high heels and evening dresses in the darkness.

Crouching amongst the rubble and long grass, we surveyed the scene. A ditch ran either side of the track and behind us the hedge ran parallel down to the road, open farmland lay behind the hedge. Beyond the ditch on the other side of the track a barbed wire fence could be seen behind a thinner, smaller hedge which formed the boundary to a sparse, over grazed paddock. The two geldings Dom had shown me were sharing a large, round bale of hay in the middle of the bare field. Each horse was wearing a thick rug complete with neck cover.

The heavily chained and padlocked gateway to the paddock was opposite the ramshackle building where we were hiding. The yard looked empty and there was no sign of the dog. I pointed to the stables. The coloured mare appeared to be dozing with her head over her half door. We checked once more and being satisfied that the yard was deserted, we ran across the yard to the stables.

There was no sign of the chestnut mare, her stable was empty, but the other four were in their stables enjoying stuffed nets of haylage. Each horse was wearing a light day rug.

"Which bay mare do you think it is?" I whispered to Phoebe.

"This one." Phoebe said confidently. "The one in the horsebox definitely had no white markings which were visible on her legs or face, so that rules out the mare with the blaze."

Sliding the bolt as quietly as we could, we unlocked the door and let ourselves into the stable with the bay horse. She sniffed at the strangers who were unbuckling the front of her rug, but otherwise appeared to be unconcerned.

"It's her, look!" Phoebe peeled back the rug to reveal the white marks behind the mare's wither. She took a photograph of the mare and the markings before quickly replacing the rug.

"What should we do now?" I asked. Despite the mounting evidence I hadn't really wanted to believe that the stolen horse had been taken to Dom's yard, "do you think Dom knows?"

Phoebe gave me a withering look, "Of course, he fucking knows. I wouldn't be surprised if that's how he makes his money, stealing horses or at the very least hiding them before they're shipped on or sold. We need to tell the police."

Before we could consider the situation, we heard a car approaching. There was no time to get out of the stable so we both ducked down and peeped through the gaps between the sections of wood which made up the half door. It was Dom. He drove straight across the yard without stopping, towards the house which lay close to the wooden stables and paddocks where small groups of horses were grazing behind the trees.

"Let's get out of here before he comes back," I urged Phoebe.

Carefully bolting the door behind us, we crept out of the stable. There was no sign of Dom, so we made a dash for it towards the track. However, before we had gone far, we heard another vehicle slowly negotiating the uneven driveway towards us. This driver was either less familiar with the path and the position of the ruts and holes or they thought more about the welfare of their car than Dom.

"I think it would be a good idea to get out of sight!" I said, looking for a hiding place.

"Agreed!" Phoebe dragged me after her out of the open and once again we found ourselves crouching in the weeds and broken masonry at the corner of the track. The car, as it approached was familiar. As was the driver.

191

"What the hell is Pierre doing here?" I asked in horror as we watched him park in the yard. We clambered over the stones and old bricks to the edge of the building. Pierre was out of his car and fussing the dog which had come bounding across the yard. Someone shouted and the dog darted away, only to return a few moments later with Dom. Both men shook hands, and they chatted for a few minutes before walking towards the stables. We were close enough to see them and to hear the sound of their voices, but too far away to discern what was being said.

"I can't believe it! Do you think Pierre is involved?" I whispered to Phoebe as we watched him and Dom going into one of the stables.

"I'm as shocked as you, but it would explain why he was keen for us to 'leave well alone' as he put it!"

As Dom and Pierre had disappeared into one of the stables we were left with the choice of either risking being seen and creeping back to the yard in an attempt to hear the conversation between the two men, or option two; take advantage of the fact that no one was watching and make a run for it.

We decided to take option two.

*****

The policeman declined a cup of tea and he didn't want a slice of cake. Phoebe thought he was probably still wary about the incident with Susan AKA Patricia.

"The horse is not stolen!" he insisted.

"Yes, she is!" we insisted back.

"I know it's the mare from the field, I recognised the white marks on her wither! Did you look at the white marks?" Phoebe demanded showing him the photograph on her phone.

"Yes madam, I saw the marks and I saw her passport and details of ownership."

"A passport isn't proof of ownership," I muttered.

"In this case it pretty much is. The animal in question was bred by the owner. He is the only person to have ever owned her."

"But…" I persisted.

"No buts. Now, we have wasted time and energy investigating this non-crime, so please let it drop before you find yourselves in trouble. The gentleman who owns the horse was very understanding but this is the end of that matter. Do you both understand?"

We hung our heads and nodded like naughty school children who have just been reprimanded.

"Now, the owner doesn't know who made the complaint so do yourselves a favour and accept that the horse has not been stolen!" He closed his little book with a snap and left.

"That's that then," I said resignedly.

"Are you joking?" Phoebe looked at me, "we know that there is something dodgy going on."

I agreed and cut myself a slice of ginger cake, "I don't know what we can do though."

"We just need a plan," Phoebe looked thoughtful, "but I think we should keep this to ourselves until we know for sure what's going on, and who we can trust."

Chapter 24

Life continued as normal for the next few days. Felicity spent hours pampering her horses but not riding, Izzy and Phoebe ignored each other, and the Thompsons continued to spend a fortune on private trainers, including Klaus, for Chantelle; a cost which looked set to rise now that she had two horses. Hannah continued to arrive really early to ride. She was friendly enough with the other liveries but mainly kept to herself; she did, however, prove to be a bit of an expert using clippers.

Felicity was constantly battling with Romeo's shaggy coat; due to an illness he struggled to shed his coat naturally and clipping him was a regular ordeal. Watching Felicity fighting to remove the excess hair, Hannah produced a pair of clippers and quickly whipped off the pony's coat, leaving him both cooler and looking much smarter.

Felicity was thrilled, "Look," she showed me proudly, it's so smooth and Hannah's used a tiny pair of clippers to leave a little pattern made up out of my initials on one side of his hind quarters and some stars on the other side. It's amazing!"

The only dark cloud appeared in the form of the obvious, growing tension between Marc and Henry.

Phoebe and I were discussing recent events as we rode around the edge of the fields which bordered the woods. Some earlier rainfall had left the ground very soft and slippery but had resulted in the release of a fresh and aromatic scent being released from the trees.

"Poor Marc," said Phoebe, "he's convinced Henry is having an affair."

"No way! That's ridiculous!"

"That's what I said," Phoebe continued, "but apparently Henry keeps sneaking out and won't say where he's going or where he's been."

"Even so, I can't believe Henry would cheat on Marc. I hope they work things out."

"Have you seen Pierre since we saw him at Dom's the other day?" Phoebe asked.

"No. You? Has he been into the pub?"

"No, but I did see Cam and Steve. I asked them about the woman with the stallion. Apparently, she was a really successful rider when she was younger, she's called Mary or Marilyn somebody, Anyway, she did up to five- star on that horse."

"Wow!"

"I know! They had a bad fall at Bramham though, and he damaged his tendon, or was it his hock? Anyway, she doesn't ride now but she does a bit of freelance teaching, occasionally she does special demonstrations or clinics at the Academy. The horse is retired from being ridden but lives life as a stud horse."

"So, do you think she is involved in whatever dodgy shenanigans is going on?" I asked.

"Hard to say but Cam spoke really highly of her... I think we should go back and see if we've missed anything, perhaps have a look in the stable or whatever it is at the bottom end of her field."

When we arrived back at the stables after our ride, Hannah was bringing Secret in for the night and Marc was leading both ponies in behind her.

"Here, let me help," Felicity took the lead rope for one of the ponies and followed Marc to their stables. "Where's Henry tonight?" she asked.

Marc shrugged, "Working late. Again."

"Hi!" James waved as we rode through the gates, "have you seen the new boy Phoebe?"

195

"He's lovely," Phoebe smiled as we dismounted and led our own horses into their stables.

James grinned, "The saddler's coming to fit him for a new saddle tomorrow then Chantelle can get started with him!"

"We're all going to the pub tonight, are you coming?" Felicity asked.

"I'm working," Phoebe sighed.

"And I don't have a car," I reminded everyone.

"Ah, that's a shame, we're trying to cheer Marc up," said Felicity lowering her voice.

"We could give you a lift," James offered.

"In which case I can bring you back when I finish work," Phoebe said, "I can stay over if you like and help with early turn out tomorrow."

*****

The Dirty Dog was busy, but Felicity and Marc had managed to claim a table. I followed Margaret and James to the bar where we were served by Phoebe. We chatted about the new horse and tentatively considered competitions for the future. There were several dressage competitions coming up and Phoebe and I were taking Skye and Treasure to another one-day event the following weekend; this was an affiliated event and (fortunately, several of us thought secretly) Chantelle had been too late in applying to get an entry accepted. Marc and Henry were taking their ponies to a show the same weekend.

"Assuming he still wants to," Marc traced the trail of condensation around his glass with his finger, "I've barely seen him for nearly two weeks. I think he met someone at the ball."

"Don't be daft," Felicity gave Marc a hug, "Henry adores you."

"Really? Doesn't feel that way right now!"

"I thought you said he was working," Felicity continued.

196

"That's what he said."

"He must have finished early then," I said, "'cos he's just come in."

Marc twisted around in his seat and scanned the crowded bar. Henry spotted our group and waved, "Hi, what's everyone drinking?" He dropped a kiss on Marc's cheek.

"I didn't think you were going to make it," said Marc.

"I finished and came straight here," Henry squeezed Marc's shoulder, "same again everyone?"

I followed him through the crowd to the bar. Henry looked flushed, almost excited and he had clearly just had a shower. I opened a packet of crisps and leaned against the bar as we waited for Phoebe to complete the drinks order.

"Is everything alright?" I asked.

Henry's eyes sparkled, "Brilliant Abi, just brilliant."

He paid for the drinks and loaded up a tray before weaving his way back to our table.

"What's going on?" Phoebe asked, pretending to wipe the bar.

"I'm not sure, but I'm as certain as I can be, he's up to something and I'll be amazed if he's genuinely been working late."

The pub gradually emptied as the evening wore on. Felicity yawned, "Well that's me, does anyone need a lift?"

I watched as our group left, amid many goodbyes and kisses on cheeks, before perching myself on a stool at the bar. Phoebe cleared tables and stacked glasses into the dishwasher. The manager, Andrew, looked at the few remaining stragglers and glanced at his watch. "Just check there's no one in the ladies for me and turn the light off Phoebes then you can go if you want. There's no point both of us hanging around."

We stood in the deserted car park and Phoebe changed her little black work shoes for a pair of leather paddock boots similar to my own. It was late and the roads were empty. This time we knew where we were heading to, so it didn't take much more than twenty minutes for us to find the field. As we approached, we saw the same unsteady torch light shining ahead.

"Oh my god, I can't believe it, they're here again!" Phoebe dropped our own car's lights to nothing more than side lights and slowed the vehicle down to a crawl.

Just as we came to the bend in the road, she pulled the car off the road into a gateway and turned off the engine.

Unlike the night of the ball, we had a good idea of what to expect and we hurried down the road on foot; our hearts hammering. Turning the corner, we both paused; we could see the silhouette of the horse box. It had been reversed fully into the actual gateway of the field, rather than being parked on the side of the road. The gate had been pulled to one side to make space for the vehicle and the ramp was down. We glanced at each other and moved silently to the hedge line at the side of the road.

As we crept ever closer, we could hear the voices of at least two men and the shriek of a horse. The animal sounded excited. Phoebe pointed to a gap in the hedge. I nodded and followed as she pushed through the hawthorn and undergrowth. We found ourselves in a field which showed the short green stumps of winter wheat, more importantly, we were in the neighbouring field to the one with the horsebox.

Staying in the shadows of the hedge which lay between us and the road, we inched our way closer to the fence line with the next field. The boundary was a mix of stone wall and hawthorn hedge. Finally, we were close enough to crouch low into the overgrown verge which ran around the perimeter of the wheat field. We pressed ourselves against the wall and crawled under the cover of the hawthorn.

There were three men in the next field. One was standing with his back to us and was holding a brown and white coloured horse not far from the bottom of the ramp of the horsebox. The horse was a mare and was trembling with excitement, she was lifting her tail and squirting as she squealed. Behind her, the cause of her excitement, a stallion was being held by the other two men.

"For Christ's sake, hold her still!" barked one of the men holding the stallion.

It was Dom.

The man holding the mare grumbled and adjusted his hold on her bridle, and on the rope, which was attached to the mare's hind leg, presumably to stop her kicking… The mare's tail was bandaged, and she appeared to have some kind of soft boot or bandage over the hooves of her hind legs, she was also wearing a heavy canvass cover extending down her neck. Dom and the third man were standing either side of the stallion; it was wearing a leather headcollar to which a chifney bit had been attached. Dom was holding a rein of leather and chain; it was clipped to the central ring on the bit and the third man was standing slightly to one side holding a whip in one hand. The men were all wearing hard hats similar to the one I wore for cross country but without the silk covering.

Suddenly, it became obvious what they were doing. The third man stepped forward and helped guide the stallion into place. The horse snorted and leaped forward as Dom released some of the pressure on the bit and allowed the stallion to mount the mare. She screamed and tried to kick out as the stallion, following his instincts, bared his teeth to grasp her neck through the canvass cover as he plunged his erect penis into her.

I grasped Phoebe's arm in the darkness. She looked at me as I mouthed, "I know that horse!" Phoebe nodded to show that she also recognised the mare. It didn't take long for the stallion to complete his task and the mare was led quickly into the horse box. Dom waited until the ramp had been raised and the gate lifted back into position on its hinges before he took the headcollar off and released the stallion. The horse bucked and plunged towards the gate but one of the men flicked a whip in the direction of the horse, sending him careering away up the field. Dom shone a torch first around the area where they had been and then over the hedge. We cowered down among the nettles and weeds until, satisfied that they had left no sign of their intrusion, Dom vaulted the gate and joined the others in the cab of the horsebox.

Seconds later they were gone.

The only evidence that they had been there was the churned mud in and around the gateway. We crawled out of our hiding place and ran back to Phoebe's car. Keeping far enough back from the horsebox, that we could follow their lights but avoid being seen ourselves, we drove cautiously behind Dom and his companions until we saw the lorry swing off the road. Phoebe pulled up at the end of the track as the horsebox disappeared from sight where the track curled away towards the stable yard in the distance.

*****

"What the hell was that about?" Phoebe drove quickly home.

"It was definitely Dom, wasn't it?"

"Oh yes, no doubt about it. But why sneak about covering a mare in the darkness!" Phoebe glanced at me as she turned through the gates and parked in front of my cottage. "Apart from the utter weirdness its bloody dangerous!"

We got out of the car and locked the gates before wandering across the yard to give the horses a final check and hang up their late-night haynets.

"Dom has his own stallion," I said as I tied a net for Eric, "so why go to the expense of taking a mare to someone else, especially in the darkness?"

"Unless…" Phoebe began slowly.

"Go on," I prompted.

Phoebe paused as she locked a stable door after hanging another net, "What if the woman who owns the stallion doesn't know Dom is using her horse."

"Okay," I followed her towards the pony boxes and watched as she hung a net for Solo, "but why? What's the point?"

Phoebe bolted the door and we took a net into Symphony. "I'm not sure," she said, "but I'll work it out. Let's get these horses done."

I picked up the last net from outside of Secret's stable. Phoebe followed me in as I fiddled to replace an empty net with the full one. Not wanting to wait, the horse greedily snatched at the sweet smelling haylage pulling the nylon net tight against my fingers.

"Get back and wait, you're a greedy sod!" I grumbled.

Phoebe pushed the horse back into the deep shavings of his bed and out of reach of the net for a moment, "Christ how long must it take for Hannah to muck out?" Phoebe looked at the depth of the bed which completely covered the horse's hooves and extended past his fetlocks.

I laughed, "She is a bit like Felicity and rather OCD about his bed. The worst thing is that she insists on using that really thick black hoof dressing every day, so the shavings stick when she brings him out and they leave a trail across the yard."

"It's not just his bed she is so anal about," Phoebe continued, "she goes mental if anyone else touches his rugs or does anything to help and I mean anything! I'm surprised she lets you hang up his net! You should've heard her rip into Marc when he said he'd borrowed her hoop-pick! And, I was washing Treasure's legs the other day; it had rained, and they were all coming out of the field absolutely caked in mud. Marc asked me to hose the ponies' legs while he was holding them, Hannah came past with this one," Phoebe nodded towards Secret, "he had mud nearly to his ears, I took one step towards her and asked if she wanted Secret's

201

legs washing while I was busy and Jesus, her reaction! You'd think I'd offered to take the horse to have it turned into fucking meatballs! I'll not offer to help her again mind!"

I smiled at the thought of very precise Hannah being horrified at the sight of Phoebe bearing down on her with a hosepipe.

"There's something odd about this girl," Phoebe said thoughtfully, "it's no coincidence her horse is called Secret!"

"Let's not get carried away with conspiracy theories." I warned her.

"I'm telling you there is something about Hannah. Look at how she denies knowing Dom. I've seen them together loads and you saw them fighting," Phoebe persisted.

"Perhaps she was just embarrassed."

Phoebe wasn't convinced.

Chapter 25

The second one day event was a much quieter affair than the one at Stonecross. Felicity was with Henry and Marc, helping them with their ponies at the BSPS show, Izzy was competing at a local venue who were hosting a championship event to mark the end of a series of dressage competitions which had been held at the venue and the Thompson family had gone along to watch her. The only unusual activity came in the form of Hannah announcing that she was going for a lesson with Secret.

"Where are you going dear?" Margaret asked.

"A place close to the Scottish Borders, "said Hannah with her usual vagueness, "they have a visiting instructor."

"Oh, if you'd said we would have booked Chantelle for a lesson and we could have given you a lift."

"I've been trying to get a place for ages," Hannah said apologetically, "they have quite a waiting list. Sorry."

Hannah had decided to hire a small self- drive horsebox. She left early for her lesson.

Phoebe and I drove out of the yard soon after Hannah. The sky was ominous and threatened to rain, the further South and West we travelled, the darker the sky became, by the time we arrived a steady drizzle was falling. The event was just over an hour's drive away with the horses; we had already been the day before to walk the cross- country course so we knew what to expect. There were several steep hills, which if the rain continued could become quite slippery, but the actual jumps were similar to those at Stonecross; several log piles, a wide solid table fence. The water jump a straightforward run into a lake, but a few strides into the water, horses were expected to jump a combination of two narrow hedges. Further round the course sloping fences and drops, designed to test the nerve of the riders, accentuated the slope of the hills.

We parked our lorry and collected our numbers before unloading the horses and tacking up ready for our dressage tests. We rode to the collecting ring together and checked in with the stewards in charge of our respective arenas; we were in the same class, but luck had contrived that we were in different sections. After wishing each other luck, we separated in order to warm up in different parts of the collecting ring, we didn't want the horses to be unsettled due to the proximity of their stable and travelling companion.

The rain continued to fall and even though it was light, the persistent wetness gradually began to soak through our jackets and breeches. Water droplets stood out like tiny gemstones on the hair of the horses and their coats darkened as they became wetter and wetter.

A lot of the spectators had chosen to watch from the dry indoor arena of the showjumping phase or even to brave the cross country course, where they were unlikely to be asked by the stewards and fence judges to put down their brightly coloured oversized umbrellas; the dressage officials were much more likely to request that the potential distraction of an umbrella be removed. The rain itself seemed to act like a muffler, softening the sounds and noises of the competition.

The quieter atmosphere meant that Skye was far more settled and relaxed than at her first competition. She was responsive to my aids and worked without resistance throughout the test. I grinned and fussed her enthusiastically after my final salute to the judge who was sitting in her car.

I rode back to the horsebox on a long rein. A light wind had dispersed the clouds and although it wasn't sunny, the threat of any heavy rainfall had passed, and the falling rain had given way to an all-encompassing dampness. It didn't take long for me to change my dressage saddle and replace it with one more suited to jumping. I added some protective boots to

Skye's legs and buckled a neck strap into place before heading towards the showjumping arena; I was just in time to see Phoebe.

Showjumping was Phoebe's favourite phase of the competition. Treasure was neat and careful but fast when he jumped.

"Well done!" I congratulated Phoebe as she rode out of the arena after completing an easy clear round. She grinned and leaned forward to give Treasure a mint.

"Clear the entrance!" shouted a steward.

"I'll wait over there," Phoebe pointed to a corner of the collecting ring with her whip, "good luck!"

The fence heights in our class were restricted to ninety centimetres, though it was permissible for two jumps to be ninety- five centimetres. The course builder had ensured that the jumps were inviting and although they were all as high as permitted there were no fences set at difficult distances. Some of the solid fillers which sat under poles were garish colours and patterns, but Skye ignored them. A pole on the last fence bounced precariously in its supporting cup but somehow it stayed in place and just like Phoebe and Treasure, we turned in a clear round.

We rode back to the horsebox together, chatting and reliving moments of the dressage and showjumping phases. "Don't make it obvious that you're looking," I said, "but I'm sure the box third from the end of this row belongs to Dom."

We continued to chat or at least give the impression that we were talking as we slowly rode past Dom's lorry. The ramp was down, and various pieces of tack and grooming kit were scattered around the vehicle.

As we rode past, a horse stamped and whinnied from inside the lorry. I glanced towards the open end and saw the slightest movement from within the dark interior.

"That was definitely Dom's horsebox," said Phoebe as we changed into our cross- country colours and dry breeches.

"I couldn't see much of the horse, could you?" I asked as I adjusted my body protector.

"No, it was too dark. I wonder if he is competing," said Phoebe.

"Mm. He must be," I said, contorting my arms through the loops on my number tabard, "the gelding he showed me, was black, so that would match with it being difficult to see in the lorry."

"He's in a different class to us," Phoebe was flicking through the programme. "Here he is number 105 riding Silverwood Obsydian II. He's doing the BE100," she pointed a gloved finger at a line in the booklet, "I suggest we go for a little wander after our cross-country. What do you think?"

"I think it would be rude not too!" I grinned.

Phoebe tucked the programme into a box containing her grooming kit, before climbing onto the ramp and using it as a mounting block. She waited while I did the same, before we both rode away towards the cross-country course.

*****

Having washed and attended to the needs of both horses and settled them with full nets of haylage in the horsebox, we set off to see what we could discover, in or around Dom's lorry. As we approached, we could see Dom. He was adjusting his spurs, standing with one leg raised his foot resting on the side of the ramp.

Phoebe and I watched from the row of parked lorries opposite. Satisfied with his spur, Dom picked his gloves and short jumping whip up from the ramp. Someone was holding his horse. Whoever it was, had their back to us. She, we both thought it looked like a woman, had her hair tucked into a hat. She was wearing a pair of blue jeans, tucked into a pair of wellies and was swamped by a large waxed jacket which looked as if it belonged to someone else, possibly Dom.

His mystery assistant was now shielded from view as she was between the horse and the lorry. As Dom rode away from the horsebox the other person hurried up the ramp and disappeared inside.

"Hi there!" Dom called as he rode past, "I thought I saw your box when I went to collect my number," Phoebe and I stepped out of the row of parked horseboxes, "how did you both get on?" Dom continued.

"Great!" Phoebe told him, "we both finished on our dressage scores, so fingers crossed for a place."

"Excellent!" he grinned down at both of us, "listen you couldn't do me a favour and take a couple of pictures, or better still a short video over one of the fences could you? I want to sell this chap and some video of him cross-country would be great."

"Er. Yes. I suppose," Phoebe answered.

"Fabulous!"

And that put an end to our snooping, at least in the short term.

We followed Dom to the warm- up and Phoebe took a couple of photos on her mobile as he popped over a log and a raised telegraph pole.

"Thanks. I really appreciate this," Dom said before heading off towards the starting box.

"I wonder why his bloody helper couldn't take his stupid pictures," Phoebe grumbled as we positioned ourselves close to a drop fence set into the hedge line. From here we could see horses coming down the hill towards us as well as having a good view of several fences in the surrounding fields

"Always assuming his helper is actually with him and not some random passer- by he commandeered, like he did us," I suggested.

"Possible I suppose. Either way, we'll have a chance to see in his lorry when we go to show him these video clips."

We could see the starting box from our position and Phoebe tracked Dom as she filmed him at a distance setting out on the course and clearing the first three obstacles. He disappeared from sight for a minute or two before thundering towards a jump heading uphill very close to where we were standing.

"You've got to admit, that's a lovely horse," I said, as Dom vanished into the distance.

"Mm," Phoebe was non comital.

"Don't you like it?" I asked.

"Oh, the horse is gorgeous, but it's one of those beautiful warmblood types, in my experience, the prettier the horse, the crazier the horse!"

I started to laugh.

"You can laugh at me... but it just happens to be a coincidence that every horse like that who I've had dealings with has been... well... awkward...difficult..."

I wiped the tears of laughter from my eyes, "What about Secret, Hannah's horse? He's identical to Dom's horse and is a saint to handle."

Phoebe shrugged, "I've never ridden him though, he might be fucking mental when you get a saddle on him. And that's another thing..."

I braced myself for Phoebe's next 'Hannah conspiracy' theory.

"Hang on, don't want to record us talking on his Lordship's video."

Dom's distinctive black and white hat made him easy to spot as he galloped towards our fence, Phoebe turned the camera back on. His horse took a line of narrow brush fences almost in his stride. We watched as Dom sat up and took a pull to steady the horse before they flew over a drop before continuing downhill into the last section of the course. Phoebe checked her phone to review the video.

"Black horses with absolutely no white are-,"

"I know," I interrupted, "very often high spirited!"

"I was going to say rare."

"Oh. I suppose..."

"Not in a rare breed, nearly extinct way, just not very common. Think about it, while we've been watching this fence, how many grey, bay or chestnuts have we seen?" she didn't wait for an answer, "dozens. How many black horses? And I don't mean dark brown, or nearly black with a blaze or white leg marking."

"Your point?" I asked.

"I just find it a coincidence that there are two perfectly black horses within what ten, possibly twenty miles of each other."

"They might be by the same stallion, or mare," I suggested.

"It said in the catalogue that Dom's horse is home bred, so I suppose there might be a connection," Phoebe mused, "but I still think it's odd."

We headed back across the course towards the collection of tents where the officials were busy working out scores. The results of our class weren't quite ready so we each bought a burger and set off to find Dom.

Any hope of snooping inside the lorry were dashed. Our delay in the hospitality area, coupled with the speed Dom had been able to reach the end of the course on a galloping horse compared to us on foot, meant that the horse had been washed and rugged by the time we caught up.

Dom had exchanged his body protector and cross-country top for a fleece. He looked up as we approached. "Hi! I'll be with you in a second."

He quickly wrapped some cooling leg bandages around the horse's tendons and offered him another small drink of water to which he had added some electrolytes.

"Come on, walk with me while I take him for a wander," Dom untied the gelding. His words were more of a command than a suggestion.

"Who's in there?" Phoebe asked as we walked away from the horsebox.

"Just his travelling companion. Did you get any pictures?"

Phoebe sent the photographs and short bursts of video from her phone to Dom's. "These are great!" Dom enthused as walked away from his lorry, "remind me to buy you a drink next time I see you in the Dirty Dog."

Before we could continue our conversation, the tannoy crackled into life announcing that the results for our class were ready. We left Dom and headed towards the small group beginning to congregate near the score board.

We were both thrilled to be placed! I was fourth in my section and Phoebe was second. If she had been in my section, she would have won.

"Wow, what a brilliant result!" I declared, examining my rosette and small envelope containing my prize money.

We hugged each other. "Your dressage has improved beyond belief," I looked at Phoebe's test sheet, "have you been having secret lessons somewhere?"

Phoebe took her sheet back and grinned, "Bow ties must be awfully expensive."

I wrinkled my brow, "Eh?"

"Well in return for me promising to keep his tie and the little gold key… well, let's just say I promised to keep them safe, Klaus has been giving me lessons when Izzy isn't around."

"Oh, my life! Are you blackmailing him?"

She laughed, "Absolutely not. He offered. And if my lesson is particularly productive, I do give him a rather nice tip."

I held up my hands, "I don't want to hear another word."

Dom's horsebox was closed, and the ramp raised by the time we made it back to the lorry park. The public address system informed us that he had won his section in the BE100 class. There was no sign of Dom and as there was no way to see inside his lorry, we set off for home.

*****

210

"Where was Hannah going?" Phoebe asked as we unpacked the horsebox.

"Not sure exactly, somewhere in the Scottish Borders. Why?"

"'cos this is her just getting back now," Phoebe stopped mixing feeds to watch as Hannah drove into the yard.

"Hi," I called, "how was your day?"

Hannah grinned, "Great thanks. Oh, I say congratulations."

I looked down and saw the ribbons from the rosette tails fluttering from within the armful of tack and spare jackets I was carrying.

"Do you need a hand with anything?" I asked.

"I'm fine thanks."

By the time we had unpacked and mucked out our own lorry, Hannah had settled Secret in his stable and driven off to return the hire vehicle.

"Was she having a jumping lesson or flatwork?" Phoebe asked.

"Dunno, why?"

"No reason really. Just curious about how far she must have travelled to have a lesson when Klaus is here so often. She never has a lesson with him."

"Well maybe she was jumping then."

"I suppose."

Chapter 26

Life continued without any great drama for a week or so. Chantelle had lessons, on both her new horse Shadow, and Zeus, with Klaus; Izzy watched Klaus like a hawk and although her own training sessions were clearly intense, her leg length and hence stirrup length remained static. Hannah resumed her early morning exercise routine with Secret and Felicity seemed to have acquired another male admirer.

"I think he's the trumpet player from the band who were playing at the ball," Marc confirmed as we watched from what we hoped was a discreet distance.

"What happened to the drummer?" Phoebe asked.

"Not sure," Marc said slowly, "I think he was allergic to horses."

"I haven't seen Pierre recently," I tried to sound casual.

"No. I think- Oh at last!" he cried in exasperation.

"I'm so sorry," Henry called across the yard, "I got caught in traffic. Road works near Longframlington."

Marc sniffed.

"But look, I've brought cake from the Deli," he held up a cake box and tried to make exaggerated puppy eyes.

"Did you come through the village?" asked Marc. "I thought you were going to the dentist."

"I told you, traffic! I was diverted. Now do you want this cake or not?"

"What about your tooth?" Marc persisted.

"Temporary filling. And I've got to eat. Honestly, what are you like!"

"Well… I suppose." Marc took the box and let Henry peck him on the cheek. They walked away together towards the stables.

"He is definitely up to something," Felicity said quietly making me jump.

"What do you mean?" asked Phoebe.

"I work at his dental practice and I can guarantee he wasn't there today."

"You're a dentist?" Phoebe looked at Felicity closely.

"A receptionist. I only work part-time, but I know for a fact that Henry was in a couple of days ago for a check- up. His teeth are perfect."

"Maybe he damaged his tooth somehow…" I was desperate to find a plausible reason to explain Henry's comment.

"Perhaps," Felicity was unconvinced, "but there were no roadworks or diversions when I left work!"

"But why would he lie?" I asked.

"Dunno. But he better not be messing Marc around."

"That's rich, given her apparent track record for fidelity," I muttered as Felicity re-joined her trumpet player.

"Sorry did you say something?" asked Phoebe.

"No," I sighed, "not a word."

The following Saturday Phoebe and I took Skye and Treasure to another One Day Event. This was quite local and buoyed up with her recent success, Phoebe had entered the BE100 class. "Dom's competing again," Phoebe commented, flicking through the programme she had picked up the previous day while we were walking the course. "He's in the Novice section. That young horse of his can't half jump."

"The yard's going to be quite empty today," I noted as we drove out and turned right towards the village.

"How so?" asked Phoebe as she continued to search through the programme.

"Well, the Thompsons are coming to look at the course with Chantelle ready for her unaffiliated class tomorrow and

213

Marc 'n Henry have offered to walk the course with her this afternoon."

"What about the others?" Phoebe asked, glancing up for a moment.

"Izzy has a dressage competition down at Richmond and Felicity is going down to give her a hand."

"Hannah will have the place to herself."

"Nope, she's going out too, she is off for another lesson somewhere," I said.

"It's either all or nothing with her," Phoebe snorted, "do you think she's secretly competing and doesn't want anyone to know?"

"God knows," I commented, but look, isn't that Henry's car ahead? I wonder where he is off to so early."

"It certainly is him," Phoebe sat up, "hurry up. We might see where he turns off."

However, because Henry didn't need to consider two equine passengers, he soon began to pull away from us on the twisting country lane. We caught sight of him as we entered the village and then his car seemed to simply vanish.

"Where the hell, did he go?" Phoebe twisted in her seat.

"No idea," I scanned the mirrors, "he must have turned into one of the houses or turned down the lane that curls round the back of the academy."

"Odd," said Phoebe turning her attention back to the programme and the map of the course.

The competition was held at a large equestrian centre with views over the valley and across to the Cheviots. It was busy but well organised and because we were in different classes, it was much easier for Phoebe and me to help each other.

The various phases flowed seamlessly, and the cross-country course was exhilarating. There were the usual combinations of stacked logs, hanging telegraph poles and brush fences along with drops, ditches and spreads disguised as haycarts and tables. The water jump was positioned just in front of the hospitality and official tents. The jump in was a simple log, of varying height depending on the class, with a narrow jump carved to represent a giant duck, fish or crocodile, again, class dependent, in the middle of the water.

Skye dropped a pole over two fences in the showjumping which put us out of contention for a place despite a brilliant dressage and clear cross country. Phoebe again finished on her ever- improving dressage score and was third in her section.

We were about to leave and head home when we saw Dom warming up for his dressage. "That horse has lovely paces," I said, "he practically floats."

Phoebe glanced at her watch. "Another quarter of an hour won't hurt our two." Phoebe said referring to Skye and Treasure waiting on the horsebox. "I wouldn't mind watching his test. What do you think?"

We positioned ourselves near a small group of spectators close to the dressage arenas. Dom trotted from the collecting ring, past us and on to his arena. He paid no attention to the people spectating; he was simply focussed on the horse he was riding. He circled the arena, keeping close to the white boards and giving his horse the opportunity to see the floral arrangements and judge's car from both a clockwise and anti- clockwise direction. An arm extended from the open window of the car and a small brass bell signalled the start of the test.

Phoebe took out her phone and filmed the test.

"Just something to watch later. I'm not a fan of Dom, but this test is amazing," she said, "I mean did you see how straight he was when they did that leg yield?"

I nodded, "And the simple change of canter lead over X, you'd think the horse had read the dam test!"

As we drove carefully between the rows of horseboxes and trailers, we saw the Thompson family with Marc and Henry. They all waved.

"It's a lovely course," I said through the open window of the horsebox.

Henry jumped onto the step of the passenger door, "How did you do?"

Phoebe grinned and waved her rosettes in his face. "Well done! Abi how did Skye do?"

"She was great. We had faults in the show jumps but fab dressage and cross- country."

"As long as you both came home safe. Are you coming tomorrow to watch Chantelle?" he asked, jumping down.

"If I can swap shifts at the pub," Phoebe waved as we drove away.

Chapter 27

The yard was deserted when we arrived home. "Do you fancy getting something to eat at the pub?" Phoebe asked, "I have a change of clothes in my car."

I took no persuading and as soon as the horses had been rugged and turned into the field Phoebe and I quickly showered and changed into clean clothes.

"Don't you have a jacket?" I asked Phoebe, looking at her bare arms, "I know we'll be in the car, but you'll freeze."

"It stinks of horses," Phoebe shrugged, "funny, I love the smell on the actual animal, but it turns my stomach when I get a whiff of the stale smell of horse or stables on someone's clothes or hair."

"I know what you mean," I shuddered, "it's like when you go in someone's house and the smell of dog knocks you out!"

Phoebe laughed, "Exactly!"

"Borrow one of mine if you like." I searched through an assortment of jackets hanging near the front door, "Here, try this." I handed Phoebe a dark coloured, slightly quilted jacket from the collection.

"This is nice," Phoebe slid into the coat.

"I hardly ever wear it," I confessed, "in fact the last time I wore it was to 'not Susan's' funeral."

"Ah. Poor woman," Phoebe reflected, "but very nice jacket."

"Keep it."

"Are you sure? I'll buy it off you."

"Honestly, you're fine. You do loads to help me, and I never wear it."

"Well if you're sure." Phoebe posed in front of the large mirror hanging in the hallway, turning to see what the jacket looked like from behind. She pushed her hands deep into the pockets as I ushered her out of the house towards her car.

"Hang on Abs, you've left something in the pocket."

She fumbled to pull out a folded flyer. "What's this?" she asked.

"Probably rubbish," I held out my hand as Phoebe unfolded the paper.

"It's the order of service from the funeral." She studied it carefully before muttering, "It can't be!"

"Can't be what?" I asked.

Phoebe didn't answer, instead she set off across the yard, past the stables towards the field where Shadow, Romeo and Jasper were grazing. Carefully avoiding the muddy area inside the gateway, I followed Phoebe as she hurried across the field.

"Look!" she pointed triumphantly towards Shadow with the order of service.

"Look at what exactly?" I asked in exasperation as I tried to balance on tufts of shorter grass and thus protect my one pair of half decent non-horsey shoes from the mud.

"It's him, Shadow, he's the horse from the picture at Susan's funeral!"

"Patricia," I corrected, "but I suppose her name isn't actually relevant. Are you sure? That it's the same horse I mean... it can't be. Can it?"

"I said I recognised him!" Phoebe gave Shadow a mint to distract him as she lifted his forelock to show off his tiny patch of white alongside the photograph on the front of the order of service, where a much younger version of what looked to be the same horse stood, neatly plaited, beside a proud and smiling Patricia.

"Good grief!" Forgetting the mud, I stepped forward to examine the mark on the horse's forehead more closely. I took the order of service from Phoebe and compared the two horses; the actual horse standing patiently in front of me and the horse depicted in the photograph.

"There's a fair amount of grey near the actual mark, but I think you're right," I handed the service sheet back to Phoebe.

"I know I'm right!" she declared, "the thing is, what do we do about it?"

*****

The lunchtime rush was over by the time we reached the pub, so we had no trouble securing a private table tucked away in a corner. We pondered the problem of Shadow and the unsuspecting Thompson family.

"I suppose there is no doubt that Shadow is the horse in the photograph," I said using a final chip to soak up the last trace of curry from my plate.

"Everything would point to it being the same animal. The age, his real age I mean, the marking… I wonder if he's microchipped." Phoebe carefully arranged her cutlery on her own empty plate.

"That's a point." I agreed.

"Of course," when Susan-,"

"Patricia." I corrected.

"When Patricia, bought the horse, microchips and passports weren't something you considered for your average neddy. People sometimes used freeze brands to permanently mark the coat but that was personal choice."

"That's true," I agreed, "but, Chantelle said her dad had been given a passport for Shadow. I wonder where that came from?"

"Yeah, I was wondering that. But more than that, I'd like to know how Dom came to have the horse in the first place," said Phoebe.

"He told me that he was helping out someone who used to keep the horse at his place."

"I didn't realise he had liveries."

"Nor me," I said, "apparently the woman would help around the yard and she looked after things when he was away competing."

"What happened?" Phoebe asked.

"I think she got divorced and needed the money."

Phoebe sat up, "Definitely divorced?"

"I'm not sure," I said slowly, "why? Is it important?"

"Depends," Phoebe chewed her lip for moment as she concentrated, "if Dom got the horse from someone who needed the cash due to a divorce it means someone owned him after Susan. Sorry, sorry after 'not Susan'."

"Patricia."

"Yeah, yeah whatever. The point is, if there was a third person involved then perhaps Dom genuinely sold the horse on using whatever story he had been told and with the paperwork he had been given. But…" Phoebe left the comment hanging as we were briefly interrupted by Andrew clearing our plates. He had a brief conversation and agreed that Phoebe could have the next afternoon off in exchange for working that evening.

"But…" I prompted.

Phoebe glanced around. There were a couple of tables occupied at the other side of the room and a young man with wavy hair was playing on the fruit machine near the door; Andrew was polishing glasses behind the bar. She lowered her voice to a whisper, "But, if there was no-one else involved then things become a little more sinister, especially concerning Dom, because we know Patricia, or whatever she's called, didn't split from her other half and have to sell the horse, the poor bugger died, in your kitchen! Now think. Did he definitely say the previous owner was getting divorced?"

I stared into the remains of my lime cordial and in my mind replayed the conversation with Dom. "Let me see; Marc made a joke and said he hoped the horse wasn't doped, then

220

I was trying to make polite conversation about the new horse, and I got fed up 'cos Dom was being so evasive and well, 'Domish'."

Phoebe nodded, understanding exactly what I meant by the term.

"He wanted me to see his stallion, so he started helping me to move some bags of feed and said the owner's circumstances had changed so she needed to sell the horse and I said, 'ah is she getting divorced?'"

"So, you, suggested divorce, he didn't offer that as a specific reason?" Phoebe persisted, "can you remember his exact words?"

I closed my eyes for a moment, "His exact words were, 'she had an unfortunate change in personal circumstances' which I took to mean divorce."

"But he didn't actually say divorce?"

I began to feel uncomfortable, "Not in as many words. But he didn't deny it either. He just…" I remembered Dom smiling at me, "he just… smiled. What are you getting at?"

"Think about it, Abi," Phoebe hissed, "circumstances don't get any more fucking unfortunate than being dead, do they?"

I opened my eyes wide and gasped. "Shit. Do you think Dom murdered Susan?"

A man and woman from one of the other tables looked across.

"Shush!" Phoebe put her hand on my arm, "calm down. She died in your kitchen and Dom was nowhere near. Besides, what motive would he have?"

"I don't know, to get the horse?"

Phoebe snorted, "Listen to yourself. It's a nice horse but it's not bloody Shergar."

"Poor horse," I said, "he must be bloody ancient. Should we tell James?"

"I'm torn, truth be told," Phoebe chewed her lip again. "Dom has clearly sold them a horse and said it was much younger than it obviously is, but," she dragged out the word,

221

"James and Margaret chose not to have the horse vetted. They seem to have some paperwork to validate whatever they were told and all we have is a photo from a funeral service."

"Even so…"

"What would happen if we went straight to Ma and Pa Thompson, right now, and said, 'oi mate you've been fiddled'?" Phoebe asked.

I hesitated.

"I'll tell you what would happen," Phoebe continued, "James and Dom would have a huge row and either the old horse would be returned and then passed on to God knows who, or Dom would persuade them, and anyone who would listen, that we are wrong and a bit mental; they'd keep the horse but move him and Zeus somewhere else."

"Then what do you suggest?" I asked.

"First thing, I'd like to see the passport. Something dodgy is going on, I'm just not sure how serious it is. Let's keep this to ourselves for now. Until we have some stronger evidence."

*****

Chantelle's experience at the One Day Event was less stressful than her first effort. Her dressage was still without any finesse, but Klaus had certainly helped to improve things since Stonecross; riding Shadow had also helped as she now knew what she was aiming to produce. Zeus took charge in the showjumping and although we all held our breath as we watched, she somehow managed to steer him around the course with only one pole lost.

Marc and Henry were on hand to anchor the excitable horse and rider combination and they safely escorted them to the beginning of the cross-country course. Phoebe and I watched from a vantage point as Chantelle clung like a limpet and let Zeus take her around the course. There were several times when we gasped and held our breath, but the horse knew his job and somehow brought her home in one piece.

Zeus' bay coat was shining and flecked with white foam and sweat, his veins were standing proud and his nostrils were flared; but his eyes were shining, and his ears were pricked.

"That was fab!" Chantelle declared as she slid to the ground. Margaret tried to feed a mint to Zeus, but he was far too excited to notice, and it was only Henry's quick thinking and his ability to practically lift her out of the path of the horse's swinging hind quarters, that prevented Margaret from being trampled.

"Oh, he's dropped his sweetie!" Margaret began searching the grass, terrifyingly close to the snorting animal's hooves, apparently oblivious to any potential danger.

"Don't worry," Henry intervened, "he can't have anything until he's untacked and cooled down."

"Really? Why?" Margaret stopped searching.

Phoebe grinned at Henry, waiting for an explanation that would stop Margaret's innocent but at times frustrating stream of questions.

"Erm," Henry paused for a moment, "because it's the rules."

Apparently, that was good enough and Margaret put her tube of mints back in her handbag and took up her camera. James handed his daughter a bottle of water and they led the way back to their trailer.

"We'll just bring your horse, then shall we?" Marc shook his head and slackened off the girth a couple of holes before leading Zeus in the wake of the Thompson family.

"She's just out of the placing for her section," Phoebe pointed out looking at Chantelle's name on the score board, "If she hadn't had that pole down in the showjumping she would have been tenth I think."

"That could be a blessing in disguise," Henry said quietly, as he and Marc handed cups of scalding hot coffee to Phoebe and me.

"What do you mean?" I asked.

"I have a sneaky feeling that if she was placed, the Thompsons would take that as a signal to step up to a class with higher fences," Henry continued. "It's a big enough risk for her to bang around with only a modicum of control over these fences but can you imagine the carnage on a course where she actually needs to ride and present the horse safely?"

"That's a good point," I agreed.

The Thompsons joined us. Chantelle shrugged when she saw the scores, "At least I wasn't last."

"There's an unaffiliated dressage at the Academy on Wednesday evening," Henry said, "why don't you take one of your boys? It would be good experience."

"How do you know about dressage competitions at the Academy?" Marc asked.

"I heard Izzy mention it the other day," Henry replied with only the faintest suggestion of a blush. "Let me give Camilla a call and see if she will squeeze you in as a late entry."

Henry took out his phone and went in search of a quiet area to make his call. James and the rest of the Thompson family followed him.

Marc looked troubled.

"What's the matter?" I asked.

"I can't see Izzy bothering herself with an unaffiliated competition at the Academy," Marc sniffed.

"Just because she was talking about it, doesn't mean she's riding," I pointed out, "she might have simply made a comment, or perhaps she's writing for one of the judges. In fact, she might even be a judge!"

"I suppose," Marc conceded reluctantly.

Chapter 28

My car had been returned by the garage and I was enjoying a sense of regained freedom and independence, now that I was no longer relying on my friends for lifts. Phoebe and I had toyed with the idea of taking a horse to the dressage competition, but neither of us were great fans of evening events as they often drag on until quite late; instead we decided to attend, purely as spectators.

The Academy was set back from the main street which ran through the village. A narrow lane led past some holiday cottages and curled away from a small camping and caravan site between a row of smart bungalows which sat on either side of the lane; all of which boasted impressive gardens with roses which were particularly noteworthy.

Just past the bungalows, almost at the end of the lane, a pair of decorative iron gates marked the entrance to the Academy. The lane continued in front of the gates, and past the red brick house where Steve and Camilla lived, until it ceased to resemble a road and turned into a narrow track which in turn disappeared as it reached the open farmland and moors which surrounded the village.

Phoebe had arrived a few minutes ahead of me and had already parked her car. She was waiting and directed me to a vacant spot in the crowded carpark. "I didn't expect it to be this busy," I said, looking at the collection of trailers, horseboxes and cars.

"Ma and Pa Thompson have just followed Chantelle to the warm- up area which seems to be in the outdoor school, over there," Phoebe pointed, "Marc and Henry are with them."

"Okay then, let's go." I began to walk in the direction of the outdoor school, but Phoebe grabbed my arm.

"Which means there is no one at the Thompson's trailer," she said slowly and deliberately.

"I know," I replied, equally slowly, "you've just said, everyone is over there, so come on."

"You are quite dim at times," Phoebe sighed.

"To be fair, you're not the first to say so, but in this instance, I feel that criticism is a tad unjustified!"

"If there is no one at the trailer we might be able to sneak a peek at Shadow's passport. It might be somewhere in the trailer," Phoebe explained, "I've searched in the tack room at home and I can't find it, they must keep both passports for the two horses at home. Come on, it's too good an opportunity to miss."

"Oh! I see!"

We hurried across the parking area to the Thompson's trailer. Both front and rear ramps were down, and a collection of grooming brushes were spilling out of a box placed near the wheel arch close to the front ramp. A headcollar dangled from a lead rope which was tied to a piece of orange bailer twine inside.

"Nothing here," I said rummaging through the grooming kit.

"Dam. They must have it with them," Phoebe said, as she scrutinised an almost empty tack locker.

We decided to avoid the drama of the warm -up area; Chantelle was riding Shadow in the outdoor school and was following a range of instructive suggestions from her father, as well as Marc and Henry, she didn't need us adding our opinions, so Phoebe and I headed straight to the indoor arena where the actual competition was taking place.

There were two entrances to the indoor arena: a large wide sliding door, which gave access to the enormous indoor riding arena, this was the entrance for horses. It was also large enough to allow a range of vehicles to drive in if necessary, to aid the removal or delivery of jumps for example.

226

The second entrance was more akin to a normal door, it opened onto a long corridor which ran the length of the building. To the left a solid barrier of about four foot in height separated the walkway from the actual arena. A door to the right led into a café and beyond the café rows of plastic tiered seats rose to give spectators an uninterrupted view of whatever was happening on the other side of the barrier. At the far end of the building a flight of wooden stairs led to a small commentating box which overlooked the entire indoor area. Music was playing through the public address system.

"Oh, those bacon sarnies smell lush!" I breathed in the aroma of crispy bacon and onions. "Come on let's get something from the café and take it with us to eat while we watch."

We opened the door into the small café. At once we were enveloped in the slightly damp steamy atmosphere. Small rivulets of condensation were chasing down the windows which would normally allow those inside the café to watch the riders in the arena. I took my place in the queue and scanned the groups of people clustered around the collection of plastic tables and chairs. I nudged Phoebe, "There's Margaret. Do you think she's alright?"

Margaret was searching through her handbag and was looking increasingly flustered.

"I'll go and see what's got her in a tizzy." Phoebe left me and squeezed through the crowded café.

"Hello, is everything alright?" Phoebe asked.

"Oh, hello dear. I seem to have lost my camera," Margaret said with a tremor in her voice. She upended her handbag onto one of the plastic tables and searched the lining and each one of the now empty pockets. As she returned the contents and it became obvious that there was no camera in the bag, she became more concerned.

"Check your pockets," Phoebe suggested.

227

Margaret did as she was told, placing each item on the table as she searched each of her pockets. "Hanky, sweeties for Shadow, James' car keys. Oh! The keys, I've remembered!" A wave of relief swept over her face, "I had my camera in my hand because I had just taken a lovely picture of Shadow coming out of his trailer with his new travelling coat on, and James asked me to lock Shadow's licence in the glovebox. I couldn't manage with one hand, so I put my camera down on the floor in the footwell of the car. I must have forgotten to pick it up!"

"Licence? OH! Do you mean his passport?" Phoebe asked.

"Yes, sorry. Silly name. As if a horse is going to go on holiday!" Margaret chuckled.

"I'll go and get it for you if you like," Phoebe offered.

Margaret looked puzzled.

"Your camera," Phoebe smiled, "If you give me your keys I'll nip out and get it for you."

"Oh, I don't want to put you to any trouble dear. I'll-,"

"Honestly, it will be my pleasure," Phoebe grinned and grabbed the keys from the table before Margaret could say another word.

We waited until we were comfortably seated in the spectating area away from the crowded café, before discussing Shadow's passport. "Look, I took some pictures on my phone." Phoebe showed me the screen on her mobile.

The passport had been issued by Weatherbys and showed the horse as only having one previous owner. "A Smith. Breeder," Phoebe rolled her eyes, "As if!"

"Let's see the diagram of his markings," I said.

Passports were usually completed alongside a qualified vet or someone recognised as being qualified by the passport issuing agency and any distinguishing marks and featured were drawn onto a generic pre -printed outline of a horse by that person; in this instance by the breeder.

"It looks like him." I said, squinting to see the diagram on Phoebe's phone.

The date of birth corresponded with the horse being twelve.

"According to the passport, he is just a horse. Stallion's name is Twilight, no specific breed and no stud prefix, just a thoroughbred cross and the mare is recorded as Chezimare. Again, no specific breed mentioned, another thoroughbred cross, just like the stallion," Phoebe read out.

A quick Google search on my phone revealed several stallions by the name of Twilight, none had done anything significant and all were simply nondescript bay horses. A similar search for the mare produced thousands of results as we discovered the name was a common nickname for 'the chestnut mare'.

"Well that was a waste of time!" Phoebe flicked the screen and dismissed the images of the passport.

"Not necessarily," I said, "was there anything else you noticed?"

Phoebe reopened the images and scrolled through them.

"Well, the actual passport did seem very new, you know given that it was supposed to be twelve years old."

"Anything else?"

"Only that his breeder didn't bother to get any of the usual vaccinations done."

I wrinkled my brow. "What do you mean?"

Phoebe expanded the image on her phone to show the vaccination history of the horse. "Here, see? There is no record of any vaccinations until a couple of months back, in fact he's only had the first two in the flu and tetanus cycle. He's due the last one round about September."

"That's odd," I agreed, "I know it's easy to forget the yearly booster but for a horse of that age to have no vaccination history at all...especially if, as the family were told, the horse has competed. And there's no mention of the woman who kept him at Dom's yard, in fact the only transfer of ownership is from the breeder to the Thompsons."

"I think the passport is as dubious as the age of the horse!" Phoebe declared putting away her phone, "Here comes Chantelle."

James and Margaret came and sat a few rows further down from us with Marc while Henry went into the arena with Chantelle. He took up a position to one side and carefully read out the movements of her test.

Her parents leapt to their feet and applauded as she delivered her final salute and walked calmly out of the white boards of the dressage arena.

Phoebe and I joined in the applause. "That was a decent test! How many lessons has she had with Klaus?"

"Dozens," Phoebe smiled, "he is very, very good."

I nudged her, "Shut up."

"Are you staying to watch the next dance?" Margaret called up to us, raising her voice over the background music which was still playing. Marc rolled his eyes good naturedly. "She's doing the Novice class and that's harder!" Margaret added.

"Yes Margaret," Phoebe called back, "we're staying to watch her do the next dance."

"You really shouldn't encourage her," I said laughing as James and Margaret headed back outside to watch Chantelle prepare for her next class under the watchful eye of Henry. Marc climbed over the empty rows to sit with us.

"What did you think of that?" he asked.

"It was great. The horse has certainly got some experience doing dressage," I said cautiously.

"My thoughts exactly," Marc agreed, "they certainly seem to have struck lucky, mind you, I think he's older than twelve. I wonder if he's done any affiliated competitions and has some points." He took out his phone and quickly tapped some details into his phone.

"Nope. Nothing. Not unless he's had his name changed!" he laughed, "I'm going to get something to eat. Do you want anything?"

As Marc clambered back across the seats Phoebe looked at me, "It's possible."

"What? You think someone changed the horse's name? Why?"

Phoebe pursed her lips. "I have no idea, you can downgrade a dressage horse, unlike a showjumper so I really don't see why you would bother. Of course, if you want to give an animal a new, younger identity to boost its price…"

Chantelle was one of the last riders in her class and again Henry stood to one side and called out each movement for her. After the applause we were about to leave when the final rider in the class rode into the arena and began to trot around the outside of the white boards, waiting for the judge to signal the start of the test.

"Well, well. I didn't expect to see him here!" I said.

"Shall we watch?" Phoebe asked, "I love this horse, despite my certainty that it is probably bat shit crazy, or would be if I was riding it," she added laughing.

We sat back down in our seats as the judge rang a bell and watched as Dom trotted uncertainly down the centre line. His horse, the black gelding, pricked his ears as they approached the small wooden judging box at the end of the arena and lifted his head slightly as they turned right.

"I wonder if the horse doesn't like the indoor arena," I whispered to Phoebe as we watched the horse and rider combination. The test we had observed at the horse trials had been smooth and a joy to watch. The horse had almost floated over the ground producing text -book examples of the movements; today it was difficult to believe it was the same horse and rider attempting exactly the same test. Rather than the seamless balanced transitions, the horse appeared tense and resistant to the aids of the rider, throwing up his head and becoming what riders describe as 'hollow' and unbalanced in some of the movements.

"Perhaps he's having an off day," I suggested, "the horse is quite young; it might be tired after the one -day event."

"That was several days ago!"

"Or it might be spooky because it's not used to the indoor arena. Dom doesn't even have an outdoor ménage, he schools on grass, apparently that's one of the reasons he was after livery at my place."

"I suppose," Phoebe was still watching as Dom rode out of the arena, "but it performed well enough jumping indoors."

I shrugged, "Well whatever the reason, that wasn't his best."

We stayed to watch Dom ride a second novice test which was slightly better than his first, but nowhere near the quality of the dressage he had ridden at the one-day events where we had seen him compete.

As we prepared to leave, the judge and her writer left the wooden judging hut and were replaced by a different combination of officials.

"I recognise her from somewhere," I said to Phoebe, pointing discreetly towards the judge.

"Me too," Phoebe scrutinised the judge and the young man walking with her, "I'm sure I've seen him somewhere as well. Probably in the pub."

I was about to agree when it struck me. "It's her!"

"Who?" Phoebe looked alarmed.

"The judge, I'm sure it's the woman who owns the stallion. You know the one-,"

"-in the field where the horsebox and the stolen, not stolen, horse was taken from!" said Phoebe, finishing my sentence as she too suddenly recognised the woman. We paused before continuing our conversation and looked around to see who might be listening.

"Yes. I'm sure it's her," I said.

We hurried after the judge and the young man who had written her comments and marks on the official test sheets and followed them into the café. By the time we caught up with them, the judge was chatting to Camilla, who was thanking her for her time and pressing a bottle of wine into her hand. The young man with her was standing to one side laughing with Henry.

Camilla spotted us as we hovered in the doorway and she waved us over. "Marilyn, let me introduce you to Abi and Phoebe."

"Have we met somewhere before?" Marilyn asked.

"They were both at the ball," Camilla volunteered, "and Phoebe works at the Dirty Dog."

"That must be it. You both definitely look familiar."

I laughed nervously.

"Abi lives at Fellbeck," Camilla pressed on with her introduction.

"It's a nice spot up there," Marilyn extended her hand, "I see you've done a lot of work, tidying the place up."

I smiled again, "Thank you."

"Marilyn has a nice stallion, unless you've decided to use Dom." Camilla grinned, amused at her own inuendo, "I mean his stallion."

"I'm still thinking about it," I said vaguely.

"I've only seen his horse a couple of times," said Marilyn, "seems to throw some nice youngsters but not very consistent. A lot depends on the quality of the mare of course…"

"Did you say you have a stallion?" Phoebe asked.

"No. But my friend here did," Marilyn raised her eyebrows in the direction of Camilla.

Camilla ignored the slight tension, "Abi has a lovely mare. She would make a fabulous wife for your boy," she laughed.

"Maybe, but not this year. He's all done and dusted, samples taken and in storage at the A.I stud down in Shropshire. As there's a waiting list, I don't imagine you will be lucky this year."

"What do you mean?" I asked.

"A.I."

I looked blank.

233

"A.I," Marilyn repeated, "artificial insemination. I don't agree with live covering, so I don't allow him to cover visiting mares; too dangerous. The vet at the A.I stud takes a limited number of samples each year and that's used to artificially inseminate mares."

"His, 'stuff,'" Camilla hesitated to find a word she was comfortable with, "you know, his love juice, it gets sent all over the world!"

"Really?" I was surprised to hear of the horse's popularity.

Marilyn smiled like a proud parent, "I have to say he is popular. That's another reason I limit his availability," She lowered her voice and rubbed her fingers together, "it keeps the price high."

As she was speaking, Marilyn opened some photographs on her phone. She passed it across to me, "Some of his children."

I opened my eyes wide in amazement. "But surely this is - "

"Olympic team. Yes," Marilyn beamed as she clarified the success of her stallion's offspring. "Charlie, or should I say High Charlton Boy, has produced some very successful young event horses they are regulars on the podium at five-star competitions. He's also thrown a couple of showjumpers who are proving very successful at the higher levels and some are excelling as pure dressage horses. Of course, as I said a lot depends on the quality of the mare."

"But you never do live covering?" Phoebe interrupted, "you know girl meets boy, girl squeals, boy sticks his –,"

Marilyn bristled and interrupted, "I know what a live covering is! And no. It's A.I, or nothing."

"Who was your writer?" I asked.

"He works for me," Camilla explained, "he's called David. A lovely lad, but very much married, if you've got your eye on him!" Camilla winked, "first baby's due in July. You stick to Dominic."

"Have you seen the scores?" James appeared in our group before I could correct the misunderstanding Camilla obviously had about me and Dom. "Fantastic night Cam! Top notch!" James continued as he dragged me away; Phoebe followed.

Margaret was crying and kissing Marc, "Look!" she pointed to the results. "My baby girl's won a rosette!"

Chantelle was third in her first class and had managed sixth place in the much harder Novice class where Dom was unplaced! He had secured fifth in the second of the Novice classes I noticed. We all congratulated Chantelle who was uploading her success with photographs of her rosettes onto social media.

"That's done her confidence the power of good!" James said quietly, "she needed a pick me up after today."

"Why today in particular?" Phoebe asked.

James looked over his shoulder to check the whereabouts of his daughter before answering, "She failed the theory part of her driving test again this afternoon."

Margaret left Marc and joined us.

"I was just telling the girls about Chantelle's test." James explained to his wife.

"Wait, how old is Chantelle? I thought she was taking her GCSE exams this summer," I said.

"Resits," James dropped his voice to a whisper, "we've got her a tutor."

Margaret snorted, "Stupid tests. I think they're fixed; how can they say she can't do English? She speaks it every day; we all do!"

James nodded, agreeing with his wife.

"Oh, poor thing," Margaret continued, "James has promised to buy her a little car to learn in, but we think it's better for her to get her theory sorted first."

I agreed that it did sound like a good idea.

"It isn't that she doesn't know all of the stuff," Margaret continued defensively, "we bought her the app thingy for her phone so she can practice, and she does so well at home, doesn't she James?"

235

James nodded, "She does. It's her nerves when she goes into the room for the test. Poor kid."

"It breaks my heart," Margaret added, "I wish I could pretend to be her and do it for her!"

"She'll get there," Phoebe assured Margaret.

"And at least she's done brilliantly well here," I added.

As I left, I noticed Marc. He looked crestfallen. I followed his gaze and saw Henry deep in conversation with David. As I watched, Camilla joined them, a few moments later Henry appeared to be saying good- bye.

"Who's your friend?" Marc asked accusingly.

"Friend? Oh, I dunno just met him. I think he works for Cam. Are we done here?"

"I think we might be," Marc replied sadly.

Chapter 29

My plans to compete the following weekend were thwarted when Skye succumbed to a foot abscess. It was nothing extreme in terms of severity and my farrier managed to locate the source of the problem and relieve the painful pressure very quickly. However, the combination of a now bruised and slightly sore foot and time out of our training schedule meant the sensible option was to withdraw. Phoebe had already decided not to enter as money for her was rather tight; she was working at the Dirty Dog from early evening.

"I was looking forward to a lie in tomorrow," I moaned.

"Yeah, me too, but I'm curious about Hannah."

"Do you still think she is secretly competing somewhere?" I laughed.

Phoebe leant her elbows on the kitchen bench and peeped through the blinds towards the stables. Hannah was in the car park pulling off her wellies and changing them for a pair of trainers before getting into her car. "She's doing something she wants to keep quiet about. Did you know she has another 'lesson' tomorrow?" Phoebe made a sign with her fingers as she said the word 'lesson' to suggest a pair of quotation marks.

I sighed. Phoebe's conviction that Hannah was living some kind of secret or double life had at least distracted her from her feud with Izzy.

"I believe she might have mentioned it."

"Why is she so secretive about where she goes? And," Phoebe pressed on before I could suggest that Hannah might simply want some peace away from the crazy of the livery yard, "have you noticed that her lessons always coincide with the one-day event calendar?"

"I think that is just a coincidence, you know what with them both happening on a weekend!"

Phoebe snorted, "Hmph. We'll see."

"Will we? Why what are we going to do?"

Phoebe grinned and helped herself to a hefty slice of ginger cake, which she cut in two before passing half to me.

"Oh, we're not, are we?" I paused to look closely at my friend, "Phoebe? Are we getting up at stupid o clock in the morning because you plan to follow Hannah?"

Phoebe's only response was another grin as she polished off her slice of cake.

*****

As with previous weekends Hannah arrived very early, in fact it was still dark, and she let herself in using the new coded locking system which Paul the electrician had recently installed on the gates. I had fed and turned out our horses and was in the middle of mucking out when she drove into the yard in the hire box which was becoming a regular feature.

"Morning!" I called from inside Flame's stable. "I fed Secret the feed you'd left form him over an hour ago and left him with a small hay-net so he should be fine to travel."

"Thanks Abi. Crikey, you gave me a fright, you're up early, I thought you weren't competing today."

"I'm not, but I thought I might have a drive down later to see the course. There's another event at the same place at the end of the season so I thought it would be helpful to see what type of fences they have."

I paused with my full wheelbarrow on my way to the muck heap. Hannah was on her knees in the deep shavings bed, wrapping travelling bandages around Secret's black legs. The container of thick black hoof dressing stood close by and the shavings which were clinging to his hind hoof, showed that she had already painted at least one hoof wall.

Satisfied that the bandages were secure, and his rug was in place, Hannah left Secret in his stable while she lowered the ramp of the small horsebox. I followed with a net of haylage which she accepted before assuring me that she was fine and could manage to load the horse and close the ramp without any assistance.

By the time she was actually driving out of the gates I had managed to have a quick shower and was contemplating breakfast when Phoebe burst into the house.

"Come on, why aren't you ready?" She demanded.

"I am, nearly. I just need –,"

"No time!"

"But -,"

"No time for that either. Come on. Hannah was about to drive out as I drove in. I have coffee in the car," Phoebe picked up the tin containing the last of the ginger cake, "and here's breakfast." She hustled me out of the house, thrusting my phone, keys and jacket into my arms as we went.

Stumbling across the yard with my boots only partially on, I grumbled that more haste usually resulted in less speed, but Phoebe ignored me. The engine was already running, and we shot out of the gateway in a cloud of dust and gravel before I had closed my passenger door.

"Steady on!" I braced myself before fumbling to secure the seat belt.

"Sorry, but we need to catch up with Hannah! There's coffee in the cup holder."

We sped down the road towards the village and I silently wondered how Phoebe ever had the audacity to criticise my driving. I thanked which ever god was listening that the roads were mercifully empty this early in the morning, as we bounced around corners and swerved to avoid potholes.

Suddenly we saw a vehicle ahead, and thankfully, we slowed down.

"That's her!" Phoebe shouted gleefully, spotting the small horsebox with the self- drive hire company's livery and contact details emblazoned across the back of the vehicle.

I sat up and studied our surroundings as we drove at a much more sedate pace, keeping Hannah in view, "I wonder where she's going."

"Wherever it is, my guess is she is planning to turn off somewhere, look her brake lights are on."

"No signal though," I commented, "I wonder if she knows we're following and doesn't want us to know she's turning off."

"Now who thinks our Hannah is up to something? Oh, there she goes, she's turned off up that track, you can see the horsebox over the top of the hedges."

"Phoebes? Do you realise where we are?" I asked as we stopped at the foot of the track where Hannah had turned off the road.

"Sort of," Phoebe looked out of the window at the surrounding countryside. With each minute the sky was becoming lighter. "To be honest, I didn't take much notice of road signs or anything in the darkness, I just followed her," said Phoebe referring to Hannah, "but now you mention it, this does look familiar."

I waited for a moment until Phoebe recognised the overgrown gate and rutted track.

"She can't be; is she going to Dom's place?"

"Looks like it." I said.

We sat for a few minutes pondering the situation.

"Do you think he's her mystery teacher?" I asked.

Phoebe shrugged, "Beats me, but it would in part explain why she is so cagey about telling anyone where she goes."

"But surely if that was the case, he would come to teach her at Fellbeck. He said himself his own facilities are rubbish," I said.

"Well," Phoebe began, "Perhaps she's embarrassed. I still don't understand why she pretends not to know the guy when clearly she does."

I nodded in agreement, "What should we do now? We have no reason to follow her, other than being nosey."

"That's true," Phoebe agreed, "okay, let's head to the horse trials then when we get home ask how her lesson was, see if she lets on where she's been."

Satisfied that there was nothing else to do, unless we wanted to walk head first into what was sure to be a negative altercation with Hannah, Dom or both of them, we set off at a much more dignified pace through the lanes until we reached the motorway and ultimately the horse trials in North Yorkshire.

The spring sunshine was shining, and daffodils were dancing in gardens and along the side of the grass verges. Close inspection revealed the early promise of blossom as buds began to form on branches, although there was still a nip to the air, and it would be several weeks before the buds had swollen enough to produce flowers.

Phoebe and I decided to collect the obligatory bacon sandwiches to eat as we walked around the cross- country course which was set in undulating farmland and pasture with some additional loops running through small areas of woodland.

Due to our early start, we managed to complete our course walk and still make it back to the main hub of proceedings in time to see some of the riders in the Novice section, complete their dressage tests.

"Do you see the rider warming up in the far corner?" I pointed, "I think it looks like Dom."

Phoebe followed my gaze, "I think you're right. Hang on."

She left me and ventured into the collecting ring where she homed in on a volunteer who was clad in Hi-Viz and a tabard broadcasting the official title 'Dressage Steward'. I watched as Phoebe had a brief conversation and the steward showed her a list of names and times. She hurried back to me.

"It is him. He's next in the third arena down there."

We left the collecting area and positioned ourselves close enough to the arena that we were able to see clearly but far enough away to avoid being noticed. I'm not sure why we felt the need to stay out of sight but both of us agreed that life would be simpler if Dom was unaware of our presence.

The rider preceding Dom completed his test, saluted the judge and walked out of the arena to be greeted by a small group of supporters. Dom nodded and acknowledged the other man before giving his own horse a squeeze with his leg to ask him to trot. The horse and rider then began to trot calmly around the outside of the marker boards passing in front of the car where the judge was watching, protected from the cold weather.

Eventually the judge signalled she was ready for him to begin the test. Rather than a bell, this judge simply used the car horn. I had expected the horse to spook when the horn sounded, given both its proximity to the vehicle when the judge gave her signal, and based on the tense nervousness we had observed a few nights ago at the Academy.

Today Dom and his beautiful black gelding produced a fabulous test. The horse was relaxed but alert with bounce and energy, responsive but without attempting to anticipate the moves; he displayed balance and precision, his ears flicking outwards as he 'listened' to the silent aids of his rider. Together they presented a picture of harmony and unity.

"That was fabulous!" I muttered to Phoebe as Dom patted the horse and left the dressage phase. We watched as he disappeared into the rows of horseboxes and trailers.

"Let's watch his showjumping," I said.

Taking care not to be seen, partly because we didn't want to get roped in as Dom's team of grooms, we made our way to the showjumping arena. Unlike most of the events we had attended so far, today this phase was outside with riders able to warm up indoors.

There were more people watching what many consider the more exciting phase of showjumping than were watching the dressage, so it was easy to find a spot where we could see the action without being noticed.

After watching several riders complete their rounds, Dom appeared in the collecting ring. We watched as he declared his number to the steward. Unlike the dressage stewards, of which there were three or four each responsible for their own dressage arena and judge, there was only one steward here in the showjumping. The riders, or a helper acting on their behalf, let the steward know they had arrived, then at their appointed time the steward called to them and allowed them access into the jumping arena; as one rider took off over the last fence the next competitor entered and began to canter around the jumps, only beginning his or her round when signalled to do so. Today that signal was an electronic bell.

Suddenly my heart skipped a beat. Dom had stopped for a moment to speak with someone. It was Pierre.

I nudged Phoebe, "Do you see who he's talking to?"

"I wonder what he's doing here?"

"Dunno," I said moving to a position further into the depth of the crowd, "but they seem quite friendly!"

It was impossible to even guess what they were talking about, but the conversation between Dom and Pierre was brief. Pierre ran his hand down the horse's neck and patted his shoulder before Dom rode away towards the practice fence and Pierre headed to the collection of trade stands, burger vans and official's tents.

"Do you think he saw us?" I asked, referring to Pierre.

"I don't think so. Look, here comes Dom."

Dom rode a flawless clear round and immediately left the phase to return to his horsebox. Phoebe and I followed him at a discrete distance. It was clear that someone was with him; helping, but it was difficult to see who the person was because they were not only wearing a baseball cap, but had pulled the hood of their jumper up over the cap as extra protection against the cold of the day. Curious to see who was helping him, Phoebe and I approached Dom and his open horsebox. As we drew closer, his mysterious assistant gave him a leg up before disappearing back into the lorry.

"Hi there!" Dom waved and rode out to greet us, "not riding today?"

"Not today," I replied, "nice dressage test by the way."

"Oh, were you watching? He is a brilliant event horse, this guy," Dom patted the horse. "Wish I'd known you were here; I'd love a video of his dressage to put with his advert."

"Couldn't your helper film your test?" Phoebe asked innocently looking towards the dark recess of the horsebox.

"Who? Oh, that's just a groom with one of the big event teams. I give him a tenner to help with tack changes and stuff if he can spare the time."

"How many are you riding today?" Phoebe continued.

"Just the one. It's difficult to organise more than one if you're on your own."

"Oh, I thought there was another horse in your box," Phoebe pressed on.

Dom smiled, though the expression didn't quite reach his eyes and rather than the twinkle I usually associated with his smile his eyes reflected something closer to a harsh cold glint. "His travelling companion, I'm sure I said last week that I like to bring a friend to keep him company on long journeys," Dom took a breath and seemed to recover his composure, "are you coming to the cross-country?" he asked riding slowly away from the horsebox, "it's a lovely course."

We found ourselves walking with him. "We're on our way home actually," I said, "we came for a look at the course but Phoebe's working later, so we have to get back."

"Shame, I was hoping to take advantage of your filming skills again," Dom winked, "ah well, another time perhaps."

By now we had walked to the edge of the cross -country course, I glanced over my shoulder back towards the horseboxes. The ramp on Dom's lorry had been raised back into place, blocking any access or view to the inside without lowering it again; standing next to the lorry watching us as we walked with Dom was Pierre.

Chapter 30

"Did you believe him? About the groom helping for a tenner?" I asked Phoebe as we drove back towards home in North Northumberland.

"I'm not sure. Whoever it was certainly didn't want to be seen."

"Mm. And did you notice that as soon as we moved away, someone put the ramp up?" I continued, "Pierre was standing right by Dom's lorry. Do you think it was him?"

"Maybe. I hate to think that Pierre is involved with whatever shifty business Dom is involved in, but it is certainly starting to look like he might be," said Phoebe, "I wonder if that's why Felicity dumped him in favour of the bloke, or blokes, from the band."

"I know what you mean," I sighed, "but I was really starting to like Pierre."

"I know you were honey. But hey, better to find out he is a shifty bastard now than later when you'd completely fallen for him, eh?" she gave me a sad, understanding smile and squeezed my arm.

When we were a few miles from home Phoebe left the main road and started to follow the narrower lanes. "How do you feel about a little detour?" she asked.

"Where do you have in mind?"

"Dom's place. We know he isn't home and even if you don't consider the time to ride his cross-country and sort out the horse, he can't drive as quickly in the lorry as we did in the car…" She glanced across at me.

"So, we have time for a quick visit I suppose."

"We do indeed!" Phoebe turned her car up the now familiar track.

"What if someone's here?" I asked hanging onto the handle above my door with one hand and bracing myself against the dashboard with the other as we ricocheted up the unkempt track.

Phoebe steered around a particularly large hole, "We simply say you wanted to have another look at the stallion you are considering using with your mare."

She swung the car into the yard and parked, "Okay, where first?"

"I thought you had a plan," I said.

"This way then," Phoebe led the way from where she had parked towards the stables and the barn "keep your eyes peeled for that dog!"

Each stable was empty, and some had been mucked out. We could see the distinctive brown and white mare in the distance, grazing with what were probably the other mares. A trail of dirty straw and muck led away from the stables.

"There are some other stables round here," I said quietly, "and this is where the stallion is."

We crept along the side of the barn and I pointed in the direction of the stables and the hemmel. Turning the corner, we were suddenly confronted with a familiar vehicle.

The small horsebox which Hannah had been hiring recently, and which she had used to drive Secret away from Fellbeck earlier in the day, was parked, with its ramp lowered, behind the barn.

We peeped cautiously around the corner before dashing from the security and protection offered by the barn wall across to the horsebox. The cab was unlocked but showed nothing to indicate who had last driven the vehicle. The tack lockers and rug- store were all empty as was the horse travelling area apart from the haylage net which I had given to Hannah earlier that morning. A horseshoe shaped grease mark showed where Shadow had been standing before the thick hoof oil had dried.

Suddenly we both heard voices.

I peered out of the small window. Two men were tipping wheelbarrow loads of muck onto a large trailer via a homemade ramp. One of the men was slim and his tight, filthy jeans accentuated the shape of his bandy legs as they disappeared into a pair of paddock boots. His angular features were hidden by a baseball cap pulled low over his eyes with the hood of his sweatshirt drawn up over the cap. Even the layers of hooded sweatshirt and a grimy looking body warmer couldn't disguise how much thinner he was than the second man who was heavily built with a jowly, stubble covered face. This second man looked slightly older than the first; he was wearing a pair of dirty, loose fitting track suit bottoms which had probably started out as grey in colour and a pair of cheap wellington boots. The hood of his sweatshirt was protruding from the neckline of his greasy waxed coat. It was impossible to be sure, but I was as certain as I could be that they were the men we had seen with the mares in the field with Marilyn's stallion.

We held our breath and shrank back against the inside of the horsebox as they made their way from the trailer towards the stone stables which Dom had shown me on my previous visit. One of the men, the thinner man, stopped, level with where we were hiding, to light a cigarette; his companion walked on a short way before pausing to wait for him.

"Better not let him catch you smoking round here mind, you know what he's like."

"Aye, but he's not here is he."

"Soon will be," the larger man continued, "he's just sent a text to say he's on his way back."

"Since when does he send you updates?"

"It wasn't a fucking up-date, it was a warning to make sure the shit's been cleared before they get back."

"Is she with him like?" the speaker leant against the panel of the horsebox and smoke from his cigarette drifted in through the window.

"Aye. Dunno what she sees in him."

"Think she'd be better with you like?" laughed the smoker. "Fuck off!"

The horsebox rocked slightly as the man with the cigarette shifted his weight. "Hey, I don't blame you. Marks out of ten? I'd happily give her one. Just thinking about her has given me a stiffy," he laughed.

"Well unless you want to stick it in one of them horses, you'd best tie a brush on the end and help me finish these stables 'cos there's only me here and I'm not gonna help you tip off ya load." grumbled the older man.

We heard the other man groan as he laughed at his friend's comment. "I need a lass. Do ya know how long it is since I had a shag?"

"What? Are you saying you can't find some tart willing to drop her knickers for you?"

"Don't care if she's willing or not!"

Both men roared with laughter.

"Old habits die hard eh?" said the older man. I couldn't tell if it was a sick joke or a reference to something more sinister.

"Well I don't know about habits, mate, but I'm certainly hard and dying for it!" Again, the two men laughed.

"Well like I said, there's no one but y' self here and these stalls won't clean themselves."

"More's the pity."

We felt the horsebox rock as the man shifted his weight again. I could feel my heart hammering in my chest. I glanced at Phoebe. She had gone white. I wasn't sure if the last comment was because the stables required work, or a reference to the fact there were no women around. I hated to think what would happen if the men outside found us hiding in the horsebox listening to their filthy conversation.

After what felt like hours but was probably seconds the men moved away with their wheelbarrows. We waited until we were sure they had gone before carefully peeping out of the window. Confident that they had moved away we left the horsebox and ran back to the barn. Keeping close to the wall, we hurried around the building in the opposite direction to where we thought the men had gone before making a final dash to Phoebe's car.

We didn't speak until we had put some distance between us and Dom's yard; and the men.

"Urgh," I shuddered, "what vile specimens of humanity!"

Phoebe shuddered, "I couldn't agree more. If they entered the human-race they'd probably get disqualified! I'm sure they are the blokes who were moving the bay mare out of the field the night of the ball."

"Yeah. I saw no sign of them when Dom took me to see his stallion, but I agree, I'm sure they're the same men. I recognised their voices from when we were hiding in the barn."

"Yeah and from the other night when Dom was there, and they had the brown and white mare with Marilyn's stallion." Phoebe confirmed.

"Who do you think 'she' is?" I asked, "you know the woman those dreadful men were talking about."

"I was wondering that. Given the fact the horsebox she was driving is parked behind Dom's barn I did wonder…"

We pulled up in the yard at Fellbeck. Felicity was leaning against the fence watching Izzy who was riding Eric under the instruction of Klaus. There was no sign of anyone else. Phoebe dropped me off before heading back to the village to go to work.

"Are you okay?" Felicity asked, "You look rather pale."

I smiled weakly, "Phoebe's driving left me a bit queasy. I'll be fine when I get some fresh air," I assured her.

The quiet yard erupted into a hive of activity as the Thompsons arrived, closely followed by Marc and Henry. Felicity disappeared to help Chantelle prepare Zeus for a lesson with Klaus; Henry and Marc collected headcollars and went to collect their ponies.

Izzy had left and Felicity was attempting to lift the air of tension which had settled over Marc and Henry, when Hannah drove into the yard with Shadow.

"Good lesson?" I asked.

"Yes thanks."

"Gosh, are you just getting back?" Felicity asked, "where have you been?"

Hannah smiled, "Just for a lesson." She offered no detail and led Shadow down the ramp and into his stable.

"Suit yourself," Felicity muttered under her breath at Hannah's retreating back.

"Now, now. Put those claws away little cat," said Marc.

"Well honestly, would it kill her to say where she's been!" Felicity continued to mumble.

"Exactly!" Margaret joined our little group, "I don't know why she doesn't have lessons with Klaus. We think he's marvellous!" She sniffed. Margaret was still annoyed that Hannah would rather hire a horsebox and go to her lessons alone than include Chantelle.

"Well wherever she goes, it must be posh!" Felicity continued.

"What makes you say that?" I asked thinking of Dom's untidy yard.

"Well she's obviously reapplied hoof oil before coming home, 'cos there was bits of hay and shavings from the horsebox still sticking to his back hooves."

"And she's jazzed his hair up," Margaret was determined to contribute to the Hannah bashing.

"Jazzed his hair up?" Marc looked baffled.

"Yes, his hair. It's all permed like when you take their knots out after a competition."

"You're right Margaret!" Felicity was happy to have someone back her up, "it must be really posh if she plaits him up for a lesson!"

"Phoebe thinks she's secretly competing," I confided cautiously.

251

"Possible…" Marc said slowly, "but why not say so?"

"Perhaps she's shy." I offered.

Felicity and Margaret snorted. "Rude yes but not shy," said Margaret.

"Or not very good," Felicity added.

"Has anyone here seen her ride?" Henry joined in.

"She rides really early. Sometimes super late," I said, "and yes, I've seen her a couple of times. She's alright."

"Well I still think she's up to something," Felicity picked up a brush and resumed working on the tangles in Solo's tail.

"Now you really sound like Phoebe!" I laughed despite the feeling of unease I could neither explain nor shake off.

Chapter 31

A few mornings later, I drove into the village to stock up on some essentials; mainly fresh bread, chocolate and a large bottle of gin. As I was coming out of the shop, I saw Henry driving past. He slowed his car and turned up the narrow lane towards the Academy.

Normally, I probably wouldn't have noticed his car, but today he had asked if I would bring in the ponies to have their feet trimmed; Marc was working, and he had been unable to arrange time off himself.

Dealing with Solo and Symphony was not a problem as they were well behaved, but I was curious to know why Henry had felt he needed to lie. Following my clients, and unfamiliar vehicles for that matter, seemed to be rapidly turning into a daily occurrence I thought wryly as I drove after Henry.

There was no sign of his car near any of the bungalows in the lane. I wondered if he had arranged a clandestine meeting at the end of the track near the moors. As I contemplated driving past the Academy towards the moor, I decided that confronting Henry was probably none of my business and I had no desire to stumble upon him and any illicit partner in flagrante, so turning around and going home to enjoy my recent purchase of chocolate seemed the best option.

The lane was narrow, so I drove through the gates to the Academy with the intention of using the car park to turn around. However, the sight of Henry's car parked at the far side of the tarmacked space caused me to stop and turn off my own car's engine.

There was no sign of Henry, or anyone else for that matter so I locked my car, zipped the keys into my pocket and headed in the direction of the stables. I wasn't surprised to find the yard to be so quiet as it was midweek and most of the Academy's business took place either early evening or weekends with daytime activity confined to individual clients having private lessons.

The stable yard was neatly swept and tidy and there were no signs of activity. A long line of stone stables were identical in their outward appearance with black wooden half doors. The interiors were also uniform; all internal walls were painted white with black rubber matting for ease of mucking out. Most of the stables were empty but one or two were occupied and as I drifted about the yard several heads appeared over the half doors to observe me, before returning to the much more interesting business of eating hay. A stack of recently washed feed buckets were waiting near the tap.

The outdoor arena was empty, as was the office. I wandered towards the indoor school. The heavy double doors were closed but the small door to the side of these opened easily when I touched the handle. I peered inside and could detect no sign of life. Closing the door, I looked around, baffled. I had definitely seen Henry turn into the lane and his car was parked outside, close to my own; so, where was he?

I left the arena and was about to return to my car when I decided to have a final look around the yard, which turned out to be as deserted as it had been when I arrived. However, as I left the concreted area in front of the stables, I glanced across towards the fields, two figures were walking away from the stables. Henry and the man he had been chatting to at the dressage competition, David. The sun was in my eyes, casting their outlines into silhouettes, but it was clear from their body language and movements as they headed across the field that they were laughing and sharing a joke about something.

Suddenly, I felt that I was intruding. The moment, however innocent, or not, was clearly private and I had no right to be here. I hurried back to my car and drove home.

I spent the rest of the day catching up on chores both in the house and around the yard. Skye's abscess had just about cleared up, but her foot was still bruised, so she was still enjoying an unplanned holiday from the serious business of becoming and event horse. I changed the dressing on her foot, it seemed clean enough, but I wanted to be certain. So far, I had managed to avoid an expensive vet's bill, relying on the expertise of my farrier and my own experience. I strapped a new section of dry poultice in place with a sticky bandage and held the whole lot in place with a nappy; the purchase of which from the village shop had raised many eyebrows especially combined with the large bottle of gin!

I turned Skye out into the field before spending a quiet hour hacking around the woods on Flame. Henry was busy grooming Solo when I got back.

"Hi!" he smiled and waved at me, "was everything okay with the farrier?"

"They were fine," I reassured him, "I left the receipt and your change in an envelope on top of your feed bin."

"Thanks, I found the envelope."

Henry left Solo and walked across to Flame's stable where I was untacking her. He stroked the mare's nose absent mindedly.

"Erm, Abi? I know it sounds daft, but would you mind not saying anything to Marc about you dealing with the blacksmith this morning?"

I placed my saddle on the half door. "Are you asking me to lie to him?"

"Gosh no! Not at all, just don't say anything. He doesn't need to know I wasn't here, that's all."

"Why?" I asked, "what's the big deal? I bring horses in for most of my clients and deal with their farriers."

"I know, it's just we've been having stupid arguments recently mainly about trivial stuff, but if he finds out I forgot to book time off work it'll be just one more thing to spark a row."

I was about to say that I had seen him at the Academy but instead I simply shrugged, it was none of my business, "Whatever you think is best, as long as I don't have to lie."

Henry gave me a peck on the cheek, "Abi, you are an angel."

I was pondering the situation when Phoebe arrived. I was sitting in my 'office' watching the sky turn to a deep shade of orange across the fields. The tabby cat who was now an official resident, had made herself a cosy nest in a box of newly washed travel bandages on the chair opposite my desk.

"Just me!" Phoebe shouted. I listened as she kicked off her boots. "Where are you?"

"Office."

"Don't often find you in here at the end of the day," Phebe joined me, "how's Skye's abscess?"

"Better, but not better enough."

"Dam. Does it need a vet's attention?"

I sighed, "No, the farrier has been back and I'm certain all of the yukky stuff has drained out, I just need to keep it clean. She's nearly sound."

Phoebe moved the box of bandages and the cat from the chair and sat down. "Apart from Skye, how has your day been?"

I thought for a moment, "Well, I tackled Hannah about her livery bill. The chunk of cash she gave me the other day brought her up to date, but she still hasn't set up the electronic bank payments and she owed me for extra feed supplements, plus she gets through a stack of shavings!"

"And did she pay?"

I threw a roll of cash across the room which Phoebe caught neatly. "Wow!" she whistled, examining the money, before throwing it back.

"Odd, isn't it?" I said, "but at least she's up to date again."

"Mm. Very odd." Phoebe agreed thoughtfully.

I stretched before crossing the room to lock the cash in the safe. "That's not the only odd thing about today," I said before telling her about Henry.

"Hell's bells!" Phoebe declared, "are you going to say anything?"

"Like what? I was so taken aback when he asked me to not say anything to Marc that the moment passed. I think it's probably best to keep quiet, for now at least," I said.

"I agree! We need to sort out Dodgy Dom first!" Phoebe stood up, decisively.

"Do we? Why?" I asked.

"Because Abigail, if we don't sort out his dodgy dealings then no one will!"

"And how can we be sure there are dodgy dealings to be dealt with? You sound like *Nancy Drew*, or one of the *Famous Five*, and please, I beg you, no more alliteration!"

Phoebe laughed and followed me into the kitchen, "Sorry, I was getting a bit carried away. But seriously, we know there is something at least weird, probably illegal going on. For all we know Hannah is involved and they are using you to launder money from their ill-gotten gains!"

I turned white.

"That could make you some sort of accessory to the fact or whatever the expression is." She added calmly.

I sat down. "Oh, my life! What should I do?"

"Don't worry-,"

"Don't worry!" I interrupted, "if you're right, I could end up in prison!"

Phoebe put a mug of tea down in front of me. "Here, drink that, I've added sugar for the shock. You aren't going to prison… Probably."

257

"What do you mean, probably? I haven't done anything!"

"And that's exactly what we'll tell the police."

"But it's true! If Hannah and Dom are involved in some scam it has nothing to do with me!"

Phoebe sipped her tea. "Actually, there might be some kind of reward… Anyway, I've been thinking."

"Why does that make me feel worried?" I said weakly.

"Probably because you're quite highly strung," Phoebe said, seriously, "I'm sure I've mentioned that before. Perhaps less sugar in your diet and more fibre." She moved the sugar bowl out of reach, "Now, as I said, I've been thinking and I'm fairly sure I've solved at least one part of our puzzle, I just need to check something."

I ignored the sugar comment, "What do you mean?"

Phoebe stood up and looked out of the window at the empty yard before glancing at the clock. "I take it everyone's been and gone for the night."

"Yes, there's just us. Why?"

"Come on," Phoebe turned from the window and pulled me to my feet. Without a word she led the way to the door and pulled on her boots, waiting while I did the same.

Chapter 32

Once outside Phoebe made a beeline for the barn where Tom and Little Tom, the builders had left the remains of the equipment they had used when they had completed the renovations. Phoebe scrambled around among half used tins of paint and varnish, until happy with an almost empty bottle she had managed to unearth she headed to the tack room where she collected a small bowl of hot water. I watched as she added some liquid soap and a sponge. "Bring that will you." She pointed to Hannah's grooming kit as she picked up a small brush with hard bristles. Thinking she was mistaken I picked up her own container of brushes.

"No, Hannah's, bring her grooming kit, please."

I shrugged but swapped boxes before following Phoebe to Secret's stable. Despite knowing we were alone I felt uneasy as I followed Phoebe into the stable. I watched as she slipped a headcollar onto the horse before tying him to his haynet.

"Phoebe, what is going on?" I whispered.

"Why are you whispering?" she asked, glancing out of the door towards the gates.

"I don't know, probably because you're making me nervous. Stop changing the subject, what are you doing?"

"Okay, promise you'll hear me out?"

I nodded, nervously.

"Can you remember when we were so impressed with Dom's horse when we watched his dressage at the horse trials the other week?"

Again, I nodded.

Phoebe continued, "And then when we saw the same horse at the Academy when Chantelle took Shadow, it produced a dreadful test. Hell, Chantelle beat Dom it was that bad!"

"Yeah, I remember all of that, but why are we in Secret's stable?"

"Hold on, I'm getting to that bit. A few days later we saw Dom down at the trials in Yorkshire and his dressage was amazing; so much better than at the Academy in fact that we joked it looked like he was riding a different horse. Well, maybe he was!"

"What do you mean?" I asked slowly.

Phoebe took a deep breath, "I'm not one hundred percent sure, yet, but we also agreed it was unusual to see a completely black horse, you know, no white at all and even more unusual to have two such unique horses in such a small area; stabled a few miles apart. Well, I got to thinking, what if it was too much of a coincidence?"

I wrinkled my brow, "Every time I think I know where you are going with your idea, you lose me."

"I know it sounds crazy and it took me a while to convince myself, but I've been watching that video I took of Dom's test over and over and the more I watch it, the more I'm convinced I'm right!"

"About what?"

"The horses, Abi. What if the horses aren't identical?" Phoebe knelt down in the shavings.

"Which horses?"

"This one and Dom's black gelding."

"Well, then they'd be different! What are you driving at?" Shadow stepped back as I raised my voice.

Phoebe stood up and looked at me to be certain she had my full attention, "Let's imagine you make your money from selling horses, competition horses; the more talented and successful the animal the greater the price tag, yes?"

"Okay, I'm with you so far," I nodded.

"Now, let's suppose you have a horse that is brilliant cross-country, pretty good showjumping but crap at dressage, or the other way around," Phoebe waited for me to demonstrate my understanding before continuing.

"Go on," I said.

"Well, you could sell a medium or advanced level dressage horse for a stack of money, easily forty thousand plus according to the website I was looking at. There were showjumpers for similar prices and some intermediate eventers on the same website were advertised at sixty-five thousand pounds! However, an eventer is worth a lot less if its flat work is dire and of much less value as a showjumper if the horse's real talent lies in having the speed, stamina and courage required to complete a big cross-country track…"

"Go on," I said.

Phoebe continued, "What if you don't have the time or the patience to spend developing a horse's flatwork and let's face it, some horses just don't enjoy dressage; or maybe or you just want to make a quick profit, the emphasis being on quick?"

She paused for a minute while I considered what she was saying.

"I suppose," I said slowly, "you would have to either take less money for the horse as an eventer or sell him as an okay show jumper, either way less money."

"Or," said Phoebe dropping to her knees again, "you find a horse that looks the same and substitute it to make your eventer appear better or more talented than it actually is."

"And you think Dom is riding a different horse but pretending it's his eventer?"

Phoebe nodded, "Something like that."

"And we're in Secret's stable because…?"

"Because I think this is the horse he is using as a substitute!" Phoebe announced, "have you stopped to wonder why Hannah is so neurotic about anyone having anything to do with her horse?"

"I thought she was just very particular," I confessed.

"Me too, at least to begin with, then Ma Thompson said something the other night that got me thinking."

"Margaret? What did she say?"

"A couple of things actually, but the first was when she told us that Chantelle keeps failing her theory test and Margaret said she wished she could pretend to be Chantelle and do the test for her. I've heard of cases where that happens, you know, someone takes a test on behalf of someone else. That made me wonder if you could disguise a horse to do a test in place of another very similar but less talented animal."

Suddenly I had a light bulb moment of understanding. I gasped.

"I can tell from your face that you've caught up with me," Phoebe grinned, "If we accept that this horse and Dom's horse are very similar but not identical then it stands to reason that one of them has had its appearance altered in some way."

I stood back and appraised Secret.

"What makes you think the second horse Dom is using is Secret?"

"To be honest, it was only the other day when we saw Hannah turn into Dom's place and then later, we saw the empty horsebox there. Plus, another comment by Ma Thompson. Marc was telling me about a conversation, and he was laughing at how Margaret had thought Hannah had permed Secret's mane or something because her 'lessons' were held somewhere ultra- posh. Well we know that a horse's mane has that wild home-perm appearance when you take the plaits out and when do we plait up?"

"When we compete," I concluded for her.

"Exactly."

"Assuming that you're right, what do we do with this information? Who do we tell? The police won't be interested, especially after their dismissal of the information about the horse being taken out of the field in the middle of the night," I pointed out.

"To begin with we tell no one. We need to have as much information as possible then we can decide the best course of action. First, we need to be sure this horse is being used as a double or a ringer in some way," said Phoebe.

"Okay, how?"

Phoebe grinned, "Look at him."

"I am looking," I said.

"Really look at him," Phoebe insisted, "what do you see?"

"I don't know, a black horse. Stop being obtuse," I moaned.

I walked slowly around Secret looking at him, trying to detect whatever tiny detail Phoebe had spotted.

"Okay, I'll give you a clue," she said.

I sighed but Phoebe ignored me and continued, "What is it about Secret that makes him stand out, "she put her hand up before I could answer, "and I don't mean his black coat or the colour of his rug. How did we know he had been in the horsebox we found parked at Dom's?"

"Well it was the horsebox Hannah had been driving, number plate, hire company info written all over it…" I began.

"And we knew he had been in the box because...?" Phoebe encouraged.

"I saw her load him that morning," I continued.

"No, you didn't!"

"Yes, I did!" I insisted.

"No! You said you offered to help but she said she was fine which is how you had time to have a shower and she was only driving out when I arrived to pick you up!"

"Oh yes, you're right."

"Come on Abi. Think about it. The minute we looked inside that box we knew this horse had been there because…"

"Because of the hoof oil!"

263

"Brilliant! Apart from Hannah, who do you know who puts hoof dressing on their horse so often? And look at how thick it is," Phoebe opened Hannah's grooming kit and held up the plastic container of hoof dressing. "I googled this stuff, it's really expensive. The main people who use it are involved in showing or sometimes dressage. If a horse has a white mark on the hoof wall or one hoof is white, and the others are black it can create an optical illusion of the horse being uneven in its paces, so this stuff darkens the hoof wall and all four feet appear black. If Dom's horse has four black feet, this horse needs to have four black feet?"

"That's a bit extreme," I said doubtfully, "who would notice the colour of one hoof?"

"It might be more than that!" Phoebe took her soapy water and began to scrub at the outer wall of Secret's hoof on his hind leg with the small brush she had brought.

I bent down to watch her more closely, "How could it be more?"

Phoebe paused from her scrubbing "Go and look at the legs and hooves of every horse on this yard then tell me what you notice."

"I don't need to," I realised suddenly, "a white hoof accompanies a white leg or at least a white marking on the leg!"

Phoebe smiled then set about scrubbing at Secret's hoof again. After a few minutes of scrubbing with the hard bristles of a hoof brush and the grease dissolving qualities of the hot soapy water we were able to clearly see the natural pale colour of the hoof wall showing through. One white wall, and three naturally coloured dark feet. "I always wondered why she was so particular about dressing his feet." I sat back in the shavings while Phoebe took a photograph using her phone.

"I know, and always this one hoof. Why not all four?" Phoebe added. She pulled the bottle she had brought from the barn, out of her pocket and tipped some of the remaining contents onto a rag she had brought from the tack room.

"What's that?" I asked.

"White spirit."

"It won't hurt him, will it?" Secret curled his top lip in a comical fashion as the strange smell filled the air.

"No, I'm only using a drop or two and I'll wash it off with the rest of the soapy water. Can you pass me a brush first to get through the mud?"

As I watched Phoebe remove the dried mud from the horse's leg, I commented how strange it was that Hannah took so much time to carefully apply the thick greasy hoof dressing, yet she never thought to wash the mud from the horse's legs.

"Remember when I told you how she reacted when I offered to hose them off the other day?"

I nodded.

"Looks like now, we know why!" Phoebe said as the white spirit-soaked rag dissolved a patch of black dye to reveal a spot of white on Secret's back leg, it was roughly the size of a fifty pence piece.

"She must be terrified that any washing or brushing will allow the white hair to show through," I said.

Phoebe scrubbed at another area and the same happened; the white spirit dissolved the black dye to expose white hair on Secret's back leg. After several more efforts we decided that at the very least this horse had a white fetlock, or sock rather than the completely black leg Hannah wanted us to think he had.

"But why bother?" I was baffled at the need for such subterfuge. "If this horse is so much more talented, why not simply sell him as the eventing star he clearly is and sell the other horse as a showjumper or something? Like the chestnut! Dom was really open about that gelding being a great horse for the lower levels of eventing."

"Mm. Chestnuts are a bit more common and if that horse is just okay at everything and not brilliant at anything it's a slightly different situation," she said after some thought.

"I suppose," I agreed, "but, now what should we do?" I asked looking at the patches of white which stood out on the horse's otherwise black leg.

Phoebe again, took some photographs before answering. "Now, we colour it all back in again!" She rummaged in Hannah's grooming kit and eventually held up a small bottle of hair dye.

"What do we do with it?" I asked, "it takes ages to dye your hair and it's quite complicated."

Phoebe squinted at the bottle, "I think this is some kind of pre-mixed solution, she probably has it to touch up any little spots that get rubbed or soaked in the field."

Phoebe continued to search until she found a small neat brush. After carefully reapplying several layers of dye and the ubiquitous thick hoof grease, we stood back to admire our work.

"Good as new. She'll never know we were here!" Phoebe declared.

"The mud," I said.

Phoebe looked at me blankly.

"She'll notice his leg is clean. Look, compare it to the others! We need to make it muddy."

"Good point!"

We led Secret out of the stable. It was almost dark, and he snorted as we crossed the yard. "What do we do now? Just walk about?" I asked leading the horse towards the field.

"We could try it."

We walked up and down the field a few times, but Secret was very particular and walked carefully avoiding the puddles and after five minutes I was soaking wet and filthy; he was not.

"We could just turn him out," I suggested as Secret dropped his head and began to nibble at the grass.

"That could take ages. And, we'd have to take him in, change his rugs… No, there's only one thing for it, watch yourself."

Before I could object Phoebe bent over and began to scoop handfuls of dirty water out of the puddles. She then proceeded to throw the water over the horse's back legs. "That looks a bit better, but it still doesn't match the other one." Phoebe shone the torch from her phone to inspect her handiwork. "Bring him closer to the gateway Abi, over here where it's really muddy."

I followed her instruction and stood with the rather confused gelding in the gateway while Phoebe threw a handful of sticky mud at his back leg. Satisfied that we had hidden all traces of our investigation we took Shadow back to his stable and fed him several slices of apple as a reward for his good behaviour and by way of apology for pelting him with mud.

We retired to my living room where, after serious consideration and a great deal of chocolate,

we decided that a visit to Dom's yard, however unpleasant was probably necessary.

Phoebe opened the outer layer of the wrapper from the chocolate and turned it, so the white inside was facing upwards on the coffee table, where she also found a pen. After a few minutes of scribbling down notes and drawing lines to connect ideas she sat back.

"No doubt about it, all roads lead to Dom!" she declared.

I left my armchair and joined her on the floor at the table where I was able to study her diagram.

"Strange things happening with horses in a field at the dead of night, horses taken to Dom's yard. Horse we see being taken belongs to Dom, apparently. Dom and vile men in the same field on a different night with a different mare, Hannah and Dom pretend to be strangers, we know they actually know each other. Dom has a horse which we have seen do a brilliant dressage test, yet we have also seen Chantelle of all

267

people beat Dom and his apparently brilliant horse. Hannah has a horse who, for whatever reason, has had his white markings hidden and again, we know that horse has been taken to Dom's yard! The Thompson family have a new horse, we know it has a false passport, but we can't prove anything, yet, and once again we are back with Dom who sold them the horse! Have I missed anything?" Phoebe asked when she finally paused for breath.

"Probably, but I also think it's enough to be going on with." I studied the piece of paper. "Do you think Hannah's horse is stolen and that's why his markings have been hidden?"

"I hadn't thought of that," said Phoebe, "but it's certainly a possibility, I just thought he was a ringer."

"And what about Pierre?" I asked with a sigh.

"I really don't know where he fits into all of this, but it is looking more and more likely that he's also involved."

"He seemed so genuine the night of the ball," I said sadly, "he was so concerned and helpful."

"I couldn't agree more, but then he was happy to let things go when the police weren't overly interested, and he was quite insistent that we stop looking into things ourselves." Phoebe reminded me.

"You're right. Plus, he was at Dom's yard that time when we went looking for the bay mare."

"Don't forget he was at the competition in Yorkshire too."

I yawned, "It's still early but I'm bushed!"

"Me too. I've had more gin than I planned Abi, too much to drive. Is it okay if I crash here tonight?" asked Phoebe.

"That's absolutely fine. I think you still have some overnight stuff in the spare room."

Phoebe smiled. "How about we get ourselves over to Dom's place tomorrow then?"

Chapter 33

As we approached Dom's yard, or his lair as Phoebe had recently begun calling the place, I felt a particularly strong sense of dread. I watched anxiously out of the windows as we drove in silence. Our previous visits had been made spontaneously, this was planned, and unlike the other occasions, today we had a good idea of what or more to the point who, might be there.

Before leaving, Phoebe and I had decided that we should try to approach the property from the woods behind the house rather than risk the very open and exposed track. If we arrived by car we would more than likely attract the attention of someone and while we could easily bluff our way out of any encounter by feigning interest in Star, Dom's stallion, we both agreed that our chance to have a good snoop would be greatly enhanced if our presence could go undetected.

We pulled off the road into a woodland car park popular with ramblers and people with dogs. A large wooden sign told us that the area was owned by the Forestry Commission and urged us to take any litter home and to avoid lighting fires. I opened a map on my phone.

"We are here," I pointed, "and these fields which skirt the edge of the wood, join the fields which surround Dom's house. This spur of woodland," I compared the map on my phone with the map provided by the Forestry Commission as an aid to walkers, "is this patch of woodland."

Phoebe nodded, "I see, so we can stay close to the trees and then it should be a simple dash across this field," she pointed, "to his house and stables, is that right?"

"That's right. We shouldn't miss it if we keep close to the edge of the woods."

The first part of our venture was very pleasurable. It was almost June and the thick layer of pine needles released their perfume as we walked through the woods. A late carpet of bluebells added a splash of unexpected colour as our path came through the trees into a small clearing. It was very easy to follow the track around the edge of the woodland which wound steadily uphill.

Eventually the path forked with the wide and gentle track disappearing into the trees. In order to stay close to the edge of the woodland and the fields, we found ourselves negotiating a steep, narrow path which was rutted with tree roots. The bluebells were replaced by the lacey heads of cow-parsley in the hedgerow at the edge of the woods. I was thankful for the stone wall and occasional wooden fence which had separated us from the farmland as this provided a support when the terrain became especially steep. Before too long the ground became level once again and the trees broke away from the fence line, as the forest marched away to the North.

Small sections of the stone wall had crumbled and had been replaced with lines of barbed wire; we found ourselves looking through the wire towards a small group of trees about fifty meters way, beyond which lay Dom's house.

I tentatively touched the wire fence before turning to Phoebe, "Are you ready?"

"As I'll ever be!" she replied.

The barbed wire was taught but neither of us felt like climbing over it, instead we retraced our path a few metres and scrambled over the stone wall before dropping down into the field. There didn't appear to be anyone around so together we hurried from the wall, across the short section of open field to the trees.

I had hoped that the trees close to the house would be denser and provide some cover where we could hide but they were tall and slender silver birch trees. Their trunks were pale in colour with black notches creating, diamond shaped fissures along the white bark. We moved through the trees, keeping as close as possible to their silvery trunks.

"Now what?" I whispered.

We had discussed our idea to approach Dom's house from the woods rather than the road and we had a vague plan to sneak into the yard and search in the buildings for something which would prove that Dom, and probably Hannah, were involved in some kind of potentially illegal activity including substituting her horse as a ringer for his in some competitions; now that we were standing on the edge of his property, we realised how much detail our plan was lacking.

The house, or bungalow to be more accurate, appeared to be separated from the stables and barn by a rough track or driveway similar to the one which led from the country lane to the stable yard at the other side of the property. A combination of broken, wooden post and rail fence and barbed wire created a distinction between the garden and the surrounding fields. A hawthorn hedge battled with brambles; both were growing wildly through the remains of the fence which surrounded the bungalow on all sides. The track seemed to have been created by years of repeatedly driving over a combination of gravel and old tarmac road chippings. Weeds poked through the gaps between the small stones and dictated the width of the path from the house to the stables.

Glancing nervously across the field I nodded at Phoebe; she nodded back to me and we ran from the trees to the dense hawthorns. We crept around the hedge line, constantly checking and listening for signs of life in the bungalow or surrounding fields.

"I wonder where the dog is," Phoebe whispered.

"I don't know but it all seems to be quiet here," I whispered back.

From our position we could see across to the wooden stables where Star, Dom's stallion and his fat pony companion were kept. Both horses were pulling hay from a round metal feeder in the hemmel in front of their stables;

apart from the two horses there was no sign of life. Dom's horsebox was parked behind the barn and a thin tendril of steam was curling from the muck heap but there was no sign of the two men Dom seemed to employ to muck out.

"Where do you think we should look first? The barn or the stables?" I asked.

"Well," Phoebe peered across towards the wooden stables on the far side of the barn, "I don't think there's anything to be gained by visiting the stallion, Dom is really open about showing him off; what about those stables over there, where his event horse is?"

I nodded, "Okay."

Again, we checked to be sure there was no one around before leaving the cover of the overgrown hedge to run along the short stretch of track, to the back of the barn. We paused again before hurrying past the steaming muck heap and the spot where Hannah had previously parked the small horsebox and on towards the stone- built stables.

Both the black gelding and his chestnut neighbour looked out of their stables to watch as we hurried towards them.

"There must be someone around," Phoebe whispered, "I think these horses have only recently been brought in from the field."

"How do you know?" I wrinkled my brow, trying to spot the clues which Phoebe seemed to have picked up.

"Haynets are full, and the beds are clean and tidy, looks as if they were turned out while someone mucked out the stables. And they're still in turn out rugs," Phoebe continued, "These rugs hanging on the doors are their stable rugs."

"Then we should hurry up before whoever brought them in comes back to change their rugs! What exactly are we looking for?" I asked nervously as Phoebe stroked the black gelding before pushing him gently back from the doorway.

"I'm not entirely sure," Phoebe confessed, "but I think we'll know when we find it!"

Weirdly, I knew exactly what she meant, and I followed her into the stable. The horse was friendly, if slightly confused by the attention he was receiving from two strangers. Working together we were able to remove his rug in a matter of seconds.

Phoebe ran her hands over his body while searching for any obvious marks and I dipped my paper hankie in his water bucket before rubbing away the dry mud from his hooves.

"He really is completely black!" I marvelled, fussing the gelding.

"And so much like Hannah's horse, apart from the white leg and hoof!" Phoebe added as she quickly replaced the rug.

Suddenly the horse lifted his head and pushed past Phoebe as his attention became focussed on some activity outside.

"Shit, someone must be coming!" I hissed. "Come on!"

I fumbled with the bolt on the door. Phoebe left the rug and followed me out of the stable.

The smell of a cigarette warned us that someone, probably not Dom, was close by. "Which way?" Phoebe looked wildly around for somewhere to hide.

"Behind the stable!" I grabbed her arm and dragged her with me.

We crouched low in the weeds behind the stables, hoping that the piles of rubble, rusting farm machinery and discarded bales of rotting straw meant that it was an unlikely place for anyone to come. However, the small mound of cigarette ends did suggest that this was used as a secret smoking corner by someone.

"Hallo there, son."

We heard someone greet the horse.

I looked at Phoebe. It was obvious from the look on her face that, like me, she recognised the voice as one of the men we had hidden from on our last visit when we had discovered 'Hannah's' horsebox.

"Hey, ya lazy bastard!" we heard the man call out.

"Are you talkin' to me?" a second voice replied.

273

We shrank deeper into the weeds as the second man emerged from the opposite side of the barn with a wheelbarrow. I silently thanked our lucky stars that we had decided not to look at the stallion as it was now quite clear that at least one of these men had been there, probably mucking out.

"Well I'm not chewin' a fuckin' brick! Yes, I'm talkin' to you, cloth heed!"

"What's the marra now?" we heard the second man ask.

"This!"

This was a pause; we guessed the first man was showing something to his companion.

"What am I supposed to be looking at?"

There was a clatter as the second man abandoned his wheelbarrow.

"The bolt! How many times do I have to tell you? Always do both bolts, top and bottom."

"I did!"

"Really? I suppose Syd here just unbolted his door his sel' did he?"

There was the sound of someone kicking the door before the second man responded.

"Well he's managed to undo his leg straps, so a bolt's probably a piece of piss!"

"What?"

This time it was the turn of the first man to sound surprised.

"Look!"

We heard a bolt sliding open and the sound of the horse walking around his stable on the other side of the stone wall.

"Some fucker's been in here!"

We heard the muffled conversation through the wall.

"Where's that bloody dog when it's needed?"

"Tied up in the barn, there must be bitch on heat nearby and the randy sod kept runnin' off. I'll go an' let it out."

"Hang on, help me get these rugs changed first."

274

"Quickly!" Phoebe mouthed as she stood up and hauled me to my feet.

"Are you mad?" I mouthed back.

"It's our only chance!"

Phoebe set off running from our hiding place towards the muck heap; I followed her and after a quick check to see that the men were still occupied changing rugs, we bolted for cover at the far side of the barn.

We rested with our backs against the corrugated metal which formed part of the wall at the end of the building, gasping and out of breath. Phoebe closed her eyes, gulping in air and I bent over clutching my side in an attempt to ease a stitch.

"Tell me again why we are here?" I gasped, while silently resolving to join a gym.

"To expose the truth!" Phoebe panted.

"About?"

Phoebe paused to control her breathing before answering, "All kinds of stuff; stolen horses, fake documents and possible money laundering, not to mention links with dead pensioners in your kitchen!"

"Crikey," I felt myself turn pale, despite having been bent over for so long as a result of the stitch in my side, "do you really think they're all connected?"

"I really do and the more I think about it the more convinced I am that Dom is at the centre of it all, but probably not just Dom!"

I deliberately ignored the implications of the phrase, not just Dom. "Well now what should we do? I don't fancy running into those blokes or the dog."

"Yeah, I know what you mean," Phoebe agreed, "we need to get away from here in case they come back, but let's think logically."

"That would make a nice change!" I muttered.

"What?"

"Nothing."

"Let's see," Phoebe counted our options on her fingers with each comment, "I don't fancy searching about in the barn if that is where the dog is; we already know the bay mare in the stables and the skewbald mare are the same horses we saw being taken in the middle of the night from the field where Marilyn's stallion is kept, so we have no need to look at them again; and we now know for sure that Dom's black horse looks very much like Hannah's horse."

"So, what are you suggesting? Do you think we should go home?" I asked. The thought of getting away from Dom's yard to a place of safety, possibly accompanied by a strong cup of coffee and a very large slice of cake, filled me with mixed emotions; on the one hand a sense of relief, yet also a feeling of anti- climax. We had, as Phoebe pointed out, a list of strange events and uneasy coincidences which all seemed to be connected to Dominic, I had thought or at least hoped, that our search today would unearth some answers.

"Well, there is one place we haven't searched," Phoebe looked at me a she spoke.

"Really? Where?"

She looked away from me across the field which lay beyond the hemmel and the wooden stables, towards the group of silver birch trees.

I frowned, "The copse?"

"No, not the trees..."

"Well there's nothing else over there except the field and the... oh no. You have got to be kidding."

Phoebe's eyes twinkled. "It makes sense. If Dom is involved in any shady business, he's going to keep any records or... or... stuff he wants to keep secret, in his house, not out here!"

Reluctantly I was forced to agree with her. We were about to make a dash for the bungalow when we heard the sound of vehicles and car doors slamming. We shrank back towards the protection of the barn wall.

276

A dog barked once or twice but the sound was muffled, suggesting the animal was in a stable or at the far end of the barn. We could hear voices, but the speakers were too far away to be identifiable or to discern what was being said.

"Are you ready?" Phoebe whispered.

I nodded and followed as she darted from the barn towards the bungalow. We ran straight through the open gateway and found ourselves screened from the view of anyone who might be watching from the stables or the barn, but in plain sight of anyone looking out of the windows of the bungalow.

"Do you think anyone saw us?" I asked as I peered back through the prickly hedge towards the stables.

"I don't think so, but if they did, we can always say we were just looking for Dom," Phoebe reassured me, "let's see if there's anyone at home, shall we?"

We hurried up the path towards the door. A slightly discoloured area of gravel with fewer weeds and an oil stain, showed where Dom was in the habit of parking his car. The front door was wooden with a large, heavily curtained bay window to either side. It was impossible to see inside so we followed the cracked paving slabs, which formed a path to the rear of the building. The garden was unkempt and had mainly been left as grass; it was clearly many years since the area had boasted the title 'lawn'. A long time ago, someone had planted some shrubs, but these had been swallowed up by the hawthorn and brambles; an old- fashioned washing line was suspended between the end of the bungalow and a metal pole.

The path led past several windows which were all shrouded by heavy net curtains before it opened out to become an uneven patio area between the back door and the grass. A handful of cracked pots and plastic containers showed an attempt to brighten this area with plants, but these too had been neglected and succumbed to weeds.

The back door was partially glazed and appeared to lead into a utility room which housed a washing machine and a large freezer; a collection of coats and jackets were hanging on the opposite wall and several pairs of boots lay scattered across the floor.

We couldn't hear anything; no radio, television and could detect no sign of movement from behind the heavy curtains. Before I could stop her, Phoebe tried the handle on the back door. It swung open.

"Hello?" she called, "is there anybody home?"

Silence.

She looked over her shoulder and grinned at me, "Wipe your feet as you come in, unless you fancy leaving your boots at the back door," and then she vanished inside.

I had a final glance around before following her, I half expected to see Dom standing behind me, but there was no one. Wiping my feet, I followed Phoebe.

Chapter 34

The utility room led into a long narrow kitchen which stretched across the width of the house, it was unremarkable and felt functional rather than homely. A handful of rosettes had been left on the windowsill and their brilliant colours had faded in the sunlight. Beyond the kitchen we found ourselves in a small hallway; directly in front of us was the front door, to the left were three doors and to the right, set into the middle of the wall was one door.

The door closest to us on the left led to a small bathroom. Most of the items on the shelves and in front of the mirror, pointed to the main occupant of the bungalow being a single man; shaving items, aftershave, one toothbrush, everything clean but purely functional. However, a bulging toiletry bag on the windowsill with some make-up and travel sized shampoo bottles indicated that a woman was at least visiting. The other two doors each led to a bedroom, the second of which was at the front of the house with one of the large bay windows. The door on the right- hand side of the hall opened into a long living room; at one end there was a polished dining table and a piano, while the other end of the room, the end with the second of the large bay windows, looked more lived in, though shabby.

A large television and a worn sofa and armchair dominated this part of the room, along with a low wooden coffee table which was laden with unwashed coffee cups and old copies of *Horse & Hound, Eventing Magazine* and *The Racing Post*. Photographs of horses, some jumping, others being presented in the showring covered the walls of the entire room.

Against the wall behind the sofa a large old-fashioned desk was covered in boxes which were stuffed with index cards, discarded rosettes and an open file containing breeding records. Stacked beside the desk were several cardboard boxes.

"Phoebe, look at this!" I called her over to where I was sifting through the sheets of paper and small notebooks.

"What are these?" she asked, flicking through one of the boxes of index cards.

"I don't understand all of it," I said, "but these are stud records to show mares that have been covered, the stallion used, and offspring produced. And these," I picked up a small book containing carbon counterfoils, "are carbon copies kept when a covering certificate is given to the owner of a mare."

Forgetting the precarious situation, we were in, I sat down at the desk and became engrossed in studying the breeding records while Phoebe rummaged through the collection of cardboard boxes.

"These are all records of mares covered by his stallion." I flicked through the pages, "this book is for coverings which have taken place this year," I said, "and they match entries in this diary." I turned the page to show Phoebe, "Each entry seems to be accompanied by some kind of code or symbol which I can't make sense of, look."

"Mm. Perhaps the symbol signifies which are his mares and which are visiting mares."

"I suppose…" I put the stud records down and pulled open a drawer. "Oh, look here, I've found some passports."

"Me too!" Phoebe announced, "dozens of them and all brand new."

I looked up from the drawer, "Eh?"

"What type do you want? I can offer a breed society, British Warmblood, Sports Horse, one of our native breeds perhaps or if you want to prove you have a Thoroughbred, I can fill in a cheeky little number from Weatherbys."

280

"Seriously?"

Uh huh, there's boxes of them, look." Phoebe opened another box and flicked through bundles of new passports. "Or if registering with a specific breed isn't your thing, I can offer something from a recognised discipline. Polo perhaps? Or carriage driving? Maybe showjumping is more up your street!"

"Crikey!" I left the desk and took one of the bundles from Phoebe. She gave another one of the drawers a tug.

"I can't get this one to open. Something's jamming it!" She pulled harder and there was a sharp crack as the drawer suddenly flew open, spewing several ink stamps and handfuls of more rosettes across the floor.

"What are they?" I asked leaving the collection of blank passports.

Phoebe picked up one of the stamps and removed the protective cover. "I can't read it, it's back to front." She pressed the stamp against the back cover of one of the books of covering certificates, "Oh, my life!" She picked up a second then a third stamp, "Abi, look. They're authorisation stamps. This one is for the BSJA, this is Weatherbys and some of them seem to be for a veterinary practice," she added stamping the back of her hand, "did you say you had found some passports; are they blank too?"

"No, these are for his own horses."

"Okay, not so interesting then," Phoebe continued to investigate the stamps.

"Oh, I wouldn't say that, look at this one." I handed one of the plastic passport wallets to her and watched as she flicked through the pages.

"This is for Silverwood Obsydian ll, the black eventer," she said, turning the booklet sideways to read the medical and vaccination history.

"It certainly is," I grinned and handed her a second passport, "and here's another one."

281

"Eh? He has two identical passports, for the same horse!" Phoebe turned the first document over to compare the front covers, "why?"

"They aren't completely identical," I pointed out as Phoebe compared the breeding and veterinary pages. I took both passports from her and turned to the horse identification diagrams where a vet had detailed the marks and identifying features of the horse in red pen. "Look!"

"Bloody hell," she gasped, "the passports are exactly the same, except for that tiny detail on the diagram, one passport shows a totally black horse and this one shows the horse with a white back hoof and a small white sock extending just over the fetlock! It's Hannah's horse, isn't it?"

"I think so!" I looked at the ink stamps scattered across the floor and the open drawers and boxes, "We should clear this up and get out of here!"

"Good idea," Phoebe agreed, "I just want to get a quick picture of these first."

I began to gather up the ink stamps and colourful rosettes while Phoebe captured a record of the black horse's passport, or rather passports, there appeared to be several, on her phone.

Suddenly we heard a sound that made my blood run cold. The back door was opening, and someone was coming into the house.

We froze.

"Shit!" I hissed at Phoebe.

She quietly slid the drawer back into place as I looked wildly around the room for a way out.

There was only one door, and that led into the hall.

We could hear movement in the kitchen but before we were able to decide, whether or not we could make a dash for the front door someone came into the hall.

"First door on the left," I heard Dom shout from the kitchen, "do you want a coffee?"

"Er, is there time?" the person in the hall called back.

"Sure, we can take it back over with us if you like," Dom replied.

We heard the bathroom door open then click shut while at the same time we heard a kettle being filled.

"Come on!" Phoebe whispered and we began to creep cautiously across the room towards the door.

Unfortunately, as we were approaching the door from inside the living room someone else was heading in our direction from across the hallway! There was nothing for it but to hide, although our choice of hiding place was severely limited. Phoebe shot behind the long heavy curtains in the bay window, there wasn't room for both of us, so I flung myself onto the sofa and prayed that whoever was coming didn't intend to sit down and watch television!

I held my breath as I heard the door open.

I could see the outline of a figure of a man reflected in the television screen. The man came into the room and glanced around; his attention was drawn to the desk. He flicked through a few pages of the stud records before looking at the box containing the bundles of unused passports. He slid a couple of the passports into one of his jacket pockets and was about to leave the room when something else appeared to catch his eye. He took a step closer to the sofa and bent over; I closed my eyes and tried to press myself into the leather.

I felt the sofa respond to the pressure of his hand as he used the back of the furniture to support his weight as he stood up.

There was a momentary pause and I was certain I had been discovered, but rather than confronting me, the man turned and swiftly left the room.

I couldn't see Phoebe and didn't dare to move myself for fear that the man, or Dom, was still somewhere in the room or the hallway.

As I lay, wondering how long I should wait before moving, I heard Dom's voice, "Is everything alright?"

283

"Yes fine," the other man replied, "I just got disorientated for a moment, then I couldn't help but admire this fabulous photograph. Is that you riding? Where was it taken, Floors Castle?"

Dom laughed, "It certainly is, a good few years ago mind!"

The other man chuckled, "It's a lovely horse. Homebred?"

"Yes," replied Dom, "I have a photograph of her sire in here if you're interested."

The living room door was once again pushed open and I could see the silhouette of Dom standing in the doorway reflected in the television.

"Another time," Dom's companion answered, "we have a lot to get through."

"I suppose," Dom pulled the door towards him and the voices faded as the two men made their way towards the kitchen.

Phoebe waited for a moment before peeping out from behind the curtains. "I think they've gone!" she whispered creeping from her hiding place.

"Did you see who was with Dom?" I asked.

Phoebe nodded, "I couldn't see much, but I thought I recognised the voice. Did you?"

This time I nodded, "I think so."

Suddenly a shadow fell across the window. Phoebe dropped to her knees and I rolled gently from the sofa onto the floor before crawling towards her. The shadows were cast by the two men outside, walking past the window. We knelt in the bay of the window and watched as Dom and Pierre left the bungalow; they were chatting as they headed towards the stable yard.

We waited an agonising few minutes until we saw them turn the corner and disappear towards the barn, then we hurried to the backdoor, which mercifully was still unlocked. Once outside we carefully followed the path around the bungalow and with a final check towards the stables, we ran a short way up the track before climbing the fence into the paddock and bolting towards the safety and cover of the silver birch trees.

"Oh my God! I can't believe we did that!" I cried, leaning my back against the papery white bark of a tree trunk.

Phoebe laughed, "I can't believe we got away with it!"

"I don't know whether to laugh or cry." I panted as we made our way through the trees.

Once we had managed to climb over the stone wall and were back in the woods, we both relaxed. It was an easier and quicker walk back to the car as this time we were going downhill. As we drove home, we discussed our adventure and everything we had discovered. Dom's involvement in something shifty and possibly illegal was almost a certainty, though the exact details of what he was up to and who else was involved were still unclear. We were also uncertain about what to do with our new-found information.

"I think we should wait until we know exactly what is going on and then inform the relevant authorities," I said, "at the moment we only have half a story."

"I think we have the halves of several stories, but I know what you mean," Phoebe agreed.

Chapter 35

The only sign of activity at home was in the form of Izzy riding in the arena. "Poor bloody horse," Phoebe muttered as we got out of the car, "he must be dizzy with all those circles she rides. I bet he'd love a good gallop!"

"Just leave it," I warned my friend, "the horse is healthy and well cared for, so please, let it go."

Phoebe snorted but said no more and followed me into the house.

"Do you have any paper?" she asked as we kicked off our boots.

"What are you up to?" I asked, handing her a notepad.

Phoebe extracted the chocolate wrapper which she had been using to make notes and began to transfer the information onto the larger sheets of paper, tearing pages from the notebook to create a large interactive diagram on my kitchen table. Seeing the 'evidence' we had collected spread across the kitchen in this way was like being allowed to see the picture of a jigsaw puzzle you have been trying to complete while blindfolded; the separate pieces suddenly began to make sense.

We worked together, writing unanswered questions on a sheet of paper in a different colour while moving 'the evidence' around into a coherent order. "Phew!" Phoebe stood back to admire our handiwork and to accept a second slice of ginger cake.

"So, if we are right, Dom is selling horses with false paperwork, I doubt the Thompsons are the first to buy a horse from him with a bogus passport, especially given the boxes of unused papers and ink stamps we found," I said, "then we have the mystery surrounding the black horses, it seems very probable that Hannah is involved in at least some of Dom's dealing and the horse we have here at Fellbeck -,"

"Ironically called 'Secret,'" Phoebe chipped in.

"Yes, that's a point," I agreed, "anyway regardless of names, the horse in my stable is very talented in terms of dressage-,"

"Brilliant compared to most event horses competing at that level, but average in terms of horses doing pure dressage!" Phoebe interrupted, "can Hannah's horse jump?"

"I've never seen him jump so I don't know what his capabilities are, but Dom's black horse is a brilliant jumper."

"But shit at dressage!" Phoebe interrupted again.

"Exactly! Given the secrecy surrounding Hannah's outings, it looks likely that Dom is somehow riding her horse and pretending it is his gelding and that's why she is going to so much trouble to black out the horse's white fetlock and hoof. It's a lot of effort and quite a risk if we are right, I suppose it hinges on how well Hannah's horse can jump..."

Before we could ponder an explanation, we heard a car pulling up outside. It was Pierre.

Phoebe and I exchanged glances. "I wonder what he's after?" I said, watching as Pierre hurried across to the stables.

As he disappeared from sight, Phoebe began to gather the loose sheets of paper into a pile. "We still don't know whose side he's on," she explained.

Reluctantly, I was forced to agree that no matter how badly I wanted Pierre to be a hero, it was beginning to look like he was not someone we should trust.

"I think he's coming to the house!" I said.

A few seconds later there was a sharp knocking at the back door.

"Yes?" I asked opening the door, "can I help?" I confess to sounding colder and more aloof than I really felt, but if Pierre was involved in Dom's shady business I couldn't allow any misguided personal feelings to sway my judgement because as Phoebe had pointed out, I had just pulled myself together after my disastrous marriage and I still wasn't clear about the rather open relationship Pierre appeared to have with Felicity.

Pierre coughed and shuffled rather nervously on the step in a manner quite unlike him. "Erm, can I have a word please Abigail?"

"Of course, is something wrong?" I asked.

Pierre looked around as if checking to see who might be listening.

"Would you like to come in?" I opened the door a fraction wider.

"No, I won't if you don't mind, I'm in a bit of a hurry."

"Okay, then how can I help?" I folded my arms across my chest defensively.

"Well first, if you wouldn't mind, could you tell Felicity I've left her something in Romeo's stable? I mean Izzy said she'd pass the message on but…"

"Is that it?" I was beginning to feel irritated and did not want to play the role of Cupid's delivery driver between Pierre and Felicity.

"Erm, no there was one more thing," Pierre studied my face before continuing. I tried to return his gaze and found myself drowning in his eyes. I gave myself a shake.

"Well what is it?" I asked.

"The thing is, it's a bit personal," he began.

"Come on then, spit it out!"

Pierre took a deep breath, "I know your relationships and who you choose to sleep with are none of my business, but-"

"Dam right its none of your bloody business!"

"But," he ploughed on, "I must ask you to reconsider your relationship with Dom."

"What?"

"I know, I know," Pierre held his hand up as if in surrender, "everyone loves him, but he is not the person you think he is."

"And you are I suppose?" my patience finally snapped.

"Me? Well I…"

"Yes you! How dare you lecture me on my friendships. You should take a good long look in the mirror mister!" I shouted at him.

Pierre took a step back, "I'm not sure what I've done to offend you, honestly I'm trying to look out for you."

"Well I'm just fine thank you. Goodbye!" And with that as my parting comment I shut the door and left him standing on the step. I returned, shaking, to Phoebe in the kitchen.

"Did you hear that?"

"I certainly did! The cheeky bastard!" Phoebe was as furious on my behalf as I had been myself.

"Why on earth does he think I'm sleeping with Dom?"

"No idea, but even if you were it's got bugger all to do with him! Do you think he saw us this morning and is trying to warn us off?"

I shook my head, "Who knows!"

"But, hey never mind him come and look at this." Phoebe had the excitable look on her face which, if recent experiences were anything to go by, meant trouble!

"What is it?" I asked cautiously.

"Horse prices. I know that Dom has black gelding for sale, I haven't found his advert yet, but look at these prices."

Phoebe handed me her phone and pushed another sheet of paper across the table towards me.

I read the numbers and gasped, "Seriously?"

"Seriously, some of the four and five year olds on this site have made it to the final of the Burghley Young Event Horse, not winners, just made it to the final and are advertised at the thirty thousand plus mark," Phoebe pointed to a column of numbers. "These are foals, not even weaned, but because the stallion has previously sired horses who have gone on to compete at four and five -star events, their price tag is upwards of ten thousand!"

I sat down to study the lists of numbers and Phoebe continued, "I found a couple of horses competing at BE 80 or who are still unaffiliated who are advertised for less than six grand, but most are going for at least nine thousand. Once you get into Novice classes there's nothing on this website for less than eighteen thousand and most are closer to twenty- five thousand!"

"Bloody hell! But our horses cost nowhere near that, at least mine didn't!" I gasped.

"Oh, I agree, Treasure was about three and a half thousand but he's just a normal horse without any fancy bloodlines or pedigree."

I nodded, "Same with mine and I put all the work in myself to get them to a competition standard, that's why even a small success or improvement means so much."

"I know, me too, but if you have the money to buy a ready-made point and go type, there are several three- star eventers listed, and their prices start at sixty thousand!" Phoebe explained.

"I knew that horses of that standard were expensive but ..." I was lost for words.

"And remember Abi, these are on a bog- standard website. Horses produced or sold by famous people or being placed at the higher levels have price tags that I can't pronounce 'cos I can't count that high!"

"What about prices for dressage horses?" I asked.

"Same ball- park."

"Crikey. I'll never be able to afford to buy a horse again," I said weakly.

Phoebe smiled, "But look here." She slid another sheet of paper across the table, "Your average all- rounder is closer to four thousand, give or take, depending on age previous experience and where they are in the country, down South is pricier than up here for example."

"No wonder Dom is anxious to sell his horse as a great eventer!"

Our sleuthing was cut short as Felicity drove into the yard. I sighed as I watched her get out of the car. She was followed by a tall well-dressed man.

Phoebe looked at me, then followed my gaze out of the window.

"Who's that with Felicity?" she asked.

I sighed again and stood up, "No idea."

"Are you going to pass on the message from Pierre?" Phoebe asked as she gathered the remaining sheets of paper together.

"I suppose."

By the time I had pulled on my boots and dragged myself across to the stables Felicity was busy mucking out. Her companion was watching from a safe distance, anxious to keep his smart shoes and expensive suit clean and un-sullied. I could hear Felicity laughing as she threw forkfuls of muck and wet shavings into a wheelbarrow.

"I thought you horsey girls were all about long leather boots and skin- tight breeches!" He sidestepped to avoid a stray forkful of dirty bedding which, having been thrown with too much vigour, had missed the wheelbarrow and landed at his feet.

"Oh, we keep those outfits for special occasions," she winked.

"Yeah, wellies and tracksuit bottoms are usually our items of choice," I added.

"Hi Abbi," Felicity threw another load into the barrow.

"Hi," I smiled, "erm, Pierre was here earlier. He said to say he had left you something..." I glanced at the man in the suit. He smiled back at me.

"Oh, I found it, thanks. He is such a sweetie, isn't he?" Felicity swapped her pitch- fork for a broom and began sweeping.

I shrugged, "I suppose. Anyway, he asked me to tell you and I have, so I'll let you get on." I looked again from Felicity to the handsome stranger.

Felicity grinned and I left her to continue mucking out as the Thompson family drove into the yard.

"Yoo hoo, Abi!" Margaret waved as she got out of the car.

"Hi," I waved back.

I followed Margaret across the yard towards the stables and we were soon joined by Phoebe. After a few minutes of polite chatter, we were interrupted by the arrival of Klaus. Chantelle was having a lesson.

Klaus greeted us and Phoebe grinned at him; he winked at her before heading to the arena. Chantelle clattered past on Shadow.

"Oh, I'd better go, I don't want to miss anything," said Margaret and she followed Chantelle in a flurry of tweed and feathers.

"I'm going for a ride, I need to clear my head," I said, "are you coming Phoebe?"

Phoebe looked at her watch, "Sorry, I don't have time. I'm working tonight. Are you coming down for a drink later?"

"I might," I said heading towards the tack room, "I'll text and let you know."

"Okay, but… be careful okay? And don't stress about you know who!" Phoebe called after me, before she followed in Margaret's footsteps towards the arena.

Phoebe rested her elbows on the fence and blew a kiss towards Klaus.

Margaret was becoming flustered.

"What's wrong?"

"Oh, Phoebe love, you know about these things. I can't turn the mirror off!"

"Mirror? What do you mean?"

Margaret was holding a phone. She gave it a shake and turned it over in her hands, "Our Chantelle gave me her

292

phone 'cos she wants me to film her lesson and I can't make it work."

"Here, let me see," Phoebe held out her hand and examined the phone. She smiled at Margaret, "You've flipped the screen round so you're filming yourself."

"Oh, I thought it was a mirror. She'll be so disappointed if I do it wrong again."

"Would you like me to do it for you?" Phoebe offered.

"Oh, that would be wonderful dear, would you?"

Phoebe took the phone and after tapping the screen a few times she re-positioned herself against the fence.

"Thank you so much." Margaret whispered.

"No problem," Phoebe whispered back.

"Thing is I prefer to use my camera, but Chantelle likes watching videos of herself riding."

"It's a useful technique to help identify your faults," said Phoebe, "I like to have my lessons recorded."

Margaret settled herself on a wooden bench to watch the lesson, happy that Phoebe was successfully recording the event on Chantelle's phone.

"There you go." Phoebe handed the phone back to Margaret as Chantelle's training session drew to a close.

"I wonder, would you mind just double checking that the recording is filed?"

Phoebe smiled kindly, "It'll be fine but if it will make you happy, give it back."

Margaret handed the phone back to Phoebe before the device had time to close down and lock. Phoebe tapped the screen and opened Chantelle's store of videos. Each clip was neatly titled and bore the date of the recording.

She was just about to confirm that all was well, when one of the recordings caught her attention, it was from the unaffiliated dressage at the Academy where Dom's horse had performed so badly. There were several videos all relating to that competition, but one in particular was of interest to Phoebe; it had been taken in the warm- up area and the still image at the beginning of the recording showed other competitors who were also warming up.

Phoebe glanced at Margaret who was anxiously watching her, "Is everything alright dear?"

"Think so. I'm just double checking," Phoebe reassured her as she selected the video of Chantelle warming up at the Academy and calmly sent a copy to her own phone before closing the app. and handing the phone back to Margaret, "there you go."

Chapter 36

The Dirty Dog was quiet when I arrived. A few locals were propping up the bar, sipping their pints as they mulled over the events of the day and a family were enjoying a meal at a table close to the window.

"Thank goodness, you're here!" Phoebe greeted me, "Andrew, is it alright if I take my break now, while it's quiet?"

The bar manager looked around the quiet pub, "Sure."

Phoebe picked up two glasses of lemonade and directed me toward a table tucked away in the corner of the bar.

"Phoebes, what's wrong?"

"Nothing. Sit here."

Phoebe put the drinks down and ensured that we were both sitting side by side with our backs to the wall, facing out into the room. She pulled out her phone. "Did you know that little Chantelle has a rather extensive video record of her training and competitions?"

I laughed, "Yeah, she is very active on social media."

"Well, by some stroke of luck, while her parents were filming her warming up at the Academy dressage, they also happened to record someone else. Look."

Phoebe slid her phone along the table to me. "What-?"

"Shh!" Phoebe put her hand on my arm and raised her eyebrows slightly as she tilted her head a fraction towards the door. I flicked my eyes in the same direction and saw the men we had previously seen at Dom's yard coming through the door and ordering drinks at the bar. We watched as they carried their drinks and sat at a table near-by. I shrank back into the shadows and whispered, "What am I looking at?"

"Just watch."

I focused on the screen and the image of Chantelle riding around the warm -up arena at the Academy. There were several shots of the sand and the carpark as well as Henry and other riders who were also warming up. The video came to an end. Phoebe looked at me expectantly, "Well?"

"Well what?"

Phoebe sighed in exasperation. "Watch it again, ignore Chantelle and look at the people in the background," she whispered.

I did as she instructed and was about to profess my ignorance when suddenly I saw what had sparked her enthusiasm. "Ah. Okay. So, it's-,"

"Shh." Phoebe glanced at the men sitting close by.

I lowered my voice to a barely discernible murmur, "It's him warming up in the background."

Phoebe grinned.

"So?"

"So," Phoebe leaned in towards me, "it's the proof we need."

"What proof? How?"

"Proof that he is riding two different horses but passing them off as one."

"Really?"

Phoebe sighed. "I have to get back to work, but look carefully at the horse he is riding, I'm sending it to your phone. Then watch this. I'm sending the video from the horse trials as well."

As Phoebe returned to work, I flicked between the two short videos. To begin with I couldn't understand what it was I was supposed to see. What had Phoebe spotted that I hadn't?

Then I saw it.

I paused the screen and switched videos, then back again. And again.

And again.

I looked across to the bar and made eye-contact with Phoebe. She grinned and I smiled back. She made a pretence of gathering some empty glasses and paused at my table, "It's obvious when you know, isn't it?"

I nodded, "The horse at the Academy doesn't move as straight as the other one, it throws a front leg and it has a slightly wider forehead."

"Did you see the tail?" Phoebe asked.

"Yeah, not only do they seem to carry their tails differently but if it is the same horse, its tail has magically grown by several inches in the few days between the horse-trials and the dressage competition at the Academy!"

Phoebe looked around to where Andrew was signalling to her from the bar, "I've got to go, let's talk about this later."

"Do you want to stay at mine tonight?" I asked.

"Now that sounds like a plan. Tell you what, leave your car here and I'll drive us home, that way you can have a drink with this lot."

I looked up as Felicity came through the door with Marc, James and Margaret. Felicity waved and Margaret joined me as the others headed to the bar.

"No Henry?" I asked as Margaret wriggled out of her coat and began spreading beermats across the table.

Margaret looked over her shoulder before answering. "He was here, they gave Felicity a lift but him and Marc had a huge row outside in the carpark just as we got here."

"Where is he now? What were they arguing about?"

Margaret shrugged and the conversation went no further as James and Felicity carefully delivered a selection of drinks. "Phoebe said she's driving you home, so we got you a red wine," said James as his wife placed each glass onto one of the beermats she had previously arranged.

I took a sip, "Thanks, and cheers!"

"Oh, he's on his phone, I think he's texting." Felicity said looking across at Marc.

"What's going on with those guys?" James asked.

"I'm not sure, they've been bickering all day," said Felicity.

Suddenly Marc left his drink on the bar and stormed out through the doors. As he left, his place was taken by Dom who neatly side stepped to avoid being knocked over by Marc as they crossed paths in the doorway.

Dom paused on his way to the bar. He spoke to the two men who worked for him, they finished their drinks and left.

"I'm just nipping to the loo," I said quietly to Felicity.

Phoebe followed me into the ladies. "Those blokes were talking about one of Dom's horses," she said after checking we were alone.

"How do you know?" I called from within my cubicle.

"I heard them when I was collecting glasses."

Phoebe waited until I had washed my hands so that she could speak quietly rather than compete with the roar of the hand-dryer. "Apparently, one of the mares has scanned as not in foal and Dom is raging and blaming them, the blokes I mean, 'cos they just turned the mare into the field and left her with the stallion rather than holding both of them and presenting her properly!"

"Crikey. I wonder if that's what they were up to the night of the ball."

"Maybe. I don't know which mare they were talking about, or which stallion for that matter. Anyway, I'd better get back. It's quiz night and things get a bit hectic after nine."

I re-joined everyone else and discovered that Dom had joined our group. Andrew was handing out sheets of paper and encouraging people to enter the quiz. Marc had returned, and so had Henry. They were both sitting at the other side of the room; a very fragile peace seemed to have settled, at least temporarily between them.

"At the risk of being told to bugger off, I'm going to see if I can ease the atmosphere between those two," said Felicity standing up, "in fact," she added taking a sheet from Andrew, "I'm going to make them do the quiz with me."

"Well that works out nicely," said Dom, "thanks Andrew, a team of four here."

"Oh, no I don't –,"

Margaret caught my arm as I began to stand up, "You can't leave me on my own, sit down."

Andrew began testing the microphone as the doors opened, "Just in time my friend."

Pierre looked around the bar. His eyes rested on our table for a moment and Margaret waved. He nodded in reply to her before ordering a drink.

"Are you joining a team?" Andrew asked.

Pierre looked from Dom to me before answering, "No. I'm just after a quick drink."

"Oh no you don't. He's our number four!" Felicity crossed the room and linked her arm through Pierre's before she swept both him and his drink back to her table. Pierre laughed and shrugged in surrender as he allowed Felicity to take him to join her team with Marc and Henry.

"Are you okay love?" Margaret asked.

I broke my gaze from watching Pierre and Felicity. "I'm fine Margaret."

I was aware of Dom watching me closely.

"Don't worry about Pierre joining their team," Margaret continued, "James has sport covered, I'm quite good at media and celebrities and Dom is good at…" at this point she hesitated.

"I am good, no very good, actually I am amazing, in bed!" Dom declared with a salacious grin.

"You are so naughty!" Margaret reprimanded him; she slapped his leg playfully with a beermat. "I think Dom probably has a good general knowledge."

The night became a drunken raucous blur as my wine glass never seemed to be empty, teams shouted and cheered as each round became louder and more enthusiastically received. Despite my best efforts I found myself laughing, along with James and Margaret at Dom's quips and borderline inappropriate comments. I forced myself to ignore Pierre sitting across the room and even managed to join in the applause when his team won the quiz.

Eventually the pub began to empty as groups and couples drifted away.

"Thank you for a most enjoyable night!" Dom shook James by the hand and slapped him on the back before kissing a giggling Margaret. He leaned in to kiss me and I ducked to one side, intending to avoid his embrace or at the very least ensure only minimal contact with my cheek; unfortunately the large amount of red wine combined with my natural awkward clumsiness, resulted in a loss of balance. Dom took full advantage of the moment and granted, he did save me from falling over, but in doing so was able to kiss me full on the lips, before sitting me back down on my chair.

"Now will you be okay, or do you want me to take you home?" he asked as he gazed into my eyes.

I shrank back into my seat, "I'm fine. And that was ..."

"Wonderful?" Dom's eyes twinkled.

"No. I was going to say - "

"As good as you imagined, better even ...?"

"Inappropriate and never to be repeated!" I snapped.

Dom laughed and winked, "Hey, you kissed me."

"I most certainly did not!" I retorted furiously.

"Are you sure about that?"

"Is everything alright?" asked Phoebe, appearing at Dom's shoulder as he leant down towards me.

"Everything's great as long as this one's not driving," Dom turned smiling to answer her.

"That's okay then, 'cos I'm driving her home," said Phoebe.

"In that case I will bid you both a good evening. Drive carefully," he gently squeezed Phoebe's shoulder before melting into the crowd leaving the bar.

"What the hell was all that about?" Phoebe asked, "are you okay?"

"I'm fine, I just feel really stupid. He was going to kiss me on the cheek, like he did Margaret, and I lost my balance. Do you think anyone else saw?"

Phoebe looked around the now empty pub. "I don't think so. People were mainly focussed on saying their own goodbyes and beating the rush out of the carpark I'll not be long, come and have a coffee with Andrew, he's cashing up, while I clear the last of the tables."

Chapter 37

By the time we were back home in my kitchen I had just about sobered up. The staff at the pub had made a take-away pack of leftovers for Phoebe; a late-night picnic of steak pie, spicy potato wedges and cheesecake went down very nicely.

"You know, I have a feeling that those blokes who work for Dom are probably back in the field, up to no good with a stallion who doesn't belong to them," said Phoebe as she licked the remains of the cheesecake off her spoon.

"What makes you say that?" I asked.

"Just the way they were talking. Fancy a trip?" Phoebe asked.

"I suppose, but what would be the point? This cheesecake is delicious by the way."

"The point is video evidence. Proof they are using the stallion in that field to cover mares. I still don't get why, but if we can prove it's happening, we might be one step closer to finding out what Dirty Dom and his creepy cronies are up to."

"Mm," I considered her point, "what are you suggesting? We hide and record them using the stallion?"

"That's exactly what I'm suggesting."

"I don't know. It's cold and I've had quite a bit to drink."

"So put on a coat, and you seem to be sober, ish. Come on, don't be boring," Phoebe stood up and dragged me to my feet.

"Oh, why do I know I am going to regret this?"

*****

"This is probably an enormous waste of time," I grumbled as I slammed the car door shut.

"Shh!" Phoebe hissed across the roof of the car to me.

"|I'm just saying…"

"Well say it quieter! Come on." Phoebe took my arm and half dragged me down the road, away from the gateway where we had parked her car. "Maybe you are still a bit drunk," she giggled as we stumbled down the dark country lane.

I giggled with her, "Perhaps. But I think it's just cos its pitch black and I can't see where I'm going. I don't think there's anybody he-."

"Shh. Look," Phoebe clutched my arm and pointed ahead. The distinctive, irregular movement of a torch could be seen flashing and bouncing in a field ahead. "Come on, it's them!"

We hurried further along the road until we were as close as we dared go to the horsebox which we could now see parked in the shadows ahead.

"This way!" I tugged Phoebe towards a gap in the hedge. We both dropped to our knees and began to crawl through the wet grass and prickly undergrowth. I paused at the hawthorn barrier and put my finger to my lips. Phoebe nodded and indicated for me to go ahead of her, through the hedge into the field beyond.

"Hurry up!" Phoebe hissed urgently.

Before I could answer I felt a hand close over my mouth and a strong arm grabbed me around the waist, pinning my own arms to my side.

I wriggled frantically and tried to scream but the person holding me was too strong. He, I guessed it was a man based on the size of the hand and strength of the attacker, dragged me as close to the hedge as possible; almost back into the dense thicket of branches.

I was aware of Phoebe crawling out of the shadows a few feet away. My assailant altered his position slightly, it seemed that he was also aware of Phoebe. His grip around my waist tightened as I tried to struggle free or warn Phoebe in some way, but it was useless. I tried to squirm and kick, but I was being held in such a way that I could barely move my legs. I watched as Phoebe slowly stood up.

"Hey, Abi? Where-?" Before she could ask me where I was, the man holding me took a step in her direction, dragging me with him. He released his grip from around my waist and grabbed her, as he had me, by putting a strong hand over her mouth.

Suddenly the men in the next field stopped concerning themselves with the horses. "Who's there?" they shouted shining their torches towards us.

The man holding us, threw himself, face first to the ground taking Phoebe and me down with him. As we fell, he somehow rolled us with him into a narrow ditch which ran close to the foot of the hedge line. I found myself crushed into the bottom of the ditch underneath the man and Phoebe, who he was still holding tightly.

The beam from the torches glanced around the field. I felt the man's muscles tense as he gripped Phoebe to hold her tighter.

"There's nowt there, I told you. Probably a fox or something." One of the men turned away.

"I suppose," his friend sounded less convinced and continued to shine his torch into the darkness.

"Come on," said the first man, "help me get this ramp up so we can get out of here. I said it would be a waste of time coming tonight, the mare isn't interested."

The men turned away and I heard the ramp crashing into place; a few minutes later the sound of the engine roared into life and the horse box disappeared into the night.

The man lying on top of me relaxed. The moment he did so Phoebe sank her teeth into his hand. He screamed and loosened his grip; it was enough for her to wriggle free. She struggled away from him and was trying to stand up when our attacker lurched forward out of the ditch and grabbed her ankle, pulling her back down to the ground. She rolled and twisted trying frantically to kick free. I took advantage of the fact that I had been, momentarily at least, forgotten about. I scrambled out of the ditch and launched myself at the man who was crawling after Phoebe.

"Let her go!" I screamed.

He did.

Now his attention was firmly on me. As he was no longer grabbing Phoebe's ankle, the stranger was able to stand up; as I was hanging onto his back, I found myself clinging to him limpet style like a dysfunctional piggy-back rider. In an effort to disorientate the man, I pulled his hat down over his eyes and then I wrapped my arms around his throat. I hung on tightly as he twisted and turned, trying to free himself of my cumbersome weight while at the same time, trying to prise my arms away from his neck.

Phoebe scrambled to her feet and turned to face our blindfolded attacker. She kicked him, hard on the shin.

He yelled out in pain; his cry muffled by the hat which was still covering his face as he stumbled forward in the darkness; his loss of balance caused me to pitch forward over his shoulder. As I fell, I continued to hold tightly onto the man, pulling him with me to the ground.

This time it was his turn to squirm and wriggle in an effort to break free. I crawled away from him as Phoebe continued to kick him and scream. The man put his arms up to protect his face and head.

"Come on, run!" I grabbed Phoebe's arm and pulled her away from the man.

We set off, running into the darkness, tripping over clods of earth and rough ground.

"Which way?" I panted.

"The hedge!" Phoebe gasped, "keep the hedge to our right, until you see a gateway. Quickly, he's coming after us!"

"I can't go any faster!"

"This way, look, I can see the gateway," Phoebe dragged me towards a spot where the blackness of the hedge was broken.

We slipped and stumbled towards the gate; we could hear the man panting his way across the field, through the darkness behind us.

"Hurry!" yelled Phoebe, half climbing half falling over the gate. I followed her and together we ran along the road, searching for the gateway where we had parked her car. Phoebe fumbled with the keys in her jacket pocket as the dark shape of her car appeared ahead. There was a momentary flash of light as the orange of the car lights illuminated the night when Phoebe activated the electronic key to disable the alarm and unlock the doors.

I was a useless mess of un-coordinated fingers and thumbs as once inside the car, I tried to lock the door and fasten my seatbelt. I could see Phoebe shaking in the driver's seat next to me, struggling in the same way.

She started the engine, or at least tried to; in typical Hitchcock style, the engine tried and stalled.

Twice.

"Third time's a charm!" said Phoebe with a nervous laugh as the engine finally submitted and growled into life.

The car skidded for a moment as Phoebe put the car into gear and pressed down hard on the accelerator pedal. In that moment the man who had been chasing us stumbled out of the darkness. He threw himself at the side of the car.

"Stop! Wait!" he yelled.

We screamed.

His face was highlighted by the lights of the car making him appear as some ghostly apparition. I stared at the ghoulish face pressed against the window of the car.

"You?!" I screamed.

The car responded to Phoebe's demands and the man was flung from the side of the car into the road. We sped away, leaving him behind.

"Did you see who -?" Phoebe began.

"Oh yes. I saw!"

Chapter 38

I poured two very large glasses of red wine and passed one to Phoebe. "If this was on the telly or a film, we would each knock back a neat scotch from a crystal glass, but all I have is wine or gin." She accepted the wine with a trembling hand.

"I can't stop shaking!" she said.

"I know." I put my hand on my chest, "my heart is pounding so hard I swear you can see it jumping right out of my chest. We didn't get any photos or a video." I said sadly, sipping my wine in an effort to settle my nerves.

"True, we got a whole heap of questions rather than any answers."

Suddenly we heard the back door burst open. "You didn't lock it?" I stared at her in disbelief.

"It's your bloody house! Why didn't you lock it?"

"Seriously? After the night you've had, and the pair of you can't even lock your fucking back door!" Pierre yelled at us from the living room doorway.

"Shit!" Phoebe leapt to her feet, brandishing her wine in front of like a weapon.

"Thanks, I could use it." He took the glass from Phoebe's hand and drained it.

"Don't you try anything mister! The police are on their way!" I bluffed.

"Really?" said Phoebe and Pierre at the same time.

I glared at Phoebe.

"Oh, yeah right, they'll be here any minute now," she confirmed.

Pierre shook his head, "You two are fucking unbelievable. What the hell are you playing at?"

"What are we playing at?" I slammed my glass down onto the coffee table, "what are we playing at? You are the one lurking in fields in the middle of the night, grabbing innocent young women and… and… and… grappling with them!" I spluttered.

"Not to mention your shady dealing with Dodgy Dom!" Phoebe added.

"What?"

"You heard," I yelled furiously, "pretending not to recognise his yard, then going back and being all pally- pally with him!"

"On more than one occasion!" Phoebe confirmed with authority.

I looked at her and nodded in agreement, "Exactly!"

"Not to mention wandering around his house, drinking cups of coffee, you were clearly quite at home in the place," Phoebe added.

"And then you hide in a field in the middle of the night and attack me 'n Phoebe, before following us home and breaking into my house!" I yelled.

Pierre stared at me open mouthed.

"Yeah, what's going on?" Phoebe stood with her hands on her hips, "I suppose you're a part of the gang eh? What are you? The look-out guy? Come here to silence us before we spill the beans eh? Well you and whose army matey? We're ready for you this time!"

"Yeah! What she said!" I echoed. Phoebe put her fists up like a boxer ready to spar, she bounced from foot to foot on her tiptoes and I began to wave my hands in what I hoped was a threatening karate style.

"What the hell are you both talking about?"

"You heard," I growled at him.

"I heard, but I didn't understand any of it!" Pierre snapped, "first, you've both got a bloody nerve accusing me of attacking *you*, I was trying to protect you and I'm the one who was bitten, kicked and punched, not to mention

309

throttled, then as if that wasn't bad enough when I try to catch up to explain and make sure you are alright, you," here he glared at Phoebe, " try to fucking run me over and leave me for dead in the middle of the road!"

"We didn't attack you, we fought back in self- defence!" I shouted, "seems like it's you we need protecting from."

"Me?!"

"Yes, you! Why were you creeping around hedgerows in the middle of the night unless you're up to no good, eh?" I demanded.

"I think that's a question I am equally entitled to ask, given that I'm the one who was actually injured!" Pierre bounced back at me.

"We were there to get evidence!" Phoebe joined in.

"Evidence? What kind of evidence?"

"Photographs-," I began.

"Or a video," Phoebe added.

"Proof that your gang are up to something illegal." I finished.

"Your turn. Why were you there and why did you attack us?" Phoebe demanded.

"I was trying to get a video of your boyfriend and his brainless sidekicks, who I think are up to no good," Pierre glared at me as he said 'boyfriend', "but you were both making so much noise I was terrified they would see me and you. Have you any idea what type of people they are? I grabbed you both to save you."

"He is not my boyfriend!"

"Okay, semantics aside, your fling, friend with benefits whatever he is; who you have sex with is your business, I -,"

"I am not having sex with Dominic!" I screamed.

"Oh well pardon me, you can see why I might be confused given that every time I see the two of you together, he is either up close and personal, helping to undress you or kissing you, acting like you are very closely acquainted! You were even having a lovely relaxing nap on his fucking sofa for God's sake!"

"No! You have taken a series of unfortunate and badly timed episodes and twisted them in your warped sex crazed mind!" I shouted.

Phoebe turned her head between the two of us as we argued like she was watching a dysfunctional game of tennis.

"I have never taken a nap in his bloody house!" I continued.

"Drop the act, I saw you."

"What? When?"

"I don't know, how many nap times have there been?"

"None! Phoebe tell him."

"She's right," Phoebe backed me up, "the only time we were ever in his house was today when we broke in looking for evidence!"

"So, we can add breaking and entering to your glittering curriculum vitae!" Pierre yelled.

"Oh, just get out of my house! Go back to Felicity and your weird sex triangle or quadrangle or... I don't know, how many of you are involved in that messed up relationship? But hey, none of my business what you and your girlfriend get up to-."

"Girlfriend? She's not my girlfriend."

"Whatever," I stepped forward and ushered him towards the door, "what was it you said, semantics?"

"Seriously, I am not, and never have been in a relationship with Felicity... well unless you count our professional connection."

"Urgh!" I shuddered and continued shooing him towards the door.

"I'm her vet!"

"What?" Phoebe and I spoke together.

"I treat her horses, Dom's too which is the only reason I have ever been to his home, with the obvious exception of the night I ended up there because you hitched a secret lift in a horsebox in the dead of night!"

311

I stopped shooing him.

"What are you talking about? If you're his vet how come you didn't know where we were that night? Or was that just an elaborate act, to throw us off the trail?"

"I'm new to the area, new to the practice. I didn't know it was Dom's yard until a few days later when I went to scan some of his mares, but hey to use your word; whatever!" he yelled as he turned on his heel and stormed out of the house. He paused at the back door, "And lock your fucking door!"

He slammed the door behind him and then he was gone.

"I did not see that coming!" Phoebe stared over my shoulder at the door.

"No," I said slowly, "nor did I."

I slid the security chain into place and turned the key.

"Bastard drank my wine, do you mind?" Phoebe poured herself another glass.

"Do you believe him?" I asked sipping my own wine.

"I'm not sure," Phoebe followed me into the living room and curled up on the sofa while I encouraged the fire back into life, "the thing is, if he is telling the truth, why hasn't he said something earlier, but if he is lying, then why didn't he simply hand us over to those men?"

"Good point," I said, "unless he is on the other team so to speak, you know, he's in it for the money but isn't completely bad. Anyone with half a shred of decency wouldn't hand a woman over to those monsters."

"Also, true," Phoebe finished her drink and yawned. "how about we thrash this out after a good night's sleep?"

Chapter 39

After the drama of the previous night, I was finding the simple, repetitive task of filling haynets strangely soothing.

"Morning Abi!"

I looked up from the pile of nets, to see Marc and Henry crossing the yard.

"Hi, Marc, Henry."

"Are you competing this weekend?" Marc asked.

"I am actually," I pushed my hair out of my eyes with the back of my hand, "there's an event at Belford Park so I'm taking Skye. It's her first outing since her abscess. I was worried I was going to lose another entry fee, but fingers crossed all seems to be good."

"I thought I heard voices," Phoebe came around the corner and dropped a stack of empty feed buckets next to the feed bin, "what's going on?"

"We're talking about the one-day event at Belford," said Marc.

"Are you going?" Henry asked.

"I certainly am," Phoebe grinned, "I've got the whole weekend off work."

Marc perched himself on the end of the feed bin and held a haynet open for me, "Are you still at Uni, Phoebe?"

"No, I finished last year, why?"

"Just wondered," said Marc.

"What's your degree in?" asked Henry, passing an empty net to Marc.

"Which one?" Phoebe asked, pulling a face at Henry.

"You have more than one degree?" Henry asked.

"I have a Master's in the history of fine art."

"Why are you working at the pub," Henry continued.

"Why are you bothered?"

Henry shrugged.

Phoebe sighed, "Turns out there aren't many career opportunities in my chosen field, most of the people I was at uni. with have gone into teaching and I'd rather chew off my own leg and beat myself to death with it than teach! I'm considering my options and the money's good at the pub. Anyway, enough about my life goals, stables are done, are you riding Abi?"

"Yeah." I threw the last of the filled nets onto a pile.

"Come on, we need to crack on as well," said Henry as he pulled Marc off the feed bin.

"Okay, what's your hurry?" asked Marc.

"No hurry," Henry put a handful of feed into a scoop to act as a bribe if the ponies were awkward to catch, "just no point in hanging around."

Marc pursed his lips, clearly annoyed but unwilling to have a row in front of us, "When are you course walking?" he asked.

"Tomorrow, probably after lunch. Are you coming?"

"Sounds like a good idea. Henry's been persuaded to go with the Thompsons."

"Is Chantelle riding?" I asked.

"She's competing on a day ticket; can I hitch a lift with you two."

*****

"I think Henry's up to something," said Phoebe as we rode out of the yard and waved at Marc who was leading Symphony towards the arena, "did you notice how he wouldn't look Marc in the eye when Marc asked why he was in a hurry?"

"Yeah, I did actually. But they'll have to sort themselves out. Have you thought any more about last night?" I asked.

314

"I've thought about nothing else!"

We turned off the road at our earliest opportunity and followed a winding track across the moor. The horses were happy to walk side by side as we discussed the events of the previous day, and night. We seemed to have all the pieces of giant jig saw puzzle but no idea of the final picture we were trying to build. By the time we returned to the yard, we were no further forward in our attempts to untangle the mystery surrounding Dominic, the passports, Marilyn's stallion and the likelihood that Hannah was in some way involved with her horse; nor had we come to a consensus regarding whether or not we could trust Pierre.

"Are you still messing with that poor woman's stirrups?" I asked Phoebe as I hung up my bridle; she was busy occupying herself with Izzy's saddle.

"Poor woman my eye! But yes, occasionally, it amuses me. Though I haven't seen her for a while. What's the old witch up to? Brewing spells around a bubbling cauldron somewhere?"

"Close, she is pre-occupied planning the wedding."

We came out of the tack room and found ourselves facing Pierre. He was holding a cake box, emblazoned with the distinctive pink and silver livery of the village coffee shop.

"Truce?"

Phoebe and I stared at him but neither of us spoke.

"I'll take that as a maybe," Pierre held up the cake box, "I've brought cake."

Phoebe stepped forward and took the box from him before returning to stand by me.

"Look, I think things became a little heated last night. We all said things…" Pierre looked around the yard as Felicity drove through the gates, "can we go inside and talk somewhere that's a little more private?"

We didn't move.

"What did you give her?" I asked.

"Who? What did I give who?" Pierre looked puzzled.

"Felicity. You asked me to tell her you'd left her a gift, yesterday."

"Oh that. It wasn't a gift."

"You said it was a gift," I insisted.

"Did I? I don't remember that, but if I did, I wasn't being literal. I was saving her a drive to the surgery by dropping off Romeo's medication for his Cushing's disease."

I looked at Phoebe; she shrugged.

"I'm not saying I believe you, but I'll hear you out."

I headed across the yard towards the house and Pierre fell into step beside me.

"I'll just be a second," said Phoebe as she veered off to speak to Felicity.

*****

Pierre stood awkwardly in the middle of the kitchen, watching as Phoebe opened the cake box, "Chocolate brownies, safe choice." She helped herself and sat down while I filled and switched on the kettle

"Well," I said, "are you going to stand there all day, or explain yourself?"

Pierre took a deep breath, "What do you want to know?"

"Everything," I said, "from the beginning."

"I'm not sure there's time to tell you every-."

"Oh, I knew it!" I turned away from him.

"- but I will try to tell you as much as I can, to be honest it doesn't all make sense; yet!"

"Get on with it then," Phoebe accepted a coffee.

"Okay. First off, I'm a vet. I'm new to the area which is probably why we hadn't come across each other until the day I came to see Romeo for his annual health check. I hadn't met Dominic, though I had certainly heard plenty about him, most of it not very complimentary I might add, until the one-day event at Stonecross. I was one of the vets on hand for any emergency or welfare issues and Camilla decided it was

316

the perfect opportunity for me to meet people; that's when she told me that you and Dom were… involved-."

"What? Oh, how many times-," I interrupted.

"Alright, but see things from my point of view, how was I to know she was wrong, and he was just messing with me?" Pierre said.

I paused for a moment and reflected. I remembered seeing Pierre and Camilla looking down at me after Dom had helped free me from my self- inflicted straight jacket and then later his comment to Pierre about making babies when we were discussing the suitability of matching my mare to his stallion, "Okay then," I said grudgingly, "go on."

"Then the night of the ball, I was late because I was on call, also the reason I wasn't drinking. I had no idea what was going on when I found you, and to be honest at that point I was as convinced as the police that you were both reacting to a combination of shock from the crash and overly active imaginations."

"What changed your mind?" asked Phoebe.

"My visit to scan some mares at Dom's yard. I recognised the place, and the dog, but what could I do? I could hardly accuse him of stealing a horse which obviously belonged to him. So, after the visit I drove up and down the lane until I found where I thought the horsebox might have been parked. That's when I met Marilyn. I'd seen her at the Academy a couple of times, and she was happy to show off Charlie and tell me about his eventing history and his subsequent breeding success."

I pushed a coffee in Pierre's direction, "Go on."

He sipped the drink before continuing. "I couldn't understand why Dom, or the people who work for him, would be taking a mare from someone else's field, especially at night. As far as I could understand there was only two explanations; either they were stealing a horse, or they didn't want anyone to know the mare had been in the field. It didn't look like the horse was stolen so that left the second option."

317

"But why?" I asked, "I know that Dom's grazing isn't the best but surely he isn't desperate enough to need to steal grazing in the middle of the night!"

"Well after my chat with Marilyn I looked more closely at Dom's stallion," Pierre continued, " there seems to be a disproportionate degree of competition success between the offspring of Dom's own mares compared to the young stock produced by visiting mares, all apparently covered by the same stallion."

"I noticed that!" Phoebe interrupted, "hang on."

She rummaged through one of my kitchen drawers before pulling out the sheets of paper she had used to make notes about the youngsters by Dom's stallion, "Here, look!"

I put my hand on the papers before Pierre could read them, "So, it's decided, we're trusting him then?"

Pierre looked from me to Phoebe.

"Well," she said slowly, "he was telling the truth about the stuff he left for Felicity and…"

"…and?" I pressed her.

"Let's just hear him out. He can find out all of this stuff on the internet like I did. I thought this might save time that's all."

"She's right. And I've already looked up the same results," Pierre said.

I let go of the papers and pushed them towards him, "Go on then."

"I know the quality of the mare is massively important, but even so…" Pierre shuffled through the papers.

"What's he up to then?" I asked.

"We saw him and those men -," Phoebe began.

I held up my hand, "Hang on Phoebes, let's hear what he has to say first."

"I think he is using his stallion to cover some mares, probably those belonging to other people, and using Marylin's horse to cover his own mares. Charlie is far superior to Star, but if he can somehow pass off all of the

318

offspring as being by Star, his own horse, then it improves his horse's record and means he can charge a lot more for stud fees."

Pierre waited, giving us a chance to process the information.

Phoebe looked at me, questioningly. I nodded and sat down between her and Pierre.

"We went back to the field a few nights after the ball and we also saw Marilyn, apparently she doesn't like the idea of live covering and Charlie is only available via artificial insemination."

"She told me the same," said Pierre.

"Which is why," Phoebe continued, "we were rather surprised to see Dom and the chuckle brothers using Charlie to cover the brown and white mare in the field by torch light, close to midnight."

"So, I was right," Pierre finished his coffee and inspected the empty cup. I took the hint and put the kettle back on.

"I took a picture of some of the counterfoils of the covering certificates and these," she showed Pierre her phone, "this is some kind of code in his records of mares and dates of coverings. But we can't understand these," Phoebe pointed out the symbols.

Pierre studied the image.

"Mm." He took out a pen and scribbled some notes on the corner of one of the sheets of paper Phoebe had shown him.

"Mm, what? I asked, "do you know what they mean?"

"Maybe. Here are the dates of the coverings, that's fairly obvious. I think the 'V' after the horse's name means visiting mare."

"That's what I thought, said Phoebe "and the 'O' means own. What I don't understand is the asterisk and the 'H'."

"But what if the 'O' is actually a zero, then the 'H' means home?" Pierre suggested.

Phoebe frowned, "That still leaves the asterisk and now the zero unaccounted for."

319

"Star!" Pierre announced triumphantly, "it's not an asterisk it's a star, code for Dom's own stallion. See how most of the star symbols are beside a 'V' while most of the names marked with 'H' also have a zero."

"Oh my God, it's a record of the mares his horse has covered and which ones he has covered with Marilyn's horse!" Phoebe declared.

"Well done! But that's not all he's up to," I said.

"Oh, I know. He's got fingers in more pies than I can count, unfortunately he is also clever which is how he seems to get away with so much," Pierre sighed.

"What else do you know about?" I asked.

"Well, let me see," Pierre began counting on his fingers, "I'm pretty sure he is falsifying documents, passing non - descript horses off with passports belonging to horses with fancy bloodlines and great competition results; the usual doping to hide lameness or withholding water to subdue animals who would ordinarily be difficult to ride and that's just the beginning."

"We can add a couple of things to your list," I said passing him another coffee.

Pierre accepted the drink, "Really? Such as?"

"Dodgy passports to falsify the age of horses he sells," said Phoebe.

"I'm not surprised, especially given the boxes of fake passports and make- believe veterinary stamps he has in his house," said Pierre.

"And using ringers in competition," I said.

"Yeah, I know. That chestnut for example has been round the jumping circuit with at least three different names if that's what you mean."

I looked at Phoebe before continuing, "We think the last bit is a tad more complicated."

Between us, Phoebe and I filled in Pierre with all we knew about Dom and Hannah.

"Wow, you have been busy!" Pierre leaned back in his chair.

"You'd think there would be someone who would be willing to turn him in. Surely not everyone falls for his creepy brand of charm," said Phoebe with a shudder.

"From what I can work out, there was someone actually. A woman, she kept her horse at Dom's yard, had done for years and she helped him with the mares and foals. I don't think she approved of what he was up to and I'm fairly sure she had reported him anonymously."

"Well who is she? Where is she now?" I asked.

"Dead," said Pierre simply.

"Oh my God! What happened? Did he kill her?" cried Phoebe.

"I don't *think* he was responsible for her death," he said.

"What was she called, what happened to her?" I repeated.

"I think she was called Pat, and as far as I know she just died, nothing suspicious."

"Shit!" Phoebe splashed coffee onto the table as she slammed her mug down, "Pat? Do you mean Patricia?"

"I suppose, why?" Pierre looked at Phoebe with concern, "did you know her?"

"I didn't," said Phoebe, "but Abi did... well she sort of knew her."

"Did you know her well?" Pierre asked me, "sorry I didn't mean to be disrespectful about your loss."

"I only met her briefly," I said to him, "crikey, who'd have thought Susan was Dom's livery," I added to Phoebe.

"It explains how he got hold of Shadow," Phoebe pointed out.

"Sorry, Susan? What are you both talking about? Who's Susan?"

We ate the last of the brownies while we told Pierre about Patricia's sudden death in my kitchen, the horse Dom had sold the Thompsons which Phoebe had recognised from the

321

funeral order of service; plus the very new and obviously false passport Dom had provided with the horse.

"So, what do we do now?" I asked, "should we tell the Thompsons? And what about Marilyn? Surely she deserves to know that someone is interfering with her horse."

"We've already talked about the Thompson family," Phoebe reminded me, "what good would it do? I say we keep quiet about that one, at least for now."

Pierre nodded, "I agree. I think they've been conned for sure but it's a drop in the ocean compared to everything else and apart from a very old photograph it's his word against ours."

I smiled at his use of the word 'ours'.

"What about Hannah?" I asked.

"Again, it's her word against ours at the moment," he said.

"But we can prove she is hiding his white bits," Phoebe protested, showing Pierre the photographs on her phone.

"Yes, but that in itself isn't a crime," said Pierre.

"Unless the horse is stolen…" Phoebe left the comment hanging in the air.

Pierre's mobile broke the silence. He spent a few minutes chatting, "Sorry, work calls, I have to go," he stood up, "I'm glad we've sorted out… well a few misunderstandings." He smiled nervously, "Please promise me that you won't do anything stupid, or rash."

Phoebe snorted.

"I'm serious. If Dom suspects that we know what he is up to he will get rid of any evidence, like the passports and stuff, then we're back to his word against ours."

"I suppose," I said, "but what about Marilyn?"

"I'll try and contact her and make something up, kids feeding horses or poachers cutting through fields; anything to make her either move the horse or step up security. Are you going to Belford Park?"

I nodded, "Yes, we both are."

"We're course walking tomorrow after lunch," Phoebe looked from Pierre to me and grinned.

His phone warned him that a text had been delivered, he glanced at the screen.

"I'm sorry, I've got to go. Remember: slowly, slowly catch the monkey!"

"That is so frustrating! How dare he waltz in here with cake and take over, I mean we found everything out, why would we screw it up now?" I exclaimed as Pierre's car left the yard.

"We wouldn't. But I see no harm in hanging fire for a day or two…" Phoebe said as she cleared the crumbs and empty cups from the table.

"You've changed your tune," I snorted.

"No, but I'd hate to see Dom and his bitchy side kick wriggle out of this just because we were careless and wanted to beat Pierre to a big television detective style reveal of the crime."

Chapter 40

Despite being called a one- day event, the competition at Belford Park actually ran over two days with the bigger tracks being jumped on the first day, Saturday, and the smaller jumps, those of one metre or less, being contested on the Sunday. This meant that our course walk on Saturday afternoon was rather more exciting as we had to be mindful of the competitors who were still on the course.

Flags danced in the wind as despite the fact it was almost June, the weather was closer to early, rather than late, Spring; a crackly tannoy relayed the progress of the riders who were tackling the cross- country course. I parked my car behind James and Margaret's four- wheel drive. Chantelle waved at us as we left the cars and made our way towards the collection of tents and trade stands.

"Come and look!" she called, "these boots are to die for!"

Chantelle held up a pair of long leather boots. They were a combination of natural and patent leather with a trim of Swarovski crystals.

"Very nice, but the mud will ruin the crystals," said Phoebe.

"Then I'll keep them for dressage or showjumping," Chantelle grinned, handing her father's credit card over.

"You should be charging them more for livery if they can afford these prices!" Phoebe whispered.

"Come on, the start's this way," Marc led us away from the hospitality area towards James and Margaret who were waiting near the starting box with Henry.

"Hi, you took your time, we've been here for ages," Henry joked.

Marc gave a wry smile, "Well it would have been easier for us to come together. I thought you were busy until later."

"I was, but I switched things around," Henry grinned.

"Where were you again?" Marc persisted.

"Just busy, you know errands. Now come on, it's freezing just standing here. I don't think anyone's told the weather that it's June tomorrow!"

We all set off to inspect the course; standing clear of jumps when the volunteer jump judges blew their warning whistles. There were long galloping stretches which separated areas where technical clusters of jumps were designed to test the rider's control and the athleticism of the horses who would be running long and flat in the galloping sections but who would need to be gathered and bouncy to clear the jumps.

The course builder had been creative and inventive, building many of the jumps to either replicate or pay homage to a nearby steam railway and priory. As well as the 'novelty' fences, straw bales and natural mounds of earth were used to add height to telegraph poles and giant logs or tree trunks. Weeping willows and lilies made the water jump look particularly natural; a decorative island in the centre invited horses to jump a carved serpent. Competitors jumping the larger fences needed to tackle the serpent closer to his head, while the obstacle became lower towards the tail.

Phoebe took photographs of each jump and we discussed the best approach to the fences. Marc marvelled at the size of the jumps, especially those in the more advanced classes, while enjoying the walk. Henry meanwhile was with Chantelle, pointing out the safest way to negotiate the course; where to sit up and take a pull, where to kick on and the best line to ride into each obstacle.

"Don't get me wrong," Phoebe began, "I'm glad Chantelle has a babysitter who can advise her like this," she raised her eyebrows and looked across to where Henry was guiding Chantelle and showing her how to tackle a drop fence.

"But?" Marc asked.

"But, how does he know so much about eventing?" Phoebe continued, "I thought you guys produced show ponies."

"Well, to begin with people can be involved in more than one discipline you know," Marc replied with a smile.

"What happened?" I asked, "did he lose his nerve?"

"What do you mean?" Phoebe asked.

"It's obvious when you think about it," I said, "only someone who has ridden these types of jumps could talk about them the way he does."

Marc sighed, "You're right Abi. Showing was always more my thing, after I damaged my back in a car accident I turned to breeding and producing ponies; showing in-hand rather than under saddle. Turns out I loved horses but could take or leave the actual riding. Henry only got involved with the ponies after his accident." Marc lowered his voice and waited until Henry and Chantelle had moved away, towards the next jump before continuing. "Henry loved to event. Hell, with the right financial backing he could have gone professional, I'm sure."

"What happened?" Phoebe asked softly.

"Abi guessed right. There was an accident, about five years ago," Marc continued sadly. "Henry had a fabulous horse, Sovereign; we'd had him since he was a youngster. We broke him ourselves… anyway Henry was riding him at a One-Daye event near York. There was a freak accident. Sovereign slipped as he landed over the first part of a combination," Marc's voice broke as he recalled the details. "It all happened so quickly. One minute they were this perfect partnership, literally flying; the next, they were a tangled heap of limbs and blood. Sovereign's leg just snapped! He rolled and landed on Henry. Oh, the image of that poor beautiful horse, thrashing about, trampling Henry… the horse kept trying to stand up you see, but his front leg…"

I put my arm around his shoulders, "Hey, it's okay."

"I'm so sorry," said Phoebe, "I shouldn't have asked."

"No, no you weren't to know. Actually, it's strangely therapeutic to tell someone," Marc pulled his phone out and flicked through some photographs, "this is him."

"He was gorgeous," I said handing Marc's phone back to him.

"Was Henry seriously hurt?" Phoebe asked.

"Broken bones, concussion… he escaped with remarkably few injuries; well, physical injuries. The real damage was psychological. He kept having flashbacks and no matter how much he said he wanted to, he simply couldn't get back on a horse."

"Oh my God, that's awful!" I said.

"Friends offered Henry horses to ride, but there was always a reason to say no; it was too windy, he was working, tired, busy…the horse was too small, too young, too much like Sovereign or not enough like him. We never replaced him. We made half- hearted attempts to look, but… well… Henry reached the point where he couldn't even watch people eventing, that's why it was so amazing when he went with you guys to walk the course at Stonecross."

I remembered how concerned Marc had been when we all arrived back at the yard that day.

"It looks like by helping Chantelle, he's found a way to help himself," Marc concluded as we continued to walk towards the next fence.

"But, isn't that a good thing?" Phoebe asked slowly.

"It would be, but I feel that he is slipping away. One thing I don't miss are those parties. Boy, people think the showjumping crowd are wild, but those eventers know how to party, I'm sure he's seeing someone else; I'm wondering if it's one of his old eventing 'friends',"

"No. Surely not!" I protested.

Marc shrugged, "We'll see. There's something going on that's for sure."

A whistle cut through any further speculation and we hurried to the side of the track as another horse and rider combination thundered past.

We followed Henry and the Thompson family around the rest of the course. Chantelle went back to the trade stands to collect the boots she had bought earlier, and Margaret disappeared into the secretary's tent. I followed her with Phoebe, to double check our starting times for each of the phases the following day.

"What are you reading?" I asked Margaret.

"The order book sweetheart. I like to keep them all 'cos they have Chantelle's name in."

I smiled and turned back to scanning the lists on the notice boards.

"I think I'll get one of those. They usually have a course map in them," Phoebe said.

I turned from the lists and looked at Phoebe; she looked up from reading the programme.

"Dom's riding here tomorrow," we both said at once.

"He must have really bad handwriting," Phoebe mused.

"What makes you say that?" I asked.

"It must be difficult for people to read his entry form details," Phoebe continued, "it's the only reason I can think of to explain why they keep spelling the horse's name wrong. I'm sure this isn't how it was spelled last time I saw it."

Chapter 41

"You don't have to bring gifts every time you want to talk to me." I laughed taking he bottle of wine off Pierre and leading him into my kitchen.

"I know, I thought it would make up for the large glass I drained, without invitation the other night. But if you don't want it…"

"Oh no, this looks nice. Fancy. Expensive," I said looking at the label, "I might save it until tomorrow though, if that's okay."

"That's fine," Pierre's face fell for a moment before he recovered his composure, "I just thought…"

I looked at his face and smiled, "I'm riding tomorrow, I need a clear head, and this looks very strong."

"Ah," a look of understanding spread across his face, "sorry, I should have realised."

"Don't worry, do you have time for a coffee?"

"I certainly do," he shrugged out of his jacket and sat down, "are you by yourself?"

"Yes and no. Phoebe is finishing off outside, then she's staying here tonight so we can get an early start tomorrow," I put a coffee down in front of Pierre before turning to retrieve the milk from the fridge.

"I'm surprised she doesn't just move in," he laughed.

"I sometimes think she is doing exactly that," I joined in laughing with him, "you know, bit by bit without actually telling me."

Suddenly we were interrupted.

"Abi! Abi! I think I've worked it out!" Phoebe came crashing into the kitchen. "Hi Pierre, nice wine. Abi, where is the programme for tomorrow's competition?"

"Here," I passed the small glossy booklet to her.

She began flicking through the pages, muttering to herself.

"Did we keep any of these from the other competitions?" she asked.

"Yeah, I think so," I began to rummage through a drawer.

"Oo, I've just remembered I have one upstairs in my room, from the event where we saw Dom, but we weren't actually riding ourselves. I'll be back in a sec."

"Her room?" Pierre said smiling.

"She means the spare room, but yeah I heard."

Phoebe came bouncing back into the kitchen, "Got it!" she waved the programme.

"Erm, Phoebe?" Pierre began, "your room? Have you moved in?"

Phoebe paused and put her head on one side, "Mm. About that, I was going to ask you Abi, if we sort out whatever mess Hannah and Dom are involved in, you might lose her livery."

I sighed, "I am aware of that, though to be fair she is so bad at paying-."

"Anyway, you might want to consider renting out your spare room to make up the money, and if you do make that decision, I'd be happy to help... given the shit hole I'm living in at the moment and-."

"And given that you practically live here anyway..." grinned Pierre.

"I was going to say it's handy for work," Phoebe retorted, "anyway, what's it got to do with you?"

"Nothing at all!" Pierre laughed.

"Hmph," Phoebe snorted, "by the way, did you know that's the exact spot where Susan was killed?"

"Who?" Pierre looked around in alarm.

"Patricia," I said, "and she wasn't killed, she just… died… unexpectedly, although to be fair she was sitting in that chair when it happened."

Pierre shuffled uncomfortably in his seat.

"Let's discuss the room later," I said, "but yes it sounds like a good idea, at least in principle. Now, why are you so excited about seeing your name in a booklet?"

"Not my name!"

Phoebe took the programmes and flicked through each one until she was satisfied that she had found what she was looking for.

"There!" she pointed, "I thought it was a spelling mistake but now I think its deliberate."

"But why?" I asked.

"To cover his tracks," she answered simply.

"Would one of you please explain what is going on? What have spelling mistakes got to do with anything?" Pierre glanced at the programme before passing it back to Phoebe, "I presume you're talking about Dom."

"Yes, look here, do you see his name and the details of the horse he is riding?" I pointed to an entry in one of the programmes, "And then here and then again here… Sometimes the name is Silverwood Obsydian ll with an 'S' and a 'Y' sometimes the spelling is Obzidian with 'ZI',"

"At first we thought someone had made a spelling mistake when the information was passed to the printers, but actually, I think it might be deliberate," said Phoebe.

"Why?" I asked.

"Yes, why would someone deliberately want to have their details misspelled?" Pierre asked, looking at the programme again.

Phoebe took a deep breath, "To begin with we couldn't figure out why Dom was riding two different horses and pretending to only ride one; the prize money is okay and if it meant he could improve his chances of winning, well, maybe… but doesn't really outweigh the consequences if he gets caught. It's only worth his while if it means if he can make a lot of money! We know he can make a decent profit if he can sell the horse as an excellent eventer, rather than a bold cross country, crap at dressage horse or-."

Pierre looked at us both, "okay, I'm with you so far, you explained this yesterday. What does it have to do with spelling mistakes?"

Phoebe grinned. "I was watching Hannah getting her stuff ready, she has another 'lesson' tomorrow by the way."

"Why am I not surprised?" I said rolling my eyes.

"Anyway…" Pierre prompted.

"Anyway, while I was watching I thought, why not keep the two horses together? It would make things so much easier but then I realised, keeping them on different yard puts an element of distance between Dom and the second horse and it eliminates the risk of any potential buyer seeing the two horses in the same place and joining the dots if the horse doesn't perform quite as expected when they try it out before parting with their cash. It's a common dealer trick isn't it a buyer rides and thinks he's bought one horse but a different one is delivered."

"Again, the spelling?" Pierre asked.

"I'm getting to it."

"Well get there faster!" Pierre ran a hand through his hair.

"The spelling means he has two brilliant event horses to sell, not one."

I wrinkled my brow. "I don't get it."

"Oh, come on, catch up! Having two is obviously better from a financial point of view than one, yes?"

"Obviously," I said.

Phoebe sighed, "Let's imagine you bought one horse off Dom."

"Which one?" I asked.

"It doesn't matter. Let's just imagine you buy one and Pierre buys the other one."

"Go on," Pierre encouraged.

"What's the first thing you do when you take possession of your new horse?" Phoebe asked.

"Take it home, give it a day or so to settle…" I began.

"Christ I could slap you at times!" cried Phoebe in exasperation.

"I'd change the passport into my name," Pierre interrupted.

"Not a problem, I've given you a shiny new passport. What else…?"

I struggled to see what she was hinting at.

Pierre frowned, then he suddenly shouted out, "British Eventing! I'd contact BE and tell them I was the new owner, check out the points the horse has on its record, how much prize money and so on."

"Hallelujah!" cried Phoebe.

"But, so what? We know the horse is registered; it has to be to compete." I said.

Phoebe and Pierre looked at each other. "Seriously, I sometimes wonder how do you manage to stand up by yourself?" Phoebe cried in exasperation.

"What do you mean?" I sniffed; I was pretty sure I had just been insulted.

"Think about it. You contact British Eventing or British Dressage, even the showjumping association-," said Phoebe.

"Or all of them!" declared Pierre who had obviously had a lightbulb moment and understood the point Phoebe was trying to make.

She grinned, "Yeah, if you like. But Pierre has also bought a horse and both of you think you are now the proud owner of Syd. The stable name doesn't matter, there must be thousands of horses called Misty or Jet, but the official registered name is unique."

"If I tell British Eventing, I'm the new owner and without knowing about me, Abi tells them she owns the same horse then Dom's fraudulent plan very quickly unravels," Pierre nodded.

"Okay…" I said slowly.

"Boy this chap is clever." said Pierre.

"I still don't see why he needed to have spelling mistakes in the programmes." I said.

"Because this way, both horses get points accredited to their name," said Pierre, " he enters the event at one venue using one version of the name and enters at the next venue using another version of the name; as far as British Eventing are concerned he simply has two horses with similar names but anyone who is considering buying the horse, anyone who has watched it compete, will simply think as Phoebe did, that the organisers have misspelled the details. Both names sound the same so anyone hearing the horse's name on the loudspeaker won't know if they are hearing Obsydian with 'S, Y' or Obzidian with 'ZI'!"

"But I still don't see why he needs to bother." I said feeling annoyed that Phoebe and Pierre were sharing some secret knowledge that I was failing to grasp.

"This way, when the new owner contacts British Eventing or whoever, the horse will have a credible number of points on its record," Phoebe explained, "think about it, if you had seen the horse win and there were no points recorded you would be suspicious. This way-."

"I get it," I cried, finally understanding, "what about the fact that one of the horses has a white fetlock?"

"I doubt this is the first time Dom's pulled this stunt," said Pierre, "though most horses are less eye catching than the black one he has now, again making the horse more valuable so it's worth taking the risk. I suppose he explains away different markings by putting it down to seasonal coat changes or mud, or even, as in this case I guess, pretending the marks have been hidden by boots and bandages or simply, just not noticed."

"Gosh, it's a risky game he's playing if we're right," I said.

"But worth it as far as he is concerned given the potential amount of money he could be making," Pierre said.

I yawned.

"Oh, now you've set me off!" Phoebe stretched and yawned too, "I think I'll have an early night."

Pierre stood up, "I'd better go. Good luck for tomorrow. I might see you there."

I followed him to the door, "Thanks again, for the wine."

"You're welcome, perhaps I could erm, I mean if you want…unless…"

"Why don't you come 'round tomorrow night and help me drink it," I said.

Pierre smiled.

"Sounds like a plan," Phoebe shouted from inside the house, "we should get a take-away to go with it and celebrate me moving in."

Chapter 42

The following morning dawned cold but bright. Hannah had already loaded Secret into her hired horsebox and was driving out of the gates when I came out of the house. By the time Phoebe and I were following in my own horsebox with Skye and Treasure, the yard was a hive of activity with the Thompson family fluttering around; Marc and Henry were sorting out their own ponies and Felicity was mucking out.

I slid on a pair of sunglasses and swung the horsebox out of the gates, following the same direction as Hannah had driven almost two hours earlier. Phoebe was sitting in the passenger seat, mentally riding the dressage test, leaving me to concentrate on the road ahead.

Arriving at our destination, we bumped across the field, following the waving and pointed directions of the Hi-Viz wearing volunteers, one of the horses in the compartment behind me whinnied.

"Someone's excited!" Phoebe laughed, checking the screen on the dashboard which was linked to a video camera in the horse area.

"Keep an eye open for Dom's horsebox," I said.

"I'm looking but can't see it."

We parked without catching any sight of Dom or his horsebox.

"He hasn't collected his number yet," said Phoebe as we left the secretary's tent.

"How do you know?" I asked.

"I gave his number and waited until she was ready to hand it over then pretended that I'd made a mistake and gave my own number."

"Sneaky!" I said admiringly.

Phoebe grinned, "Thanks."

The warm- up area for the dressage phase of the competition was busy. I tried to find a quiet corner, but Skye was excited and was clearly enjoying her pony party after being away from the action due to her abscess. She spooked and shied at invisible dragons and monsters only she could see lurking in the grass or the fence line.

The collecting ring steward called me over. "You're in the third arena, the one with the blue car and the judge is using a bell to start the test. You can walk down now."

I thanked him as he ticked my name off his list.

I was glad that Marc and Henry were coming later with Chantelle and her parents. This was not our best dressage test. "You clearly need more work missy!" I muttered to Skye as I gave the judge a very forced smile with my salute.

We bounced back to the horsebox for a quick tack change before heading towards the showjumping.

"Good luck!" Phoebe held onto Skye as I used the ramp as a mounting block, "I'll be starting my stressage or at least be in the collecting ring when you get back, will you be able to manage?"

"Yeah, I have everything laid out ready. See you later," I called as we jogged away.

Skye was strong but she listened to me more than she had in the dressage and somehow, we managed a clear, though not very elegant, round.

"How was the showjumping?" Pierre asked. He was leaning against the back of the horse box when I got back.

"Well that depends. Style, horse and rider harmony, skill, definitely 'nil points'; luck and dogged determination, however, means we scraped a clear."

"A clear's a clear. Come on I'll give you a hand." Pierre held Skye while I dismounted and helped me to prepare for the cross -country phase.

"Have you seen Dom?" I asked as I pulled on my gloves.

"Not yet, at least I haven't seen the man himself, but his box is parked a few rows back," Pierre gave me a leg up, "the ramp was still up. Maybe we could try sniffing him out when you get back?"

I smiled down at him as we walked towards the final section of the competition.

"I'll see you at the finish," he said.

"Okay, it's a date. I mean not a date, date but... I mean I'm not opposed to a date if you... but..." I stammered.

Pierre laughed and reached up to put a hand on Skye's neck; as he did so, she grabbed at the bit and pulled forward, meaning that rather than the horse's neck, Pierre's hand landed on my thigh.

We both looked at his hand. "

Oh, I'm sorry! I didn't mean," he snatched his hand away, "be safe, okay. She's really on her toes today."

I gave my girth a final check, "I'll be fine, I'll see you soon."

Skye snorted and tossed her head impatiently as we circled the starting box, waiting for the official to begin the countdown and set us on our way.

I was breathless but exhilarated by the ride. Each fence had been built to its maximum height and spread. Skye relished the long gallops and responded each time I asked her to slow down and listen. At one fence, constructed from timber to resemble a steam train, I misjudged the approach and we almost came to a nasty, and premature end, as Syke scrambled over the jump. Somehow, she put in an extra effort and stretched to regain her balance while slowing down as I found my own balance and retrieved my lost stirrup.

I leaned forward and hugged my brave little mare as we flew past the finish before slipping from her back.

"That looked amazing!" Marc suddenly appeared on the other side of Skye. He ran my stirrup up the leather and helped to slacken the girth as we returned to my horsebox.

"Thanks!" I grinned, "when did you get here?" I asked as I undid the chin strap on my hat.

"About an hour ago. Henry's helping Chantelle but I wanted to see your cross-country."

"Have you seen Pierre by any chance?" I asked looking around.

"I'm right here!" said a voice behind me, "Crikey you were fast, and lucky! I thought you were a gonna at the train."

I laughed, "Me too, but she saved us both." I kissed Skye on the nose.

With both Marc and Pierre to help, it didn't take long to untack and cool down Skye. Phoebe returned and made a switch from dressage to jumping kit, made easier by the extra pairs of hands. Marc went with her towards the showjumping, leaving me with Pierre to settle Skye.

Pierre stood on the corner of the ramp while I tied up a hay-net for Skye. "Hey, come and look at this?" he called.

"What are you doing?"

He handed me a small pair of field glasses and pointed across the carpark towards the dressage arenas, "Can you see him? In the first arena."

I scanned the area until I was able to pick out Dom. I watched as he rode a beautifully balanced test.

"That horse practically floats!" I declared passing the binoculars back to Pierre.

"It certainly does," Pierre watched for a few more minutes than gave the glasses back to me.

I refocussed, "Oh, Phoebe is two arenas down, they're in the same class but different sections. She's saluting. They're both leaving their arenas. Ahh! He's looking straight at me!" I screamed.

Pierre laughed and took the field glasses, "They're small but have excellent magnification."

"Oh, thank God. I thought he was looking right at me for a second."

"He's saying something to Phoebe. Oh, and Henry's there too," Pierre explained.

"What's she saying?" I snatched the binoculars and tried to find them.

"I don't know, I don't lip read and long-distance hearing isn't one of my superpowers. But she'll be here in a second or two and you can ask her."

"Ask who what?"

I spun around to see Phoebe sitting on Treasure.

"Where did you spring from?" I asked.

"One of the stewards let me out at the bottom of the dressage section, saved me having to ride all the way back to the warm-up and then all the way back round. I cut through the horseboxes. Help me change saddles."

"Were you talking to Dom down there?" I asked, sliding off her dressage saddle.

"How on earth do you know? But yes, we exchanged a few words," she glanced from me to Pierre and back again, "he was doing his test at just about the same time. That black horse has paces to die for."

"We saw," Pierre waved the binoculars before slipping them back into his pocket.

"Nice one. I wondered how you knew I'd spoken to him. Henry was watching. I was going to ask him to record my test, but he was already filming Dom."

"Is that what you were talking about?" I asked.

"Not really," Phoebe answered slowly, "we were just passing the time of day, being polite, you know."

"Oh, nothing interesting then," I said.

Phoebe lifted her saddle flap and used her head to keep it raised while she fastened her girth. She smiled and looked around before answering, "Well, I wouldn't say that exactly," she teased.

Pierre jumped off the ramp and the three of us huddled together.

"When Henry gave Dom his phone back, he was congratulating him and admiring the horse, blah blah blah, but before Dom rode away, Henry said how much better the horse had gone since the last time he'd seen it. Dom acted all surprised and was like 'what do you mean? this horse always does an amazing test' and Henry said, 'maybe he doesn't perform as well indoors' and Dom got all defensive, so then Henry said something about the dressage at the Academy and how it had almost looked like a different horse!"

"No way!" I gasped.

"Way!" Phoebe confirmed.

"Then what happened?" Pierre prompted.

"Well Dom was clearly rattled but then Henry said he supposed that Dom must have put a lot of work in," Phoebe lowered her voice even more and Pierre and I leaned in closer to hear her. I took a deep breath and inhaled the wonderful spicy smell of his aftershave, "are you okay?" Phoebe asked looking at me.

"Yes, sorry," I gave myself a shake, "what happened next?"

"Well Dom took the compliment and said the horse had just been a bit off because he was still a bit stiff after the one day event and," Phoebe gave a small laugh, "this part was genius, he said the horse was freaked by the wooden judging box! He said the dressage judge always sits in a car at horse trials and it was the first time the horse had seen one of the wooden hut things! He even made a joke and said he was going to invest in a garden shed."

"Wow! I wish I'd been there to see his face," I laughed.

Phoebe checked her watch, "I've got to go."

"Alright, good luck. I'll hang about here to help you get ready for cross country," I said.

We watched Phoebe ride away towards the showjumping. Suddenly she was joined by Dom as he emerged, riding from the line of parked horseboxes and trailers. Pierre pulled the field glasses out of his pocket, "When you know what to look for, you can tell it's a different horse." he said.

"It also explains the super- fast tack changes," I added, "I wonder where his little helper is."

"I was thinking something similar," said Pierre, "you hang on here and I'll nip over to his lorry."

Before I could object, he was gone.

I stood on the ramp and peered into the lines of parked trailers and horseboxes but there were too many. I sighed and sat down on the ramp to wait, with my flask of coffee and a chocolate bar.

Phoebe arrived back in a whirl of excitement. "Hell, some of those fillers!"

"I know, real rider frighteners," I laughed, "how did you do?"

"Clear, just. I really rattled the last fence-,"

"That flimsy little gate thing?" I asked.

"That's the one. I was convinced it had gone but somehow it stayed in place," Phoebe laughed with relief, "it's ages since I had such a precarious round. I hope he's more careful out there." Phoebe nodded towards the cross-country course.

"I know exactly what you mean," I put an over-girth over Phoebe's saddle, "I think me, and Skye hit every pole on every jump!"

Phoebe tightened her body protector and pulled her number back over her head. Treasure stood patiently while Phoebe used the ramp as a mounting block then I walked with her towards the cross-country course.

I watched her canter calmly towards the practice fence. "What are the chances that Chantelle and 'Zeusy' will look anything like that?" I turned to see Henry standing behind me with Marc.

"Oh, hi!" I gave Henry a hug, "where is she? She isn't on her own, is she?" I panicked.

"No, don't worry," Marc reassured me, "Klaus turned up to watch so he's supervising her in the collecting ring for her dressage test."

"So, we escaped for a bit to watch some of the cross-country," Henry added.

"Klaus? I didn't think he considered horse trials civilised enough to grace them with his presence!" I laughed.

Henry rubbed his thumb and two fingers together, "Money. He was judging the dressage in one of the classes this morning, he probably hung around for the fancy lunch."

"There's Phoebes going to the starting box," Marc pointed down the hill.

Treasure leapt out of the box and flew over the first fence before disappearing from view. We hurried from our vantage point towards another spot where we could see several more fences.

Phoebe and Treasure were making the challenging course look like a walk in the park. They were meeting each fence on a near perfect stride; until the water complex. Treasure took a huge leap over the log into the water, meaning that he was much closer to the second element, the serpent on the island in the middle of the water. His massive jump had clearly taken Phoebe by surprise and though she managed to regain her balance, her now soaking reins slid through her fingers and Treasure plunged straight past the second element and out of the ornamental lake. Phoebe quickly gathered up the long lines of slippery leather and guided Treasure back into the water and over an alternative, much longer, route.

"Dam, that's blown it!" I said, feeling for my friend, "they were doing so well."

The rest of their round was far less slick and controlled as Phoebe struggled to control Treasure's speed and keep a balanced rhythmical pace as her wet reins were effectively useless, offering no grip as they slipped through her hands.

We hurried to wait for her at the finish. Once she was safely through the flags she sat up and tried desperately to slow down the horse who was fighting his rider to control the situation. Marc and Henry rushed after her, and as

343

Phoebe did her best to slow Treasure by altering their balance and circling, they put their pincer movement into action and intercepted her as we had seen them previously take control of Zeus and Chantelle.

Treasure was snorting and blowing, his veins standing out against his wet glistening skin.

"Thanks guys!" she was bright red and gasping for breath, but smiling, "I thought I was going for a swim at the water!" Phoebe laughed as jumped off while Treasure was still walking, being led by Marc and Henry.

"So, did we," joked Henry, "we had our cameras ready!"

Phoebe punched him half-heartedly on the arm, "you are such a cock!"

"I try my best," Henry replied proudly.

"Come on, let's get you both back," I said following Marc who had taken temporary control of Treasure.

"Listen, I'll follow you in a minute, I just want to watch someone," Henry called after us.

Phoebe stopped walking and turned around, "Who?" she asked with a scowl.

"No one special, just hoping I can see someone get through the water without a lead rein or a life- boat."

Phoebe stuck her tongue out and hurried to catch up myself and Marc.

"Where's Henry?" asked Marc looking around when we reached our horsebox, "has he gone to help Chantelle?"

"He erm, said he wanted to watch someone," Phoebe mumbled.

"Who?" Marc looked at her.

Phoebe shrugged and disappeared inside the bib with her number to avoid any further questions from Marc.

He turned his attention to me, "Who's he watching?"

I busied myself swapping Treasures bridle for a headcollar, "I honestly don't know. I think he wants to see a few riders so he can give Chantelle some final pointers," I bluffed. It wasn't altogether a lie; I genuinely didn't know who Henry wanted to see and I was sure he would have some extra tips for Chantelle after watching a few more riders.

"Hmph," Marc wasn't convinced, "can you manage without me?"

"Yes. Of course. Thanks for your help…" Phoebe began but Marc had gone.

Pierre returned while Phoebe was changing her clothes and I was bandaging some special leg cooling gel over Treasure's tendons to prevent any risk of injury.

"You're right, he's definitely got two horses here." Pierre said, following me as I moved around Treasure, bandaging each leg in turn, "and there's someone in the horsebox."

"What did you see?" asked Phoebe, re-joining us now that she had changed out of her wet riding clothes.

"Not much to be fair," said Pierre, "the ramp was up so I couldn't see inside but I could hear a horse moving about inside while Dom was still out on the cross-country. There was someone in the living as well. The door was locked but I definitely saw someone moving around."

"What should we do?" I asked.

Pierre shrugged, "Not much we can do at this stage. It's not against the rules to have a second horse as a travelling companion and some people would argue it is common sense to lock everything and to lift the ramp if you have a horse left unattended."

"But he rode a different horse in the dressage and pretended it was the same horse he was jumping!" Phoebe protested.

"Our word against his, the stewards didn't notice anything."

"That's because the stewards at each phase act in isolation," I grumbled.

"So that's it then, Dom's going to continue cheating and riding ringers and there's nothing we can do about it. It's not bloody fair!" Phoebe threw the protective boots Treasure had worn for cross-country into a tack box with such force that the horse leapt back in alarm.

"Steady on!" I jumped out of the way to avoid being kicked.

"Sorry Abi."

"Let's not give up. He's bound to make a mistake and when he does…" Pierre tried to reassure us.

"I suppose," I agreed reluctantly as I stood up and stretched my back, "There you go Phoebes, all done."

"Thanks Abi. Look there goes Chantelle. She must be going to show jump," Phoebe pointed. Chantelle was being escorted by Marc and Henry on either side and her parents following on behind; she looked like one of the riders being taken to the start of the Grand National. Zeus was bouncing and jogging between his escorts.

"He's almost doing piaffe," I commented as we watched the procession.

"Shall we go and watch?" Phoebe asked.

"If we take a slight detour," said Pierre, "we can pass Dom's lorry and we might see what's going on inside. Surely, he'll drop the ramp to untack and sort out his horse."

Fate was against us; by the time we had negotiated the lines of vehicles, avoided horses and messengers on quad bikes not to mention the seemingly hundreds of people who wanted to stop and say a few words to Pierre, (almost entirely female I noted) Dom had dealt with his horse and the ramp was firmly back in place.

"Dam." Pierre was furious.

"Never mind," I said," you said yourself there isn't much we can do, in fact if we tackle him or report him today it will only make him more careful."

Chapter 43

Chantelle and Zeus stormed around the showjumping. She definitely had more control than at her first event, but it was still nerve wracking to watch. She sat, or perched, and simply steered allowing the horse to make his own decisions about striding and take off.

"She doesn't help him much, does she?" I whispered to Phoebe.

"Probably safer this way. Oo shit, that was close!" Phoebe gasped as Chantelle swung Zeus around a corner and into a blue and yellow jump. The poles bounced as the horse flew over the fence but luckily, they landed back in the supporting cups.

She wasn't so lucky at the next jump; a double built from black and green striped poles. As Zeus charged towards the combination, his attention was on the last jump, a multi coloured fence with a rainbow shaped filler sitting under the poles, rather than the green combination. His lack of attention caused him to get too close, or too deep, before taking off for the first part of the double; consequently, he tipped the top pole off. Hitting the plastic rail refocused his attention, slightly but without any help from his rider he ploughed through the second element sending poles flying.

As the arena team of pony club volunteers leapt into action to rebuild the jump, Chantelle pointed Zeus at the rainbow fence. Sensing that she might be in trouble, Chantelle gave Zeus, who was actually already preparing to take off, an almighty, and unexpected, kick. The horse responded and leapt into the air, tucking his legs up tightly. As he landed Chantelle was propelled up his neck towards his ears, but she hung on and managed to wriggle back into the saddle.

"Well done darling, well done!" Margaret shouted from the side of the arena.

The commentator congratulated Chantelle on managing to remain on board before announcing that she had acquired eight faults as a result of hitting both parts of the double.

Margaret turned to Marc, who was standing between herself and Phoebe, with her pen poised over the event programme. "Now do explain the penalty thingy please."

"Basically, the less penalties the better," said Marc. He sounded distracted and I followed his gaze to where Henry was leading Chantelle away from the collecting ring. Walking beside Henry was another man who looked vaguely familiar; and Dom.

"Excuse me, I'll see you for the cross-country," said Marc as he hurried through the crowd after the retreating back of Henry.

"Wait up," called Pierre as he also followed the small group surrounding Chantelle.

Margaret sighed and fell into step between Phoebe and me as we followed more slowly. "Well that doesn't help. I mean I'm not stupid!"

"Of course, you're not stupid. What don't you understand?" Phoebe asked kindly.

Margaret smiled, "The man with the microphone said Chantelle and Zeusy had eight faults."

"That's right," Phoebe confirmed.

"Oh." Margaret stopped walking and considered this for a moment. "Ah!" she continued, it seemed that she had just experienced a light bulb moment of understanding, "so she gets a bad point-,"

"A penalty," I said.

"Yes, a penalty," Margaret corrected herself, "she gets a penalty for every stick she knocks off!"

"Stick?" Phoebe mouthed at me looking puzzled.

"She means pole," I mouthed back.

"No-," Phoebe began.

348

"What about the flowerpots and the pictures? Oh, and what about the wings, is that what you call the bits that the sticks are balanced on?" Margaret interrupted her.

"Yes, the sticks, sorry, the poles are supported between wings-," Phoebe tried again.

"You see, I'm learning," Margaret beamed as we continued towards a vantage point where we could see the cross-country course. This wasn't as straightforward as it should have been as Margaret shared her daughter's lack of concern for her own safety and self- preservation. She was oblivious to the horses tied up at the side of trailers and horseboxes, and also of those being ridden between the vehicles. Somehow, Phoebe and I managed to prevent her being trampled, kicked or ran over by horses or quad bikes.

"Now, as I was saying, these penalties," Margaret emphasized the word, "does she get one for each stick she knocks off and do you get the same amount of penalties if you break the pictures or the wings and what happens if the flowerpots fall over?"

"No. It doesn't work like that…" Phoebe tried to explain again and then she stopped to process what Margaret had said, "pictures?" Phoebe looked at me for help.

"No idea!" I said.

Margaret looked at both of us as if we were mad and stopped walking. "The pictures. Under the sticks."

"Fillers!" Phoebe and I both realised at the same time.

"I'll get some coffee," I said, leaving Phoebe to explain that regardless of the degree of devastation four penalties are given for each jump knocked over, assuming the horse and rider don't completely part company.

"Who's that with Henry, down at the start?" I asked Phoebe.

She squinted into the distance, "Not sure… I can see James and Marc just off to one side and I think I can see Pierre right over near the starting official."

349

"Yes, but right beside Henry. There, that bloke who has just jumped out of the way to avoid being trampled by Zeus," I persisted.

"Oh yes, I see who you mean."

"Who is he?" I continued.

"Dunno. He looks vaguely familiar… but from here I couldn't say. Looks like he knows Dom though."

"What do you mean?" I asked, shielding my eyes with my hand.

"I think that third person down there, on the other side of Zeus is Dom."

"Oh, she's started!" Margaret shouted, "come on Chantelle!"

"There, now the horse has gone and the three of them are left, that's definitely Dom down there with them," Phoebe said.

"I wonder what he's up to. I hope he isn't trying to sell James another horse!" I muttered.

We stood with Margaret and watched until Chantelle was out of sight. Do you want to go over to the finish Margaret?" I asked.

Henry and Marc were already hurrying towards the end of the course with James.

"No pet, I think I'll just wait here then meet them all where the horses come back to the trailers," Margaret said.

We waited with her and kept up with Chantelle's progress via the loud-speaker public address system. She was flying around the course and had cleared each obstacle so far. However, as in the showjumping, too much speed meant that she was unable to gather Zeus together and they galloped straight past a narrow fence at the bottom of a hill. She circled around and had more success at her second attempt.

By the time we had followed Margaret back to the Thompson's car and trailer, Chantelle's band of supporters had untacked and cooled down Zeus. Chantelle was recording the activity and updating her various social media accounts. "I think I'll start a vlog," she said to me, "I can post videos and inspire up and coming riders."

"Oh," was all I could think of saying.

"That's a wonderful idea sweetheart," Margaret enthused, "you could become an influencer and get sponsorship!"

Phoebe turned away, shaking her head, "She thinks the jumps are made of sticks and pictures but this terminology she understands. Come on, let's check the results board. I'm fairly sure we are both out of the running but I'm curious to see if Dom placed."

The results indeed showed that neither Phoebe nor I had been placed but Dom was first in his section. We watched as he posed, grinning for a photograph as he received his rosettes and prize from the event organiser. Afterwards he seemed to melt into the crowd and disappear.

"He's like a bloody phantom." I said.

"I wish he was a phantom," Phoebe laughed, "then we could call in an exorcist to sort the bugger out!"

My phone beeped.

"Who's that from?" Phoebe asked, as she watched me read the text.

"Pierre," I tried to control the grin spreading across my face, "he wants to know if I want to share that bottle of wine and have a takeaway tonight."

"You're getting cosy," she teased.

"Oh, you're welcome to join us."

"No, it's alright. I think I'll go back to the flat and pack. I'll move in tomorrow rather than tonight if that's okay."

"That's settled then is it?" I asked.

"Yeah, I want to give you and Pierre some privacy, I'll come tomorrow instead," Phoebe confirmed, missing the point I was trying to make.

I had to confess that I was looking forward to having some company; and if, correction *when*, things came to a head regarding Hannah, the extra money would be a help.

351

Threading our way back to my horsebox we literally bumped into Marc. He was hurrying through the lines of vehicles with his head down, clearly distraught.

"Hey, are you okay? What's happened?" I asked catching his arm.

"Nothing, nothing," he shook his head and tried to look away, "I'm fine."

"No, you're not," I said.

Phoebe gave him a tissue, "It's clean," she assured him.

Although this made him laugh for a brief moment, the laughter soon dissolved into a strangled sob.

"I'm sorry…" Marc was obviously upset and embarrassed that we were witnessing his distress.

"Come on," Phoebe directed him towards my horsebox. She sat him on the steps, "Sit there and take deep breaths. In through the nose and out through the mouth. There we are. Now what on earth has happened?"

"Has someone died?" I asked cautiously.

Marc shook his head, "No, at least not in the literal sense."

He began to cry again, and we had to wait until he had regained enough of his composure for him to tell us what had caused his breakdown.

"You know I've thought for some time that Henry was… was seeing someone else?"

"Yes, and you know that we all-," I began but Marc put up his hand and I stopped talking.

"It's no use Abi. He's been so secretive, slipping off without telling me. Lying about working late or meetings… oh all sorts of excuses. He must think I'm stupid."

"But how can you be sure that he was lying?" Phoebe asked.

Marc sighed and accepted another tissue, "The shower. Every time he came back from wherever he claimed to be, it was obvious he had just taken a shower. I mean who has a shower in a traffic jam?"

Phoebe and I exchanged glances.

352

"Then today he was deep in conversation with that bloke, David." Marc practically spat out the name. "He didn't introduce me, and Henry always introduces me to people. But I recognised him from the dressage at the Academy. The two of them were thick as thieves that night too."

"Of course, the Academy," said Phoebe, "I knew I'd seen him somewhere before!"

"He works there according to Pierre," Marc sniffed, "anyway, all day I've seen Henry sneaking off to have little chats with his new friend."

I thought back and realised that I had seen David and Henry chatting on several occasions, I hadn't read anything into it because Dom had often been close by too.

"I'm sure he's married, with kids," I tried to reassure Marc, but he ignored me and continued.

"And then, just as they were all loading Zeus, Henry got a load of text messages and he was so excited each time he read one. When I asked what they were he said they were just Facebook notifications, but he wouldn't show me," Marc took a deep breath, "then, just now he said he was going to the loo before we went home and I... I followed him. He didn't go to the loo; he went to make a phone call. I heard him! 'Stop texting' he said, and he was laughing!" Marc looked at the shocked expressions on our faces.

"It gets worse," he said, "'stop texting, Marc's getting suspicious.' Then he made arrangements to meet whoever he was talking to at the 'usual place' but half an hour earlier and that he would bring him up to speed about 'the situation' when they met!"

Phoebe enveloped Marc as he burst into body wracking sobs, "Wait 'til I get a hold of him, I'll-,"

"No, please don't say anything," Marc pleaded between gulps.

"But surely you can't just ignore this and let him get away with it!" Phoebe was indignant.

"I'll tackle him, but in my own time. I want to be rational and in control of the discussion."

"If you're sure," Phoebe said, "cos say the word and -."

"I'm sure, but thanks."

"Do you want a ride home with us?" I asked, "it'll give you time to…calm down… you know get over the sudden shock without being squashed into a car with Henry and the Thompsons."

"That would be amazing. Thank you," Marc climbed into the cab and Phoebe sent a non -comital text on his behalf explaining to Henry that we had simply kidnapped Marc.

The drive home was tense and because Marc was with us, we couldn't discuss Dom or his horse. Phoebe tried to lighten the mood by telling Marc that she was moving in as my housemate.

Chapter 44

"I didn't know if you wanted Indian or Chinese, so I brought pizza," Pierre held the large boxes out. "Great."

"I mean, everyone likes pizza, right?" he laughed nervously.

"I don't know about everyone, but I do."

I led the way into the kitchen.

"And I didn't know if you were a veggie, so I've brought a selection."

I looked at the stack of boxes and laughed, "I like meat, but I also eat vegetables. Shall we use plates or eat straight from the boxes?"

"I'm happy to eat picnic style, less washing up," said Pierre.

"Then follow me," I swept up the wine and two glasses before taking Pierre into the living room where the fire was crackling in the hearth. It was the beginning of June, but the evenings were still quite chilly. We sat on the floor with our backs against the sofa and the pizza boxes between us.

As we ate, we chatted about ordinary, mundane things; the state of the roads, the cost of bread in the village shop compared to *Tesco*, even the weather. He was easy to talk to and eventually I found myself telling him about to my decision to set up the stables as my post marriage fresh start."

I cleared away the empty boxes and we settled down in front of the fire to enjoy the wine. "It's a shame we didn't get some proof that would help sort out Dom," I mused.

"I know," Pierre slid his arm behind me like an awkward teenager, "I tried to sneak another look in his horsebox while he was at the prize giving, but no luck."

I smiled and settled into his embrace.

"Then I got caught up with the course builder; that bloke can talk for England! But I did stop off and I managed to have a word with Marilyn on my way home." he said.

"What did you tell her?" I asked.

"Not too much, I didn't want to scare her. I just said there had been reports of poachers in the area and suggested that she move Charlie until the police either catch them or they move on to a different area."

"Do you think she will, move him I mean?" I asked, enjoying the closeness.

"I don't know, but I feel better for saying something," he said, sipping his wine, "I'm sorry you didn't get placed today."

I shrugged, "Doesn't matter. We got home safely so that counts as a win."

"Good attitude, I'll drink to that," Pierre clinked glasses with me.

"But," I said, "you did miss all the drama."

"Oo, do tell."

"Are you laughing at me?"

"Mm. A little bit, but come on, tell me. What's the drama?"

I told Pierre about Marc's suspicions regarding Henry. Pierre sat up, "Oh hell, no it's all wrong!"

"I know, who'd have thought it. They seem, sorry seemed, so happy."

I was surprised that Pierre was so concerned, "I didn't realise you knew them so well."

"I don't. I mean I know them to chat to, pass the time of day, but I'm as certain as I can be that Henry isn't having an affair and most certainly not with David!" he laughed.

I leaned forward and put my glass on the coffee table, "How do you know?"

"Henry is seeing David, a couple of times a week as far as I know, but not romantically," Pierre leaned back again.

"Urgh. Is it just sex? Is Henry paying him to do dirty stuff that Marc won't?"

"What? No! At least not to my knowledge," Pierre leaned towards me and lowered his voice conspiratorially, "and from the conversations I've overheard, I don't think there's much off the table where those guys are concerned, if you know what I mean. Plus, David is happily married, to a woman."

"Well what is Henry up to?" I asked.

Pierre smirked. I punched his arm and laughed, "You have a filthy sense of humour! Now tell me."

"He's having riding lessons, and I mean horse riding!"

"No! He can't be... can he?" I gasped.

"Why not? He clearly loves horses and knows a fair bit about them. Why is it so odd that he would learn to ride? The only odd thing is why he hasn't told Marc."

I told Pierre about Henry and his accident, "Do you think I should tell Marc?" I asked.

Pierre shook his head, "No, Henry obviously has his reasons. We should respect his decision."

"If you're sure," I said uncertainly.

"I am, at least for now," he looked at his watch, "it's getting late, I'd better be making tracks."

"This was fun. We should do it again," I said.

"Or, perhaps I could take you out for dinner?" Pierre said as I walked with him to the door.

"What like on a proper date? I mean that sounds great, but only if... I mean I don't want you to feel-,"

"You over think things and you talk too much!" he said.

"Wha-,"

Before I could be indignant, he kissed me.

"That worked," he grinned, "just to warn you, I may need to do it again if I feel you are starting to over think things!"

357

I put my arms around his neck, "In that case it is only fair to point out that I love over thinking things and I never stop talk-,"

He kissed me again, "I did warn you!" he said with a warm smile that made his eyes twinkle.

I kissed him back, "It's a habit that might be hard to break."

"Challenge accepted," he murmured into my neck.

Chapter 45

If the strained atmosphere between Henry and Marc was anything to go by, Marc still hadn't confronted Henry and it was two days since the competition. Phoebe was riding Flame and I pushed Skye to match the other horse's long stride as we hacked through the village.

"How was your lesson this morning?" I asked.

"Amazing. Just thinking about it makes me all … fizzy!" she giggled.

"What do you mean?"

"Klaus! That guy has moves-."

"Stop! I do not want to hear. I meant your actual lesson, on Treasure. What did you work on?"

"Sitting trot and extension mainly," she smirked.

"Phoebe, I'm warning you!"

She laughed, "Sorry."

"Yeah, you sound it, "I slapped her good naturedly on the back with my whip, "you do know he's marrying Izzy in September, don't you?"

"Of course."

"And it doesn't bother you?" I asked.

"No, why should it? The cheating bastard's not marrying me. Come on, shall we trot?"

We arrived home in the middle of Marc and Henry having a huge row. They were in the tack- room but we could hear their voices across the yard.

"What the hell's going on?" Phoebe looked at me.

"I don't know, but it doesn't sound good."

I was wondering whether or not to ignore Pierre's advice when Henry stormed out of the tack-room. He got into his car and disappeared in a cloud of dust and gravel. We stood outside, one either side of the tack room door, with our arms full of tack.

"Do you think it's safe to go in?" Phoebe mouthed at me.

In reply, I shrugged," It seems very quiet."

"Too quiet. Why don't you go in?" Phoebe prompted.

"You go in," I retorted

Suddenly a voice behind me asked, "What's going on?" Phoebe and I both screamed.

"Bloody hell, Pierre! Where did you spring from? If I had a spare hand, I'd punch you," I shrieked.

"Sorry. I thought you'd heard me drive in. That was hilarious."

"What's going on?" asked a voice from the doorway.

Again, we both screamed as we spun around to see Marc in the doorway.

Pierre leaned against the wall clutching his sides with tears running down his cheeks.

"Oh, man! I think I've stumbled into a *Carry- On* film or something." Pierre gave up trying to control his hysterics and gave in to the laughter which developed from a chuckle to side splitting guffaws as he slid to the ground.

"Get up," I kicked him.

"You are such an arse," Phoebe snorted and turned away from him into the tack room. Marc followed her.

"Phoebe could you do me a favour?"

"Of course, what's up?"

"Please don't judge me, but I want to follow Henry."

"Okay, do you want me to come with you?"

"I'd like you to drive. He'd spot my car in a flash, besides we both came in his car so I'm sort of stranded here until he comes back."

"Don't worry, I'll get my keys."

"Where are they going?" Pierre asked.

"I have no idea. But I have a bad feeling," I said as I watched Phoebe and Marc drive out of the yard, "do you have time for a coffee?"

"Sorry, I was just driving past, saw you, and thought I'd drop in to say hi," he took a step towards me.

"Hi," I grinned, "should I overthink this visit?"

"If I remember correctly, the way to stop that annoying little habit was-,"

I didn't wait for him to finish but leaned in and kissed him.

"Cute move," said Pierre looking at the saddle I had transferred to his arms, "how did you do that?"

"Come on, I'll show you," I said leading him into the tack-room in what I hoped was a coquettish manner.

"God, I wish I could stay here," Pierre groaned.

"I wish you could stay here," I agreed.

"I've stayed too long already. I have a string of visits. Are we still on for dinner tonight?"

"Pick me up at seven. Unless you'd prefer me to meet you -."

"I'll be here at seven."

He gave me a final kiss and left.

I was still sitting in the tack room when Felicity arrived. "Was that Pierre I saw driving away?"

I nodded and turned to hang up my bridle in an attempt to hide the grin on my face.

Returning to the house I looked at my reflection in the mirror and I decided that a luxury girlie pamper session was in order before my date with Pierre.

It was my first date in ages. I had been on a few 'blind pity dates' organised by friends before I had moved to Northumberland, but this was the first time I had felt properly attracted to a man in a very long time.

I looked in the bathroom and even counting Phoebe's contribution I could only find cheap store brand discount shampoo and combined conditioner. I wanted, no I needed, some scented body lotion and shampoo to make my hair smell like a summer meadow I decided.

I picked up my purse and keys and set off to the village.

*****

The shop was opposite the Dirty Dog. It sold an array of basics from gin to air fresheners for your car and most things in between. I collected a basket and selected a range of hair products and bubble bath and I threw in a fancy body lotion just for good measure. I paused on my way to the check out and selected a bottle of red wine, just in case the body lotion has the desired effect I told myself, and a large bar of chocolate in case it didn't.

I was about to leave the shop when Phoebe came in looking very flustered.

"Hey, Phoebes."

"Oh Abi. Thank heavens. Wait here. I need to get some chocolate and a packet of tissues for Marc."

"You should have told Henry to pick them up," Jan said as she rang the purchases through the till, "he was in earlier buying champagne."

I looked around, hoping that Marc hadn't heard.

"Where's Marc?" I whispered.

"In my car. Crying."

"Well that explains the tissues," I said watching her pay, "what's going on?"

Phoebe sighed as we walked slowly towards her car, "This afternoon apparently, Henry suddenly said he needed to go back to work because he'd left something he needed, and before you ask it doesn't matter what, it just matters that Marc didn't believe him and they had a huge row. Marc accused Henry of lying and of shagging someone else, so Henry stormed off and Marc wanted to follow him, but Henry had the car…"

"So, you drove him in your car," I filled in the gap.

"Exactly, and all the way he was swinging between wanting to either apologise or confront him and end it all."

"Shit! Which did he decide on?" I asked, fearing the worst given that Marc was in Phoebe's car in floods of tears.

"Neither yet. We couldn't find him. We drove through the village; we even did a lap of places he might be in Alnwick. No sign of him."

I shuddered to think how fast she must have been driving and looked at Marc. He was a mess.

"I hope I don't live to regret this," I said opening the passenger door of Phoebe's car, "Marc, I think I might, might, know where Henry is."

"Seriously? Where?" Marc asked scrubbing his eyes with the back of his hand.

"I don't want to interfere, but it's dreadful, seeing you like this."

"Abi, you've got to tell me. Please, this is killing me!" Marc grabbed my hand.

"If I happened to drive somewhere, and you happened to follow me, and I didn't say anything would that count as me interfering?"

"Get in your car," Phoebe instructed.

I did as she told me and drove a few meters down the road before turning off the main street towards the Academy. I kept going and drove into the Academy car park where I pulled up; alongside Henry's car.

Phoebe parked behind me and got out of her car with Marc.

"What's going on? Why are we here?" Marc asked.

"Seriously, I don't know. But I think maybe you should just trust him," I said.

"How can I when I know he's lying to me."

"I've done too much," I said, "give him some time, it might not be what you think."

"You know something," Phoebe looked directly at me.

"I've told you; I don't know anything."

"But you have a good idea. Come on," she began pulling me out of the car.

"No, I don't want to. I want to go home," I wailed, "heavens you're strong. Ouch, alright, I'm coming!"

Against my will I found myself sandwiched between Marc and Phoebe as Marc led the way from the carpark to the stables.

"Where do you think he is?" Phoebe asked.

"Probably shagging that David bloke in one of these stables, or the hay store!" exclaimed Marc with a catch in his throat.

I stood awkwardly while Marc and Phoebe scurried around the yard, checking all of the possible places where they thought Henry might be having sex.

"I'm quite relieved I haven't found him," said Phoebe, "it's one thing watching people, strangers, have sex on the telly but I'm not sure how I'd react if it was someone I knew in real life. I mean what do you say, what's the etiquette? Do you interrupt them straight away or wait until they reach a certain point?"

"How the hell would I know!" I replied, "I'm going home."

"Oh, I don't think so. How did you know he would be here?" she asked.

"A lucky guess and to be fair we haven't found him, just his car!"

Marc came back from checking the stables. "No luck, come on, I want to check the indoor school."

"Really?" Phoebe sounded surprised, "isn't that a bit exposed?"

"I was actually thinking they might be in the café." Marc said.

I put my hand on his arm, "Don't worry, she applies her own sexual boundaries, or lack of them, to other people."

"I can't say I'm surprised," Marc whispered as he set off towards the indoor school.

I grabbed his arm, "Stop, you can't just charge in, someone might be having a lesson. If you are determined to go in at least use the side door."

"Or better still the fire door." said Phoebe triumphantly, "Come on!"

She led the way around the side of the building to where a fire door was slightly ajar.

"Someone's going to be in trouble, this shouldn't be open," I muttered following Marc and Phoebe.

The door opened into a space behind the tiers of layered seating. We crept through and crouched down behind the seats. We could hear the voice of someone instructing.

"Stop looking down. Are there five pond notes on the floor or something?"

We pressed ourselves against the wall as the shadow of a horse went past and the rhythmical sound of hooves cantering on the dusty surface thudded by.

"Okay, bring him again and don't let him get too deep to the fence."

We couldn't see, but we could hear the horse canter with a steady thump.

"Shorten him, make him use his hocks, more come on!"

The rhythm altered and sounded bouncier before the sound stopped altogether for a moment as the horse took off over the jump before landing. "Good, now remember to ride him away, straight. Better, much better. Give him a long rein and catch your breath while I change this around."

"That's that bloody David!" Marc hissed.

"How did that feel?" we heard David ask the rider.

"Great. Much more balanced. I can't thank you enough. I feel like me again."

Phoebe began to speak, "That's -."

"Henry!" Marc went to stand up, ready to confront Henry and demand some answers.

"Please, wait," I begged him, "he must have a reason for keeping this a secret."

"Have you told Marc yet?" David asked.

Marc froze and we all held our breath.

"Not yet."

"For fucks sake man! You said you were going to say something on Sunday. Are you having second thoughts?"

"No, I just wanted to be sure," Henry answered.

Marc stood up, "Please!" I implored.

"And are you sure?" we heard David ask.

"Yeah, I'm certain. I've got a bottle of champagne in the car. I'm going to do it tonight. I can't wait."

"Well let's give this another go but on the other rein, remember balance the horse as you come around the corner and don't let him get long and flat, keep him short and bouncy."

Marc stumbled out of the building and we followed. I peeped back inside and saw Henry riding a large grey thoroughbred horse towards a jump. I watched as he cantered around the arena, popping over the three jumps which I could now see.

Marc was ashen, all colour had drained from his face. "That's it then. He's going to dump me tonight."

"It didn't sound like that to me," I said.

"You heard them. David asked if he'd told me and asked if he was having second thoughts."

"He also said he had a bottle of champagne," I pointed out.

"That's probably to share with his new lover," Marc said miserably as he turned away from the arena and headed back towards the car park.

*****

"What are you going to wear?" Phoebe asked. She was sitting on the end of my bed, watching me put my make up on.

"I'm not sure, 'cos I don't know where we're going. There, how's that?"

"Good, not too much but enough to show you've made an effort," said Phoebe, approvingly.

"Thanks, I think."

366

Phoebe picked up the body lotion I had bought earlier. She unscrewed the lid and gave it a sniff, "This is nice, may I?" She squeezed a sample onto her arm.

"So, is this where we do the stereo type thing where you try on everything and despair because you have nothing to wear and once all of your clothes are piled on the floor you resort to a cashmere sweater and tight- jeans?" she asked.

"Not something I was planning to do, if I'm honest. To begin with I've never owned anything cashmere and all my jeans, tight or otherwise, are in the wash."

"Oh," Phoebe sounded disappointed.

"I was thinking about my black trousers."

"Not very fancy," Phoebe was still hankering after recreating a scene from every romantic fiction she had ever read.

"We are going for a meal; I'll be sitting down," I insisted.

"I suppose. What top?"

"That is where I am uncertain." I held up a silky black top with skinny shoe- string straps.

"Too much black."

"How about this?" I showed her a cream blouse, "maybe with a jacket?"

"Nope, you'd look like you were going for an interview, plus splashage."

"'Splashage'?"

"Mm. Splashage. You might be going for an Italian, nothing more off putting than pasta sauce splashage," Phoebe waved her hands over the area of her chest most in danger of the dreaded 'splashage'.

She got up off the bed and went to my wardrobe, "What about this?" She held up a dark teal coloured top. It was silky to the touch but with long loose sleeves and the wrap around style created a v shaped neckline.

"That was going to be my third choice!"

*****

367

Dinner was not Italian. We drove to a small country pub, about twenty minutes from Stonecross. Outside there were tables with closed up umbrellas and overhead heaters. "It's lovely to sit here when the weather is nicer," Pierre said, "you get a fabulous view across towards the Cheviots."

The sound of laughter and convivial conversation drifted out of the windows into the air, becoming momentarily louder as a door opened and closed. Pierre led me towards the front door, which he held open for me. Inside there was a polished wooden floor and the low beams were festooned with old horse brasses and pieces of tack, there was even an old side saddle balanced on one of the beams. The stone walls were decorated with hunting prints and delicate lanterns illuminated the ornaments and equine memorabilia which sat on crowded window ledges. Fairy lights were entwined around the higher beams and small candles burned in jars on each of the tables. The bar was full, and a round - faced, woman waved as we came through the door.

She waited until we had jostled our way through the crowd, then led us to a table. "I've put you here, it's a bit more intimate," she smiled before handing each of us a menu and taking a drinks order, "the specials are on the board above the bar."

"Thanks, Mel. This place is an absolute hidden gem." Pierre assured me as Mel left to get our drinks.

"Is this your local?" I asked.

"Used to be. Before I moved to the practice at Stonecross, I worked out of a surgery about half an hour further on. I still try to come back when I can. Special occasions and the like."

I smiled and hoped this counted as special occasion, "What do you recommend? Everything sounds delicious."

"I confess, I have tried most things on the menu, several of them more than once, but I do have a weakness for the scallop starter."

"That's a good enough recommendation, that's what I'll start with."

"Good choice," said Mel as she placed our drinks down, "Pierre?"

"I'll have the same, followed by the rack of lamb."

She wrote down his order then looked at me with her pen poised, "I think I'll try the chicken in white wine please."

"Excellent, give me a wave if you want more drinks."

"Are you sure I can't tempt you with a dessert?" Mel asked as she cleared away our empty plates.

Pierre leaned back in his seat, "Sorry but I will absolutely burst if I eat another thing."

"Same, I think I've broken a rib I've eaten so much," I groaned, "which is such a shame as I had my eye on the cheesecake."

"Don't worry, you can try it next time, can't she." Mel grinned at Pierre.

I blushed.

"She certainly can," he smiled, "but for now, just two coffees please."

Pierre reached across the table and gently took my fingers and entwined them with his own.

"I've had a lovely evening," I said.

"Me too."

We drank our coffee, slowly.

"I hate to be a kill joy, but we are closing." said Mel putting our bill down on the table.

I looked around and realised that the pub had emptied, apart from ours, the tables had all been cleared and reset.

"Gosh I'm sorry," Pierre released my hand and we both stood up.

I reached for the bill. "What do you think you're doing?" Pierre snatched it away and handed it back to Mel with his credit card.

"At least let me pay half, you bought the pizzas and the wine."

"I asked you out. No arguing."

"But-." he stopped me talking with a kiss.

"It's ready for your pin number." Mel interrupted.

Pierre tapped his number into the machine and slid a ten pond note into Mel's hand. "For you, not the tip jar, I'm really sorry we kept you so late."

Mel tucked the money into her pocket and winked at Pierre, "Thanks. See you both soon."

Once outside I continued to protest. "You could at least have let me leave the tip."

"Okay, next time you pay. Happy?"

"Oh, so there's going to be a next time is there?" inwardly I cringed at the corniness of the line.

"What do you think," Pierre said flatly before he kissed me again.

We kissed for a long time, standing in the deserted carpark under the starry night sky. Eventually I began to tremble. "What's wrong? Are you okay?" Pierre looked at me with concern.

"I'm just a bit chilly," I shivered.

"Oh, of course you are. Didn't you bring a jacket?"

"No, I didn't think…"

"Come on, you can have mine, it's in the back of the car."

He took my hand and led me to his car. "Here it is, excuse the junk," Pierre handed me his coat and I shrugged my way into it while he scrambled around picking up the bits of plastic tube and empty wrappers which had spilled out of the car onto the ground.

"What's this?" I asked picking up a flat plastic device.

Pierre closed the back door and opened the passenger door for me, "What's what?" he asked settling into the driver's seat.

I held up the unfamiliar item.

"Oh," Pierre took the small object out of my hands, "it's a micro-chip scanner. Correction, a broken micro-chip scanner." He gave it a shake to demonstrate an odd rattling sound before throwing it over his shoulder onto the back seat, "I need to get a new one from the surgery in the morning."

"What happened to it, or is it a victim of the back seat?"

Pierre glanced at the mess in the back of his car and laughed, "Surprisingly, no. A horse didn't want his microchip to be checked and the short version is the horse stood on the scanner and now the scanner is broken."

"That's a shame," I said as Pierre drove us out of the carpark and headed towards home.

"Mm. It's okay though, I just need to remember to pick a new one up before I head out tomorrow."

"Yeah, but if it wasn't broken, we could have used it tonight."

"Really? That sounds different." He raised an eyebrow and smirked suggestively.

"Idiot! Keep your eyes on the road. I didn't mean to use on me."

"Pity."

I laughed, "Stop it! I'm being serious."

"Believe me, so am I."

I chose to ignore the comment, "I meant, we could check to see if Secret, Hannah's horse, has a microchip."

"That's a good point actually. I could drop round tomorrow, if you like," Pierre reached across and took my hand in his.

I squeezed his hand, "I like."

"Good night?" Phoebe asked when I finally said goodnight to Pierre and locked the door. She was in the kitchen, wearing a onesie in the style of a unicorn, waiting for the microwave to heat a mug of hot chocolate.

"Yes thanks."

"Where did you go?" she asked, carefully taking her drink.

"It was called The Horse and Hounds. I've never been before."

371

"Was it on one of those little back roads, past Rothbury?" Phoebe asked.

I nodded.

"I've heard the food is great there," said Phoebe.

"Mm. It was lovely."

Phoebe blew to cool her drink down, "Are we still talking about the food?"

Chapter 46

Phoebe had already turned out and mucked out our horses by the time I made an appearance on the yard the following morning. "Good afternoon!" she greeted me with a smile.

"Sorry! You should have given me a shout."

"Don't worry, I thought you deserved a lie in. I wasn't sure how tired you might be."

I rolled my eyes and followed her to the barn where a pile of empty nets were waiting to be filled.

"I've done Felicity's horses, she sent a text asking if she could have them on full livery today, she confused her dates and had to take her car for a service or something, and Hannah is off for a lesson."

"This early? How long did I sleep?"

"She was driving out at about half seven, eight-ish. Interestingly, she hasn't plaited up. Oh, did you hear, Henry and Marc have made up," she added.

"Brilliant. How do you know?"

"Marc texted me, I forgot to say last night. Apparently, Henry had candles and rose petals all over their house and he told Marc that he's been having riding lessons for the last couple of months. He hadn't wanted to say anything because he didn't want Marc to worry, or to get his hopes up. He said it took the pressure off him if no one knew. Anyway, they'll tell you all about it later."

"I'm so glad they've sorted it out."

"Marc said he didn't mention that we had been to the Academy yesterday and I promised we wouldn't say anything."

"Of course," I agreed.

We continued to fill the haynets and wash out the feed buckets while we chatted about my date with Pierre and I told Phoebe about the plan to scan Hannah's horse.

"That's a good idea."

"Why is Eric in? Does Izzy have a lesson?" I asked.

"Farrier I think."

"And here are the Thompsons," I nodded towards the gates as James drove in.

"Hi Abi!" James waved, "I'm just leaving our Chantelle to muck out and everything. She's going to hold Eric for the farrier as a favour to Izzy, I'll be back in a bit; I have to drive Margaret to the hairdresser."

"Okay, bye," we both waved.

"The dirty little minx, I know what 'everything' means," Phoebe snorted.

"I don't," I said, "what am I missing?"

"Really? Brad and Chantelle? She's been shagging him since the ball. Her parents would have a fit if they knew!"

"Brad? And Chantelle?" I remembered the episode I had unwittingly witnessed through the kitchen window at Stonecross Hall, "urgh. I think I need a coffee to get over that news!"

"And cake. I've heard cake is good for shock," Phoebe linked her arm through mine.

Before we could get as far as coffee and cake in my kitchen, Marc and Henry arrived. They crossed the yard together; they were both positively glowing.

"Good morning," I greeted them.

"It is a good morning." Marc linked his arm through Henry's and the pair exchanged a look which was full of so much love that Phoebe felt compelled to comment, "Hey, enough of this loving couple shit. Stop rubbing your successful relationship in the face of us singletons!"

"Singleton's plural?" Henry looked at me, "I have it on good authority that one of you is enjoying the delights of our gorgeous new vet."

"How on earth…?" I looked at Phoebe.

She held her hands up, "Nothing to do with me, I swear."

"And you," Henry turned his attention to Phoebe, "I don't know about relationship, but you're getting your quota of German sausage."

Phoebe gasped.

Marc and Henry laughed but Henry tapped the side of his nose and refused to be drawn on the source of his knowledge. He did, however, tell us about his secret riding lessons.

"I'd tried to get back in the saddle before," he explained, "I mean, everyone says 'get straight back on after a fall' don't they? But it didn't work for me. I felt like I was doing it for other people, not for me. People expected me to brush myself down and get on with it."

"I'm so sorry," Marc squeezed Henry's arm.

"I've told you; I don't mean you. You couldn't have been more supportive, but in a way, I can't explain, that almost made things worse, I felt I was letting everyone down, especially you."

"So, what changed?" I asked anxious not to let the mood become down beat.

"To be honest, it was Chantelle. When I saw her bouncing around having so much fun on that crazy horse of hers, I began to feel, not jealous but… oh I can't explain. It was as if I was waking up. Anyway, when we did the course walk at Stonecross, I began to see the sport through her eyes. I had such a blast helping her… that's when I realised, I wanted to start riding again, for me, no-one else. Then at the ball I got chatting to Steve and Camilla and they suggested I drop round and have a potter on one of the school horses."

"And that's where you've been going?" I asked, anxious to clarify the situation.

"Yes. I didn't mention it because I didn't want anyone to get their hopes up for me. For all I knew I would have a panic attack or discover I no longer enjoyed actually riding."

"I still think you should have told me. I was so worried," Marc said.

"I know and I'm sorry. I shouldn't have put you through that. But the good news is that after having several lessons a week either with Cam or David, riding all shapes and sizes of horses, I am now ready to start horse shopping again," Henry said.

Marc stood beside him beaming, "Can we reserve one of the empty boxes please Abi?"

"Of course, you can."

"Oh, I'm so happy for both of you!" Phoebe burst out, hugging both Henry and Marc in turn.

"Have you found a horse? What are you looking for?"

"I don't know if I'll compete again, especially at the level I was at, but hey, never say never. I've got my eye on a couple, but I haven't been to try any. Yet"

"But," said Marc, "we thought it would be a good idea to reserve a stable. Just in case. I mean we'll pay from today to make sure you don't lose out if someone else wants it."

"Don't worry about that. The stable is yours."

After more excited hugs, Marc and Henry headed off to muck out their ponies and I went indoors with Phoebe for coffee and cake.

We were still eating cake to celebrate the fact that Marc and Henry had sorted things out when they left. Before driving away, Henry came over to the house and shouted through the window, "Do you fancy getting together for a drink at the Dog tonight?"

Phoebe gave a thumbs up through the glass.

"I'll text the others!" he waved before leaving.

Phoebe gave another, thumbs up.

"What was that last bit?" I asked.

"No idea. But here's Pierre. Are you inviting him tonight?"

"I'll mention it..." I said.

"Is everything okay? I thought you had a brilliant night out."

"We did. It's just…"

"Just what? Come on Abi, spit it out the bloke's out of his car already."

"Nothing. It's nothing. We'll talk later." I said.

True to his word Pierre arrived armed with a microchip scanner.

"Hannah isn't here," I said.

"Good," Pierre waved the scanner, "let's get started."

"And neither is her horse," I added.

"Less good." Pierre stopped waving the device, "where's she gone?"

"No idea. She said it was a lesson, but we know what that usually means," Phoebe said.

"Of course," Pierre looked at his watch, "well that throws a spanner in the works. I wonder how long she'll be."

"Can you wait until she gets back?" I asked Pierre.

"I wish," he said taking my hand, "but I am supposed to be working."

"Oh, get a room!" Phoebe reminded us she was still there. Taking the scanner, she asked, "Are these hard to use?"

"Not at all. I could show you both and leave the scanner with you, then come back later to pick it up," Pierre suggested.

"Good idea, then we can scan Secret when Hannah brings him back."

"Can you take a microchip out?" I asked taking the scanner from Phoebe and turning it over in my hands.

"Not without leaving a fucking massive scar!" Pierre said, "but you can sometimes render them unreadable with magnets."

*****

"They're really easy to use," Pierre assured us both before giving me and Phoebe a quick lesson in how to turn on the device. We just need the horse to keep still while we locate

377

the chip. They sometimes move away from the spot where they're inserted."

Eric was still waiting patiently for Brad to arrive. Chantelle was in the tea- room re-applying her make up.

"Come on, I'm sure Eric will oblige for a minute. Quickly while no one is looking." Pierre ushered us into the stable.

"I'll grab a head collar," said Phoebe.

Eric was glad of the company and stood obligingly while Pierre demonstrated.

"Keep close to his neck and move the scanner in a small circular motion. Make sure you keep this button held down while you are scanning."

We watched before trying for ourselves.

"If nothing shows, it's worth checking both sides." Pierre said, "And remember that it doesn't become law for a horse born before 30th June 2009 to be chipped until October. Of course, any animal born after that date should be microchipped either by six months of age or the last day of December in the year of birth, whichever is later."

"I don't know how old Secret is," I said quietly.

"Here's Eric's chip." Pierre showed us how to read the information on the scanner before we slipped out of the stable.

"Should we write down the information from the display?" I asked.

"Or take a picture?" Phoebe added, "so we can pass the information to you later."

"No need. This scanner saves the information so you can read it again later. It sits on a little memory card until you either delete the information or the card fills, then it starts to over- ride itself."

"Like a dashcam in a car, or the CCTV at the pub?" Phoebe checked.

Pierre nodded, "Exactly the same. Now I must go."

"A few of us are going to the pub tonight, Marc and Henry are celebrating the fact that Henry's got his mojo back… if you fancy coming…?" I said to Pierre.

"Sounds great. But I'm on call."

"Oh," My face fell, and I couldn't keep the disappointment out of my voice.

"But," he continued, "I was going to suggest meeting you there."

"Oh," this time I smiled as I spoke.

"In fact, I could give you both a lift home if you like. Just to collect the scanner you understand."

"I think she understands" Phoebe laughed, "but I accept the lift."

Chapter 47

"Isn't she back yet?" Phoebe asked looking out of the window.

I turned the scanner over in my hands, "I really wanted to check that horse today."

"There's time yet. In fact, here she is," said Phoebe.

I looked up as Hannah drove into the yard in the usual small hire box.

"I think I'll go and ask if she's coming to the pub," I said.

"Oh Abi, why would you do that?"

"Well for one thing it's a nice thing to do, and for another, I might get an idea of how long she's going to hang about," I said.

"Okay then. I suppose."

"Is that Brad, just leaving now? How long does it take to shoe one horse?" I asked as I watched his small van driving away.

"Which reminds me," Phoebe added, "I'm going to go over the tea- room with some bleach in the morning. Just in case."

"I don't think you need to worry. Unless Chantelle's trailer was the only vehicle affected by a very localised gale of wind about half an hour ago, I think the tea-room is safe." I reassured her with a shudder, "are you off to work?"

"Yeah, I'm working an early shift, I'll be finished about half six, so I'll see you in the Dog later. I'll leave my car and pick it up tomorrow if I'm okay for a lift back with you and Pierre."

"Of course. I might see if I can grab a lift with someone to get there…"

"Good idea. Now, I'm off, I'll see you later."

"Phoebe," I called as she was about to go.

She turned to look at me as she pulled on her shoes, "Yeah?"

"Phoebes, it's ages since I was … you know, seeing someone…"

"Uh huh," she grinned at my obvious discomfort.

"How long would you say you should wait before… you know… sleeping with someone?"

"Sleeping? I dunno I have to be really serious before I let someone hear me snore," she teased.

"I will stop making cake," I threatened.

Phoebe laughed, "Okay, if you mean how long before having sex, well that depends. Are you taking the base of your timeline from when you meet someone or… how far into the date? It depends on all kinds of things: where you are, does the door have a lock, does he have a wife or a fiancée and if so where is she…?"

"Forget it. Go to work, it doesn't matter."

"I'm sorry," she laughed sounding anything but sorry, "I take it we are talking about you and Pierre."

I nodded.

"Oh," she became serious, "do you think he doesn't want to?"

"Quite the opposite. I know he wants to."

"So, what's the problem? Ah, you don't want to. I see. Well, don't let him push you into anything you feel uncomfortable about. No means no! I mean think of sex like a cup of tea, you might think you want one but then just before you drink it you decide you're not thirsty after all. You can change your mind and decide not to drink that tea at any point you want!"

I was beginning to feel rather confused, but Phoebe continued, "And if you did decide you didn't want the cup of tea, you would never sit back and happily allow someone to pour the scalding liquid into your mouth and force you to drink it just because earlier you thought you were thirsty and might quite like a cup of-."

381

I stopped her, "Aside from the fact that I prefer coffee, I think I understand the complicated metaphor you are trying to deliver, so you can get off your soap box. No one is forcing me, I'm just a bit nervous."

"Nervous? About what?"

"You know…" I shuffled awkwardly, "I haven't been with many people and I haven't had any visitors, down there," I looked down to emphasise my point, "for a long time. For all I know it's healed up, there are probably cobwebs …"

Phoebe burst out laughing, "You are making a shag sound like a scene from Raiders of the Lost Ark. Tell Pierre to wear his head torch. I'm sure it will be fine. Do you want me to crash somewhere else tonight?"

"No, of course not."

"Stop overthinking things. When it's the right time, you'll know."

I decided that Phoebe was probably right, I should stop overthinking things. Even so, I decided, it wouldn't hurt to shave my legs again and tidy things up a bit, just in case.

*****

I fed the horses and settled them down before heading to the shower. Hannah had finally gone home but Felicity was waiting for Romeo to finish his feed and Izzy was still pottering about. She seemed to be quite friendly with Hannah so I didn't want to risk being seen scanning Secret; Hannah always made such a big deal about ensuring no one but her ever touched him, Izzy would be bound to comment if she saw me.

"I thought he'd never finish eating!" Felicity said. I was collecting the empty buckets from my own horses when she spoke, "thing is, if I just leave him to it, I don't know if he's eaten his painkillers and tablet or tipped it into his bed."

"Pity we can't explain how expensive those little pills are," I agreed with her, "but he definitely ate the pill for his

Cushings, I fed it to him myself; I didn't expect to see you today."

"I told Phoebe I'd pop up with their carrots. It's good news about Henry isn't it?" Felicity said as she carefully wiped Romeo's bucket.

"I know, I was starting to worry about those two."

"Are you coming down to the Dirty Dog?" she asked.

"Yeah, it should be a good night."

"Do you want a lift?" Felicity offered jangling her keys.

I hesitated, looking to see if I could gauge how long Izzy would be. Felicity misunderstood my hesitation, "don't worry the car passed its MOT."

"Oh, it's not that," I assured her.

"Or were you waiting to get a lift from someone else?" Felicity winked, "okay, I don't blame you. I'll see you later." She hurried across the yard to her car and tooted a good-bye as she left.

I felt the scanner in my pocket and decided to give Izzy another ten minutes. I went back indoors and watched from the kitchen. If she hadn't left by the time the ten minutes were up, I decided, then I would set my alarm clock and get up early to check Secret's microchip in the morning. Or I could even do it when we got back from the pub later tonight.

I was about to give up when Izzy finally left.

I grinned to myself. I wasn't sure why it was so important to me that I was the one to scan Secret. Perhaps it was because so far Phoebe had managed to do so much. She had been the one to take the risk and hide in the horsebox and put all the pieces of the puzzle together so far. Maybe, deep down I felt that I wanted to prove something and do my bit. Afterwards, I might even phone Pierre and ask him for a lift to the pub. I smiled at my own daring; Phoebe must be rubbing off on me, I thought.

I pulled on a jacket and my boots before sliding the scanner into my pocket. The door clicked shut behind me and I hurried to the stables.

"Good boy." I crooned to Secret. "I just want to see if you have a little chip, the size of a grain of rice in this beautiful neck of yours."

He was surprised at the late visit from me, but once he'd established that I had no treats, he ignored me and concentrated on his haynet.

I unfasted the neck cover on his rug and rolled it back. "It's too hot for this, isn't it, eh?" I wondered about getting a head collar and tying him up, but he was quite relaxed and happily pulling at his haynet, so I pulled out the scanner and set to work.

Remembering Pierre's demonstration, I kept the scanner close to the horse's neck and moved it in slow circles. I was beginning to wonder if I should try the other side of his neck when the device in my hand suddenly lit up and made a sharp beeping noise.

The horse jumped at the sudden high- pitched sound. "It's okay," I reassured him as I checked the small screen, "I'm all done. Now let's get you ready for bed again."

I put the scanner carefully into my pocket and pulled the zip closed before replacing Secret's neck cover. I reached over the half door and pulled open the bolt before stepping outside. The moment I set foot through the door I felt an incredible force under my jaw, forcing my head upwards and sending me backwards into the stable.

Everything went black before I even hit the ground.

Chapter 48

There was a lively atmosphere in the Dirty Dog. Jan from the shop was sitting with Paul the electrician and Tom the builder was leaning on the bar with his son, both enjoying pints of local ale. James and Margaret were sitting on a bench seat in the window, with Hannah perched on the end, Marc was at the head of the table to Hannah's left. Then next around the table was Henry, facing those in the window. Chantelle was balanced on a stool at the bar sipping lemonade, topped up with vodka from a flask in her bag. Tucked in beside her was Brad.

"Where's Abi?" Henry asked as Phoebe pulled a stool from a nearby table.

"I don't know, I've texted but she hasn't answered," said Phoebe sitting down next to him.

Henry wrinkled his brow, "Do you think everything's alright?"

Phoebe looked around the pub then whispered to Henry, "Pierre isn't here either."

"Oh, do you think they're together, as in 'together' together?" Henry nudged Phoebe and winked.

"Let's just say that based on a conversation I had with Abi earlier, I wouldn't rule it out."

"Hi everyone!" Felicity called as she made her way across the crowded bar, "can I get anyone a drink?"

"I'll help you," Phoebe offered, "Henry pull that other stool over for Felicity."

"Did you see Abi before you left?" Phoebe asked.

Felicity nodded, "I offered her a lift, but I think she was waiting for a visit from the vet."

"I thought as much. Hey, Andrew! I'm dying of thirst down here. Shall I come and serve myself?" Phoebe called down the length of the busy bar.

"Hold on, I'll be with you in a sec."

"Have you told Hannah yet?" Marc asked Henry.

"Told me what?" Hannah put down the gin and tonic she was sipping.

"Well, nothing's been decided yet, but it's possible that you and I might, just might become pony twins!" Henry declared.

"What do you mean?" Hannah asked slowly.

"I am very interested in the black gelding Dom has been eventing," Henry explained, "I had a chat with Dom on Sunday and I, sorry we," he smiled at Marc before continuing, "we, went over this morning to have a proper look."

"Oh, he is such a pretty horse, just like your boy," Margaret turned to Hannah, "you'll have to make sure they have different colour blankets and things, or we won't be able to tell them apart, proper peas in a pod they are."

Hannah ignored Margaret, "You've been to see this horse, where? At Dominic's yard?" she pressed Henry, "when? Have you ridden it?"

"We didn't go to his yard," Henry confessed, "apparently Dom doesn't have very good trial facilities, so he drove the horse to the Academy, and we used the indoor school."

"Today? You definitely rode this horse today?" Hannah was quite insistent.

"Yes," Henry said slowly with a smile, "today, at the Academy."

"Did you jump?" Hannah persisted.

"Just a little cross pole. Dom thought it was best for me to just try him on the flat, because I'm just getting my confidence. But I liked him, he just floats, so…"

Hannah leaned forward, "So?" she prompted.

386

"So tomorrow we're going over to Dom's yard and if the vet gives the horse the thumbs up…"

"Oh, this is so exciting! James, I think this calls for something special."

"I'm one step ahead of you my peach," he stood up and made his way to the bar.

Hannah leapt up and grabbed her bag, "Excuse me."

She pushed past Marc, rocking the table and causing drinks to splash out of their glasses onto the table. She continued to elbow her way towards the door, pulling out her phone as she went.

"What's up with her?" asked Marc, mopping up the spilt drinks with a pile of tissues which Margaret had produced from her bag.

"I don't know but she's giving someone serious grief on the phone," said Henry, "I can see her in the carpark."

"She's furious," Marc gasped, "I'm glad I'm not the one she's screaming at. Boy, what a temper!"

"Do you think she's been stood up?" Henry asked.

"What makes you say that?" Marc asked.

"Not sure, but I thought I caught something about meeting her…" Henry said, straining at the window.

"I wonder if she kisses her mother with that mouth! Goodness me!" Margaret turned away, shocked.

"Oh, she's off!" Henry announced as Hannah sped out of the carpark.

At the bar, James intercepted Felicity and Phoebe ordering drinks, "Two bottles of Moet and some glasses please Andrew."

"Oo, is that for our table?" Felicity asked.

"It certainly is. To celebrate with the boys in style. Margaret didn't think gin and tonic was special enough."

It took a while for Andrew to complete the drinks order before he was able to get the champagne for James.

"I wouldn't have given you the night off if I'd known it was going to be this busy," he grumbled to Phoebe, "I don't suppose I can tempt you to jump back here and lend a hand."

"No chance. But I will go and find a couple of ice buckets for James and I will even fill them with ice cubes."

"Here we are everyone," Phoebe put the two ice buckets down, "Thank you, James. Cheers."

"Yes, thank you, this is so kind," everyone echoed.

"It's a pleasure," James blushed as he popped open the first bottle and poured out a glass of champagne for everyone. "To Henry and Marc!" James proposed.

Everyone echoed the toast.

"And to their new horse!" Margaret announced.

Again, everyone echoed the toast.

"We haven't decided to buy him yet," Henry said with a note of caution.

"I know," Marc raised his glass, "to Henry and his mo-jo, may they never be parted again!"

"Hi everyone, I'm guessing this is the fun table."

"Pierre! Come and sit down, join us in the naughty corner!" Margaret giggled.

"Yes, come and have a glass of champagne," James invited.

"I'd love one but I'm on call so I can't drink I'm afraid. I'm just going to grab a coke then I'll be right back."

"So, no Abi," Pierre said looking around the table.

"No, she isn't here yet," said Phoebe, "I've been texting her, but she hasn't answered any of my messages. What time did you leave her? Is she following?"

"What do you mean? I haven't seen her since I saw both of you earlier, you know when I dropped off the 'thing'. I thought she was getting a lift with one of you guys."

"I thought she was waiting for you," said Felicity winking at Pierre.

"No," said Pierre blushing, "we agreed to meet here, 'cos I'm on call. I'll text her."

"Are you and Abi…?" James asked, "well that calls for more champagne."

"We can't have a proper celebration until she gets here," Margaret cautioned James, "and what about Hannah? Is she coming back?"

"Oh yeah, where's she gone to?" asked Phoebe.

"Didn't you see her storm out?" Margaret asked.

"No, what happened?" Phoebe put down her glass with a growing sense of unease.

"Well we were just hearing about a lovely horse that Henry is going to buy," Margaret began.

"Might be buying," Henry interrupted.

"Might be buying," Margaret corrected with a smile, "but you said you liked him when you rode him this morning."

"Well… yes I did. Actually, Pierre, I've arranged for someone from your practice to come and give the horse a provisional inspection tomorrow, is it you?"

"Er, I don't know yet, I'll get my list of visits tomorrow. But you were saying about Hannah…"

"Yes," Margaret picked up the story again, "Henry was saying how they might be pony twins and suddenly, poof she was off and in such a temper!"

"Help me out here Marc," Pierre looked between him and Henry, "twins?"

Marc laughed, "Yes, Henry is interested in the dark gelding that Dom has been eventing. I mean he's asking a lot of money, but wow, can that horse move, and we've seen him jump. He really is the whole package. He could even show, he moves so straight…"

"Anyway," Margaret took control of the conversation again, "Henry was explaining how much he'd enjoyed riding the horse at the Academy, Dom hasn't got an arena you know. We actually viewed Shadow at the Academy didn't we James?"

"Yes, Dominic very kindly met us there with the horse in his wagon. As he pointed out, it showed the horse was good to travel."

"What?" Pierre began to stand up.

Phoebe looked at him, "Why did this make Hannah take off?" she asked.

"No idea," Marc confirmed, "she just stormed out, spilling drinks everywhere."

"But we think she might have been stood up," Margaret added.

"I might have pressed myself into the window to listen when she was screaming at someone on the phone," Henry confessed, "she yelled something about meeting and, cover your ears Margaret," Marc stretched across and shielded Margaret's ears before Henry continued, "we heard her yelling, 'you'd better fucking be there or that's it! but with a lot more swearing and venom!"

"Then she jumped into her car and was away!" Margaret concluded the story.

"Phoebe, can I have a word with you please."

"Yes. Back in a sec," Phoebe stood up and followed Pierre outside, "I have a really bad feeling."

"Me too, jump in," said Pierre unlocking his car.

Chapter 49

"Her car's still there!" Phoebe shouted, running towards the house, "Abi! Abi!"

"I'll head over to the barn and the stables; you check the house," Pierre called.

Phoebe raced through the house checking each room and shouting as she went.

"Phoebe!" Pierre yelled, "Phoebe out here. I've found her."

Phoebe ran across the yard, following the sound of Pierre's frantic shouting, "In here!"

Pierre was on his knees in Shadow's stable.

"Oh my God! Is, is she…?"

"She's breathing. I've phoned an ambulance. I wonder what the hell went on here."

I blinked my eyes open, trying to make sense of my surroundings. I was cold and I had a strange plastic mask over my nose and mouth.

"Just leave that there for a minute pet," I struggled to identify the speaker, "there now, that's better, nice to have you back with us."

Slowly a pair of blue gloves swam into focus and I was able to see that the speaker was a man wearing a green uniform.

"My name's Keith and you've had a bit of an accident love, so we're taking you down to Cramlington so they can have a little look at you in the hospital. Okay? Do you understand?"

I nodded, slowly as a band tightened around my arm for a moment or two.

"Alright then let's take this off," Keith said gently removing the mask.

"Now, can you tell me your name pet?"

Satisfied that I knew who I was and where I was going, Keith shone a little torch into my eyes and monitored my blood pressure as the ambulance took us to the new emergency hospital in Cramlington.

Phoebe was sitting behind Keith, white faced and tear stained, "Pierre's following in his car. There was only room for one of us."

*****

"You took quite a blow to your jaw," said the Doctor, referring to my notes which he had on a clip board, "but fortunately nothing seems to be broken. Have you any idea what it was that hit you?"

"None at all," I said.

I could see Pierre and Phoebe hovering behind the Doctor.

Phoebe snorted," I'm willing to bet I know what, or should I say who, happened!"

The Doctor turned towards her, still holding my notes, "Were you there?"

"No, but it doesn't take a brain surgeon to work out who it was, does it."

The Doctor smiled, "Ah, that'll be it then, I'm not a brain surgeon."

Phoebe scowled at him.

He turned back to me and scribbled something onto the sheets of paper on his clip board. "But as your x-rays are clear, I'm happy to let you go home, assuming you have someone to stay with you."

"Yes, she has someone," Pierre said from behind the Doctor.

His sentiment was echoed by Phoebe, "So, is that it then, she can go?"

"I don't see why not," the Doctor turned back to me, "we'll sort you out with some pain meds and anti-inflammatories to

392

go home with. I'll be sending your x-rays over to the maxillofacial unit at Newcastle. They'll contact you within three days if they think there's anything we've missed, but I'm happy that you've got away with nothing more serious than a nasty bruise. You're lucky you landed on something soft. If you'd hit a hard surface when you went down, this would be an entirely different scenario. I'm sure the police will want to talk to you."

He handed the clip board to the nurse who was waiting at the foot of the bed, "Can you sort out the painkillers?"

"Of course," she tucked the board under her arm and left the small examination room.

"Good-bye. Take care of yourself," the Doctor shook my hand and followed the nurse.

"Back in a second," Phoebe followed the Doctor.

"You gave us such a fright!" Pierre took my hand, "have you any idea who did this to you?"

"I didn't see anyone. One minute I was standing in the doorway, the next I was in the ambulance."

"Shadow's gone," he said flatly.

"What do you mean?"

"We found you in his stable. The door was open, and you were lying, spark out. Thank God for the deep shavings."

Before we could say anymore the nurse returned with the drugs, which the Doctor had prescribed, in a white paper bag. She handed it to me with a card, "If you develop any of these symptoms, feel unwell or are worried there's a number here."

Pierre took the card and put it into his pocket before escorting me out of the room. Phoebe caught up with us as we reached the doors.

"What were you up to?" Pierre asked her.

She smiled and held up a business card, "I think it's just common sense to be friends with a Doctor."

Pierre drove the three of us home. "I'll sleep on your sofa," he announced when we got back.

"Thank you but there's really no need," I said as I kicked off my shoes.

"I disagree. Phoebe's car is still at the pub, and while I'm sure you will be absolutely fine, I would feel happier to be here. Phoebe I can take you to collect your car in the morning."

"But aren't you on call?" I pointed out.

"I phoned and explained that I was having a personal emergency, so someone has taken over for me."

"Okay, if you're sure," I was too tired to argue.

"I'm going to check the horses and see what's what out there," Phoebe told us as she switched her shoes for her yard boots.

"Let me come with you," Pierre began to put his own boots back on.

"No, someone should stay with Abi," Phoebe insisted.

"Then you stay here and let me go."

"Stop playing Alpha male. I can look after myself."

"But-." Pierre began.

"How are your ribs?" Phoebe reminded him of the episode a few nights previous when we had mistaken him for an attacker.

"I'll be fine," I insisted, "please both of you go, I need to know if Shadow was taken, or if he's wandering about in the dark."

They set off, armed with a torch, towards the stables and fields.

I watched from the kitchen as their torches bobbed towards the buildings. I could track the progress of their inspection as the lights in the barn, stables and other buildings were turned on for a few minutes casting a harsh glare in the midst of an otherwise dark landscape. The torches disappeared as Pierre and Phoebe left the stables in favour of the fields.

"Should you be drinking?" Pierre asked as I greeted them with a glass of wine.

"It's the first I've had all night and I feel that I deserve a drink. Besides, if I do have a funny turn Phoebe can phone her new friend."

Phoebe accepted her glass, "If you don't want yours Pierre..."

"No, I think I'll be fine. I'm not the one who has been to hospital after being rendered unconscious because of a bang to the head," Pierre took his glass.

"It was a blow to my lower jaw actually, not my head."

"I think boxers call it a drop upper cut," Phoebe added.

"Oh well, if we know the name that makes it all fine then doesn't it! I give up," Pierre took a slug of wine.

"Anyway, Shadow has definitely gone," Phoebe said sitting down.

"Shit! We need to phone the police. That's it, I'll lose all my customers when they hear that a horse has been stolen."

"I phoned the police when we found you," Phoebe explained, "someone's coming to take a statement tomorrow."

"Do they know a horse has been stolen? We should phone them so they can start searching. Are the other horses okay? Oh, and Hannah; I should phone her! What'll I say?" I panicked.

"Calm down, they are all fine and I fancy Hannah already knows," Phoebe said calmly.

"What do you mean?" I asked, still panicking.

"Her stuff, it's all gone. Tack, grooming kit, rugs...the lot," Phoebe explained.

"But how? Why?"

"Something spooked her, that's for sure," Pierre added.

"My head's spinning," I said, "and it's not the wine, it's a different kind of spinning. I'm confused about everything that's happened."

"It's a pity you didn't get the chance to scan the horse before you were knocked out," Phoebe said.

"Oh, but I did! I forgot about it in all the mayhem. I was on my way out of the stable when I was attacked. The scanner's in my coat pocket, unless whoever bashed me has stolen it."

Pierre put down his wine and hurried to retrieve the scanner.

"I just need to upload this serial number and check it against the information on the data base… Can I borrow your laptop?" He carefully removed the tiny memory card from the handheld device and slotted it into the computer.

"Oh, my goodness!" Pierre exclaimed.

"What is it?"

"The horse has been stolen alright, but not from here. Look."

Pierre showed us the information which proved that the horse registered to the number on Secret's microchip had been reported as stolen about five months earlier from an address in the South of England.

"We've got to tell the police now!" I cried.

"I agree, and I'll have to alert the surgery before they are contacted by someone wanting to know why this particular chip has been scanned here in Northumberland by one of our machines," said Pierre, "but it can wait a few hours. We all need some sleep."

"I agree. Goodnight all," yawned Phoebe.

"This isn't quite how I imagined it would be the first time you slept here," I said as I handed Pierre a bundle of blankets.

"So, you have imagined it then?" he laughed as I blushed.

"Are you sure you'll be okay down here?"

"I'll be fine. You need to rest. And I don't want you to think I'm taking advantage of you."

"I wouldn't think anything of the sort. I just mean you might be more comfortable … not on the sofa. I promise I'll keep my hands off you and just go to sleep," I assured him.

"You have no idea how tempting that sounds, but you obviously have more self-control than me." He kissed me gently before turning me and pointing me towards bed, "Goodnight, I'll see you in the morning."

Chapter 50

My jaw ached and a purple patch of bruising was spreading up towards my cheek.

"Ouch, that looks sore," Phoebe winced when I joined her in the kitchen.

"It feels sore," I tried to smile before swallowing some painkillers.

"You'll probably have a million text messages when you turn your phone on. I did!"

I closed my eyes.

"What am I going to tell people? You know how rumours spread," I groaned.

"Already on it. When people couldn't reach you, they texted me, so the story is: Hannah took advantage of everyone being away from the yard and did a flit because she owes you livery money."

"That bit's true," I interrupted, "but how do I explain this?" I gingerly touched my swollen jaw, "or explain why I didn't turn up last night?"

"Again, I've gone for damage limitation. Personally, I think Hannah, or possibly Dom was your mystery assailant but, we don't want them to know how much we know."

"Simplify please, my head hurts. And where's Pierre?"

"Pierre's at work, he said he'd call or text later on. As for your injury, if Dom or Hannah suspect that we know about the stolen horse and everything else they'll get rid of any evidence and, what's the expression, 'go to ground'?"

"Okay, so what do we say to that lot out there?" I asked.

"You were mugged."

"What? Where?"

"At the cash machine in Alnwick. That will explain why the police are here and stop the liveries worrying that it isn't safe here," Phoebe calmly explained.

"Impressive. What about Hannah?" I asked.

"Why don't you phone her? Say you thought she must be out for another early lesson but since all of her stuff is gone…"

*****

"I tried several times to phone Hannah and each time her phone went to voice mail," I explained to the policeman who was sitting in my kitchen drinking tea and enjoying a large slice of fruit cake. "I've left messages and sent texts," I showed my phone to the policeman.

"It does appear likely that your suspicions are correct, and this lady has packed up and left without giving notice of her intention, possibly because she owes you money," he agreed.

"Are you going to arrest her? She gave a false address; I've checked it on Google maps," I didn't add that I had checked it because I had planned to go around and confront her.

"I'm sorry, but this is a civil matter. It isn't a criminal offence to not pay your bills, unless its council tax or income tax, television or road tax where non- payment is a specific offence."

"You have got to be kidding!" I exclaimed.

"Sorry," he shrugged, "you can pursue the money she owes through the small claims court…"

"But what about me being attacked? I was left for dead!"

"That was unfortunate and I'm sure the experience was very unsettling, but…"

I snorted, "But?"

"But," he continued, "there is no evidence to suggest who your attacker was."

"But it's obvious!" I cried.

He shrugged again, "There is no actual evidence, no matter how circumstantial."

"What about the stolen horse?"

"That is another matter which we will look into. However, as you were given specific instructions by the owner not to interfere with the animal…"

"Stop right there," I replaced the lid on the cake tin, "the contract all my liveries sign, points out that regardless of prior agreements, I have the right to intervene if I believe it is in the interests of safety or animal welfare. And as the horse is more than likely stolen, she isn't the owner!"

"Okay, well anyway, I'll drop by the vet's and have a word there. In the meantime, here's a crime number and feel free to contact me on this number if you think of anything else." He underlined a telephone number and wrote his personal identification number on a card which he left on the table.

*****

"He's bloody useless. We should ask for a different policeman!" Phoebe cried, "and he's eaten most of the cake! It's obvious, even to a blind man on a galloping horse at midnight, that you were attacked by Hannah. Or Dom!"

"I think you're right. But I can't understand why."

"I was wondering about that, I think you were just in the wrong place at the wrong time; she was trying to get away, quickly," Phoebe picked at the crumbs and remaining bits of cake which had crumbled across the bottom of the tin.

"Yesterday, Hannah was away with Secret really early. Usually her 'lessons'," Phoebe made the sign of quotation marks with her fingers in the air, "coincide with a competition, the horse comes back with a mane that has clearly been plaited blah blah. But yesterday there wasn't a competition-."

400

"Do you think she really had a lesson?" I interrupted, replacing the meagre remains of the cake with a packet of biscuits.

"No, I think she took the horse to Dom, then I think he loaded it into his own wagon and drove to the Academy where Henry rode it, thinking it was the horse he had seen Dom eventing. I mean we know it sort of was or is the same horse, but the horse Henry tried has only done the dressage phase."

"Why bother? I mean why not just take the horse Dom already has at his yard?" I asked.

"Henry and Marc would notice the difference in the quality of the horse's flat work. Henry had already asked why the horse was so different at the Academy's dressage competition. I'm sure Dom wouldn't have gone that night if he had known we were all going to be there. It was important that the horse Henry tried out had fabulous paces."

"Gosh what a risk."

"I think Hannah panicked when she realised that the potential buyer who had ridden Secret or Syd was Henry. That's why she freaked and left the pub in such a hurry and why she was so angry. I think she was furious that Dom was prepared to shit on his, or to be more precise her, own doorstep," Phoebe continued.

"Surely whoever fell for their scam would soon realise that the horse wasn't the amazing eventer they had paid for and come back asking questions!"

"Dom would probably blame the new owner and their riding ability, or point to changes made to the horse's regime, different tack surroundings and so on," Phoebe listed the excuses she imagined Dom would use, " I'm guessing that Hannah realised Henry and Marc, armed with the videos they had taken on Sunday would realise it was a different horse and seeing Secret everyday they would soon put two and two together."

"But if this all happened in the pub last night, how did Hannah get the horse and all of her stuff out of here so quickly?" I asked.

"Dom. He was probably the person she was arguing with on the phone and rather than arranging to meet up with a date or someone who'd stood her up she was telling him to meet her here asap!"

"Wow. That does kind of make sense."

"I know!" Phoebe smiled smugly and sat back to enjoy a chocolate biscuit, "they might have taken the horse, then come back to empty all of her stuff from the tack room while we were at the hospital."

"Pity she didn't manage to muck out. Leaving that enormous bed without mucking it out and owing me money just adds insult to injury."

Chapter 51

"That was Pierre," I said, putting down my phone, "he's going to call by when he finishes work."

"That's unexpected," Phoebe managed to keep a straight face as she spoke.

"Guess where he is going later this afternoon? Dom's yard," I said without waiting for an answer.

"Oh, my life! Really? I wonder if he'll see Hannah or her horse."

"Do you think that's where she's gone?" I asked.

Phoebe nodded, "It's the first place I'd look. Why is Pierre going over there? Is he treating one of the mares? Dom does seem to cover them really early."

"No, it's a bit awkward actually. Henry arranged for a vet to go and look at the horse he's thinking about buying and the practice have sent Pierre."

"Now you mention it, Henry did say something yesterday, but it was right before we realised something was wrong and we came looking for you. Is that allowed, ethically I mean, since that is the practice who treat Dom's horses, don't they have to declare an interest or something."

"I'm sure we'll hear all about it when Pierre gets here," I said, "look, Henry and Marc are here."

I waved at them out of the kitchen window and they hurried over to the house.

"Sweetheart, these are for you," Marc pressed a bouquet of flowers into my arms before crushing me in a bear hug.

"Lilies! My favourites! How did you know?"

"A little bird called Phoebe," Henry tilted my chin towards the light, "crikey they planted you a good 'un."

"What did the police say?" asked Marc.

403

"Oh, you know," I tried to be vague, "they'll do their best but …"

"They're overstretched that's problem," said Henry, "anyway, we're here to cheer you up."

"Do you feel well enough for a little trip out?" Marc asked.

Henry drove slowly, negotiating each individual pothole on the track from the road to Dom's stable yard. "He needs to get some gravel in these bloody craters," Marc grumbled as we were thrown around in the car, "there's Pierre's car, park next to him, in front of the horsebox."

"What the hell are you two doing here?" Pierre hissed as Phoebe and me climbed out of the back of Henry's car, "are you fucking mad?"

"Hi Pierre!" Henry called across the car, "I hope it's alright that we brought the girls. We thought a little outing would cheer up Abi after her dreadful ordeal yesterday."

"Dreadful ordeal," Dom appeared from behind the horsebox, "what happened?"

"Afternoon Dominic; Abi was mugged at the cash point in Alnwick," Henry explained.

"Oh, no! Are you alright? What happened, did they hurt you?" he asked with concern.

"Look what they did to her," Henry continued indignantly.

"That looks nasty, what did the police say? You have told the police I presume?" Dom continued.

"Yes, I've told the police."

"And what did they say? Do they know who it was?"

"You didn't see who it was did you?" Henry answered for me, "and they knocked her clean out and just left her lying there so she can't even remember properly what happened, can you?"

"That's right," I agreed.

Dom came closer and examined my bruised jaw. "Bastards," he said is a low voice, whoever did this needs a good hiding." He held my gaze and stared deeply into my eyes, "I'll see to it myself if I ever find out who it was."

"And as if that wasn't bad enough," Marc continued, oblivious to the rising fury in Pierre's face, "when the girls got up this morning, they found that Hannah, do you remember Hannah? I think you met at the ball."

"Mm, maybe, what about her?"

"Well she's fucked off without saying a word to anyone. She didn't even muck out!" Marc explained, "no one knows where she's gone."

"Really?" There was the slightest hint of a twinkle in Dom's eyes.

"And, she owes Abi money!" Marc concluded.

The twinkle vanished, "What a bitch." Dom was still staring, it felt as if he was trying to read my thoughts.

"So, where's this horse?" Pierre stepped forward. His jaw was tense, and I could see him clenching and unclenching his fist by his side.

"This way," Dom answered, still gazing into my eyes.

"Come on then," breezed Henry, forcing Dom to tear his eyes away from me in order to lead us away from the cars.

"You have some lovely horses," Marc said, as Dom led us past the barn.

"Thanks. Mainly brood mares and youngsters. The guy you're interested in is down here."

Phoebe and I dropped a few paces behind the others as we followed Dom.

"I think Dominic has a thing for you," Phoebe whispered.

"He makes my skin crawl. What did you make of his comments?"

"Not sure," said Phoebe, "but did you see how furious Pierre was when Dom was staring into your eyes? I thought Pierre was going to punch him."

"Do you think Hannah is here?" I whispered looking around and trying hard to hide how pleased I found myself feeling after hearing Phoebe's comments about Pierre.

"I can't see her car, but that doesn't mean she isn't here somewhere," she whispered back.

"Come on, keep up," Marc called causing the small group to stop and wait.

"Here he is," Dom let the black gelding out of his stable, "Silverwood Obsydian, or Syd to his friends."

The gelding's coat glistened in the sunlight; his mane had recently been pulled to maintain a neat short line as had the top of his tail. Dom handed the horse to Henry to hold while he stripped off the gilded day rug which helped to preserve the quality of his coat. He stepped back to allow us to admire the animal before picking up a brush from a basket of grooming tools which was sitting by the stable door. He used the brush to remove an imaginary fleck of dust.

"Well, Pierre, what do you think, isn't he gorgeous," Henry beamed.

"Oh, enough about me, what about the horse?" joked Dom.

Pierre pursed his lips and pulled a pad out of his medical bag. He arranged a sheet of card beneath the second carbon page and filled in the date and the address of the stables. "Before we continue," he said, "I need to point out that Dominic is a client of ours so potentially there could be a conflict of interests. I am honour bound to recommend that before you make a purchase you get a second, independent opinion."

"You've never treated this guy, though have you? I usually just refer to your practice for the brood mares."

Marc and Henry looked at each other before they both nodded for Pierre to continue.

"If Secret has been brought here, where do you think he is?" Phoebe whispered.

"He'll be tucked away somewhere out of sight. They wouldn't dare take the risk of anyone recognising him today."

"Even with a rug, he would stand out if he was spotted in one of the fields…" Phoebe said slowly.

"The barn!" I said.

Phoebe nodded.

Pierre was completing a diagram, noting down any confirmation points including whorls; a patch of hair growing in the opposite direction of the rest of the hair. On an identification diagram such as this they were similar to fingerprints. "Okay, we'll take him into the stable to look at his eyesight, then I'll need to have him lunged or trotted up on a hard surface to check for lameness," Pierre explained, "if you are still happy, we need to tack him up, to check his wind and breathing. Is there somewhere we could take him for a good gallop?"

"There's the field behind the house, is that any good?" Dom offered.

"Perfect," Pierre nodded.

"Phoebe, I have a plan." I whispered.

Chapter 52

As expected, Syd passed each stage of the examination.

"I'll just tack him up then we can head over to the field," Dom moved a saddle from where it had been balanced against a bale of haylage. He hung it on the half door of the stable and picked up the bridle. Marc stroked the chestnut who was watching from his stable next door. "This guy has a lovely kind eye," he said.

"He's coming along nicely as a showjumper, I'm just taking it steady, don't want to over face him." Dom said as he took the saddle from the stable door.

As Dom was busy preparing the horse, Pierre quickly drew Henry to one side.

"What is it? Is there something wrong?" Henry asked.

"Do you trust me?" Pierre asked, keeping his voice low.

"What's going on?" Marc asked.

"There isn't time to explain, but please, I am begging you, do not buy this horse off this man."

"Why? Is something wrong with him?" Henry asked.

"Nothing I can write on a certificate based on any examination of this nature. Please, I will explain when I can. Just don't make any decision today."

Pierre moved away from Marc and Henry.

"Are you feeling okay?" he asked me.

"I'm fine. What were you saying to Henry?"

"I'll tell you later. What are you up to?" he asked looking closely at me.

"Nothing, why?"

"You've both got *that* look," he hissed.

"What look?" Phoebe asked innocently.

"She's got that look in her eye," Pierre glanced at me then back to Phoebe as he continued to whisper, "and you look…excited. I don't know how to explain. But I don't like it, it makes me nervous; whatever you're planning, don't do it!"

"Do you want to ride him, or shall I?" Dom asked Henry as he brought Syd out of the stable.

"You please. I haven't galloped in a wide- open space for a while and like an idiot I've forgotten my hat."

"No problem," Dom sprung onto the horse's back, "follow me."

We all followed Dom as he rode away from the stable towards the field behind his bungalow. As we reached the point where the track turned away from the stables, Phoebe and I peeled away from the group.

We ran, keeping close to the wall of the building until we reached the front of the barn. "If he's anywhere, he's got to be in here," I said.

"Come on then, we don't have much time."

It was naturally dark in the barn, and after the brilliant sunshine outside, it was even more difficult to see, and we had to waste several precious minutes for our eyes to adjust to the gloom.

The first half of the barn seemed to be a dumping ground. To the left of the doors a stack of old jumping wings were jumbled in a heap. Rusting jump cups and ropes spilled out of buckets or lay in dust covered piles alongside broken poles and old oil drums. A tractor and an assorted collection of farm machinery lay behind the wings. Half assembled motorbikes peeped out from beneath dust sheets and opposite them, on the other side of the barn behind a stack of haylage was an old car. The car was covered in cobwebs and a thick layer of dust.

Beyond the assorted detritus there were internal stable dividers; proof that someone had considered turning the space into an American Barn style of stable.

409

We crept over the rough earthen floor, picking our way over the broken ladders and old tyres towards the back of the barn and the partially constructed stables. A beam of sunlight through the open door provided some light to illuminate our way through the dark building, showing particles of dust dancing in the air.

The stables were piled high with rubbish; old mattresses, unwanted furniture, bales of straw with grass growing out of them, even some rusted bicycles and an old lawnmower.

As we ventured further into the gloom, I heard a familiar sound. I put my hand on Phoebe's arm.

"I can hear it." she whispered.

Somewhere in the darkness we could hear the sound of a horse munching hay. Phoebe pointed to the far corner. We followed the sound and discovered that not all the stables were filled with junk; two stables were inhabited.

One stable was home to a small chestnut pony. His net was empty, and he banged his door as we approached, anxious to be out. He put his ears flat back against his head and rolled his eye angrily in warning as we got closer. His neighbour was far more welcoming and familiar.

I put my hand out and stroked the dark head. "It's him, isn't it?" I said quietly.

"I think so," Phoebe shone her torch over the door, "what a fucking awful place to keep horses. Even you, you miserable bugger," she added to the grumpy pony who stretched towards us with his ears still back and his teeth bared.

"What should we do now?" I said to Phoebe.

"Yes, what are you going to do now?"

We spun around and saw a figure standing in the doorway. The sun cast the speaker into a silhouette, but the stance and the voice were familiar, it was clear that the person was Hannah.

"What does it take to make you keep your fucking nose out of other people's business?"

"Really Hannah," Phoebe flicked the screen of her phone and quickly tapped out a message as she spoke, "you might have knocked Abi out when you took her by surprise," she said into the darkness, "but there are two of us."

"And there are two of them," Hannah said with a smile.

She moved to one side and the two men who worked for Dom stepped out of the shadows.

I was aware of Phoebe moving slowly beside me. "Get ready, and at the first chance…"

I squeezed her arm to show I understood. She pushed me behind her and suddenly she flung open the door of the pony's stable. "Garn, whoop, get on!" she screamed. The pony leapt out of the stable towards her, but we pressed ourselves against the wall as the chestnut made a bid for freedom.

Excited by the sudden activity, Secret began to snort and stamp in his stable. He whinnied and plunged as his companion disappeared in a furious charge towards the doorway.

"Get them, you stupid fucking morons, and don't let that pony out!" Hannah screamed.

There was a moment of pandemonium as the men tried to block the pony's path, but they were wary of his teeth and in the darkness, they were reluctant to get too close.

"Quickly, let him out too!" Phoebe directed as she fumbled to find the bolts on the second stable.

The moment the door was open the black horse plunged after the pony, determined not to be left alone in the dismal darkness of the dusty barn. We ran behind him, shouting, screaming and chasing him on. He barged straight through the path of the first man, sending him reeling to the ground. As he fell, the man crashed into Hannah, knocking her into the broken sets of wings.

Finding himself, literally the last man standing, the second man stood in the doorway waving his arms. The pony hesitated and looked for another way out. I scrambled in the

411

darkness, searching for anything I could use to help our situation. My hand closed around a scrap of rope.

I flung it towards the pony and by good luck it caught him on his hind quarters. He squealed in fury and lashed out with both back legs. The pony's hooves connected with the man's chest, sending him through the doorway, where he landed in a crumpled heap. The black horse behind the pony retaliated; thinking the pony was kicking out at him Secret leant forward and bit the pony, hard on the neck.

The pony squealed and lashed out with its back hooves again. Now that the man, who had been kicked, was lying gasping in the doorway the larger horse followed the pony as it kicked and plunged in the darkness; shying at the shadows and screams which rang though the air.

Phoebe followed my example; she also found some rope which she swung above her head as we both yelled and hollered. It was too much for the horses who launched themselves through the doorway. Phoebe and I hurtled after them.

Suddenly I found myself crashing to the ground as a hand wrapped around my ankle and pulled me back into the barn. "Come here you nosey fucking bitch!" Hannah screamed.

As I hit the ground, the air was knocked out of my lungs and I gasped for breath. I tried to focus but my vision was blurred as spots of light danced before my eyes. I had a brief glimpse of Phoebe who had been grabbed from behind by the man who had fallen into Hannah but who had avoided being kicked. Phoebe was struggling and screaming but couldn't get away.

"Get your hands off her!" a voice cut through the screams.

Hannah let go of me and I felt someone lift me gently off the ground. I opened my eyes, expecting to see Pierre; instead I found myself being carried out of the gloom by Dom.

"I suggest you follow your own advice and get your hands off my girlfriend."

412

Dom set me on my feet and backed away, holding his hands up in mock surrender to Pierre.

"And you pal, put her down before I-," Henry didn't get the chance to finish his heroic demand. Phoebe threw herself forwards before flinging herself back with all of her might ensuring the back of her head hit the bridge of the man's nose. Instantly he screamed in pain and let her go as a crimson stream of blood gushed from his face. Henry rushed forward and put his arm around her. "What the hell is going on?" he asked.

"I have no idea," said Dom.

Marc was holding Syd who was becoming reacquainted with Secret, his travelling and competition companion. Henry looked around and spotted a headcollar hanging by one of the stables to the side of the barn, where the brood mares were watching the proceedings with great interest. He slipped the headcollar onto Secret.

"Why are there two of them?" he asked looking at the two horses.

"That is exactly what I would like to know."

The speaker was a tall dark -haired man. He was slim and his complexion suggested that he travelled or had recently been on holiday. He was wearing an expensive suit, over which he had on a dark waxed jacket. In the confusion with Hannah and the men, not to mention Secret and the angry pony, who still refused to be caught, no one had heard the three cars driving up the rutted track.

The man who had spoken, was accompanied by another man. He was slightly shorter than his companion and his fair hair was mainly hidden beneath a checked cap. He was dressed in a similar manner to the first man, but rather than a waxed jacket, he was wearing a dark blue windproof jacket with a logo embroidered onto the front. They were joined by a grey- haired woman. Like her male companions, she was smartly dressed in a pleated navy skirt and a blue quilted jacket which bore the same logo as the one on the man's jacket. She wore a Hermes scarf around her shoulders. They had been travelling in the third of the three cars with a police officer; the other two cars were police cars.

Hannah scrambled to her feet and looked around wildly for a means of escape.

"Let me introduce myself," the dark-haired man continued, "I represent the British Equestrian Federation. I don't make house calls, as a rule but as I was in the area, I thought I would tag along with my friends who are here to have a chat on behalf of British Eventing," he looked at the messy, weed infested yard, "this looks like quite a nice horse, why is it here?"

A woman wearing dark coloured jeans and a white shirt came forward with one of the police officers. "That is a question I'd love to have answered," she said flashing an identity card, "good afternoon, I'm with the National Crime Agency and my colleagues and I have a few questions which I think you sir," she looked at Dom," and you madam," she smiled brightly at Hannah, "might be able to answer."

"I know nothing about anything he's involved in!" Hannah shouted as two police officers moved towards her and the men who worked for Dom.

"Shut up!" Dom snarled at her before turning on his familiar charm, "I'll be happy to help in any way I can, Miss...?"

The woman turned her attention to Dom, "I am a National Intelligence Officer Dominic. There'll be plenty of time for us to chat. But, before we head over to the house, I think these lovely people would like to have a closer look at your horses which you have so kindly brought out into the sunshine for us. I presume these are the animals that are of interest to these good people, Pierre."

"That's right Jo," Pierre nodded.

"You won't mind if this lady and gentleman from British Eventing take some pictures of these lovely animals and have a little look at their microchips do you Dominic?"

In reply Dom simply glowered at the woman.

"Henry," Pierre said quietly, "would you mind giving Abi and Phoebe a lift home?"

"Of course, but won't they need to ask us some questions, I mean we are witnesses," Henry was enjoying the drama.

The lady from the NCA tuned away from Dom and lowered her voice, "We will need to speak to you sir, to all of you but not here and I think this could take quite a while. Are you okay? I can organise another ambulance," she looked at us.

"Another ambulance?" I asked.

In reply she indicated the man who had been kicked. He was still curled up on the ground whimpering.

"I say, is he alright?" the lady from British Eventing asked.

"He will be. Probably got a couple of broken ribs," Jo said, "I dare say that pony's been waiting for the chance to do that for a while. Don't waste your sympathy on him. But as I was saying, you two look as if you've had quite a traumatic experience."

For the first time I became aware of our appearance. I was bleeding from the grazes on my hands and face where Hannah had pulled me to the ground, and we were both filthy from the dust we had stirred up during the struggle to escape from the barn. Phoebe was covered in blood from the man whose nose she had broken.

I shook my head, "We're fine, nothing a shower won't fix."

We were all directed to one of the uniformed officers who took our details in order to contact us later.

Pierre drew me to one side, "Let Henry take you and Phoebe home. I promise to come over as soon as I can, and I'll tell you everything."

"You called me your girlfriend," I said smiling at him.

"Sorry. I was angry with Dom and worried about you and… did you mind me calling you that?"

"No, it's just a bit quick. We've only been out twice."

"Three times if you count last night." Pierre smiled, "we've known each other for a while and you must admit, we have been through quite a lot together."

"I suppose, but this time last week I still wasn't sure if you were one of the bad guys."

"And now, have you decided?"

I shrugged, "How do you know her?" I nodded towards the woman he had called Jo.

"Are you jealous?"

"No!"

"That's a shame, 'cos I was jealous as hell when I saw Dom acting all protective and gazing into your eyes."

"Good, but there's no need," I kissed Pierre, "okay, I'll go home with Henry, but I want to hear everything tonight."

"I promise, now go."

Chapter 53

Henry and Marc chattered excitedly all the way home. Henry was especially excited because it turned out that Phoebe had sent him a text from the barn. "When I saw those words: BARN HELP, in big shouty capitals I just snapped into action didn't I Marc?"

"You did. I am so proud of you!" Marc agreed, "and then when Pierre swept you up at the end Abi, and snatched you away from Dom, it was like a scene from an *Officer and a Gentleman*."

Marc sighed and Henry made his voice as deep as possible and said, "Get your hands off my girlfriend," in the worst American accent any of us had ever heard.

"Actually," said Marc, "I think that's a line from a song by Charlotte Church."

"Good Charlotte," Phoebe corrected.

"She is, isn't she? Voice of an angel," Marc began searching in the glovebox for a c.d.

Phoebe sighed and settled back into the car seat beside me. "It seems like an awful lot of fuss over one stolen horse and a bit of cheating at a competition," she said.

"Stolen!" cried Henry causing the car to veer alarmingly across the road.

"Jeez, you drive like Abi, slow down!" Phoebe admonished him.

"Sorry," Henry regained control, "but did you say stolen?"

We gave Marc and Henry a brief rundown of the way we thought Dom and Hannah had been using the two horses at the horse trials. We deliberately avoided mentioning the bizarre night-time activity involving Marilyn's stallion.

"Bloody hell, so the horse I rode at the Academy was actually Secret, not Syd!" Henry shook his head in disbelief.

"And do you think she realised you were onto her?" Marc asked, "is that why she did a runner?"

I shrugged, "Who can tell."

"But you said stolen," Henry reminded Phoebe, "what's that about?"

"Hannah has been hiding the fact that her horse isn't jet black, he actually has white markings on his back leg. She's been hiding it with some kind of stain or dye."

"I knew it!" Marc announced, "I borrowed a hoof pick from her grooming kit 'cos I couldn't find ours and I said to you didn't I Henry, I said I'm sure there's a bottle of showing dye in her kit."

"Oh, I'd forgotten about that," Henry said, "you couldn't understand why she went so mental because you'd borrowed a hoof pick. I said, you shouldn't have even mentioned it."

"I know!" Marc said, "I mean I'd put it back and everything! Anyway, now we know, she probably wasn't bothered about the hoof pick, just worried we'd recognise the showing dye. We thought her horse must have a small scar somewhere 'cos that's mainly why people use that stuff."

"Go on though Phoebes. Hiding a bit of white doesn't mean the horse is stolen," Henry continued.

"I know, but the microchip Abi scanned in his neck yesterday certainly proves it!"

Marc and Henry gasped.

"You weren't mugged at all were you?" Henry said, looking at me in his mirror.

I shook my head, "But there's no proof that it was Hannah…"

"I'd say her behaviour today moves her up the list of suspects. I always thought she was so demure and refined but after today…" Marc said, "she's gone right down in my estimation."

418

"She's so far down in my estimation, she's fallen out of the bottom!" Henry declared. We all laughed, and the mood lightened.

"Please don't tell anyone else, at least until the police and whoever those people are, sort everything out. Apart from the microchip in Secret's neck we haven't proven anything else yet. I'd hate them to get away with it because someone heard a rumour and …. well you know," I said.

"Our lips are sealed!" Henry promised.

"Zipped, locked and thrown away the key!" Marc said as he mimed the same.

Margaret smothered me in a fur and feather embrace the moment I got out of the car, "You poor darling. Shouldn't you be in bed?"

"I'm fine, but thanks," I assured her.

Margaret pressed a small bottle into my hand. "It's arsenic, from my herbalist, to help with the bruising."

I looked at her in alarm.

"Arnica," James corrected.

I relaxed, "Oh, thanks."

"Me 'n our Chantelle have mucked out Hannah's stable for you," James said.

"Thanks James, there was no need for that, but I do appreciate it."

"Well," Margaret turned to Henry, "how did it go with the horse? Did it pass the tests?"

"I'm still thinking about it," Henry said, "I have a couple of others I want to look at before I make a decision."

"Very wise," James patted Henry on the shoulder, "don't let him think you're too keen."

*****

"Your boyfriend's here." Phoebe shouted from the doorway. The light was fading, and we had just been out to give the horses a night-time check and some apples.

419

I looked up from pulling off my boots. "It's late, I'd just about given up," I said ignoring the 'boyfriend' jibe.

"Hi," Pierre called as he came around the corner. "Sorry I'm so late." He kissed me, "I've just finished with the police."

"Good grief, have you eaten?" I asked.

"Bits and pieces but I've brought fish and chips." He held up a paper package, "I've brought extra, I didn't know if you'd be hungry; if Phoebe would be at work or…"

"Stop gassing!" Phoebe ordered, "we're always hungry. Plates or paper?"

We spread the paper package in the middle of the kitchen table and the three of us sat around the table eating the mini feast with our fingers.

"Come on then," I said as the pile of food disappeared, "tell all. That seemed to be a lot of police and fancy official people for one stolen horse."

"Believe me, there's an awful lot more going on than Dom and Hannah using ringers in a competition," Pierre began.

"And how do you know that woman?" I asked for the second time that day.

"She is called Jo and I've been sort of working with her for a while now."

"Wait, I thought you were a vet!" I pulled him up.

"I am, let me explain. About eight or nine months ago the drug squad were made aware of a fairly regular consignment of drugs coming into a ferry port on the South East coast. They couldn't find any common threads with passengers or lorries but then someone spotted that each time a fresh drop appeared to have taken place, a transporter bringing horses to the UK from the continent was also on board. No one made the connection at first because it was hardly ever the same horsebox. Anyway, turns out the horses were literally being used as drug mules; they had packages of whatever drug, cocaine I think, inserted at one end of the journey and then removed once they arrived over here."

"Oh my God, is Dom a drug baron?" I gasped.

Pierre pulled a face, "No, he is a tiny fish in this particular crime pool, but fortunately for us, a greedy fish. Once the drugs were retrieved the actual smugglers had no use for the horses, so they were sold off. Most of them seemed to go to one of two places. They either ended up with a bloke near Leicester or up here in Northumberland."

"I'm guessing Dom was the Northumberland destination," Phoebe said.

Pierre nodded, "That's right but he was quite careful. The horses didn't come straight to his yard, most went to a range of places across the county, some even went to Durham or Yorkshire; occasionally they were used in riding schools or as hunt hirlings but whenever one of them was sold, the money made its way back to Dom. It was actually the tax man who started to look more closely at him, then his fake passports came to light."

"We saw those in his house," I said, "boxes of them."

"A couple of people tried to contact the vets who had signed the passports, they wanted to see if there was a record of the horse's medical history; flu jabs previous pregnancies that sort of thing. Well, because the passports were false the vets who were contacted had no knowledge of the horses and they wanted to know why their name was being associated with the history of these horse, some passports had been signed with fraudulent signatures and some of the actual veterinary practices didn't even exist!"

"So how did you get involved?" I asked.

"The practice I used to work for was one of those Dom tried to use on his passports, and my signature was one of those he tried to falsify. I suppose at some point a passport I had genuinely signed came into his possession or maybe he just took my name from the website my old practice used… anyway, it was obvious that he was involved in more than false passports so the police, who were monitoring his movements, decided that rather than move in straight away they would try to get closer to Dom. He had no idea that I was one of the vets whose signature he had copied and when I got a job so close to the area where he lived the NCA thought it was too good an opportunity to miss. They wanted me to gain an insight into his other activities. Jo was the person I liaised with. She had been watching Hannah."

"I wondered what Hannah was bringing to this party. How was she involved?" Phoebe asked.

"Hannah was dealing out of a yard in Durham, she mainly sold ponies, 'show ponies' to rich parents with no equine knowledge. Young animals or ponies with problems, she either doped them or deprived them of water, she used some nasty methods to subdue the poor things. She's a regular on the welfare watch list apparently. She got done once for covering the 'L' which insurance companies insist on freeze branding onto horses when they pay out for a 'loss of use claim'. The brand is used to show the horse has been classed as no longer fit for purpose. Hannah used the same type of hair stain to hide the mark, that she was using on Secret. When the customer saw the 'L' mark showing after a couple of weeks, Hannah said it stood for Lipizzaner! The horse was a black and white cob! Dom sent horses to her that had the potential to be tidied up for showing or dressage! It's amazing how you can alter a horse's appearance with a hogged mane or by allowing a mane to grow long; even a clip or a change in weight... These horses and the ponies were sold from her end as 'pretty show types' or dressage horses and he concentrated on those who had some jumping ability."

"I knew there was something about that woman," Phoebe waved a chip to emphasise her point.

I nodded in agreement.

"Most of the horses coming over with the drugs were common, ordinary types who could be picked up cheaply at auctions abroad, but Dom and Hannah got greedy," Pierre continued, "Dom used his contacts to bring retired

422

competition horses over, and they used a combination of false paperwork and Hannah's skill to change a horse's appearance to compete the horses at lower levels as ringers before selling them on. When this proved to be so lucrative, they started dealing in horses stolen from the competition circuit. Dom sourced them, Hannah provided cosmetic changes and the horses were sold to unsuspecting customers, usually some distance away from either Hannah or Dom's own yards with a new identity provided by Dom and his bank of fake passports and veterinary stamps."

Pierre paused while we digested the information.

"But if Hannah has her own place, why did she keep the black horse here?" I asked, as I began to prepare some coffee.

"Her yard was too far away so they needed somewhere quiet and fairly close to Dom. She could easily whizz up and down the motorway in her car, but it was too far away to easily transport a horse, I think her and Dom had some kind of messed up 'relationship' if you can call it that; anyway I thinks she stayed at his place sometimes, especially on competition days," Pierre said, "until the black gelding showed up they didn't need to be close to each other, in fact I think Dom preferred her to be some distance away."

"When they realised the black horse was almost identical to Dom's horse it was too much of a golden opportunity. Dom had been competing for years on ringers, in order to win classes or fool customers. He realised that he could improve his dressage score by riding that phase on one horse, then switch to ride the jumping phases on his own horse. He wanted to keep the stolen horse at arms- length, then if it was recognised, he could distance himself and leave Hannah to take the blame. She must have been furious when she realised that Dom was planning to sell his horse to Henry."

"Why would he do that?" Phoebe asked.

"I think he realised that British Eventing were onto him, that's actually why the officials turned up. Hannah panicked when she found out what he was planning. Dom wanted to sell his horse to Henry, it was too close for comfort as far as she was concerned. Dom already had another buyer lined up for Secret. Once Syd had been sold, the second person would be told that the white leg had been covered for aesthetic reasons or that it had been unnoticed due to fetlock jumping boots or mud; after all, it is clearly marked on the passport! The horse would be ridden on the flat and jump a few fences like Henry did and take the horse's cross-country ability on trust due to its BE record or videos... some people actually buy horses unseen on the strength of a video!"

"They had it all worked out didn't they," Phoebe shook her head in disbelief.

"Was it Hannah who hit me?" I asked.

"Yeah. She admitted it. Apparently, Dom came with the horsebox and she was already in the yard with the horse; he didn't know you were there. He was furious when he found out that you had been lying unconscious in the stable."

"So, when we saw you wandering about Dom's house," I said, "you were looking for evidence."

"That's right. And the officials who turned up with the police today was just pure luck. One of the dressage stewards at **Belford Park** last weekend went to watch her friend in the showjumping. She noticed that there was something different about Dom's horse. It seemed to have a different way of going than when she'd seen it in the dressage, and its tail had grown!" Pierre laughed, "I can't decide whether they were getting sloppy or were just incredibly arrogant. Anyway, the steward had a word with the organisers and the rest is history. The guy from the BEF is up here for a conference and was planning to visit a new venue with the couple from BE. He thought tagging along with them to interview Dom would be a 'jolly PR jaunt'."

"What about the business with Marilyn's stallion?" Phoebe asked.

"No one had any idea about that little side-line until you two stumbled into the middle of everything. That night after the ball, I had no idea it was Dominic's yard. I only realised when I got the chance to go there and scan the mares," Pierre explained, "someone will talk to Marilyn and I'm sure some DNA testing will be done. That was a smart move spotting how successful the stock from his own brood mares were, compared to those from most of the visiting mares."

"And what about the horses? What will happen to them?" I asked.

"And the dog!" Phoebe reminded us, "where was he today?"

Pierre shrugged. "I scanned everything at Dom's place this afternoon. The paperwork for the chestnut show jumper doesn't match with the details on his microchip, so chances are he's one of Dom's ringers. Nothing else flagged as stolen, just the horse Hannah was keeping here. The owners have been contacted."

"Poor Henry," Phoebe stirred sugar into her coffee, "he was so excited at the thought of getting another horse."

"He will, there are plenty out there," I said.

"Just not that one!" said Pierre as he gathered the papers together from our fish supper.

Chapter 54

Three months later...

"Who's that with Marc and Henry?" Phoebe asked. We had just arrived back in the yard after a ride. I shielded my eyes and squinted in the September sunshine to where Phoebe was pointing.

"I'm not sure. Another friend who's come to see the new horse I suppose."

"He is lovely," said Phoebe referring to Henry's new horse, a smart liver chestnut with four white socks and a crooked white blaze down his face.

"And what a brilliant name; Swanky! It really suits him," I added.

"Look at him now, Henry's posing for pictures and he's holding a little kid on his back."

We untacked and turned out our own horses and after watching them roll, we crossed to the field where Henry was leading a small beaming child towards the gate on Swanky. The child was flanked by Marc on one side and a woman, his mother I presumed on the other side. Both were holding the child. As they drew closer Marc swept the little boy off the horse and carried him through the gateway.

Marc waved as they got closer, "Hi, good ride?"

"Lovely thanks. Have you got a saddle yet?" I asked Henry.

"Couple of days. I can hardly wait!" he almost squealed with excitement, his eyes shining.

"Have you met my sister, Charlotte?" Henry waved his hand from us to the woman who had been holding the small child, "Lotte, these are my good friends Abi and Phoebe."

A young woman with a long dark ponytail, stepped forward and extended her hand. "Hi, I've heard a lot about you both," she said shaking hands with both of us.

"And who is this?" Phoebe asked, bending down until she was at eye level with the small boy who was hiding behind Charlotte.

"This is Oliver. Come on Ollie, come and say hello to the nice lady."

The small child slowly peeped out and gave a shy smile.

"Did I see you riding that big horse?" Phoebe asked.

The child looked at her from behind his mother again and nodded.

"Was it fun?" Phoebe asked him.

The little boy nodded once more and clung to his mother. Henry bent down and swept him up tickling him, "You're not shy are you mister?"

Oliver dissolved into giggles as Henry carried him towards their car.

"See you later," said Marc, smiling after them.

*****

The entrance to the medieval hall where Izzy and Klaus had decided to get married was decorated with an arch made from twisted ivy and white roses. Gold berries and tiny orange flowers reminded guests that this was September. Inside the hall chairs decorated with russet coloured organza bows were arranged in rows.

"You look amazing!" Pierre said, pressing his leg close to mine, "you will outshine the bride."

Phoebe snorted and used a small mirror to check for lipstick on her teeth, "That's hardly a compliment, given the fact that the bride is a dried- up old bag."

"Phoebe! Shush!" I hissed.

"Why are you even here?" Pierre asked, "I didn't think you were invited."

427

"Klaus invited me," she put the mirror away and I caught a glimpse of a small gold coloured key and a man's tie in her bag.

"Phoebe," I warned, "promise you'll behave. Why did you come today?"

"I've told you Klaus invited me, perhaps I still hold the key to his heart," she sighed dramatically, "besides which, Izzy thinks I'm borderline respectable now because I'm dating a doctor."

"Where is he?" I asked.

"On duty. He's coming later." she winked.

I couldn't decide whether she simply meant he was meeting her later, or whether she was making some kind of inuendo.

"I wish Marc and Henry would hurry up, they're really good at helping her to tone it down, especially around Izzy," I whispered to Pierre, "it's not like them to be late."

I twisted around in my seat but there was no sign of them. The medieval hall where the ceremony was taking place was filling up. James and Margaret were sitting a few rows behind us with Chantelle. Margaret waved.

"Have you heard from Marc or Henry?" I asked Phoebe.

"Nothing," she checked her phone for messages.

I leaned forward and tapped Felicity on the shoulder, "What about you, have you heard from them?"

"No, and they won't get a seat if they don't hurry," Felicity turned around to answer me, "Oh look, here they are!" She waved to attract their attention.

"What happened, why are you so late?" Phoebe scolded them as they squeezed along the row of seats.

"It's a long story but we're changing Swanky's name!" said Henry as he checked his reflection using Phoebe's mirror.

"But it suits him, and it's unlucky to change a horse's name," Phoebe insisted as she straightened Marc's tie.

"Not as unlucky as fucking keeping it!" Marc hissed through gritted teeth.

"What the hell's happened?" I asked.

Henry and Marc exchanged glances before Henry took a deep breath. "Can you remember my nephew, Oliver?"

We all nodded, "Cute kid about four or five -year old," Phoebe confirmed, "what about him?"

"He started school the other day and his new teacher was asking the kids about hobbies and interests," Henry explained, "when she got to Ollie, he told her his favourite thing was visiting Uncle Henry and riding Swanky."

We all smiled.

"Oh, how cute," Phoebe gushed.

"Really? How about I tell you we were late because we've just spent many hours with some very official gentlemen and a lady from social services because my nephew cannot pronounce the letter 'S'!" Henry announced as the air became filled with the music which heralded the arrival of the bride, "we are changing the horse's name!"

Printed in Poland
by Amazon Fulfillment
Poland Sp. z o.o., Wrocław